Jaxxa Rakala
The Search

Book 1 in the
Jaxxa Rakala Saga

A Novel
Bryan Caron

Jaxxa Rakala: The Search
2nd Edition
Published by Divine Trinity Films
©2013 Divine Trinity Films
www.divinetrinityfilms.com

Text Copyright (2nd Edition) ©2013 Bryan Caron

Original Cover Art
Designed by Bryan Caron
©2013 Bryan Caron

When "Jaxxa Rakala: The Search" was originally published in 2006, I had high hopes that the novel would become a runaway hit, leading to three sequels that would be just as popular. Due to my lack of experience, though, reality halted that dream. The book stalled and I moved on to several different projects in both fiction and film. But everyone I know who did read the book continually asked when the sequel was coming out. I can now say, "Soon."

With this, the 2nd edition of "Jaxxa Rakala: The Search," I have used the experience I've gained over the last seven years to recraft the story. Though character actions, plot points and key story developments are still in tact, I've given a few characters more defined personalities and backstories, and at the same time, quickened the pace of the writing. The action is smoother, the dialogue is crisper and the emotion is deeper; all of it to prepare readers (returning fans and newcomers alike) a refreshing look at the beginning of the Jaxxa Rakala Saga, which will continue in 2014 with the release of Book 2, "Memoirs of Keladrayia: Jaxxa Rakala."

I want to thank everyone who originally supported this book (and demanded to read more). Without you, I may never have taken this next step. This is for you.

Enjoy.

Jaxxa Rakala

The Search

The Abduction
(prologue)

Blinding light slips through Ken Brody's bedroom window, consuming everything from visibility. He tries to open his eyes but it's as if he were looking directly into the sun as it races toward Earth in a mad pursuit to end everything.

Squinting through the glare the best he can, Ken rises from his bed and searches his way to the large bureau near the bedroom door. He ruffles through various nick-knacks that had been thrown on there like wasted memories over the years and finds a pair of dark sunglasses he bought when he and his first wife, Gloria, were on their honeymoon in Hawaii. Stroking his ego, she said they made him look cooler than Tom Cruise in *Top Gun*. Several years later, in one of many fights that exploded out of thin air, she said they made him look foolish. He hasn't worn them for over ten years but kept them as a reminder — for the sake of the one she left behind.

It takes a couple of minutes for his eyes to adjust to the subdued intensity of the light, but making significant shapes out of anything is still extremely difficult. He staggers to the window and sees a small, black rectangle lined with tiny square lights where the lawn should be. They rest in a large, circular void connecting both halves of the light as if it were a pathway between separate worlds.

"Stacey," Ken whispers to his wife still slumbering in their bed. "Stacey. Come over here and look at this. It's like the X-Files out here."

Ken grows concerned when she doesn't respond. Stacey, whom Ken met a few weeks after Gloria disappeared, has always been a very light sleeper — but not tonight.

Why not tonight?

Trading his focus from the light to Stacey, Ken walks to the bed. He repeats her name over and over, each time pronouncing it louder and more elongated. As he reaches the corner edge of the bed, a glimmer of movement near the bedroom door flashes past the corner of his eye. He turns, but can only see the bright white void.

It's your eyes playing games.

Ken shakes his head and turns back to the window when he hears a hushed growling — or a huffed grunting —

What's the difference?

— much like a couple of wild dogs. He can't move.

It's all in your head, Ken. All. In. Your. Head.

Just then, ripples break through the light and Ken becomes overwhelmed with fear, yet at the same time, feels more secure than he's ever been, as if he were suffering a heart attack while stealing a nap after work. Ken hears waves crashing on the shores of his life, his love —

Beauty is a picture of the one I see...

A soft air of fog hits Ken's face, sending a chill down the back of his neck.

Ken's euphoria subsides as the ripples dissipate, leaving him breathless within the silence of the light. Ken isn't sure if his heart has stopped or if it's racing for freedom, but his lungs finally take in the crisp night air, now hinted with the sweet scent of honey and roses. Ken quickly shifts around the bed, wanting nothing more than to take his wife in his arms. As he steps up to the headboard, the light casts a small shadow in the shape of his body over the flattened — and painfully empty — sheets.

He is alone.

"Stacey?" He crawls onto the bed and searches for her. Never has he been so scared of losing someone. Stacey is more than just his wife; she is a piece of him. Without her eyes, he cannot see; without her ears, he cannot listen; without her lips, he cannot speak; without her touch, he cannot feel. Unlike Gloria, Stacey has consumed his soul and replaced it with her spirit, a spirit that now calls to him — screams for him — to rescue her from a fate he is not ready for.

Ken sucks in a breath of air that sticks to his throat. Of all of the thoughts that he could have had, the one he cannot shake is the one that kills him. But he isn't dead; so Stacey can't possibly be either. It's impossible. The only other explanation is one he never thought he could believe.

The X-Files. What else could it be? But if that were true, then —

Ken whips his head to the door; it's the only thing that makes sense. Those mysterious, growling ripples, for a reason that not even Ken can fathom, came and chose their newest victim.

"Stacey!"

He leaps to the door in two giant steps but can't go any further. Across the hall, bleeding in bright red on his daughter's bedroom door, the light casts a crescent moon. The familiar shape — the sheer splendor of its radiant glow, the superiority of what it symbolizes — holds him mesmerized in a breathless grip, one of which he is more than happy to remain for eternity.

BAM!

The front door knocks Ken from his fugue state. He grabs his forehead in light-headed confusion before he remembers what's going on. *Stacey.*

"Stacey!" he screams and rips off the sunglasses. The light is extremely painful, but going blind would be an acceptable exchange to have his wife safely in his arms. He jumps down the stairs like a rabbit from a fire and runs out into the icy night, instantly overcome with consternation. The wind blows steadily from above and all he hears is a soft, soothing hum emanating from the endlessly starless night hovering quietly above the green and brown patches of his lawn. Three rows of purple lights form a crescent moon that ultimately wraps around the edges of a small ramp digging itself into the earth. Two large, burly creatures — *things?* — carry a lifeless body amidst two rows of runway lights lining the ramp.

"Stacey!" he screams to no avail. His anger and fear are enough to compel him to strike the nearest *thing* like a leopard attacking its prey — swift and quiet. It drops one of Stacey's legs as it loses its balance. After readjusting its footing, the *thing* grabs Ken by the throat and picks him off the ramp with ease. Just the sight of it (or maybe it was the stomach-inducing smell oozing from the *thing*'s drooling mouth) disgusts Ken to the point where he isn't sure if what he's seeing is real or a manifestation of too much television and hoagies before bed. Its head is almost perfectly round, bald and lumpy, and its eyes are like two slits in a piece of paper drawn approximately four inches apart from the center of the circle. Two horns protrude from both sides of its head where the ears should be and wrap around both slits, touching each other in the middle where the bridge of its nose would have been if the *thing* had a nose. A large mouth filled with sharp, fanged teeth rests approximately two inches from where the bottom of the horns wrap around the eyes.

As Ken grows faint, losing both air and his grasp on reality, the other *thing* grunts in asperity. Before completely losing consciousness, Ken is thrown thirty yards away. For a few seconds, the only sensation he feels is the sharp burn in his lungs as he searches for air. When the asphyxia does finally fade, his mind continues to find its way back from death. He composes himself with a cough and sets his wavering sights back to the *things.* He chokes out Stacey's name one last time — unable to call out any louder than his own hearing could bear — as she disappears completely into darkness, leaving only the purple crescent floating among the patchwork of light and dark. Ken reaches for it in a vain attempt to hold it in place, but in the end, all he can do is watch as everything becomes a void of disillusionment.

THE PROJECT

— 1 —

Dark and unforgiving dreams of Stacey's abduction (some longer and more allusive than others) prevented Ken from ever getting a peaceful night's rest for over five years. Sometimes he would lie awake with her visage bouncing around his thoughts like a pinball that won't ever stop moving; other times he would wake with the sun, washed in a cold sweat, his breath quick and heavy. But no matter the circumstances, one question remained front and center —

Why did they choose her?

The desire to answer that question led Ken into a long relentless journey — a project he granted himself in order to believe in something much richer than his swelling depression and thoughts of suicide. All of his friends and colleagues (even those that loved and adored Stacey as much as he did) told him he was insane, but the project gave him hope that someday he would see her again, and that was enough for him, despite its ultimate cost — seclusion. He took their lack of confidence far too personally and broke away from both recent and longtime friendships in favor of his newfound focus. What he never took into consideration was how much those relationships meant to him, and how losing them would affect him in the long run. With a complete lack of reason to counteract his passion, Ken lost more than he was able to comprehend.

Alone in bed, the bags under his deep red eyes caught the tears that tried to roll down his face. Regardless of how much sleep he was actually able to find, every morning for the past four years Ken would use the project to push him out of bed just after six in the morning. He would step into the cold shower and mindlessly wash, after which he would let the water run over his body for minutes, sometimes a half an hour. Once he found the strength to turn the water off, he'd sit and cry — for his wife… for his life — until he was able to justify why he should continue to care.

But this day — a day in which he woke without being drenched in sweat — was a day that the man staring back at him in the mirror was smiling. His eyes, usually wooden and dark, were instead as bright and alive as a child's on Christmas Eve. With a flurry of excitement that he hadn't felt since his first kiss with Stacey, Ken didn't even bother with a shower; he could barely even keep his hands from shaking to brush his teeth. And don't even ask about his wardrobe choices.

Ken took two steps at a time down the secondary staircase to the kitchen and went directly to the refrigerator, oblivious of his daughter, Tracey, eating Rice Krispies — *Snap, Crackle, Pop* — at the breakfast table. He chugged down what was left of a carton of orange juice, forgoing the use of a glass in favor of time, and tossed the carton into the sink. He let out a semi-noiseless burp and finally acknowledged Tracey.

"Sorry, sweet-pea," he said softly. "Didn't see you there." He kissed the top of her head. Even without a shower, her hair was soft and smelled like flowers. It reminded him a lot of Stacey, who smelled like honey no matter where she was or what she did. "Is Jacks still in her room?" he continued as he grabbed his watch from the bowl at the edge of the counter.

Tracey stared at the wall across from her without any response whatsoever. She simply placed another spoonful of cereal into her mouth and chewed like a drone.

Ken checked his pants as if he were forgetting something, cleared his throat of residual juice, and headed back upstairs. *I sure as hell hope she's home,* he thought as he knocked on his daughter's door, ignoring the poster that, to this day, he continued to nag her about:

TURN THE F K AROUND
I'M BUSY

The u and the c of what was easily Ken's least favorite word were covered up with a picture of a naked woman bending over, her derrière in the forefront with several lipstick kisses painted on it. If he had a choice, he would have torn it down years ago. Not once did he think his project would lead to such disrespect from his eldest daughter.

"Jacks?"

No reply. He knocked again. "Jacquline, open up."

Again nothing. He grabbed the doorknob and shook.

Locked.

"Jacks, if you're in there, open this d—"

The door squeaked open. Jacquline leaned up against the frame half asleep, her hair knotted up in a torn ponytail. The mass of holes in her ears and nose were vacant, much like her eyes, but sometime in the day they'd be filled with rings and chains that made her look more like a demon than the smart, young woman Ken knew her to be. It was her slip of a nightgown, draped so low down across her arm, that forced Ken to avert his eyes and avoid staring at the tattoo of a hawk just above her nearly exposed breast, one of only a dozen tattoos Jacquline had gotten over the last four years to spite him.

"You're not too great at reading comprehension, are you?" Jacquline said.

"Can you cover…?" Ken said, waving his hand above Jacquline's chest.

"God." Jacquline rolled her eyes as she pulled the strap up to her shoulder. "Better?"

Ken cautiously lowered his eyes, hoping she hadn't dropped the entire gown, something he knew she wouldn't be afraid to do, not if it meant embarrassing him or making him feel awkward and demoralized. It was a far cry from the child he loved to remember — the innocence of her sweet, cherubic face, the joy and excitement behind every straight-A report card, and the love she conveyed for her family and friends, not to mention the unadulterated respect she had for herself and her future. He had to dig deep for those memories, though. There weren't a whole lot of them since Stacey's disappearance.

"Good to see you made it home last night," Ken said.

"Who said I did?"

"Look," he said, ignoring the implication. "I need you to take Tracey to school today."

Jacquline sighed and shifted away, pushing the door closed.

Ken caught it before it shut completely and followed Jacquline to her bed, where she made a face plant into her pillow. Her room, by all accounts, looked just as callous as Jacquline.

"Do you have a problem with that?" Ken asked.

"Get out."

"I'm already late, Jacks. Can you just do this one thing for me?"

Jacquline looked up at Ken, more depressed than tired. "Why? So you can waste even more of your life?"

"I have not been wasting my life. You know—"

"She's dead, Ken," Jacquline stated with derision.

"She's not dead!" Ken screamed, grabbing Jacquline under the chin, pulling her face close to his. Jacquline was more than willing to jam his teeth to the back of his brain, but managed to remain as morose and calm as a dormouse.

A minute later, Ken relaxed.

Jacquline shook her head from his hand. She shifted up her bed slightly and pulled her legs in close to her body.

"I am going to find her."

"You're freakin' deluded. She's dead. Accept it and move on already."

"I can't," Ken said softly.

"Get it through your thick skull, Ken. The bitch left us, just like mom did. If you were smart, you'd take my advice — forget about her. Tracey deserves at least that much from you."

"Not yet. Not when I'm this close."

"Then do me a favor and leave me and Tracey out of it, okay."

"Just drive Tracey to school," he said and left without another word.

Jacquline followed him to the door. "Asshole," she screamed before slamming it shut.

Tracey hadn't moved an inch when Ken returned to the kitchen, though the lightly stained milk was now nearly empty and her spoon sat next to the bowl. Ken watched her a moment as she stared at the wall, silently thinking — *planning?* — about whatever it was she thought about. Ken's own thoughts strayed from that of Stacey and dwelled on his inability to really know his own daughter. On the surface, she was a normal eight-year-old girl with the exception of a birthmark in the shape of a crescent moon imprinted on her left cheek. (There used to be one on her right cheek as well, but that mark faded away about the same time as Stacey, and Ken had convinced himself that it had never been there to begin with.) But inside was something far different, and something Ken was unable to understand. She was the complete opposite of Jacquline; instead of a rebelliously sociable promiscuity, Tracey kept everything hidden and preferred stable routines in close proximity to the safety of her home. She absolutely hated communicating with anyone, including her very own family. Thinking about it brought long-buried feelings to the surface of his mind, forcing him to realize how much he had missed — had ignored — over the past five years. Time to sit with her, talk with her as a father and understand her thoughts, her pleasures and fears, had passed with the single beat of his heart. It chilled him to think that he might have lost that chance forever. In a few days, perhaps he might get his second chance, but not today. He had a project to finish — a life to find.

Tracey would have to wait.

Ken brushed Tracey's hair behind her ear and kissed her head. "I'll see you," he whispered. Tracey sat motionless, unaware of the love he was trying to give her — if that was truly what it was.

Ken grabbed his keys from the bowl on the counter and hurried out the door without another look back. He walked with confidence to the rusted pickup truck and fired up the engine. For a moment, as Ken found a more comfortable position in his seat, Ken found his thoughts once again bounce to his daughters. What he saw most clearly was a broken family — isolated and defiant. He saw two young girls, both of whom had lost a mother without a word of reason, each fending for themselves because the one parental figure they both shared in common had basically abandoned them. And for what? He hated what Gloria had done to Jacquline and somehow knew his own actions of late were bordering on just that. But he also knew, above all, that the dream he was chasing so relentlessly was the key to fixing that broken family. Gloria was a lost cause; nothing he could ever say or do would fix that. But Stacey had been taken against her will. She was out there somewhere, and only she could bring happiness back to the hell he called home.

There could be no further hesitation. The truck backed out of the driveway and shot down the quiet suburban road. As he drove, Ken's mind shifted gears faster than the pickup could. The further he got from his home, the less he thought about his girls and the more he thought about Stacey — her smile, her voice and her gracious and enlightened personality. It all melted into the night he first met her, standing in the middle of the road, the rain glistening off her body. There was an odd magnetism between them that he knew he would never feel again. From that point on, Ken couldn't concentrate unless she was with him; when he was alone, his energy drained from his pours. He loved her, more than anyone he had ever loved — his parents, his daughters, and especially Gloria, who at one point he was sure would be his one and only love.

So, what happens if the project's a failure?

Failure was on his mind every day, but Ken always suppressed that possibility with his tenacity. His project would not fail; it couldn't. He would lose everything if it did, and that was simply not an option.

All of this faded gently to the background as he mechanically pulled up to a faded-brown wooden shack in front of a black steel gate. The guard was half-asleep but he quickly became alert at the sight of the little Toyota. Ken flashed a smile and a white badge with his picture and name.

The guard replied with his own sluggish smile and turned a key to activate the gate. "Have a good day, Dr. Brody."

"Indeed, I will," Ken said, waiting impatiently for the gate (moving slower than its usual snail-pace) to open enough for him to squeeze past. He raced through the nearly empty parking lot and came to rest in a space near a black door sitting all alone among the flood of gray metal making up the foundation of the large industrial-style building. Ken hurried to the door and slid his badge across the top of a small security pad with a red light shining brilliantly above a faded keypad. He typed in a series of numbers — 0-2-1-4 (Valentine's day, the date of his marriage to Stacey) — and the red light vanished in favor of the green one next to it. A loud "*CHUNK-Clink*" soon followed. Ken vigorously stepped inside his second home and allowed the door to slowly latch itself closed behind him — *Click-CHUNK* — swallowing him once again from the outside world.

— 2 —

Tracey sipped the last of the milk from her bowl as Jacquline fell into the kitchen. She watched as Jacquline pressed the butt of her palm to her forehead to push away the remnants of her hangover. Rings and chains plugged the holes in her ears, face and stomach and she had changed into tight, slick black pants and a black top that bounced just above her stomach. Her hair was still knotted in a "messed-up" ponytail. As she would say —

Perfection.

"Come on, Squint," Jacquline said as she stumbled her way to the refrigerator. "I don't want you to be late." She pulled it open and searched the barren shelves. "Damn it, where's the OJ?" Upon slamming the door shut, Jacquline took notice of the juice carton in the sink and picked it up.

"Bastard." She tossed the carton back into the sink and headed out of the kitchen. "Hurry up. I need to make a Starbucks run. I'll grab your books."

Tracey set her bowl down and stared at the wall, stiff. Jacquline returned a minute later and dropped Tracey's backpack next to her chair. "I think it's all there. Let's go."

When Tracey didn't move even an inch, Jacquline knelt down and looked into Tracey's small, hazy eyes. She always loved the color of her sister's eyes — almost periwinkle in color. "Hey, kiddo. What's wrong?"

Tracey still didn't move.

"Is there something you want to talk about? Did something happen at school? Are you sick?" Each question was returned with the same blank stare. "Talk to me, Squint."

Talk to me; it was a statement full of hope and disappointment. Even though Tracey was completely capable of developing and functioning as a normal child, she never had been able to fully grasp the concept of speech patterns or words. Her mother had been helping her develop those skills, but all of the charisma and excitement that Tracey had exhibited in her progress all but evaporated when Stacey disappeared, most likely because of the pain she must have felt. It hurt Jacquline just as much; she always thought Tracey had the most beautiful voice, and to hear it just once more would be the best gift she could ever receive.

Jacquline lowered her head. "It's dad, isn't it?" She peered back up to Tracey. "You miss him."

Tracey blinked — the first acknowledgment of comprehension.

"So do I, Squint. But it's almost over." Jacquline wasn't sure what else to say. She took Tracey's hand and squeezed it. "Give it just a couple more days. I promise."

Jacquline displayed a tender smile. "Look, if you get up now, I'll take you out for a big waffle cone full of ice cream after school. What do you say?"

Tracey's grim stare finally gave way to the smallest of smiles, but her eyes were awash with anticipation. She grabbed her bag and tossed it over her shoulder as she left the kitchen.

Jacquline stood, pleased to see Tracey happy, even if it was only for a second. It was an extremely rare occurrence, so whenever it did happen, Jacquline did her best to savor it.

Always loving, always kind...

Jacquline placed the bowl into the sink and went to the front door. She threw on her leather jacket and joined Tracey in her beat-up red Volkswagen bug, first built a century ago. It wasn't the ideal, but it was what Jacquline could afford — and there was no way she was going to go without a car. Exhaust poured from the tailpipe as it coughed to life and rolled away from the house. *Just doing my best to save the planet,* she liked to joke.

There were a million things Jacquline wanted to say as she drove Tracey to school, but she remained as deathly silent as her little sister. She loved Tracey and had always done more than she would ever be required to do as a big sister. But with Ken having all but given up in the nurture department, she was the only one left to give Tracey a hug, or sit and talk with her about her day, even if that meant a one-sided conversation. It was a good feeling just to know Tracey could count on someone. For her, nothing cut deeper than isolation and she felt sorry for Tracey for having to go through that. At the same time, that isolation and loss helped them bond on a much deeper level, one that would allow Jacquline to help Tracey develop into the bright, young woman Jacquline always pictured her to be. In other words, Jacquline would be the mother she never had.

When they pulled up to the large brick building currently going through a multitude of renovations, Tracey stared into her lap, scared to death of leaving Jacquline to join the plethora of school kids rough-housing and running around a mere foot away from her. A school bus arrived just behind them and dumped off a slew of kids — some eager to get the day started; some already anxious for graduation; some pretending to be ill (a couple not pretending at all); and others who couldn't wait to see their teachers again — that Tracey couldn't understand. Spending the next five years in a closet was always a better idea to her than attempting to be social. What was the point? But the game always came much easier to Jacquline, who never let an opportunity to push Tracey go by without a fight. It always made Tracey a little queasy.

"Wow, they're finally bringing this shithole into the twentieth century, huh?" Jacquline said. "It's about time. This place was a relic when I went here. Here's hoping they take less than a thousand years to finally upgrade to the twenty-first, right Squint?"

Jacquline hoped for a smile, but all she saw was anxiety. "Come on, Trace. You have to go to school."

Tracey looked at her with her normal "I want to die" gaze.

"Don't look at me like that. You wants that ice-cream later, yous gonna have to get youself a serious edumacation so you cans be smart when the adulthoods takes you over."

Again, not even a hint of a laugh. Jacquline waited, hoping to see some spark of light, but when it didn't happen, she changed tactics. "Do you want me to come with you?" she asked in her best motherly voice.

Tracey slowly shook her head. She looked at the children still herding into the school by the handfuls.

"The other kids don't like you much, huh? Do they pick on you a lot?"

Tracey shook her head.

Jacquline didn't believe it for a second. She pulled Tracey's head to her. "Look at me, Squint. This is what you're going to do. The next time one of those little shits starts to make fun of you, don't run away. Don't hide. That'll just fuel the fire and it'll never end. You have to confront the little brats with their own game. You're strong; I know you can put an end to it. Don't be afraid to stand up for yourself, okay?"

Tracey's eyes glistened.

"Do anything you need to do to earn their respect? If you have to, just think of what I would do if it were me. Got it?"

Tracey nodded but it wasn't clear if she fully comprehended. Jacquline smiled nonetheless and offered Tracey her hand. She didn't want to shake it or kiss it; she simply wanted to hold it, to give Tracey a moment to feel safe. After a long pause, Tracey took her hand. ßJacquline could feel the icy sweat. Her smile became affection and she hugged Tracey tightly.

"You be strong."

Tracey tediously stepped from the car. She glanced back at Jacquline every few seconds as she walked to the school, eventually being consumed by its doors.

"Be strong," Jacquline whispered. A kid, probably no more than six, stared at her. "What are looking at?" she sniped and then pulled away from the school, a big black cloud left in her wake.

— 3 —

Sparks jumped from under the metal console that filled half of the closet-sized space. Ken was hidden half under it, welding a small line across two pieces of sheet metal. When he finished, he repositioned his dark goggles to his sweaty forehead and gently examined the smooth mold with his gloved hand. Satisfied, Ken turned off the torch and slid out. He set the torch and his gloves aside and grabbed a white-sheathed electrical wire dangling from a gap in the thin, flat plate that separated the curvature of the console's belly with its face. The red plastic had been stripped away from another wire attached to the plate in a loop, which allowed Ken to tie the organs of the white wire to the copper of the red. Letting out a relaxing breath, Ken smiled and searched the welder for something that obviously wasn't there.

"Lark," he called out. "Can you grab me the electrical tape?"

Ken pulled off the goggles and wiped his forehead as he waited impatiently. "Lark!"

"Right here," Lark said. The electrical tape rested across his shoulder.

"Oh. Thank you." Ken took the tape with a light brush of her fingers and quickly wrapped it several times around the exposed wires, making certain he had covered it all. "Where'd you take off to?"

"Just grabbing a bite," Lark said. She took a seat in one of the two cushioned chairs in front of the console and rested her feet gently on the front.

"You really need to get a fat, juicy steak one of these days," Ken said, taking notice of the small salad she had sitting on her knees. She was deathly thin and looked younger than she actually was — which at thirty-six, she absolutely loved hearing.

"When you turn Vegan," Lark said, shoving a mound of lettuce into her mouth with a satisfying grin and a wink.

Ken shook his head. "One day in Hell," he said and slid the wires into the panel.

Lark giggled and dropped her feet to the floor. She set her dish on the console and examined the blueprints that Ken had sprawled scrappily upon it. "How's it coming?"

"I think I figured it out." Ken picked up a rectangular metal plate from the floor and covered the gap, completing the panel with a light fist bump and a couple of screws. "Like I said, I think it comes down to the ion thrusters operating in opposition to the ignition."

"You didn't?"

Ken smiled and returned Lark's wink.

"Ken, we already talked about this." Lark was standing now, unconsciously stepping away from the console.

"An explosion is only one possibility, Lark." Ken stood.

"And a damn good one, too."

"No more so than jumping to the speed of light instantaneously when we start her up."

"Exactly. The simulations were clear."

"That's before I grounded the ignition."

Lark's worries dissipated slightly. "You did what?"

"The simulations were predicated on the ion thrusters working in tandem with the regular drive. All I did was give the thrusters their own private portal to the ignition."

"What does that mean?"

"The nuclear reactors can provide power independently to the thrusters, but they weren't getting any real ignition. I set up the system so when we're ready to light them up, we can trigger the ignition at the same time through the thrusters."

"So, what? You're going to pump jet fuel into the mix to help the ion thrusters burn faster?"

"And to generate more juice."

"Thus pushing us past the threshold and sending us over the barrier."

Ken gestured his acknowledgment.

"But won't that cause a faster rate of decay?"

"Possibly, but if I'm right, it'll still take over a year of travel for that to happen."

Lark smiled, her cheeks growing dimples with ease. "That might actually work."

"If we don't blow up first."

Lark's smile vanished for a second before Ken broke his own. She returned it with a playfully angry punch to the arm, followed by a nice, generous laugh that Ken found exciting and soothing at the same time.

"All that's left now is to test it."

Lark set her hand on Ken's arm, squeezing it gently. "If you're right, Ken, we'll be traveling at the speed of light by the end of the day."

"And on our way to history."

"I'll set up the simulator with the new specs."

Within seconds, Lark was on her way, her dirty-blond ponytail bouncing gracefully across the small frame of her shoulder blades. She walked with a substantial limp, having once broken both of her legs as a pilot in the Air Force. During a routine low-range speed trial of an untested fighter jet, Lark was forced to eject when the engines malfunctioned, and though she had taken every precaution to land safely, her position was far too low for her parachute to work effectively. Occasionally, on her worst days, she would need the use of a cane to get around, which she hated with a passion.

Ken took a bite of the salad and examined the blueprints one final time before gazing through the Plexiglass windows resting just above the console. Lark spouted out a few orders as she limped past some of the technicians middling about the massive room. He loved watching her bark out commands like that; authority fit her well and made her look exquisitely exotic. After she slipped through a door at the other end, Ken lowered his head and took in a deep breath, revealing an anxious demeanor that he wasn't ready to share with Lark. She was a great friend and their partnership in this project was one he wouldn't want to ever change. But Lark had made it clear from the jump — reaching space may be one of her life's ambitions, but she would never allow that ambition to endanger anyone's life. If there were any doubts at any time whether this would actually work, she'd pull the plug in less time than it would take to blink. Ken's mask of confidence was all he had to guarantee the project continued to move forward.

Ken sat down and pushed the blueprints to the floor. *Please let the simulations work,* he prayed as he gripped a pair of metallic handles. *They will. They have to.*

He leaned back in his seat, far from confident.

— 4 —

Jacquline sat on her knees in front of a double set of French doors. She took in a breath as she twisted the hairpins around inside the lock. It had taken her six months to perfect the skill, but then again, that was a little over ten years ago and her mother wasn't about to let her give up.

"That's it, sweetie," Gloria whispered into Jacquline's ear. "Concentrate."

Jacquline was eight, and for whatever reason, the lock just wouldn't make that special sound. "Keep your hands steady and breathe. You'll get it."

After hours of trying, all Jacquline wanted to do was kick the door in. "I can't," Jacquline screamed.

It wasn't clear if the memory had slipped from her lips or remained a daydream, but either way, it didn't seem to disrupt the make-out session between Jay and Harlet, the two teenage crooks who hired Jacquline to help plan the score. Both were strapped in black leather and had more holes in their bodies than a sponge. They remained clutched in an unbreakable embrace, swallowing each other's tongues.

Jacquline couldn't watch them for more than a second, resorting to staring at the brand new placemat under her feet that shouted, "Wel—me." She closed her eyes and pictured her mother kneeling down in front of their own front door, showing her how it was done. She watched carefully, trying hard to find that key to understanding what she was doing wrong.

What was it?

"Damn tongue twisters," Jacquline whispered. She stood in frustration and peeled Harlet away from Jay. Harlet whimpered, trying desperately to reattach herself to him like a leach. Jacquline wouldn't have it. She stood between their heated bodies.

"What the hell?" Harlet said, attempting to look through Jacquline to keep a scintillating gaze on Jay.

"You two sex pistols are supposed to be helping me," Jacquline said.

"We did our part," Jay said. "I should be asking you why we aren't already in this damn place. It's been ten minutes already. I thought you were supposed to be one of the best."

"Correction. I am the best. But when all I can hear are the squirt of bodily fluids flowing from one diseased mouth to the other while your tongues train for the Olympics, it's a little hard to concentrate. Besides, you two jack-offs are supposed to be making sure no one's watching. I'm not about to go to prison for you."

"I told you. Everyone around here is either on vacation or a night owl, so shut your damn mouth and get your ass back to work so we can get the goods already." Jay shoved Jacquline out of the way and pulled Harlet back to his chest.

For a second, Jacquline thought about walking away. It was never her nature to give anyone else the lead on a job. She preferred to work alone; it minimized the risk and kept the unexpected at bay. But the potential score on this job was far too much to pass up. Not only was the community a paradise, but all of the houses along the street were shrouded in fences, trees and exotic plant life. Should this job work out, it could lead to a cavalcade of riches. For that alone, Jacquine was going to have to suck it up and deal with the inevitable chaos when it arrived.

"I'm not going to jail," she repeated with a softer, distant tone.

"And we do?" Jay snapped back. "You need to stop being such a pussy and just do what we hired you to do."

Jacquline took a breath. "I want sixty-five."

"Hell no. The deal was thirty."

"The way I see it, without me, you've got nothing but pictures of a gorgeous mansion that might help you jack off a little and get to sleep at night. If this place is worth as much as you say it is, I want two-thirds. That's it, that's final."

Jay looked about ready to take a swing at Jacquline, but he gave in rather quickly. "Fine. Just get me in there."

Jacquline searched for any sign of deception as Harlet returned to suck Jay's tongue like a Popsicle. It wasn't something she was used to, but if she was going to make this happen, she would have to trust them. This place was capable of ten times more than she would ever take in on her own, so even though she couldn't escape the thought of being arrested, for sixty-five percent of the take, it was well worth the risk.

Never run from a major opportunity; you'll never get it back.

"Never," Jacquline whispered and pierced the hairpins back into the lock. After a few more failed attempts, Jacquline once again stopped and took in a long, deep breath. She pushed all noise from her mind and cleared her thoughts, allowing just one to creep back in — the first time Gloria let her pick the lock of someone else's house. It wasn't their first job together, but it was the first time Gloria trusted Jacquline enough to take point. Nothing gave her more of a thrill than hearing that first click. That one single thought gave her precisely what she needed to make it happen again.

"You got it?" Harlet said.

Jacquline hadn't heard their lips come apart. "Did you have any doubt?"

"Yeah, kind of."

Jacquline ignored her as she removed the pins. Harlet instantly reached across Jacquline's shoulder to open the door, but Jacquline was quick to slap her hand away.

"What the hell?" Harlet squealed, rubbing her hand.

"What did I tell you? We need to be cautious or else we're all screwed."

"Just hurry up," Jay chimed in.

"Just wait. I don't know what kind of alarm system they have. I need to get ready for whatever's waiting for us on the other side."

Jacquline pulled a small felt pouch from her laptop bag and sorted through numerous wire cutters and an assortment of screwdrivers, powders and brushes. The whole package was the last thing she remembered of her mother and it was the only thing, aside from Tracey, that she cherished enough to die for.

* * *

"Jacquline," Gloria whispers, waking Jacquline from her fairytale.

"What… what is it?" Jacquline moans, trying to find a glimpse of her mother through the dark of the room.

"I want to give you something," Gloria says quietly.

"A present?" Jacquline's tired eyes light up with anticipation.

"You bet."

Gloria's warm hand grabs Jacquline's wrist and something soft and fuzzy lands in her palm. "What is it?" Jacquline asks, pulling it close enough to make out its shape.

"It's a very special gift. Keep it with you no matter where you go."

Jacquline holds the gift to her chest. "It's beautiful," she says.

Only silence answers.

Jacquline suddenly feels cold.

* * *

"You all right?" Harlet said.

Jacquline shook away the memory. "I'm fine." She had to be. Over the years, Jacquline had dealt with small country homes and track homes, most of which were some of the easiest places to break into because most of them don't have alarms (unless you count the dogs, which Jacquline found out the hard way worked just as well). This was a far cry from those toy boxes; this was the big time. Her performance here had to be perfect. She strapped the pouch to the outside of her laptop bag and curled her fingers around the door handle.

Harlet held onto Jay's arm and bounced with the joy of a girl being felt up for the first time. "Open the shit up already," she said. Jacquline held up her other hand to quiet Harlet and cracked the door open.

Pillars of highly decorated wood crafted by hand lined the endless foyer. On the left, long leather couches with gold rims and oak finishings filled the majority of the living room, leaving very little room for the elegantly shaped glass coffee tables. Down the hall a ways, on the edge of one of the stairwells, was a small table with a porcelain lamp and some vases that most likely came from a foreign country. In the den to the right were a couple of computers and dozens of books lining elegantly handcrafted bookshelves.

Harlet's eyes beamed as she squeezed her head around the doorframe to get her first glimpse. "What are you waiting for?" she said, her voice cutting through the silence. "There's no alarm."

"It might be silent," Jacquline said quickly, keeping Harlet from bullying her way through the door.

"Why would you think that?"

"Because these rich bastards always have shit like that. Give me a second. Let me make sure." Jacquline reached into one of the powders and threw the contents into the house. As it settled to the floor, a thin blue beam strung across from the door hinge to the living room filtered out the powder. "You see that?"

Jacquline grabbed a flashlight from her bag and searched the house. Hanging on the wall below the second stairwell at the end of the foyer was a small black box. "Bingo," she whispered.

"What? What is it?"

"The security panel. Give me a minute to disarm it."

Jacquline tossed more powder into the house and examined the checkerboard pattern of the beams. She stepped over the first beam into the space she could make out as safe, her heart racing faster than a bullet in a hurricane. Once settled, she tossed more powder out and took another cautious step forward. More powder gave way to more beams and shakier, breathless steps. It was three long minutes before Jacquline took her last step in front of the control panel, finally able to let out a breath. She looked to Jay and Harlet, who bounced about as if she hadn't taken a piss for days. If it weren't for Jay, she probably would have already triggered the alarm. Jacquline held up her index finger hoping it would be enough to keep them from entering for another few minutes, then pulled a Phillips screwdriver from her bag. The four small screws on the cover of the control box were out in seconds. Jacquline's first thought was that the rest would be a piece of cake, but the wires connecting the panel to the deep recesses of the wall were quite overwhelming. Undeterred, she allowed the panel to dangle against the wall by its veins and shoved the flashlight between her teeth, allowing the freedom of her hands to dissect the various connections. Focusing her eyes through the building sweat on her brow, Jacquline knew there was only one way to disable this intricate of a system. She grabbed Gloria's favorite pair of wire cutters (the ones she never went anywhere without) and stripped the colored plastic from three different wires, exposing the copper underneath. After resting the cutters along the front end of the first wire, she closed her eyes and cut, letting out a long, overdue breath when nothing happened. She repeated the process with the second wire and then tied both to the center of the third. When she was through, she tucked them as deep as she could into the wall and gently rested the teeth of the wire cutters around a long black wire. She gave Jay and Harlet a wink and turned her head away from the control panel. Sparks flew from inside the box as she squeezed the handles of the wire cutters together. Jacquline let out a small squeak of pain and pulled her hand to her chest. "God damn it."

But the pain was well worth it.

The beams were no longer evident as she tossed a bit more powder into the room. "God, I'm good," Jacquline mused through gritted teeth. She wanted to flex the fingers on her numbed hand but she was afraid her arm would seize up if she did. At least it was only temporary.

Jay and Harlet giggled as they leapt hand in hand up the stairs.

"Where are you going?" Jacquline said.

"I've never had sex in a rich-bitch bed before," Harlet said and the two thieves rounded the hallways to finally consummate their excitement.

Jacquline sucked up her residual pain and checked for the wire cutters. When they weren't on the floor as expected, she realized there was only one place they could be. "Damn it," she whispered. *So much for that heirloom,* she thought. "Sorry, mom." No time to dwell on it now; she had a house to clean out.

Choosing to stay downwind of the fleshy affair, Jacquline walked to the table at the edge of the stairwell and examined one of the vases, admiring its hand-painted roses resting against the bright blue background. If she was lucky, it might net her a couple hundred dollars, but Jacquline wasn't sure if that was enough to go through the hassles of authentication, not to mention the headaches of coming up — and maintaining — a believable story of how she acquired the vase in the first place. She decided the best thing she could do was stick to the essential currencies — silver, gold and of course the most easily attained, and obvious, green. Since most people are sheep and cling to their clichés, if there was a safe in the house, it was more than likely hidden in the master bedroom, where Harlet moaned for Jay to go harder. It would have to wait.

In the meantime, Jacquline made her way to the kitchen, where she figured she'd find some nice silver that she could pawn off quite easily. It was at least three times the size of Jacquline's bedroom and probably cost more than her house. Elegant, hand-carved shelving and cupboard doors with gold ringlets lined the walls and the faucet was in the shape of a swan, highlighted in silver. The refrigerator, kept hidden within the cupboards, held nothing but vintage wine, caviar and other foods that made Jacquline gag.

"Rich bastards," she whispered to herself. "Don't they ever eat anything normal?" She looked through the cupboards for any type of trash bag. When she came up empty, she headed back. Harlet called out for God as if He were the one beneath her. Jacquline was a bit surprised Jay was able to even go this long.

"Five minutes," she said, "and then I'm coming up."

"Come join us," Harlet called back.

An awkward chill flowed through Jacquline's skin. "I'm fine, thanks." She quickly rounded the stairwell to a small hallway on the east side. A key rack hung next to the door at the end of the hall and another chill (this one pure excitement) washed over her. Jacquline wasted no time unlocking the door and switching on the light, one that not only lit up the room, but her entire soul as well. A brand new model Corvette and a bright blue Rolls Royce were parked together as the perfect couple. She was immediately drawn to the burnt-orange 'Vette like a magnet and caressed its body with the touch of a lover, completely overwhelmed by its majestic aura. Even better were the accessories hidden inside — stick shift, leather seats, MP3 and a state-of-the-art stereo system with navigation screen; everything she ever wanted in a car. Lying against it, her chest pushed up against the window as her cheek rested against the cold metal of the roof, making her flesh fill with goose bumps.

She didn't know how long she was there when she finally found the will to pull away and walk to the rear of the car to unscrew the license plate. If she could only take one thing from this house, there was no question in her mind that this car was it. No cash value could compare to what this baby was worth to her. As the plate hit the concrete, Jacquline thought she heard the light squeal of sirens. She became completely still and waited until she was able to confirm the increase in volume with each passing second.

"Damn it," she said under her breath. Without another thought, she rushed back into the house and made a beeline for the front door. Before she reached the edge of the stairwell, two squad cars pulled up to the driveway.

"Shit." Jacquline immediately ran to the door and locked it shut. Demands to open it went unanswered and Jacquline knew it wouldn't be long until they took it into their own hands. She had to think fast. Her first thought:

What's Ken going to do to me when he finds out I was arrested?

Then she thought of Tracey and knew that wasn't an option. "What the hell," she said and started back to the garage.

"What the hell's going on?" Jay called out, standing in the buff halfway down the stairs, Harlet curled up behind him.

"You're screwed," Jacquline said. She rushed down the hall without concern or remorse as the front door splintered open. Jay and Harlet rushed back up the stairs with a couple of cops in pursuit. One officer caught site of Jacquline grabbing the keys off the rack.

"Stop there," he called out.

"Make me," Jacquline said, flipping him the bird. She ignored any further pleas as she flew through the door and into the car. The smell of the leather and her tight grip on the wheel was enough to entice her to get lost in the moment. If only it could have lasted for more than a few seconds.

The cop tore open the door and made instant eye contact with Jacquline, who froze for a split second before smiling. The thrill of hitting that ignition button and hearing the engine roar to life — to take in its soothing vibration and absorb its complete essence — was more sexually gratifying than a night of drunken promiscuity. With her hand rested gently on the wheel, Jacquline cocked her head ever so slightly, sent the cop a wishful kiss, and threw the car into reverse.

The cop aimed his firearm at Jacquline as the Corvette ripped through the garage door, leaving an array of wood flying about.

The car wasn't in reverse for long.

After taking out the metal fence, the Corvette found the back end of one of the squad cars. Jacquline smashed her head against the steering wheel and it took a moment to catch her breath (and her senses), but once she had, she shifted the car into gear and slammed on the gas. The tires squealed as the Corvette spun around the back of the squad car and away from the house.

The cop started firing. With only three rounds, he found the rear tire, forcing the car to fishtail. Jacquline tightened her grip on the steering wheel in a vain attempt to keep the car from flipping. After rolling over a hundred yards, the car parked itself on its side against another large metal fence.

Faint sounds of footsteps pounded toward her. Though Jacquline's entire body ached and she could taste the blood pouring from her nose, she found enough strength to crawl out of the front window and sit against the hood. Her breaths were erratic as the cop asked her to move different parts of her body, all of which felt slightly numb. Soon, a second cop was standing in front of her, reciting a familiar speech as the first stood her up and cuffed her. All the while, Jacquline's mind wandered to thoughts of how disappointed Tracey would be when she didn't show up to get her the ice-cream; Ken's head exploding at the sight of her behind bars; but most of all, the disappointment her mother would have felt if she were still around. Gloria was never arrested — not once, regardless of the crime.

As she was escorted into the squad car, her head lowered with tremendous force, the only thing Jacquline could hear was an echo of words from her father, repeating over and over: *One of these days, you're going to do something stupid and your friends aren't going to be there to bail you out. And when that happens, neither will I.*

She just hoped that today wasn't going to be that day.

— 5 —

Tracey sat in the corner of the playground shaded by the line of trees that swarmed the hill, keeping the kids contained within the parameters of the school. This was her spot; this was where she went every lunch period to stay away from all the kids that wanted to make fun of her, or worse, hurt her. She ate her sandwich, slowly chewing each bite more than the twenty-two times she'd been told to do and carefully observed the other kids scream and run and enjoy themselves with great exuberance. They looked so carefree and happy — something she secretly longed to be a part of, yet didn't know how to be. Introductions were foreign to her; she understood what was going on, understood the need for speech, but was unaware of how to contribute — or maybe feared what she had to contribute.

She had just finished the last piece of her sandwich when a couple of boys walked up to her and stared as if she were going to combust at any moment. At first she was afraid to look up at them, feeling their eyes graze into her head. But as her mother once said, "The only way to know for sure if you can trust someone is to give them the benefit of the doubt."

Tracey finally looked up at their freckled faces. She didn't want to, but deep down, Stacey was asking her to — for her. Immediately, she felt the urge to squeeze her way into one of the gopher holes surrounding her petrified body, if only to escape the bright, glaring red hair and evil smirk radiating off the boy that made the top of her most despised list. But for whatever reason, when the boy spoke, she couldn't help but listen.

"Hey, Tracey. We just came up with this game, but we need a girl. Do you want to play with us?"

The thin jaw of the second boy (whose name may have been Robert, or Bobby, but whom Tracey always thought of as 'Coal' because of the rich black hair that grew down below his eyes) tightened, forcing back his laughter.

Give them the benefit of the doubt.

She would, only because she wanted so badly to fit in — to be one of them and to have fun. So even though trepidation haunted her gut and a spiritless gaze remained stamped on her face, she nodded.

"Cool," the redhead said as Coal ran over to a group of kids who had been watching the whole time. Most of them she knew, but there were a few fresh faces thrown in.

Tracey kept her eyes glued to them as the redhead grabbed her hand. "Let's go." He pulled her to the group and left her standing alone just in front of them. "Stand right there," he said as he led the boys into a circle around her. They held hands and stood shoulder-to-shoulder, making the circle as small as possible.

Tracey looked around at the boys — ten in all and not all of them happy about having to stand so close to another boy. She pulled her arms across her chest, rounding her shoulders forward slightly as a screaming match broke out between two of the boys she didn't know. Tracey feared it might have grown into a fist fight had the redhead been a few seconds later to break it up. After he whispered something to them (more than likely about Tracey, judging by the finger that kept pointing back at her), they finally agreed to stand next to each other but weren't about to hold hands.

"Okay, guys," the redhead said once he was back in position. "The first one to break the rhythm goes in the pot and becomes a target. Ready?"

All of the boys yelled out, "Ready!" in near unison.

"Here we go," the redhead said with a delightfully menacing grin. "Mighty Mute."

With that, the game had started. Each boy took a turn spouting an insult at Tracey, one right after the other:

"The mute."

"The black haired freak."

"Cheese from the moon."

"Planet Pluto's long lost moon."

None of the boys missed a beat in their little round-robin. Tracey stood still and quiet, her head tucked as close to her chest as possible. She ignored as many of the insults as she could as the dance made itself around the circle a second time. When it reached the redhead to begin the third round, Tracey was unable to overlook the words that echoed deep and loud.

"Mother killer."

Tracey stared at the redhead as the boys continued their attacks, all of which fell on deaf ears. Her focus was pinned on the redhead, his laughter becoming more infuriating with each new name. The last laugh was on him, though, as the insult wheel returned — and he froze, unable to come up with a zinger. His laugh faded faster than an ice cube in an oven as his friends razzed him for his brain fart. He tried desperately to call out a name but it was too late. Coal pushed the redhead inside the circle and closed it back up by taking the next boy's hand.

"I can't believe this." The redhead stood with his back to Tracey, his arms crossed in defiant disgust.

"Okay," Coal called out, taking charge of the game. "Insults are fair game on both of 'em." He then paused before addressing the redhead. "Hey, you know the rules."

The redhead sneered and reached for Tracey's hand, but she wasn't having it. She took a step back and glared at the redhead with a hint of rage.

"Hey, freak. I hate this as much as you, but it's part of the game. Now, come on."

The redhead again tried to take Tracey's hand but she was quick to steal it away and shove him toward Coal.

"What the hell are you doing?" he asked. "Don't push me!" The redhead shoved Tracey with more force than she did him. She stumbled backward to a couple of the boys, who whooped and hollered as they gleefully pushed her back toward the redhead. He inadvertently stopped her and held her for a brief, nervous moment as chants of, "Jason loves Tracey," came spewing from the group.

"Get off me hamper-diver," the redhead said, shoving Tracey to the ground. She instantly looked up at him with dark eyes, her breaths now highly erratic.

"What, are you gonna cry now?" The redhead looked back to his friends. "The big moon baby's gonna cry." He turned back to Tracey, his expression that of the devil. "Let's see those tears, mother killer."

It was those words that made Tracey's glistening eyes blossom into a deep turquoise. The laughter from the group faded as a bright white outline formed around Tracey's birthmark. The redhead stepped away in frightened confusion, unable to turn away from Tracey's ever darkening eyes.

"What's happening?" Coal said.

"What do you think?" the redhead said. "Moon baby's letting her freak flag fly."

Tracey suddenly let out a piercing screech. She leapt and clawed at the redhead as if he were her own personal cat tree.

After a quick moment of "What should we do?" stares, a few of the boys ran away as others remained petrified. Inching closer with an attempt at calming the situation, Coal touched Tracey's shoulder with the tips of his fingers. "Tracey."

Tracey swiped backward and sent Coal flying. He landed some forty feet away and rolled another few feet before coming to a stop. He lay still, unable to move — *not wanting to move?* Tracey couldn't tell, but her first glimpse of the other kids on the playground confused her. Everyone had stopped what they were doing and were looking at her as if she were the newest attraction at the zoo. That's when she realized what she had done. She turned back to the redhead. His face dripped with blood.

The glow around her eyes and birthmark softened as she stood away from him. She calmed her breaths and searched for any features of the redhead she could recognize. When she couldn't take it any longer she turned around and instantly spotted Coal, now surrounded by his friends and a couple of teachers. Tracey's knees gave out from under her and her head fell limp. With one last look at the redhead, Tracey collapsed.

— 6 —

Looking back over the calculations based on the new information, Lark rubbed her mouth, concerned that the numbers wouldn't hold up. They looked sound, but how it worked in practice was a much different beast altogether. Was it worth seeing the disappointment on Ken's face when it failed to find out if it would work? It was better than the anger and resentment that would follow if she refused to test it.

"Here goes nothing." Lark shifted the mouse, beginning the simulation. Everything was steady, producing all the right results. Then again, liftoff wasn't the issue; it was what came next that had her hands folded anxiously against her lips. After a few tense moments, Lark shifted the mouse again and clicked. Her eyes remained awash with anticipation as the screen glistened against them.

"Come on, work, damn you," she whispered. For a few seconds, Lark was in great spirits, her leg bouncing uncontrollably. But any hope she had left was lost in one split second.

"Shit!" She slammed her fist on the desk and then took a moment to contemplate the results, staring at the screen as if she could somehow make them change. Defeated, she slid her chair across the room to the large window overlooking the main room.

"Ken," she said into an intercom unit next to the window.

"Yeah," Ken responded after a short pause.

"I need you in the sim-room. There may be a problem."

"What's wrong? Didn't it work?" Ken's voice was full of hidden disappointment.

"Just get your ass up here."

"It's already out the door."

Lark switched off the intercom and peered down at the spaceship sitting in the middle of the cylindrical room. It was shaped like a rocket, just over twenty-five feet from stem to stern with a pair of wings at the rear that spread ten feet from the body. Four engines were tucked inside the tail, with two smaller engines that sat just underneath the ship, a detail Lark added to Ken's otherwise flawless plans to help better perfect the liftoff. Another edition she made early on were the two small jets on the nose of the ship that would be required for deceleration.

Ken stepped out of the ship and jogged in Lark's direction, stopping to answer a question from one of the techs before disappearing beneath her. Ken had a good relationship with everyone, mostly because of his extremely casual rules and demeanor. It was his most appealing attribute and one that pushed Lark's affection for him above simple friendship. Even with that, Lark wasn't sure she wanted to be around when he arrived — not with what she was about to tell him. She swiveled around to meet Ken's anxiety as the door to the simulation room opened.

"What happened?"

Lark pointed to the screen. "Check it out."

Ken slid over to the computer, almost in tandem with Lark's nonchalant turn away. What he saw ran deeper than heartbreak.

WARNING:

Detection of hull breach
Elapsed time: 30 seconds

"That can't be right," Ken said, taking a seat. Lark tried to avoid him as he rapped at the keys like a piano, but it was too hard to look away. "You put all the specs in, right?" Ken checked the information that Lark had updated and then ran a quick diagnostic of his own, triple checking for any errors.

"It's right," Lark barked. "I double checked it myself."

"It can't be." When Ken was through running his diagnostic, he clicked the button that read, "Launch."

"This has to work," he said, barely audible.

Lark sighed, keeping watch of the screen over Ken's shoulder. A digital model of Ken's ship ignited its engines and lifted off the ground. It floated in the center of the screen as the background transitioned from a light, sky-blue into a dark black with little dots representing the stars. Finally, a message appeared on the screen:

Ready to ignite ion thrusters
PROCEED?

Ken hit the button without hesitation. Suddenly, the back of the tiny model lit up in a brilliant white with a light green hue. The ship itself didn't move but the stars rushed from left to right, moving faster as time passed until they were simple white streaks across the screen. As it continued, Ken opened a data screen to the bottom right, where he could track the progression of the speed of the ship, the temperature of the nuclear reactors and the integrity of the engines themselves. All of it seemed to be in perfect order.

"It's working," he said with a slight lack of confidence.

"The ion thrusters, yeah," Lark said. "Your idea works like a dream. Check the structural integrity."

Ken glanced down at the numbers representing the ship's hull. The faster the ship went, the less the ship could withstand the pressure. "What's the problem? These numbers are accurate."

"Keep watching."

Ken kept his eyes glued to the numbers. When the ship's velocity reached half the speed of light, the pressure ripped the ship into a million little specs. This was followed by the message of a hull breach.

"Damn it," Ken said. He sat back and wiped his mouth, unable to look away from the disheartening message.

"I thought you said the LS-Accel would hold up," Ken finally muttered.

"I thought it would. The damn stuff holds up perfectly under pressures equivalent to more than 10 miles below sea level. It should not be failing."

"Then why is it?"

"I don't know."

"What does that mean?" Ken was exasperated.

"It means I need to take that damn stuff apart and start from scratch."

"Damn it, Lark. You can't do that."

"What do you want me to say? It's the only option we have."

"If we want to cut tail and run like little bitches."

Lark folded her arms and turned back to the window. She had only seen this side of Ken a few times over the last few years and she hated it more every time, to the point where it was becoming intolerable.

Ken knew that gesture well. He lowered his head and took a few calming breaths. "There has to be another option."

"It's not safe otherwise."

"I don't believe that. We can't abort." He looked back up. "*You* can't."

Ken was in tears. He tried to hide it but Lark knew him long enough to see through the mask he used to protect himself from what he didn't want to see — or let anyone else see.

"I'm sorry, Ken," she said. "But we both knew this was a possibility."

Ken looked back to the computer. His silence said everything Lark needed to hear.

"Let me take another look at it. There may be something I haven't factored in yet. If I find something, anything that shows this can work, then we'll reconsider. Just give me a couple of days." She waited, and though Ken hardly moved a muscle, Lark knew he was smiling. "Take that time to clear your head."

"I'm fine," Ken said, though it sounded highly disingenuous.

Just then, one of technicians' voices boomed over the intercom. "Ken, there's a call for you."

Ken wiped his eyes and walked to Lark. "Can it wait?" he replied as he hit the receiver, his voice fatigued.

"I don't think so. It's your daughter's school."

"What do they want?"

"They wouldn't say, but they need you to pick her up right away."

Ken's forehead dropped into his hand. He brushed it through his hair. "Tell them I'll be right there."

"Yes, sir."

Ken peered down at Lark. "What do you think it is?" she asked.

"I don't know."

Lark took his hand. "Go," she said, her voice more compassionate than it had ever been. It took Ken a little off guard. "Take the next couple of days."

"No. Do whatever you need to do to find out what's going on with the LS-Accel and then gather the team in the conference room. I'll be back in two hours."

"Two hours? Ken, this problem may take two years to figure out."

"You're smart."

"Not that smart," Lark said under her breath. Ken didn't notice as he was headed out the door.

"Ken," the technician called again over the intercom.

"Get that," Ken said as he turned into the hall.

Lark rolled her eyes. She adored the guy, but there were times when he could be impossible. "Yeah," she said, shoving her thumb to the receiver.

"Where's Ken?"

"He's gone. What do you need?"

His response shocked Lark to the point that she didn't even finish listening to what the young man had to say before she was out the door, racing after Ken. She caught up with him just inside the main door.

"Ken, wait," she yelled, bounding up the stairwell.

"Shouldn't you be working?"

"Ken, it's your daughter."

"Where do you think I'm going?"

"No. Your *other* daughter. Jacquline."

"What about her?"

"She needs you to post bail."

It took a second to register what she said. All he could do was shake his head. *What the hell's happening to my children?*

"Are you sure you don't want to take a couple of days to sort through all of this?"

"Two hours," he said, ripping the door open before Lark could object.

"God damn it," she hissed and walked back down the hall to try and find a solution to a problem she knew wasn't there.

— 7 —

I don't have time for this.

Time was a luxury Ken couldn't afford and his daughters were stealing it from him. *How can they be so inconsiderate?* he kept thinking as he rushed toward the school, almost forgetting to shut the door of his truck. As he raced through the halls, he thought of nothing but getting back to the ship and how excited he'd be when Lark gave him the good news. He felt so close to Stacey and yet there was still a part of him that knew he'd never see her again, no matter how far he pushed that fear to the depths of his mind.

"Where is she?" he said, bursting through the main office door.

The secretary (older but light on her feet) stopped Ken from entering the principal's office. "Where is who?"

Ken had been in this very office so many times because of Jacquline — because of her mother? — that he always wondered why he hadn't taken up residence. And yet, the secretary still didn't know who he was.

"My daughter? Where is she?"

"Sir, calm down," the secretary said calmly. She may not have remembered him since the last time he was there but she certainly knew how to control an irate parent. Ken had to respect that. "What's your daughter's name?"

"Tracey Brody," he said, matching her tone. "I got a call saying I needed to pick her up."

"Okay, Mr. Brody," she said. "Ken, right?" Maybe she had remembered him. "Have a seat. Ms. Krane will be right with you."

"I'm kind of in a hurry. Can I just have Tracey so I can go?"

"Mr. Brody?"

Ken relaxed upon hearing Linda's familiar voice. "Linda. Thank God. Where's Tracey?"

"It's been a long time, Ken," Linda said sweetly. "It's good to see you again. Of course, I wish it were under better circumstances."

"Yeah, yeah. Where's Tracey?"

Linda gestured Ken into her office. "Please, join us."

Tracey sat in front of Linda's desk. Her head was down — in shame or guilt, Ken couldn't tell — and she wouldn't look up, not even when Ken wrapped his arms around her with a supportive hug.

"How you doing?" Ken tried to lift her head but she stayed frozen. "What happened?"

"Ken, please have a seat," Linda said from behind her desk. She waited until Ken was seated before sitting herself. His eyes remained fixed on Tracey, his hand attached to her shoulder as if he were afraid that if he let go, she'd be lost to him forever. "I'll get right to it, Ken. I'm afraid I'm going to have to expel your daughter."

Ken was on his feet. "What? Are you crazy?"

"Ken, please," Linda said, matching his stance and tone with her own. "Let me explain."

"Yes, please. Explain to me why you think Tracey needs to be expelled."

Linda was unflinching. "Have a seat."

Ken was ready to pull Tracey from the office but he thought better of it and took his seat instead. A few seconds after, Linda took her own.

"What happened?" Ken finally said as calmly as he could muster.

"Tracey put two boys in the hospital this afternoon."

"The hospital? You have got to be kidding."

"I'm afraid not."

Ken looked back to Tracey, who shifted her head away. He brushed Tracey's hair back behind her ear in hopes of getting just one small glimpse of her face. "How?"

"Some of the boys who witnessed it said they were playing a game when she attacked them without provocation."

"I don't believe that," Ken said sternly. "If she fought anyone, it's because they provoked it."

"Regardless of who started what, the fact is she ripped half the skin off one of the boy's faces. From the reports I've received, he'll never be able to see out of his left eye again"

"Have you ever thought maybe he deserved it?"

"Mr. Brody."

Regret filled Ken's features. "I'm sorry. I didn't mean that."

"No one ever thinks their child is capable of something like this until it happens."

Ken still wasn't ready to accept that Tracey could do such a thing but he was going to indulge Linda in hopes of getting out of there quicker. "What happened to the other boy?"

"Apparently when he tried to stop her, she threw him across the playground. I don't know how to explain that, Mr. Brody, but he has a collapsed lung and may not make it through the night."

Linda let her words sink in. Ken's eyes remained defensive.

"I understand your anger, Ken, but the parents of both children are threatening to sue the school for what happened. I've been getting persistent calls from parents asking to pull their children out. I adore Tracey. Up until now, she's been a model student. But parents don't feel safe having her here with their kids."

Ken had no viable response to that information.

"I've also had to contact social services —"

"Social services," Ken yelled, leaping from his chair. "What the hell for?"

Linda was back on her feet. "Ken, your daughter almost killed two of her classmates. I had to contact them. It's my job."

"Screw your job. She's my daughter."

"I'm sorry. I had no choice."

Ken composed himself enough to say what he needed to say without violence. "I'd die in Hell before I'll let some crazy bitch who thinks she knows better take my child away from me." Ken pulled Tracey into his arms. "Come on, Tracey. We're done here." Tracey dug her face into his shoulder. She would have to eventually, but she still wasn't ready to look at him.

Linda grabbed Ken's arm before he could step away. "I can't let you take her." She let go quickly in response to Ken's sharp, cold eyes.

Tracey felt Ken's anger, sadness and pain in his grip. It was something she wished she could take away but knew was impossible. What she had done was unforgivable. If only she had her mother to comfort her.

Ken left the office without another word.

— 8 —

Jacquline lied on the bed in the cell. It had been over an hour since she had called Ken and her patience was wearing thin. She aimed the last of the rubber bands from her hair at the light above her and let go. It bounced off and fell to the ground with all the others. *Damn bastard left me here to rot,* she thought. Suddenly, the door leading into the cellblock squeaked open and footsteps approached.

"Well, it's about damn time," she said, swiping her jacket off the bed. She fixed her hair, which now fell to the middle of her back

The cop that busted her appeared between the cold round bars — alone. Although Jacquline hadn't expected to see Ken standing with him, a part of her was still disappointed.

"I should leave your smart ass in here," the cop said.

"What did you say to me?"

"That was a message from your father." He unlocked the door. "But I have to agree with him."

"I guess he does care about me after all."

"He must." The cop escorted Jacquline from the cellblock. Along the way, she mentally prepared for the ass chewing she was about to receive. She actively raised the walls around her vulnerability and relief so as to make sure she stayed on the offensive. It was just her luck that when she walked through the doors into the station, Ken was nowhere to be found.

"Where the hell is he?" she said.

"Waiting outside." The cop walked to the cage next to the door and pulled out a manila envelope.

"Bastard couldn't even face me," she said, walking up to the cage.

The cop poured out the contents of the envelope and named them all off. "Sign here," he said, handing Jacquline a clipboard. She signed for her possessions and scooped them up.

"Don't let me see you in here again."

"You won't." Jacquline threw her jacket on and walked out of the station. She raised her hand to her forehead to help her eyes adjust to the bright rays of the sun. It only took a few seconds after to catch sight of Ken a few yards away, pacing next to his truck. He was on the phone until he saw Jacquline and got in the truck. For a moment, Jacquline thought of walking the other way — clear her head. But then she noticed Ken talking to someone in the truck and her curiosity got the better of her. As she got closer, she finally saw Tracey.

What is she doing here? Jacquline thought. Her pace quickened; by the time she reached the truck, she was in a jog.

She opened the passenger door. "What's going on?"

"Get in," Ken said. "I'll explain on the way."

Jacquline was hesitant. He was being way too calm. She half expected him to scream and yell; part of her actually desired it. Finally, she got in, cautiously keeping one eye on Ken and the other on Tracey, who sat between them with her chin rested firmly against her chest.

Ken started up the truck and drove away.

"Hey, Squint," Jacquline said. "What's wrong? What happened?"

Tracey shifted her head away from Jacquline, making sure to keep as far away from Ken as possible. She didn't want to face the disappointment from either of them.

"Look at me, sweetie." Jacquline tried to force Tracey to turn her head but she was too strong for her. Instead, Jacquline wrapped her arms around Tracey and lowered her head next to hers. "Please," Jacquline whispered, hoping it would entice Tracey to do as she asked. It didn't work.

"What happened to Tracey?" Jacquline asked Ken, her voice strong with anger.

Ken cupped his hand over his mouth and refused to look at her.

Jacquline turned away, containing her rage — for Tracey's sake. She never let go of her hand, though it wasn't clear if it was because she couldn't, or if Tracey wouldn't let her.

"Where are we going?" Jacquline said upon realizing that her surroundings were completely unfamiliar.

"Back to the office," Ken replied soberly.

"You can't take us home first?"

"I'm already late because of you."

"Late for what?" It was becoming harder for Jacquline to contain her anger.

"I have a meeting to get to."

"What meeting? And don't you tell me this is about that stupid abduction nonsense of yours."

Ken didn't say a word.

"God, you are a piece of work," Jacquline huffed. "I thought I told you to leave us out of your messed up shit."

Jacquline pulled Tracey into her lap and combed her hair away from her face. It was amazing how much she looked like Stacey. If only she had stayed instead of Ken. Jacquline trusted Stacey — loved her, in fact; she wouldn't have neglected them the way Ken did.

But then why did he stay?

Ken stayed, Stacey didn't. Gloria didn't. It may not have felt like it, but Ken still must have held a love for them that Jacquline couldn't see — or refused to see. It was the same love that Jacquline refused to give Ken. Maybe it was time —

For Tracey.

— 9 —

Jacquline held Tracey's hand as they followed Ken into the cold hallway. As the door automatically locked behind them, Ken stopped a couple of steps down the barely lit stairwell and turned to them.

"What you are about to see is highly confidential and does not leave this building, understood?"

Jacquline rolled her eyes. "Whatever."

"I'm serious."

"Yeah. I got it," Jacquline said with bite. "What's so damned important," she added under her breath.

"Stay right next to me and do as I say."

Jacquline kept Tracey close as they walked down the stairs. She couldn't help notice the thick layer of dust and cobwebs on the light fixtures, which for a second made her think that something was crawling on her arm. There was no doubt that it was all in her head, but it forced her to pull Tracey in closer nonetheless.

When they reached the bottom of the staircase, the contrast was overwhelming. It was immaculately clean and gloriously white. Bright florescent lights streamlined the ceiling along the endless circular hallways. Glass panels lined the entire inner wall, looking out across an empty void where more windows covered the completion of the inner hallways. For a moment, Jacquline felt she was on the edge of a giant see-through doughnut. She hadn't realized she'd let go of Tracey as she stepped up to the glass. What she found, two stories below her, mesmerized her beyond belief.

"What do you think?" Ken asked.

"I —" Nothing else escaped her lips.

Ken smiled. He wrapped his hands around her shoulders and pulled her away from the glass. After a moment, Jacquline realized what was happening and shifted away from him, once again taking hold of Tracey's hand.

"What is that?" she said, taking long glances toward the ship as they walked. Tracey didn't once attempt to look; her eyes stayed focused on her shoes.

"I'll explain it all, but right now, I need you to watch Tracey while I go to this meeting."

Ken led them into one of a dozen rooms lining the outer wall. It was a large kitchen with several vending machines, a couple of sinks and a refrigerator. Three round tables sat in the middle. He pulled out his wallet and handed Jacquline a few dollars.

"Help yourself to whatever you want. Just promise me you'll stay right here, okay?"

Jacquline swiped the money away. "Yeah." She walked Tracey to one of the tables and sat her down.

Ken wanted to say something but chose to leave instead. He closed the door behind him, leaving Jacquline free to vent her anger on one of the vending machines. She sat down with her back to Tracey and buried her face in her hands. It was minutes before she felt a light touch on her shoulder. Tracey was standing behind her, looking at her with much sadder eyes than Jacquline was used to. Jacquline embraced her; whether it was for Tracey's sake or her own was unimportant.

"You hungry?" Jacquline said, walking to a vending machine. She popped in a dollar and hit the buttons for a bag of Cheetos. Tracey took them and sat back down, holding the bag without ever touching the actual chips.

"Not hungry, huh? I don't blame you." That was Jacquline's cue to start munching on them herself. Millions of questions that would probably go unanswered raced through her head. As Jacquline cleaned the residual cheese off her fingers with her tongue, a lanky man of Korean descent walked in. He stopped, startled.

"Don't mind us," Jacquline said. "We're just visiting."

"You must be Ken's daughters," the man said. His voice matched his young appearance. "I'll leave you be."

"Wait a second," Jacquline said before the man could leave. "Can I ask you something?"

The man looked down the hall and then back to Jacquline, who curled her eyebrows with just enough puppy-dog magnetism to keep him there. He walked to the vending machine. "What do you want to know?"

"What is it, exactly, that you do here?"

"I'm just an intern," he said. "File papers mostly, take phone calls."

"Right." She tossed the empty Cheetos bag on the table and stood up. "And what are those papers and phone calls about?"

"Your dad didn't tell you?"

"He likes to keep things a secret, especially from me. He doesn't fully trust me, you know, being a jailbird and all." Jacquline leaned up against the vending machine next to the young man. She rested her foot high up against her butt and crossed her arms under her breasts, pushing them up slightly to reveal an extra hint of cleavage.

"I'm sorry."

"That's all right. I'm over it. I'm Jacquline by the way." She opened her hand, keeping it tucked in close to her breast.

The man smiled nervously. "Kwan." He avoided shaking her hand.

Jacquline smirked, resting her hand back down. "You see, what does matter, Kwan, is what that thing is down there."

"You mean the ship?"

"So it is a ship. Like, a spaceship?"

"Yeah." Kwan punched the numbers and claimed his prize.

"Meant to do what?"

"I think that's something you should talk with your dad about."

"Don't you worry, I will. But come on." Jacquline took hold of Kwan's hand and pulled him close. "I just want a little context before I do." She fluttered her eyes ever so slightly.

Kwan smiled. "Talk to your dad."

Jacquline's flirtatious grin faded. She let Kwan go and plopped back down in the chair.

"Sorry. It's not my place." Kwan left the room.

"Dick." As the door closed, Jacquline pulled Kwan's wallet from her pocket and stripped it of all its money. "At least it wasn't a complete bust." She stuffed the money into her pocket and tossed the wallet into the trashcan.

— 10 —

The room hushed as Ken walked in. He looked around at the dozen sober faces without saying a word and then locked eyes with Lark. His heart stopped as she desperately tried to hide the bad news painted across her face. He'd have to leave it be — for now.

Ken slid to the empty chair at the end of the long conference table. He placed his hands on the table, his head facing the floor, and took a breath. Moments later, a familiar touch appeared on his forearm. He didn't want to look at her; he just wanted his wife back — the sooner the better.

Lark's soft whisper broke the silence. "Are you okay?"

"What did you find?" Ken said, just as soft.

"Nothing that's going to help us. I told you, I need more time."

Ken looked up to the group, shifting his arm away from Lark, hoping she'd think it was intentional. But Lark knew better. She kept her hand close to his on the face of the table.

"What do you think?" Ken asked generically.

No one was brave enough to answer. They all knew what needed to be said and none of them wanted to be the bearer of bad news.

"Anyone."

"With the latest simulation results," said Jackson, a thin man wearing wire-rimmed glasses, "I have to agree with Lark. I think it's in our best interest to postpone the live test."

Ken grimaced. "Who agrees with that?"

Everyone at the table raised their hands. Ken couldn't help but smile. "You must have had a great argument," he said to Lark.

"We just can't guarantee its safety," Lark said. "Not yet."

"The LS-Accel is too unstable," reported a portly man named Gary. "The simulations are clear. It will not hold together at that rate of velocity."

"Lark designed the LS-Accel to withstand thirty-thousand degree heat and thousands of pounds of pressure," Ken said. "I have faith that it will not fall apart."

"I don't."

"Duly noted."

"It's not just about the LS-Accel, Mr. Brody," Margerite chimed in. She was an older woman with graying hair. "Lark brought me on to continue research on the metal's integrity and real-world applications. I never once thought any human would be testing it like this, at least not this early in its development."

"Then Lark should have been more clear about that. This was always the goal."

"But at that level of speed," Margerite said, "it'll rip your body to shreds, regardless of whether or not the LS-Accel holds up. This isn't a science-fiction movie."

"I'm aware of the physics," Ken mumbled. "All I care about is whether or not the ship is a go."

"Technically, the ship is sound," Harvey said with an echo of agreement. He was one of the first to come on board the project and worked just as diligently as both Ken and Lark, sometimes even more so. If there was any person who knew more about the ship than Ken, it was Harvey. "But there are still a lot of unexpected things that might happen. I still say we should test the entire thing remotely first."

"That could take years."

"And could be what saves your life. Let's say the LS-Accel holds up and you don't get torn to shreds. The nuclear reactor and this new addition of jet fuel into the ion thrusters is concern enough. If it becomes too unstable, it can blow at any time."

"But you believe it *is* stable."

"For now."

"That mix of chemicals alone is all you need to be concerned about," added David, a balding man tucked away in the corner.

"What's your concern?" Ken asked.

"Nobody's ever tested anything like it before. You think these things up on a whim and just expect them to work."

"Our tests and the simulations show a clean ignition."

"I'd feel safer testing the mix on a drone first, to back-up that data."

"The question is, will the fuel help push the ion thrusters to the speed we need or not?"

"Yes, they will," David said hesitantly.

"Then as far as I'm concerned, we're a go."

"This isn't just about the ship, Ken," Lark said.

"She's right," Ryan, a man with a small mustache and a pocket protector, added quickly. "You're not ready, physically or emotionally."

"We've been training in the simulation tank for the last three months —"

"It takes years of training for a real astronaut to get ready for a flight like this."

"We're not going to be space walking, doctor. You know that. Besides, the gravity simulators will help us with the weightlessness problem, right?"

"In a manner of speaking."

"Then we're fine. We've been through all of the scenarios and passed our physicals. Is there anything I'm missing?"

"Your kids," Lark said.

Ken took a deep breath and lowered his head as the words sunk in. Lark's hand slid down his arm and rested softly on his wrist.

"What about them?" he whispered.

"I'm worried about them."

"They'll be fine."

"Are you sure about that? Both of them got into serious trouble today. Do you really think it will help them to have their father jettison off into space with a high probability he won't ever come back?"

"I think it will help them to have their mother back in their lives."

"If we even find her, the chances of which are minuscule at best. You're absolutely ready to give them up for that dream?"

"I'm ready to do what I have to to make their lives better."

"I think being with them would make their lives whole."

"Only Stacey can do that."

Lark forced Ken to look at her. He was lost.

"I'm aborting the project," she said.

Ken pulled away and kicked the door.

"I'm sorry for what happened, Ken, I am. But, the well-being of your kids far outweighs what I can do with this material."

"That's easy for you to say. You got everything you need to sell this to some big conglomerate for billions. What do I have to show for it? I came into this to find my wife, and that's what I damn-well plan to do."

Ken stormed from the room. Lark waited, feeling a great deal of compassion for Ken's situation. "Take the rest of the day," she said solemnly. "We'll shut her down tomorrow."

The group chattered away as Lark left. She found Ken sitting against the wall, staring at the glass with watery eyes.

Lark sat next to him. "You know I'm right."

Ken turned away.

"You love your kids, Ken, I know you do. But they need you more than you realize. Who would I be if I took you away from them?"

"It's too late," he said.

"No, it's not. They're waiting for you. Just go to them; be with them."

"And all of this is for what? Without Stacey..."

"I know how much you loved her, Ken. But if you love your kids as much as her, you need to show them that."

"I don't know how?"

"Yes, you do." Lark squeezed Ken's hand and wrapped her arm around his shoulder. "You do."

Ken wiped the moisture from his eyes. He tucked his forehead into Lark's and held it there, unwilling to leave.

— 11 —

Jacquline was staring at the ship when Ken walked up to her. "I knew you were insane, Ken, but I never thought you'd go this far."

"Come on," he said softly. "I need to talk to you guys." He opened the door to the kitchen and waited for Jacquline. She hated the sight of the ship, wanted to destroy it, but didn't want to take her eyes off it. When she finally did, she kept them away from Ken. She sat next to Tracey and held her hand. Ken took a seat at the next table. He consumed Tracey's innocence; her silent need for comfort, for love — for her mother.

"You finally ready to tell us what you're planning?" Jacquline said. When Ken refused to respond, Jacquline continued. "Let me guess. You truly believe that your wife was abducted by freaking *aliens* and you've decided to commit suicide in a damn spaceship to find the sorry bitch. Does that about sum it up?"

"I'm going to forgive you for that, Jacquline," Ken said solemnly, "but I don't ever want to hear you say it again."

Jacquline saw the anger in his eyes, yet somehow he was able to contain it, most likely for Tracey's sake, as Jacquline had done so often before.

"Yes," he continued. "I built a spaceship that I fully intended to use to find Stacey.

We had planned to test its speed capabilities today."

"Had planned?"

Ken didn't want to say it out loud. "We had to abort."

"Good. Now maybe you can take care of your daughter, you know, like a real father."

"We had to abort the test," Ken said, "because we don't need it anymore. We have enough information to safely make the jump and start looking for Stacey immediately."

"I can't believe this," Jacquline mumbled.

"I will admit, the jump is dangerous and I may end up being gone for some time, possibly a few years. But it's something I have to do. You have to understand what I've gone through for this."

"What I understand is you couldn't care less about us."

"That's not true, Jacks. I care a great deal about —"

"Stacey. You care a great deal about Stacey. Did you ever think once about us over the last five years?"

"I've been doing my best, Jacks."

"No, you haven't."

"I have. You don't know how hard it is, Jacks, not when one daughter gets arrested and the other one almost kills someone."

Jacquline's outrage immediately fell to confusion. "What?"

Ken rubbed his mouth in disbelief. "I didn't want..."

Jacquline's furrowed brow scared Ken into submission. "Apparently some boys were picking on her today," he said, "and I guess they went a little too far."

"She defended herself?"

"I don't know. Maybe."

"Good for you, kiddo," Jacquline said to Tracey.

"You told her to do that?"

"I told her to stand up for herself, yeah."

"Why would you do that?"

"Who else was going to stand up for her? Certainly not you."

"I've tried to be there for you guys, Jacquline."

"If that was true," Jacquline roared, "do you really think Tracey would have tried to kill someone? Think about that for a second." Her eyes cracked red.

Ken combed his hand through Tracey's hair. "I need you to take care of her until I get back."

"I hope you die up there," Jacquline said, pulling Tracey away from him. She pressed Tracey's head softly up against her stomach, making sure she couldn't look at him.

Ken reached out for her, hoping to hold her one last time, but knew that was impossible. He had been right — he lost them a long time ago. "I love you," he said.

"Have fun," Jacquline said, her voice cold.

Ken stared at Tracey for a while longer. "I will be back for you, Jacks."

"Yeah, sure," she said sarcastically. "I'll cross my fingers."

Ken took a deep breath and left the room.

Jacquline waited a few moments before she was willing to let Tracey go. "Looks like it's just you and me now, Squint."

Tracey looked up at Jacquline. Her eyes were empty and stale.

"Forget about him," Jacquline said. "He's not coming back."

Suddenly, the emptiness in Tracey's eyes was replaced with something Jacquline didn't recognize.

"What's wrong, Squint?"

Tracey let out a scream with a pitch so high, Jacquline could feel it more than she could hear it. She strained for air as she grabbed her throbbing ears and closed her eyes. It wasn't long before she fell to the floor as if she were melting, her body drained of life. When Tracey finally stopped screaming, she ran into the hall and looked down at the ship, her hand pressed firmly to the glass. That little box below her was Ken's pathway to Stacey; there was no reason it couldn't be Tracey's as well. She sprinted down the hall, eventually reaching a dark stairwell that she jumped down with deviating speed. Tracey knew she was vulnerable to detection as she slammed through the door that led into the docking bay, so there was no time for sightseeing. She raced through the eerily quiet space, hoping no one would report her transgressions to Ken.

As she leapt through the open hatch, the sheer beauty of the ship's interior finally enticed her to stop. It looked larger than it did from the outside. There was a door leading into a small area with two chairs and a gray, metal desk. Opposite that door was another door leading to the back of the ship. But what caught her eye were the large cabinets lining the wall in front of her. She immediately opened the one directly in front of her. Inside was a round ball of metal with a strap that wrapped around it like an equator. It was as big as Tracey's upper body and filled the entire cabinet. Tracey shut the door and opened the next one — a giant toolbox. The next one was filled with a large red canister that read:

FLAMMABLE

She was losing hope as she reached the last cabinet. To her relief, it was empty and just to her liking. She stole into the cabinet and concealed herself in its darkness.

— 12 —

Jacquline shook with pain as she lay in a tight ball attempting to catch her breath. Her body felt as if she were deep under water — her muscles constricted her from movement, her head felt as if a hammer were pulverizing it to mush, and her heart pounded as her lungs squeezed out just enough air to keep her alive.

Five minutes had elapsed before Jacquline was able to remove her hands from her ears and open her eyes. It felt as if a thousand needles were piercing them through. When she sensed some vitality return to her legs and arms, she slowly limped to the door. All she could see as she peered out into the hall were giant white voids, but none of that mattered; it was up to her to suck it up and find Tracey before something bad happened to her. Her first thought was that she left the building, but that didn't make a whole lot of sense. Tracey wasn't one to run away like that. She did what she did for a reason — to get away from Jacquline. But why did she need to get away from her so desperately that she would risk hurting her?

The answer was actually quite simple. Ken was leaving them to find Stacey and Tracey was connected to her in a way that Jacquline never was to her own mother. If Ken was this determined to find her, Tracey would be just as determined, maybe even more so. But going to find Ken would end in rejection; Tracey was too smart for that. She was going to do something more daring; she was going to do something more cunning. And based on the tiny handprint Tracey had left on the glass, there was only one place Tracey could have gone.

She was going to get on that ship.

By the time Jacquline found her way into the main room, her chest felt ten times better than it had just five minutes earlier and the aches and pains were fading exponentially.

Unlike Tracey, Jacquline was far more cautious. She hid behind a small pillar near the stairwell and looked around for anyone middling about. Her eyesight had readjusted to normal (and in hindsight, a lot better than it had been), allowing her to see clearly to the other side of the room. There wasn't anyone on the ground floor, but Jacquline needed to make sure no one was inadvertently spying through the hallways. She examined each level carefully until the ceiling caught her eye. It was so far up, she had a difficult time translating what the specifics were, but she knew it was the only way the ship was going to get out of that room. "Insane."

Movement in the corner of her eye knocked Jacquline back to the second level, where Ken walked briskly from one of the offices and around toward the stairwell.

She thought for a moment that she should wait for him; tell him what was going on. But he might not believe her — or else would yell at her for losing Tracey. Besides, there wasn't any proof that she was even in the ship, and if she wasn't, that meant he would have to take time to help find her, thus postponing his ride to death. That wouldn't go over well and Jacquline wasn't in the mood to deal with that right now.

A short, stocky man stopped Ken in the hall and gave him a handshake and a hug. This was her chance. Staying as low as possible, Jacquline sprinted as fast as she could to the ship.

"Tracey?" she whispered as she stepped inside. The ceiling was only a few feet above her head, which forced her to bend over, somehow feeling she would hit her head if she stood erect. "Tracey?" she said again, her voice scratchy and almost non-existent.

Nothing but cabinets lined the wall in front of her, none of which looked large enough to fit an eight-year-old child, so she turned her attention to the cockpit, where again, there wasn't anywhere to hide. The only possibility Jacquline could see was the door at the back of the ship.

She tried to capture the entire picture all at once as she stepped through the door. Lining the back wall were two tubes, stretching from the floor to the roof. They were dark, but Jacquline saw gray waves rippling within. The base of the tubes was connected to the rear of the ship with small pipes connecting the tubes to the large metal casing strapped to the wall, also sitting from floor to ceiling. A countless number of wires connected the tubes to the sides of the room, which Jacquline immediately recognized as a very complex computer system. Dozens of lights flashed their readiness and several meters read levels of stuff Jacquline couldn't quite make out. Above her, there was a row of grates that made up the ceiling holding various dark, circular shapes.

Jacquline walked to the panels for a closer look, her steps vibrating softly off the metal floor. Her heart raced as she saw readings of oxygen levels, gravity levels and nuclear levels. She felt dizzy and had to drop to her knee to catch herself from fainting. *What the hell is he thinking?*

Suddenly, the door closed. Jacquline stood, slightly groggy, and rushed to the door. By the time she reached it, it had automatically locked, though that didn't stop her from attempting to open it anyway.

"Help," she screamed repeatedly, pounding on the door to no effect. It was clear that the back of the ship had been designed with heavier, thicker metals to contain a potential nuclear explosion. Jacquline had to accept that it would also be sound proof because of it. She looked around for an intercom or speaker system of some kind — anything that would allow her to communicate with someone in the ship or the building. Jacquline found the absence of one to be a major flaw in the design — for this very reason.

Just then, the tubes at the rear of the ship turned from their dark gray stasis to a bright green as the engines fired up. Jacquline's heart jumped to her throat. It didn't matter if no one could hear her now. She was trapped inside the core of a potential bomb; she had to keep trying.

"Help! I'm in here! Dad, help!"

— 13 —

Lark stared at the screen in the simulation room. She wanted to run over all the tests again, but doing so would only be to appease Ken, nothing more. For her, the LS-Accel wasn't flawed at all. She designed it exactly the way she envisioned it — for the purpose of retrofitting Naval vessels and aircraft, enabling them to withstand greater punishment, in both manned hypersonic flight and wartime situations. It was never meant to go as fast as Ken was trying to push it. Ending the program now was the right thing to do, even if he couldn't see it yet.

She shut down the computer and rubbed her eyes. The excitement she felt for this achievement was bittersweet and she wasn't sure exactly what she wanted to do next. She had worked with Ken on a much more personal level than she had expected over the last four years, inadvertently becoming his mirror image; they finished each other's thoughts and complimented one another like twins. She knew this day was coming but never believed she would feel so guilty about it. Part of her wanted to bring him in closer, to keep him aboard the original plan; the other part wanted to keep him as far away as possible — for his complete protection. It was messy and there was no clear answer. Until she could rectify the love she felt for Ken as a friend, and the love she felt for him on a deeper level, there was no way out for her. She had already broken his heart, and in consequence, hers as well. She wasn't sure if either of them would ever get over that.

She grabbed a cup of coffee off the table and pressed it to her lips when a rattle vibrated the windows. She set the cup down and listened intently for what could be making it react that way. It didn't take her very long to figure it out.

Lark jumped to the window. Smoke drifted from the back of the ship and she could now hear the distinct whir of the engines. "God damn it, Ken." Lark slammed her fist against the glass and hauled ass out of the room, limping as fast as she could toward the stairwell. She almost ran over Harvey coming out of his office.

"What the hell is he doing?" he said.

"I don't know," Lark said, barely pausing to stop.

"Lark, wait. I need to talk to you."

Lark stopped and turned to him. "About what?"

"The FBI," he said as if he were trying to keep it secret.

"What about them?"

"They just issued a BOLO out on you."

Lark looked at the ship. *God damn it! Just what I needed.*

She wavered on whether she should stop Ken or get the hell out of the building. Ken won over her instinct of self-preservation. "I have to take care of this. Sit tight. And don't let him open that roof."

Lark spun back down the corridor, ignoring Harvey's further questions and objections. The ship still rested on the ground when she reached the main room, but it would be up in the air in no time. She waved her arms as she limped toward the ship, attempting to flag Ken down, but he was doing a great job of ignoring her. Frustrated, she slid across to the side and knocked away a panel next to the hatch, exposing an access keypad. She typed in her code, followed by an override code. The door hissed open and Lark jumped inside just before the engines under the ship ignited, pushing the ship a few feet off the ground and knocking Lark against the cabinets. "God..." she moaned as she rubbed the back of her head. As the ship balanced, Lark stormed into the cockpit. "What the hell are you doing?" she yelled, sitting down next to him.

"I don't want to hear it."

"We agreed, Ken. We're shutting it down."

"You agreed to shut it down. This has been my whole life for four years. I can't let it go. Not when we're this close."

"You'll have a hell of a time getting through the roof," Lark said.

"Not if I'm going fast enough," Ken countered near simultaneously.

"It's not ready."

"Simulations can be wildly inaccurate, Lark, especially with as many unknown variables as we have. I believe in you, and I believe in your idea. The LS-Accel is sound and it will hold."

There was a strong confidence in his voice, more confident than Lark had heard in a long time.

"What about Tracey? Jacquline?"

"I already talked to them."

"And they know this might be the last time they see you?"

"I'm ready for takeoff, Lark. Either strap in or get out."

Lark searched for the words to convince him to end this once and for all. When she couldn't, she left the cockpit. Ken sighed, having hoped she would have changed her mind and gone with him. But this was for the best. What he had said was true, but he didn't want to risk anyone else's life should he be completely wrong.

The light signifying that the hatch had been sealed lit up green. Ken adjusted a few more levels when Lark suddenly slid back into the co-pilot seat, pulling the buckles over her shoulders.

Ken looked at her, his mouth slightly open in confused awe.

"What?" Lark said as she tightened the belts across her chest. "You have faith in me, I have faith in you. If you say it's ready, I want to be there when it works."

Ken smiled. Lark returned it with the addition of a wink.

Lark immediately started running a few of her own equipment checks and noticed a slight rise in one of the readings. "Gravity and oxygen are holding steady but the plasma levels look to be a little high," she said, tapping the meter.

"Yeah. It went up a bit after I lit the hovers. It's still within acceptable range."

"Then let's get this bucket of bolts in the air."

"Yes ma'am." Ken slid a small lever off to the side of the console toward him and the hover engines pushed the ship skyward.

"Open the roof," Lark said into the intercom in the middle of the console.

Harvey came back a bit shaky and confused. "What about —"

"Just do it."

There was silence. The ship continued to rise. It was nearing the top of the building when Lark finally saw the edge of the roof slide open.

"Last chance to back out," Ken said.

"No way in Hell." Excitement had consumed her.

The ship climbed smoothly past the roof and came to a stop ten yards above it.

"Check out this view," Ken said, admiring the city below. "I think I see your house," he joked.

"It's about to get a whole lot prettier," Lark said. "I think it's time to see the stars, don't you?"

Ken felt like vomiting, excited yet scared to death. Lark felt the same; her hand twittered nervously as she placed it on one of two levers in the center of the console. She looked to Ken and smiled, her eyes sparkling.

"Ignition," Ken said.

Lark pulled the lever downward. The four cells in the rear of the ship immediately glowed bright white before flames and a heavy amount of smoke pushed the ship forward. At the same time, Lark slid another lever to maximum power, firing up the hover jets and forcing the ship skyward into the bright blue emptiness.

— 14 —

Both the rear cells and the jets underneath the ship had been turned off for about an hour. The ship had cleared the atmosphere with very little difficulty and its current momentum was enough to carry it beyond orbital range and into the dead of space without having to waste any more fuel. There were plenty of fuel reserves tucked away in the engine room but Ken hadn't anticipated burning it as fast as they did, and conservation was necessary if they intended to get back home.

"We've just cleared orbit," Lark said, responding to the flashing light near the navigation screen.

Ken had been admiring the view for some time, taking in the vastness of his surroundings and contemplating the ever-shrinking probability of finding Stacey. Sitting at home, imagining the possibilities, thinking only with the adrenaline of hope, was far different than the reality of what he had gotten himself into. Looking upon it now, hope had all but died.

"Ken," Lark said, snapping her fingers.

He broke from his daze. "Yeah. We ready?"

"Nav says we're in the clear."

"So, no running into Saturn?" Ken said, smiling.

Lark laughed. "We'll be lucky to even reach Saturn on this jump. My concern is what the friction of space dust might do, not to mention the asteroid belt."

"You think we'll make it that far?"

"The only thing stopping us is her." Lark pet the console lightly.

"Well, according to these readings, she looks ready," Ken said, checking the meters and gauges for the hundredth time since coasting began. "Even the plasma has relaxed to normal range."

"Then what are we waiting for?" Lark said, fastening the straps of her seatbelts. "Let's see what this bitch can do."

Ken happily joined her, licking his lips with a taste for the future. He could see Stacey in his mind; she felt closer than she had in a long time. So much so that he could almost feel her touch. Every glorious star reminded him of her, as if she were staring back at him from every possible direction — waiting.

"Ready?"

"More than I've ever been," he said. "Light her up."

Without hesitation, Lark rested two fingers on a pair of faders next to the fuel lever. She slid them upward as slowly as she could. "Beginning ionization."

The tubes in the engine room grew a dark shade of green and swirled about, funneling toward the entry into the ion thrusters.

Ken watched the plasma meter carefully. No changes occurred. His stomach turned with anticipation. It took the ship a few minutes to pick up speed, but once it had reached the necessary velocity, Lark sat back and grabbed hold of her seatbelts. "I'll let you do the honors," she said.

"Hold onto your skin." With one quick swipe, Ken pulled the fuel lever downward. A loud explosion sent the ship reeling forward, pasting Ken and Lark into their seats. They couldn't move and their skin felt ready to rip off, but nothing gave them more satisfaction. They watched breathlessly as the stars fused with each other, forming long streaks around them until it became a simple white void.

Ken strained to check the readings on the console. "Hull still holding," he said, though he wasn't sure if anything could be heard. The rattle of the ship seemed to drown out all other audible signals.

"Speed?" Lark yelled out.

Ken looked up at the speedometer gauge near the roof. His eyes hurt like hell. "Five-thousand kilometers and rising," Ken yelled back. He could feel pressure on his chest and had trouble breathing.

The acceleration of the ship soon steadied and the pressure around Ken's body waned. "Ten thousand and holding," he said with a bit of relaxation.

"The hull is in good shape," Lark said, also relaxing a bit. "Fuel and plasma levels still green."

"Begin phase two."

Lark wanted to say something to calm her nerves but anything she could say would be meaningless. Instead, she squeezed Ken's hand tightly and nodded. Ken returned her affection as Lark placed her hand on a second pair of faders just below the first. She slowly inched the first one downward.

The ship slowly sped up once again. Ken watched the speedometer rise to eleven thousand kilometers per second. Twelve thousand. Thirteen. Only the sheer pressure of the ship's velocity masked his excitement.

"Adding the last of the juice," Lark yelled. She slid down the fourth and final fader.

The ship suddenly accelerated exponentially in a smooth glide.

"Fifty —" Ken choked out — or tried to, as his lungs felt like they were being squeezed in a vice. No matter how hard he tried, he couldn't hold his eyes open any longer. Even if he wanted to stop the acceleration, he wouldn't be able to. All he could do was enjoy the ride.

To his right, Lark was dying. She was partially aware of what was happening around her, though it could have been an altered state of consciousness. Her lungs had stopped functioning and she no longer felt her heart beat.

Within a matter of seconds, the ship was sprinting along at over a hundred thousand kilometers a second and continued to rise. At one hundred and fifty thousand, the glass on Ken's watch shattered and stuck to the back wall of the cockpit. At two hundred thousand, Ken felt as if his entire body was about to do the same. Sparks flashed in the engine room as the ship's body pulled slowly inward — a small child trying hard to crush his first can of soda pop.

Two hundred and fifty thousand.

Two hundred and sixty-five thousand.

Two hundred and seventy-five thousand. Ken's body had gone numb, but he fought his natural instincts and forced himself to remain conscious. The roof of the ship was nearly touching the top of his head and the Plexiglass window was painted with a web of cracks. Sparks shot from the console like fireworks.

Two hundred and ninety thousand.

Ken thought he had died. Stacey, her hair flowing through the windless air, appeared before him in a hazy fog. The familiar green jewel she always wore around her neck gleamed like the precious sparkle in her eyes He felt her breath on his cheek, heard her heart beat, but he couldn't get close to her or say anything.

Stacey suddenly evaporated with the sound of a loud crash. A surge of pain split Ken's body as his heart tried to rip through his chest. His lungs boiled and his head pounded, but he was alive. A bed of nails couldn't have been more painful as he opened his eyes and focused them on the speedometer.

Three hundred thousand kilometers per second — and climbing.

Ken wheezed, the pressure in his lungs containing his excitement. "We did it," he said, though he couldn't tell if it was out loud or not. He grasped Lark's arm. "We did it."

When Lark didn't respond, Ken gently wiped his eyes to refocus them. What he saw was a corpse — a once beautiful woman now painted a pale white. He instantly ripped off his seatbelts and checked Lark's pulse, holding out hope that she was still alive. Her body said otherwise.

Ken had Lark's limp body on the floor in no time, fearing her heart was no more than a pound of Jell-O. Nonetheless, he pressed his lips to hers and expelled what little breath he still had in his own lungs into her before starting compressions. Not once did Ken think he would actually have to use the CPR training he was forced to get in college. The closest he ever got was in some foreplay with Gloria. She was a drowning victim and Ken would "save" her life and be rewarded with pleasure.

But this was far too real.

As he again pressed his lips to hers, guilt washed over him. What he was doing was far from cheating, but the odd sense of affection and humiliation was enough for him to second-guess his loyalties. There was no doubt Stacey would understand him touching his lips to another woman's in this type of circumstance, yet saving her life was a much bigger betrayal than any faux kiss — one that Stacey might never forgive. At the same time, Ken couldn't — *wouldn't* — sacrifice Lark for Stacey, not if he could help it. She was his best friend, and for the last four years, his life.

Ken quickly pumped her chest — one, two, three, four, five — then added more air. Sweat covered his body as he repeated the process over and over, each time growing more afraid that Lark was never coming back. After telling himself he would try one last time, he pushed his final breath into her lungs and Lark jolted upward with a violent cough, sending Ken reeling backward, holding his mouth tightly. She frantically slid away from him in confusion until she hit the wall. It took her several minutes of uncontrollable coughing before she was able to regain her composer.

"Lark," Ken said, tasting the blood from the cut on his lip. "Are you okay?"

Lark took in some deep breaths to control her waning coughs and opened her eyes, ignoring the searing pain that came with doing so. All she could see was a series of black, white and gray blurs. Unable to comprehend what was happening, she wrapped her arms around her chest and hid her face as best she could between her knees.

Ken wanted to go to her but felt it better to give her some space. That, or he felt Stacey was waiting for him to disappoint her. Either way, he held still, shaking uncontrollably among the silence. As the minutes passed, Ken's body relaxed, pain replacing his shock and adrenaline.

A loud bang made Lark jump in fright.

"The ship is holding," Ken said, massaging his neck. "A little worse for wear, but holding."

Lark could now see Ken clearly but all color remained absent. Her eyes moistened and all she could do was embrace him. For a brief moment, Ken forgot about Stacey and held Lark with a profound need to protect her until she was ready to let go.

A series of pops and snaps compelled Lark to look around the cockpit, eventually locking eyes with Ken. He smiled softly and combed some hair behind her ear. Lark replied with a smile and for the first time, felt the pain coursing her body. "God," she muttered, her voice scratchy. "I feel like I was run over by a Mack truck."

Ken laughed as she sat back, grabbing her waist. She attempted to massage the pain away, but the more she tried, the more it hurt. "What happened?"

"We did it," he said softly through a cracked smile.

"Are you serious? We're there?" Lark scanned the windows. "We actually reached the speed of light?"

Ken pointed to the speedometer. It was surrounded by several edges of the compressed cockpit walls, impossible to read from her current position. She inched her way to her knees, wincing with every small movement, and leaned in close to Ken. Her breasts brushed up against his face for a split second, enough for him to blush with innocent guilt and shift his head downward. Suddenly, he felt sick to his stomach.

"I'm sorry, Stacey," he whispered. "I love you. You are my soul. I will never leave you. I can never forget you. I am you and you are me. I'm sorry."

"Impossible," Lark hissed under her own breath. She scanned the console. Most of it was gone, having stopped working for one reason or another. She pushed the accelerators and plasma faders upward and checked the speedometer. It continued to rise as the engines remained hot. "Ken." The scratch in Lark's voice was gone in favor of strong command.

Ken continued mumbling under his breath. Lark couldn't quite make it out, but she heard a few syllables of "Stacey" and "Love." He seemed trapped somewhere between reality and madness. She wasn't sure if snapping him out of it would break him completely, but with the aches and pains of the ship becoming more numerous, Lark had to get his attention — damn the consequences.

She sat down and grabbed his head. "Ken."

Ken's muttering was instantly replaced with a strange, bright smile and wild anticipation. This haunted flash of love and devotion quickly faded as he realized that the young woman in front of him was only Lark. He averted his eyes, attempting to hide his disappointment.

"Ken," Lark said again, this time more forcefully. "You still with me, Ken?"

"Yeah," he said, moving his head from Lark's hands and rubbing his eyes. "Yeah. What is it?"

"How long have we been traveling?"

Ken checked his watch. "Damn." He covered the strap and looked back to Lark. "I don't know. Why?"

"We have to stop this ship."

"Why? What's wrong?"

"Other than the fact that our acceleration is tearing the ship apart at the seams, nothing, really."

Ken chuckled, but quickly grasped what Lark actually said. "Wait. Acceleration? How is that possible?"

"Your guess is as good as mine. But if we don't get this ship stopped, we won't get the chance to figure it out."

"Good point." Ken slid into his seat. He checked the console and found what Lark had already seen — it was all but dead. "Come on."

Ken tore open the cockpit door and rushed to the back of the ship. He punched in his authorization code —

Thank God the access pad still works.

— and pulled the engine room door open. Smoke bled from inside, momentarily blinding him.

Lark attempted to follow but the brittleness in her knees wouldn't allow her to stand upright without the fear of them shattering. But when she smelled the smoke, she knew she had no choice.

"Fire," Ken screamed.

Lark used the console to help pull herself up and she gradually added weight to her legs. After what she had had to endure after the plane crash, she wasn't afraid of the pain. Of what she remembered, the scariest part of that night was her lack of independence as she waited in the middle of nowhere for someone to come and help her. The cold wind, shock and pain had numbed most of her body and the fatigue had made her sick. She never thought she would have to face that type of situation again, especially after being honorably discharged after the incident. But that dependency had returned and it burned her heart. She was determined to fight it, though, with every ounce of strength and will she could muster. It wasn't a matter of if; it was a matter of when. All she needed was confidence that no amount of pressure was going to break her. Once that happened, she hobbled her way to the engine room.

Meanwhile, Ken pulled a small fire extinguisher from the cabinets and killed the blaze he found burning inside one of the panels near the door. He swiped away the residual smoke and peered inside. "I need a flashlight," he said, reaching in to shift a few cables from obstructing his view. The heat nearly burnt his fingerprints off. "Lark!"

Suddenly, a light cough echoed around the room. Ken saw a shadowy form move among the smoke near the reactors. He held up the fire extinguisher defensively. "Lark."

"I'm coming," Lark rang back, annoyed.

"Someone's in here." Familiar features of black leather became more prominent as the intruder coughed again and rose. Through the dissipating smoke, Ken caught sight of her hair — long, brown and knotted with several white splotches. The fire extinguisher hit the floor as Ken's body fell weak.

"Stacey," he whispered. Everything — the noise, the fear, the danger — was replaced with relief. His goal had been achieved; a dream from which he'd never want to wake from. He smiled as he absorbed the divine features he had fallen in love with and couldn't let go of. Her sparkling blue eyes and the pristine curvature of her cheekbones stopped his heart. "I found you," he whispered under his breath. Instinctively, Ken embraced the lovely image; he consumed the beat of her heart, the smell of her skin and the silk of her hair. Unable to speak, unable to let go, unable to let the moment fade into memory, he stood, holding her in his arms. But it was too pure to last. As the intruder coughed again, the beautiful image faded into the smoke with the softest of whispers.

I am always with you.

"Stacey!" Ken cried, reaching out.

The intruder shifted some hair from her face. Her green eyes, shallow and empty, dropped Ken to his knees in a release of hopelessness. He so desperately wanted it to be true, for his search to be over, that he had forgotten that his quest was going to be a long, hard fought trip to the deep recesses of both space and of his own mind if he ever expected to win back the love he lost. His frustration and stress poured from his eyes.

"Ken," Lark said as she leaned up against the engine room door. "Are you okay?" She was immediately aware of Ken's complete lack of spirit. She looked at the intruder but didn't recognize her. "Who is it?"

"My daughter," Ken choked out after Jacquline coughed and brushed some of the remaining smoke away.

"Your daughter Jacquline? What is she doing here?" Lark used the walls for support as she slid into the room. The cracks and sparks combing the ship were increasing.

"I was trying…" Jacquline said, each word slipping out under a short cough and wheeze.

"Trying to what?" Ken said. His voice was deep and full of anger. He looked to her, his eyes pierced with red lines and bubbling with water. "You were supposed to be taking care of Tracey."

"What the hell do you think I was doing?" Jacquline said with just as much antagonism.

"Not that." Ken stood, unsure if he was mad at her for losing Tracey or because she wasn't Stacey. "What were you thinking?" He swiped the small flashlight from Lark and started to play around inside the panel. "You could have been killed."

"Hey. You locked me in here."

"Just… quiet. I'll deal with you later."

Jacquline folded her arms and muttered inaudibly under her breath. Suddenly, her head started pounding and she felt queasy. She leaned over and grabbed her forehead. "What happened anyway?" she asked, fighting her nausea.

"Shut-down circuits are fried," Ken said, pulling out a series of wires fused together in a giant roasted ball.

"I'm on it," Lark said. She grabbed Ken's shoulder and used him to limp to the adjacent panel. Jacquline took in a deep breath as Lark typed in a series of codes — each faster than the last — into a control panel that looked as if it would short-circuit any second. "God damn it, work." Lark banged the wall with the butt of her palm and kicked the panel below it, ignoring the pain that scorched her body. "Lousy piece of shit," she added under her breath.

"Back-up overrides won't work?" Ken said.

Lark dropped a deadly gaze on him. "What now?"

"What else? We're going to have to shut it off manually."

Just then, a loud rattle shot through the ship and all three of them rose off the floor.

"What's going on?" Jacquline said through a light tremble.

"Quiet, Jacks. It's nothing."

"Gravity's gone offline," Lark answered, hoping it would calm Jacquline. "Ken, get into that panel and fix it. I'm going to shut down the engines."

Ken pulled his way along the walls to the cabinets where he grabbed a handheld saw. He checked to make sure it worked and then guided himself back to the engine room, keeping as low to the ground as he could. When he reached the back of the room, he fired up the saw and sliced into the wall. Sparks flew from the blade like hundreds of small fireflies, disappearing quickly into the smoky darkness.

Meanwhile, Lark drifted over to the reactors and pulled a panel from the floor. She quickly located the ion thruster grids and tried to rip them out. When that turned out to be entirely futile, she flipped around and pushed herself closer to the floor. "Sorry, girl," she said and repeatedly slammed the heel of her foot into the grids. The hum of the reactors faded with a series of sparks and a soft explosive fizzle that almost caught Lark's boot on fire. It still wasn't enough; the engines remained hot, pushing the ship forward.

"Damn it," she whispered and quickly pushed herself to a series of grated panels in the middle of the floor.

"How's it coming?" Ken called out.

"The thrusters are offline but the engines are still hot. I'm going under to switch 'em off."

"Hurry."

"No shit," Lark said under her breath as she peeled the center panel from the floor and pulled her way into the bowels of the ship. To her dismay, no matter the texture or size of each of the dozens of wires that connected the engines to the control boards, they were all essentially the same color — some hue of gray. "Damn it," she hissed and worked her way out of the hole.

"I need your help," Lark said to Jacquline, who was fixated on the sparks surrounding her father. She grabbed Jacquline's arm. "Jacquline."

Jacquline yanked it away and shot Lark an irate glare. "What?"

"I need your help."

"Help with what?"

"I need you to go down and get these engines turned off."

"You do it. It's your damn ship."

"I'm looking through the lens of a black and white camera right now, Jacks. It's impossible for me to do this alone." It was hard for her to admit that.

"Don't call me that," Jacquline said, her voice full of resentment.

The hum of the saw ended, sending a piece of metal to join the floor panel in their dance around the room. Ken peered into the hole and caught sight of a black spot near the base of the wall. Above it, an electrode had broken away from the rest of the body and a frayed wire floated from the scene. He quickly pushed himself into the other room to retrieve a small toolbox.

"Look at me, Jacquline," Lark said, pulling Jacquline to her. "You and Ken have some serious issues to work through, I get that. But if we don't get these engines shut down, we are all going to die. So stow your shit in your back pocket and give me your damn eyes for two seconds."

Jacquline wanted to rip Lark's head off. From what she could tell, this woman was the reason Ken had abandoned them. Not once had he ever mentioned her to them and she wondered what else he was doing behind their backs. Whether it was to build the ship or if it was something more, Jacquline and Tracey were the ones she eventually screwed. But the longer she looked into that woman's eyes, even under all of the fear and frustration, Jacquline saw a great deal of compassion.

She turned back to Ken, who had settled into the hole. She partially understood why he would hide the ship from her, but the only reason she could think he would hide this woman was because Jacquline wasn't good enough for him. Secrets, lies, detachment

— they had all infested themselves into the wall that separated him from everyone else except this new (and in an incredibly queasy way, much younger) companion. Whatever the reason, it was enough to fuel her desire to upstage Ken and prove to him that she mattered; that she was worth more than Ken and his mistress combined.

"Tell me what to do," she said.

Lark smiled and for a moment Jacquline saw why Ken was attracted to her. "Wait here." She used the floor to get to the toolbox and floated a pair of wire cutters to Jacquline. "You know how to use those?"

"Yeah, of course." Jacquline collected the wire cutters.

"Good. Get under the floor and do as I say."

Jacquline grabbed a hold of the floor and looked into the hole. A small ounce of respect for her father flashed through her mind at the sight of it all. Long white tubes ran each side of the duct. Near the back was a large metal panel with hundreds of different-colored wires criss-crossing each other. Two small flames burned inside clear Plexiglas casings under the nuclear reactors. Taking in a deep breath to mask her adrenaline, Jacquline slid into the duct.

"Can you see the flames?" Lark said.

"Yeah."

"Make your way to them."

Jacquline was there in a matter of seconds. "Okay, I'm here. What next?" Her voice was clear and strong.

"Find a series of rainbow wires. They should be tied in a bundle, one of each color."

"Got it," Jacquline said, grabbing a hold of the wires.

"Good. Now listen carefully. You need to cut each wire, one at a time, in the order I give you. If you cut the wrong one, it could cause one of the systems to mix with the wrong elements or simply ignite, both of which are not good for us."

"Yeah, no shit," Jacquline whispered. She separated the wires from each other with her fingers.

"Are you ready?"

Jacquline wiped a bit of sweat from her forehead, unsure if it was from the heat or her own growing anxiety. "Yeah," she answered, hiding the quiver that danced in her throat. "Give it to me."

By now, Ken had placed the end of the broken electrode back in its place against the base of the wall and soldered a small copper casing around the two strips of wire. As he grabbed a second pair of wire cutters and stripped the cover from both ends of a spare wire, he took notice of Jacquline's absence. A hint of admiration washed over him when he realized where she was. He let a slight smile slip before sneaking back into the wall.

"Cut the red wire," Lark said.

Jacquline cut the wire. "Got it."

"Now cut the blue wire, and then the purple."

After Jacquline sliced the purple wire, the flames shut off. Everything went dark except for a small green glow emanating through the crack in the floor above her. "I can't see," she yelled.

Lark grabbed the flashlight from Ken's pocket. Ken didn't take notice as he cut the blackened ends of two wires dangling above him. He stripped the ends of their coats away, exposing their copper guts.

"Here." Lark shuffled over to the hole and tossed the flashlight toward Jacquline.

"Thank you," Jacquline said. "What next?" She stuffed the flashlight in her mouth.

"Cut the yellow and then the green."

Just before Jacquline cut the green wire, Lark called out, "No, wait. Orange. Cut the orange."

Jacquline relaxed her body and pulled the flashlight from her mouth. "Is it green or orange?"

"Orange," Lark said.

"You're sure." Jacquline had a hard time believing her.

"Yes," Lark said more confidently. "I'm sure."

"You damned well better be," Jacquline mumbled as she put the flashlight back in her mouth. Lark lowered her head into her hand, fearing the worst.

As Jacquline sliced the orange wire, the soft hum that filled the room stopped and the faint green sparkle from above dissipated.

Lark and Jacquline both let out a breath of relief.

"Good job," Lark said. "Now carefully strip the plastic from the green wire without cutting the copper. Can you do that?"

"One second." Jacquline pressed the wire cutters to the plastic as soft as she could until she felt the razor-sharp needles slice through the sheath.

At the same time, Ken tied one end of the new wire to one of the leads and soldered a mound of copper over it. When he touched the other end to the second lead, everything floating about the ship fell to the ground. Jacquline jolted downward, causing her hand to twitch and almost cut the wire. "Damn it," she said, the flashlight falling next to her head.

Lark's hand was holding onto the floor when she fell, forcing it underneath her body and snapping it under her weight. She screamed and rolled over, grasping her wrist to her chest.

Ken finished soldering the final patch and ran to Lark. He grabbed her shoulders and tried to pull her hand away. "Let me see," he said. Blood seeped through her fingers rather quickly.

"How about a little heads up next time," Jacquline yelled. She found the flashlight and carefully snipped the wire's sheath. "What's going on up there?"

"She broke her wrist," Ken responded.

"Well, what do I do?"

Ken finally took notice of Jacquline's hollow, metallic voice. He looked down into the floor. "How far did you get?"

"I just stripped the green wire," Jacquline said, followed by an inaudible, *No thanks to you.*

"Okay, find the black wire," Ken said quickly. "You need to cut it, strip the casing on one end and attach it to the green wire. That should bypass the injection system and shut the engines off completely."

Jacquline worked quickly but patiently. As she tied the black wire to the green, the flames at the back of the ship flashed out.

"I'll be right back," Ken said, more to Lark than to Jacquline. He ran to the cockpit and sat down at the control panel. "Please work," he muttered as he flipped through a series of controls. The small jets at the front of the ship lit up with great force. Ken looked up at the speedometer. It was slow, but the numbers were descending.

Suddenly, sparks spit from the console and forced Ken to duck from the room. When the light show was over, he peered at the blackened, dented console. For the first time, he realized they were stuck. No time to dwell on that now. Lark was hurt and needed him to remain calm and centered.

He grabbed some rags and a medical kit from the cabinets and returned to the engine room. Jacquline had come out of the floor and was kneeling next to Lark, who sat up against the wall. The pain had all but numbed her arm.

"How come we haven't stopped?" Jacquline asked Ken.

"We can't just stop, Jacks," he said, pushing her away. "We have to gradually slow down. It should only take a few minutes."

With just the affection in his eyes, Ken urged Lark to move her hand away. He quickly wrapped several rags around it. Lark covered his hands with hers and held them there.

"Is this piece of shit going to hold that long?"

"Watch your mouth, Jacquline." Ken pulled his hands free of Lark. "What are you doing here, anyway? You were supposed to be with Tracey."

"That's exactly why I'm here."

"What are you talking about?"

"Your daughter has one mean scream," Jacquline said. "She ran away from me and I swear I saw her get on the ship."

"Well, unless she's invisible, she's not here."

"No shit."

Ken was about to rip into her — about her language, about her lack of respect — but he knew better than to lose his temper, especially in front of Lark. Besides, Jacquline had just helped save their lives. She would get a free pass — this time. "We need to get a splint on Lark's wrist," he said. "Grab that piece of metal and my saw."

Even with the urge to ignore him, Jacquline was quick to gather the items. Ken took them and placed the metal panel on the floor. "Hold it steady."

Jacquline got to her knees and pressed her hands firmly on the sides of the panel.

Ken lit up the saw. "Close your eyes."

Jacquline turned her head as Ken sliced into the metal. She held on as tight as she could, though the longer he cut, the more the heat burned the sides of her hands. "Hurry," she urged.

"Almost there." Ken finished slicing a thin piece away and turned off the saw. Jacquline let go of the metal and sat back, pressing her hands together tightly, fighting the lingering pain.

Ken grabbed a rag to pick up the metal and turned to Lark. "Ready?"

Lark nodded and moved the rags away from her wrist, which no longer resembled such. It was bent thirty degrees in the wrong direction with the bone jutting through the skin. Ken gently took a hold of her hand. "This is going to sting a little."

"Sting my ass," Lark said and braced herself. Ken placed the metal on the inner part of Lark's wrist, stretching from her palm to just before her elbow. Lark clenched her teeth and winced as her arm burned, though not as much as it might have had it not been half numb.

As the pain subsided, Ken wrapped medical tape tightly around her arm, holding the metal in place. When he felt there was enough to keep her wrist from moving, he ripped the tape from the roll and rested his head against the wall.

"I'm just a walking picture of health, aren't I," Lark said, causing a bout of nervous laughter from Ken.

Jacquline wasn't as cheerful. "What are we supposed to do now?" she said.

Ken sat next to Lark without a word. He had no idea what he was going to do but he wasn't about to let Lark, and especially Jacquline, know that. Though in his heart, he already knew they did.

THE GEM

— 1 —

Floating along as part of the cool, smooth steel floor, Qah-Shekel could see down the pitch-black corridor as if it were lined with hundreds of fluorescent lights. The only noise that echoed through the deadened silence was that of his own soft breath, making his surroundings eerily dry and sterile. Qah-Shekel stopped halfway down the corridor and caressed the wall with his fingertips. He pressed the head of his cloak to the wall and took in several deep breaths. A moment later, he pulled a long, curved blade shaped like a shark's fin from his cloak and rammed its sharp tip through the wall. The shrill call of metal against metal reverberated across the corridor as he sliced the wall from left to right, then head to toe on each side. After he had made the final cut from right to left at about the height of his knees, Qah-Shekel let the blade disappear under his cloak and muscled the wall open. It fell forward into a room, illuminating the corridor in a soft, gentle green glow. Taking his time, Qah-Shekel took in all of the various objects stored on the shelving units built around the cramped confines of the room. Some of them he knew to be very rare items that were being hunted by every last bounty hunter he was aware of (and probably others that he wasn't); others were unfamiliar, but still quite exotic and deliciously tantalizing. Part of him wanted to take everything and trade it all for a handsome bounty. But that's not what he was there for. Qah-Shekel was there for one, tiny object — the small, round crystal that floated in the center of the room, which produced the light that lit everything green. Each tiny cut of the checkerboard pattern around its surface emitted a different frequency of light that made the gem sparkle with exact precision.

Qah-Shekel walked up to the highly sought-after artifact but was afraid to touch it, not so much because of its pure brilliance, but because he knew its creator was the only being that could. It was widely known that if anyone other than the creator tried to take possession of it, they would encounter a severe shock produced by the living force field that detained it. Whether there was veracity to those rumors was still a topic of debate among a countless number of species, but Qah-Shekel was there to find out one way or another.

As he reached for the crystal, the air surrounding it burned his hand. He immediately held it to his mouth, allowing his saliva to deaden the immense sting and rejuvenate the residual wound within seconds. Rumor confirmed. But knowing that didn't keep him from completing his task; it simply hindered it. He wasn't sure how, but he was going to take this treasure with him or let it kill him. Without it, he had nothing to trade for the knowledge he ultimately sought. There had to be a way to transport the gem; after all, it had found its way here.

Qah-Shekel searched the room for anything that might help him, rummaging through several familiar objects — a flute he had stolen some years earlier that somehow found its way back to the owners he stole it from; the Garcolly of Hessinger, a small arrow that wielded a poison that would leave a being near-death for all eternity; and a rare musical instrument that gave its owner the power of sleep — none of which were of any use. But what forced Qah-Shekel to pause in remembrance and longing was a small, tawny rock that he knew had come from his home planet of Krylex. After several long heartbeats, he placed the piece of rock inside a pouch around his waist, stealing it for nothing more than his own sentimental yearning.

After discarding artifacts of Jarawada, Refitkli and Ortanagwa, Qah-Shekel found a relatively large jar holding a dark yellow, mucus-like substance. Moving around inside was a pencil-like creature that Qah-Shekel recognized with disdain. It rammed into the sides of the jar every so often, apparently trying to escape the confines of its prison, something Qah-Shekel was more than happy to help it accomplish. Even though he couldn't stand the little insect after the destruction it had caused to his own ship, it had been bred as a pure, genuine piece of weaponry, and in Qah-Shekel's current situation, it could end up working to his advantage — in more ways than one.

Qah-Shekel slid the lid off the jar and tipped it upside down. The yellow mucus slowly drained from the bottle like honey and pooled into a mound on the ground. The insect didn't try and escape or attack him after landing. Instead, it continued its chaotic bounce around the mucus, following it as the substance burrowed through the floor, leaving a thin, watery trail behind it.

Continuing to hold the jar upside down, Qah-Shekel walked back to the gem and held the jar above it, eyeballing its size. The opening had a large enough circumference so the only thing stopping him from making this work would be if the force field expanded beyond it. There was only one way to find out. He lowered the jar slightly closer to the gem, which lit up the force field, though it remained small in comparison to the jar. Qah-Shekel kept a tight grip on the jar as sparks of lightning forced it to become increasingly unsteady. When the gem had been fully encased, he felt an intense, yet soothing heat, and waited to see if the gem would shatter the jar. It didn't take long to conclude that the gem wasn't attacking it, but was simply a reaction to the jar's proximity. The lightning made a loud static scratch as Qah-Shekel flipped the jar upright and sealed it with the cover. The gem gradually turned itself around on its axis until it had reached its own upright position and came to rest in the direct center of the jar. Once settled, the lightning stopped, as if it was ready — or wanted — to be transported.

Qah-Shekel flipped his tunic open and tied a long strap around the lip of the jar. As he secured the gem with a second loop from top-to-bottom, a soothing, peaceful warmth licked his skin. Fighting the need to lie down and rest, Qah-Shekel returned to the corridor and slowly traced his way to a small passage that led into a massive control room. Dozens of figures, all shrouded in the same type of cloak as Qah-Shekel, concentrated heavily on their own private tasks. Qah-Shekel had become integrated into this group of beings after acquiring one of their robes and participating in their mundane routines. For a long time, he studied the intricate layout of their ship and their technically-precise habits. As long as each and every one of them continued as they always did, Qah-Shekel would have no problem slipping away as easily as he was able to merge in. From what he could see as he scoured the room, all of them were exactly where they should be, including him. At about this time each day, Qah-Shekel would leave his station at the end of the corridor and head for the nutriment hall, where he would get a bite of nourishment before proceeding with his tasks. Continuing that habit, he slid his way smoothly — almost floating — toward the door on the far wall like clockwork. But unlike every time before, something felt eerily off. As he reached the door, he turned and looked at the cold red glow hidden under the hood of the figure near the communication station. He wasn't sure if the figure could sense anything was different, but he also knew this race was highly alert when it came to even the smallest of changes.

The figure lowered its head, intensely searching Qah-Shekel's body. When it reached his torso, sparks from the gem warmed his skin to the point of uncomfortable irritation. The figure's eyes suddenly burned bright, ready to kill Qah-Shekel with a quick blast of fire.

Qah-Shekel didn't hesitate. He bolted from the room with breakneck speed, racing down the corridors that now wailed with loud sirens. Any minute, guards would be on him like bees to honey, prepared to kill him in a slow agonizing torture. He grabbed hold of a ladder near the nutriment hall and climbed as fast as he could. A couple of larger-sized figures emerged from the nutriment hall and sent small electric blasts in his direction from devices attached to the tops of their bone-spurred hands. For now, Qah-Shekel wasn't worried; this race was infamous for their bad aim. But he also knew that once they adjusted their targeting sensors, he'd be in for a lifetime of suffering. As Qah-Shekel jumped from the ladder and headed down the upper corridor, shots struck the metal ceiling above him. Undeterred, the figures jumped up the length of the ladder, firing in pursuit, each shot missing but successively inching ever closer.

An electric bolt ignited Qah-Shekel's tunic on fire just before he reached the massive hangar bay. He quickly tossed it away, continuing his speed in stride, knowing full well that the next shot would hit him without fail. Inside the hangar were legions of ships from all over the known universe. Qah-Shekel's was the smallest, but still almost twenty meters in diameter. He had originally brought it in as a bounty to earn the beings trust, and as he suspected, it was right where he left it, sitting nearest the large opening leading into space.

Reacting quickly to the sound of that inevitable shot, Qah-Shekel avoided the blast by jumping to the side and rolling a few meters. As he stopped, he grabbed a tiny, thumb-sized device from his belt and pushed the red button that covered almost the entire blue body of the weapon. A thin laser shot from the head of the device and sliced right through the bony structure of the figure's hand. Qah-Shekel immediately swiped his own hand downward, cutting the figure's hand in half. It let out a ghastly howl as Qah-Shekel aimed the weapon at the second figure. It instantly dropped to its knees and lowered its head, placing its hands on the ground in a gesture of defeat. Qah-Shekel took a moment to look the figure over, flashed a quick smile and pushed the trigger, sending the laser straight through the figures head. He slowly made a small circle before letting go. The figure dropped to the ground. A soft blue ooze streamed down its body and melted away as it hit the floor. Qah-Shekel then pointed the device back at the first figure and fired, striking a circle in its chest.

Qah-Shekel took a breath of victory and ran for his ship, aware of the dozen or more figures that would be arriving in mere seconds. He raced up the ramp and shot to the cockpit, firing up the smooth long engine under the ship. It rotated slowly as it rose from the ground. Sporadic weapons fire soon shot past him. He maybe had a few minutes before they were able to align their aim enough to hit any major systems, so he remained calm and allowed the ship to complete its necessary warm-up cycles. Once ready, Qah-Shekel punched a series of controls and lit up the rear thrusters, instantly burning a handful of the figures to ash.

After the ship had passed through the hangar's milky force field, Qah-Shekel pushed the engines to their top velocity. Within minutes of his departure, another large ship, the *Equinox*, appeared out of thin air. Unafraid, Qah-Shekel impulsively guided his spacecraft to the rear of what he called home and attached his ship to the small portal that had been awaiting his arrival.

— 2 —

Gloria kisses Ken softly, waking his resting body. He kisses her back with a smile, petting her light brown hair with simplicity. But wait — his wife hasn't kissed him awake for years. He sits up and shifts away from her.

"Where were you last night?"

Gloria attempts to kiss him again. Ken climbs out of bed. "I want to know," he says, staring Gloria down with piercing eyes.

"What do you want to know?" she asks, sliding out of bed and stopping him from his agitated wanderings. "That I was out looking for a good screw? Bar hopping all night to find a man that will satisfy me in bed?"

"Stop it," Ken says, unable to turn away from his wife's deceitful eyes.

"You asked. So here it is. What if I said I found a man last night? One that took my drunk, wasted body back to his place where I let him do anything he wanted."

"Stop, Gloria, just stop. How could you do this?"

"Do what? Help myself to some real pleasure. What do you expect from me? I sure as hell don't get what I need from you."

"This isn't about me, Gloria. How can you keep doing this to your daughter?"

"What are you talking about?" Gloria shoots back, unwilling to let her weakness show. "I haven't done anything to Jackie."

"That's a crock of bull piss and you know it. While you were out getting poked by some diseased dick, your daughter was here, waiting for her mother to take her to the movies and get an ice-cream like she promised."

Gloria lowers her head and rubs her eyes. "She'll get over it," she mutters.

"Maybe," Ken says, "but you never see the disappointment, the heartbreaking bed of tears she cries every time you're not there for her. She's only eight years old, Gloria. She needs a mother right now, not a friend; not a whore."

Gloria is shocked at how her husband can even think she isn't being the best mother she can be. With her silent response, Ken turns away, giving up on his attempt to unite his family with the bond he's always dreamt of.

"I couldn't care less what you do, Gloria. Just don't make anymore promises to Jacks that you know you can't keep."

I'll be her mother, a voice whispers from behind him. Ken turns around. Standing where Gloria once was is a woman, glowing in the light of the window and radiating a love he has never felt. *Love me, and I will be. Find me, and I will love.*

Ken grows lightheaded. He sits down at the kitchen table next to Jacquline. The smell of pancakes, eggs and bacon fills the air. Gloria stands at the stove wearing the apron he bought her the previous Christmas. Jacquline practices her cursive, her pigtails dangling from her head playfully as she writes:

$$\textit{I love my mom and dad.}$$

"Morning, Jacks?" he says as he always does.

"Hold on, daddy. I need to finish this. Miss Carpenter says if it's late, we don't get to help build the robot in science today."

"Don't want you to miss that." He pulls on her pigtail, making a "ding-dong" noise. Jacquline giggles and takes a bite of her thick, buttered pancake. Ken brushes his fingertips along her cheek and then goes to Gloria. He wraps his arms lovingly around her waist and kisses her neck.

"Do you think I should call in sick today," he whispers. He licks the tip of her ear, which surprisingly tastes a lot like honey, the smell of which quickly dominates the bacon and eggs that have curiously evaporated from the pan.

Your love is strong, but distance is pain.

Ken backs away from Gloria in confusion. Symmetrically separated white streaks paint across her hair.

"Gloria?" he asks. Suddenly, the room around him drops into a deep swell of darkness.

I need to be... the woman whispers before turning around to face Ken.

Keladrayia.

Ken's focus instantly fixates on the green jewel dangling from around her neck. The glow strikes a cold frost up Ken's spine as a gust of wind whips past him. The porch light illuminates his fatigued posture as he opens the door and places his briefcase against the wall. The usual smell of dinner — a roast or lasagna — is once again non-existent. For the past year, Gloria always seemed to be absent, and the idea of her being home is only a childish hope. He slowly removes his tie as he labors upstairs to his bedroom, wondering where Gloria might have run off to this time. He flips on the light. Sitting on his bed is Jacquline, staring at a picture, tears slowly streaming the course of her extra puffy cheeks.

"Hey, Jacks. Shouldn't you be getting ready for the dance?"

Jacquline is only eleven but she's been waiting weeks to go to the school dance with a boy she keeps saying makes her heart float every time she sees him. Gloria can't wait to see her daughter look and act like a woman. She helped Jacquline pick out a dress and agreed to help her with her make-up. Ken can see now that Gloria missed her all-important date with her daughter — again. He knows nothing he can do will help, but what else can he do?

"Jacks?" he whispers. He sits next to her and kisses her cheek, hoping for a reaction that never comes. "What's wrong?" He runs his hand through her curly hair and looks at the photograph of Gloria smiling brightly in the purple flowered dress he bought her on a whim after their first date. She loves that dress and wears it whenever she attends a party or special occasion. It's her reminder of him, of their love and the eternal life they would spend together. But as hard as Ken tries, he cannot think of a moment when she wore that dress after taking this particular picture.

"She's gone," Jacquline chokes — beyond tears, beyond depression.

"What do you mean?"

Jacquline finally looks up. Her eyes are bloodshot, her cheeks a rosy pink, and the edges of her nose a dark red. "Just that."

Ken's heart breaks in regret as a tear drops from Jacquline's cheek onto the windshield along side other droplets of rain. Ken drives through the darkened streets, highlighted only by the dim glow of the headlights. He is tired, having had only ten hours of sleep in the last sixteen days. But even if he were in bed right now, sleep would be the farthest thing from his mind. The image of Jacquline crying over her mother continues to haunt him.

All of a sudden, a soft outline in the road catches his attention. Adrenaline rushes his body as he slams on the brakes and turns the wheel. The car skids across the wet pavement, sliding past the figure and into a telephone pole.

Ken remains completely still, allowing the swirl of anxiety to subside before doing anything. When his body has relaxed, he turns to look at the figure still standing in the middle of the road. He steps out into the rain, which has become harder since he stopped. The headlights of his car are pointed in the opposite direction so he has to step closer if he hopes to even attempt to make out any definitive features.

"What are you thinking?" he calls out. "What are you doing in the middle of the road? I could've killed you."

There is no response but Ken is now close enough to make out the outline of a petite woman. She appears extremely statuesque as the rain glistens off of her naked body.

"Hello?" Ken says, becoming a little impatient. "I'm talking to you."

There is an uncanny warmth to her body as he grabs a hold of the woman's shoulder to turn her around. A strange sensation swarms Ken's body as his eyes fall upon the small green jewel around her neck, sparkling radiantly in the rain. His stomach tickles, causing the corners of his mouth to curve upward. As his eyes glow with stimulation, his focus turns to the woman's features, lit up as if all of the light in the world is suddenly focused on her face. Her cheekbones rise with the curvature of her thin lips and her cheeks swell inward in two small dots. Her nose sits between them like a little gumdrop and her forehead gleams without a single flaw. But what Ken is interested in most is her eyes, swimming in a deep blue that sparkle with more clarity than the most brilliant of oceans.

The woman takes Ken's hand and pulls him close, holding him against her as if she were his best friend. Ken can think of nothing better than to wrap his arms around her and accept the power and the warmth of her heavenly silky skin. After a moment, she kisses Ken with an intoxicating passion that can never be explained in words. He no longer feels his heartbeat or the outer shell of his body. The only thing that matters is the taste of sweet peaches on her lips and the aroma of roses and honey that surrounds his soul. It all suddenly feels right, as if nothing bad has ever happened.

Ken doesn't ever want it to end.

Suddenly, it feels as if his skin is being ripped from his body when an unknown force pulls the woman away from Ken and suspends her in mid-air above the wet pavement. To Ken's surprise, the woman remains completely composed without an ounce of fear. Ken reaches for her, but all attempts to retrieve his beloved send him right through her, her essence floating about him like a cool mist. As all hope drains from his body, the woman points to his car. Glowing in the light of his headlights stands a young girl, no more than three years old. She is scared and lonely.

"Keep her safe," the woman whispers, the sound emanating through the pounding rain like crystal. "Never leave her."

"I won't," Ken says.

With that, a blinding light illuminates the woman, curving her body into a crescent. The jewel wrapped around her neck lifts from her chest. The little girl reaches out for her, crying. Suddenly, the necklace snaps off the woman's neck and races toward the child. Just before it gets to her, the jewel explodes in a display of shattered light.

One forever…

The woman bursts into an array of brightly colored sparks, each falling to the ground softly around Ken. As the crystal's fade, all Ken can do is scream out the only word he can remember.

"Stacey!"

— 3 —

Jacquline sat solemnly in the cockpit, running her fingers through the white stripes in her hair, a feature that brought back memories of Stacey she had long forgotten. She had always thought Stacey's white stripes were cool and sexy and had spent countless hours brushing them as they watched television or gossiped about boys. But having hurt her family the way she did, Jacquline wasn't sure she wanted that connection, or if Tracey would accept it — if she ever saw her again.

"Stacey!" Ken screamed from the engine room. Jacquline rolled her eyes. She had gone into the cockpit to get away from Ken, but this was nowhere near far enough. Usually, when things got this tense and she needed to clear her head (which, unfortunately, was quite often), she'd be able to get miles away from him and spend the night at a friend's house somewhere uptown. Every time she would, they'd always ask why she just didn't leave. But leaving Ken wasn't the problem; it was leaving Tracey. She couldn't betray Tracey like that, but most of all, she couldn't betray herself. She had made a promise to keep Tracey safe after Stacey left and her inability to do that left her with a bad taste of guilt. And now, with her newfound association with Stacey, it made her even sicker.

Jacquline pushed open the door to get a glimpse of what was happening. Ken breathed heavily and held his eyes in tired shock. Lark was next to him, trying her best to comfort him. Jacquline felt somewhat sorry and wondered if she should go over and act like a concerned daughter. Either that or continue to ignore him, neither option being all that appealing.

"Did you have the dream again?" Lark asked, more romantically than a friend. She held her arm around Ken's shoulder, trying to massage his terror away.

"No," he choked out, trying to hide his obvious torture. "No, it was different. Gloria… my first wife… she…" He paused, unable to understand the dream. "I was watching myself lose everything I ever had… and… and the jewel." Suddenly, Ken started screaming. "No, don't lose the jewel. It's your life. Tracey will be protected. Let me protect her. Don't leave me here alone. I need you… I need you Keladrayia!"

"Ken!" Lark yelled, pulling his face toward her. His eyes were plastered with a dark, haunted glow. "Ken, snap out of it."

"Keladrayia," he whispered, searching Lark's eyes for something he couldn't explain. Finally, he realized where he was and pulled away.

"Whoa," he said, rubbing his eyes. "What happened?"

"You were going insane," Jacquline muttered. She stood at the door, watching closely.

"What?"

"She's right," Lark added. "You seemed lost."

"Completely gone is more like it," Jacquline said.

As Ken tried to wrap the events around his head, he steadily grew more frightened and confused. "Where are we?" he finally asked. "Did we stop?"

"No," Lark said. "The fuel ran out about a half hour ago. We've been traveling at around two hundred thousand kilometers for the last hour or so. But everything still seems to be holding. I think we're okay."

"Until the universe gets the best of us and we crash into it," Jacquline added wisely. She returned Ken's disdain with her own, but Ken was far too exhausted to do anything more about it. He leaned back and stroked his hands across his face.

"What's Keladrayia?" Lark asked, returning the subject to the dream.

Ken looked at her in confusion. "What?"

"Keladrayia? You screamed it just before you came to."

"Really?" Ken tried hard to remember. "I don't know. The last thing I remember is Tracey, standing in the rain, reaching out for Stacey."

"What was she reaching for?" Lark asked, genuinely curious.

"I think it was the jewel," he said, unsure of his answer.

"What jewel?"

"Stacey always wore this beautiful green jewel around her neck." Ken looked at Jacquline with a slight smile. "You remember. You used to want to wear it to dances but she always said no."

"Only because she never took the damn thing off," Jacquline added.

"That's right," Ken said with a laugh. "Not even when she took a shower or went swimming. It was like it was part of her." Ken stopped and just smiled at Jacquline.

"What is wrong with you?" she asked a bit uneasy, disgusted by the thought that he was looking at her like he did Stacey.

Ken shook his head and rubbed his eyes. "Sorry. The dream was just so real. Nothing like my other dreams."

"What dreams?" Jacquline said.

"Nothing," Ken uttered, dropping his head down. "You wouldn't care anyway."

He was right, but Jacquline was still curious. "How do you know I wouldn't care?"

"Just leave it alone."

"No," Jacquline countered with lightning speed. "You've been doing this shit for the past four years."

"What?" Ken said with just the right mix of anger and annoyance. "What have I been doing?"

"Leaving me and Tracey in the dark about every little thing you do. How can I care about you when all you do is cower behind this little bitch?"

"Don't you dare, Jacquline." Ken raised his finger at her, but she wasn't buying any of it.

"What are you going to do? Ground me? I'm dead anyway because of you."

"You just don't get it do you?"

"Oh, here it comes." Jacquline crossed her arms and leaned up against the wall.

"You know… I'm done. Go back to the cockpit and wallow in your own self-pity and leave us grown-ups to figure our way out of this."

"Whoa," Jacquline laughed. "You're calling me a child? The man who can't even admit that not one, but *two*, women ran out on him because he's so god damned dependent."

"Shut up, Jacquline. Just shut up."

"Okay, that's enough," Lark finally said, standing between the two of them. "You're both acting like a couple of children. And for what?"

Both Jacquline and Ken turned away, exasperated.

Lark couldn't help but smile. "You guys are exactly the same, you know that?"

"Shut the hell up," Jacquline bit back.

"We are not," Ken said right along with her.

"Listen to me. You're family. You should not be fighting over petty differences like this. Now let's work through it." She looked to Jacquline. "I want you to tell me what the problem is."

"He's my problem," Jacquline snipped.

Lark held up her finger to quiet her. "Ah. *Why* is he the problem?"

"Haven't you been listening?"

"I want to hear it again." Lark waited patiently for Jacquline to answer. It took some time, but she finally worked out the words she needed to say.

"I just want to know why."

"Why what?"

"Why we're all here? Why was he so adamant about this whole thing?"

Lark turned to Ken, surprised. "You never told her?"

Ken rubbed his mouth, wishing he could crawl into the ducts and die. Even though it killed her knees to do so, Lark knelt down to face Ken on his level. It frightened her to see the contempt radiating from his eyes. "She's your daughter," she whispered. "She deserves to know."

"Just stay out of this," Ken muttered.

"No, Ken," Jacquline said. "She's right. I may have spoiled all of your plans by being here, but now that I am, I think the least you can do is give me a reason."

Ken bit his upper lip. All he could see as he peered up at Jacquline was that young girl, hurt and alone, crying for a love she would never have reciprocated. She had been through hell, more than once, and now stood strong and radiant — a picture perfect representation of Ken's own lost love. For the first time, Ken understood her and knew that what she said was right.

"She deserves to know," Lark whispered, her hand rested gently on the back of Ken's neck.

Ken turned away — to hide his tears — as he accepted the fact that he had been wrong in keeping this all a secret from his children. "I was only trying to protect you," he said lightly.

"By keeping us in the dark?" Jacquline said. "What did that accomplish?"

"I don't know," Ken said. "I thought it would keep me focused."

"Oh, so that's all we are to you, then. A distraction."

"I didn't say that."

"You sure as hell just did."

"I just meant that, if I told you what was happening, you wouldn't have believed me."

"You mean, I might have thought you were insane? I got news for you — I already knew that when you started this damn project."

"Then why didn't you take Tracey and leave?"

Jacquline shifted away from Ken, who kept his eyes on her a moment longer before looking back to Lark. *Tell her,* she said with just her lips.

"Every night since Stacey went missing," Ken said, defeated, "I've been dreaming about it. The exact same dream, every single night. I just couldn't let it go; I couldn't let her go."

"Wait. So you're telling me that you did all of this, *literally,* because of a dream?"

"I don't think it was just a dream. Dreams come and go, but this... she wanted me to find her."

"Oh my god. You are certifiable."

"I knew you wouldn't understand."

"Understand what, Ken? There are no such things as space aliens. God, I can't believe I ever went along with this insanity."

"Why did you then?"

"Because I thought you needed an excuse for your own damn shortcomings. And I wasn't about to leave Tracey alone under the influence of a delusional asshole."

"Jacquline —" Lark said.

"Don't do that," Jacquline snapped. "Don't you defend him. I mean, you're just as bad as he is."

"Jacquline, please," Ken said, quieter than he thought.

"No, I want to know. Did you actually believe his bullshit?"

"Yes, of course she believed me," Ken said before Lark had a chance.

"Why?" Jacquline said, unconvinced. "Why did you believe him? What is it that you get out of this whole thing?"

Lark couldn't answer.

"That's enough, Jacquline," Ken said instead.

"Oh, that's right, always defend the mistress. But you can't tell me you're not even the slightest bit curious."

"I just want to find Stacey."

"Fine. Keep living the lie. But before we all die in this wonderful coffin you've built for us, let me pose one simple little question that I'm hoping at least one of you asked at some point during this whole fiasco. Where were you going to go when you got up here? Were you just going to stop by the nearest planet and ask directions? Hope that maybe they took a detour to get a suntan on Mars? What was your plan?"

"I would have found her," Ken said, his voice hiding under his breath.

"With what?" Jacquline said, and then added with vindictive ridicule, "Love?"

Ken lost his breath.

"And what about weapons? What did you think? You were just going to go up to the aliens and say, 'Oh, I'm sorry. You seem to have taken my wife. Can I please, please, please have her back?'

" 'Oh, we're sorry. We didn't know. Here you go.'"

"This was only supposed to be a test jump, Jacquline," Lark answered. "We were just going to test the speed and the structural integrity and then turn around and go home."

Jacquline nodded. "And we all know now how well that worked out, don't we?"

"This is why I didn't tell you," Ken said.

"Because I'm logical?"

"Because you just don't understand."

"You're right, I don't. So why don't you do us all a favor and until we get to the end credits, just stay away from me. I don't want anything more to do with you." Jacquline peered over at Lark. "Or her."

Jacquline pounded her way back to the cockpit and slammed the door (as best she could, anyway, with the frame bent as it was). She sat down and held her palms to her eyes, trying to stop the tears that slowly grew within. But as her throat clamped shut, she couldn't help herself. Ken's broken mind had conjured up an inane reason to mask his insecurities, and by not telling her or Tracey about it, he now risked all of their lives. If only he had said something, maybe she wouldn't have fallen prey to his insanity, and she and Tracey could have been happy together — as the family Jacquline was only pretending to be a part of.

— 4 —

Kahli smiled at the brilliance and warmth of the gem, which filled the jar with its bright green aura. "I have spent a lifetime hoping to see just a glimpse of what I hold in my hands right now," she said, unable to take her eyes off of it. "Everything went as planned, I assume? No trouble?"

"A small fire-fight," Qah-Shekel said. "Nothing serious."

"Nothing serious? You don't think they'll come after us for this?" Kahli never once looked away from the gem.

"I wouldn't worry," Qah-Shekel muttered, his gruff tone hiding his amusement. "I set an energy-bleeder loose on the ship. They won't be bothering us."

"Uh-huh." Kahli was too mesmerized to acknowledge any further. She took in every precise cut, every sparkle of light, intoxicated by its history and the significance of its purity.

"Kahli?" Qah-Shekel said, but the gem had her. He knew it had a magnetism unlike anything else but had never seen it quite so visibly. The gem didn't affect everyone, only those who wanted to keep it, to own it, which is why Qah-Shekel was the best suited to track it down. He didn't want the gem; all he sought was peace, and the gem was his key to acquiring it.

"Kahli!" he said, tearing the jar from Kahli's hands.

"What are you doing?" she yelled, lunging desperately for the gem.

Qah-Shekel stepped away and used her momentum to shove her to the ground. "Stop," he said. "Find your center."

For a moment, Kahli's eyes burned with rage. She sensed something had gone terribly wrong as Qah-Shekel covered the gem with a cloth and hid it behind his back. She cleansed her eyes and took a deep breath to reboot her mainframe. When she reopened them, she felt calm and free.

"My apologies," she said and immediately bounced back to her feet. She hummed through her memory chips, desperately searching for an explanation for her behavior. Kahli was normally very calm, some would say sedated, after having spent two years in the dark deserts of Haserathen eradicating all of the aggressive presets from her emotional data drive. But the gem was able to locate and extract something she must have missed, and there had to be a reason hidden somewhere in the gem's history. She was right.

"That's it," she whispered. "How could I not have seen it before?" She looked up at Qah-Shekel and smiled. "You found it, all right. That is definitely the gem of Jaxxa Rakala."

"Are you okay?" he asked.

"Yes. Now that I understand what happened, I will be able to control it."

Qah-Shekel set the jar down on a shelf with some other artifacts, mostly alien organs that Kahli had studied over the years to find medicines for inter-species healing and life-strengthening energies.

"No," Kahli said. "Don't keep it in here. Take it somewhere no one will be able to see it or touch it. No one is to know where it is, including me."

Qah-Shekel wasn't one to ignore her. He picked the jar back up. "Are we on course?" he said, holding the jar close to his side, away from Kahli.

"Yes," Kahli replied softly. "We're closing in on three hundred delias."

"Good." Qah-Shekel left the room, leaving Kahli to her own. She walked to her desk, a curved, rounded crescent with sharp, rounded curvatures at each end that extended out from within the pure white wall. A small white platform with a rounded belly floated just in front of it, but Kahli refrained from sitting, opting to stand against the desk with her hands wrapped around the smooth curvature of its edge while collecting her thoughts and attempting to understand the effects of the gem. Fear was rare for Kahli, but the emotion was powerful alongside the gem. It wasn't so much that the gem had affected her, making her feel as if she could do anything without consequence, but that it was able to access her circuitry the way it did that scared her. She had thought that she would be protected from the gem's influence by the fact that she was only a machine, but that was clearly a false assertion. And if it had the ability to control a computerized mechanism and flood her with such a mad desire to never let it go, she could only imagine the embrace it would have on an organic species. She now understood how so many wars were fought over such a small piece of rock.

Suddenly, a soft, female voice rang over the communication bud embedded in her ear. "Qah-Shekel. Report to command."

Kahli filed the encounter away and left the room. She traced her way through the tight, smooth corridors of the *Equinox* until she reached a ladder at a dead-end. She climbed to the upper level, which was alive with brilliant white light. Kahli walked through the spacious corridors before reaching a hand-built archway at another dead-end. A tall creature with pointed eyes and fanged teeth, crafted by the province of Yeosha, hovered above her, standing within an alter of plant life and holding a long sword against its side. Needing to make sure she wouldn't make any irrational or illogical judgments, Kahli ran a quick diagnostic of her decision processors to make absolutely sure she was functioning properly. Satisfied that her mind was free of the gem's influence and was fit for duty, she tapped the wall in the center of the arch as if she were typing in a code. The wall soon shimmered, allowing Kahli to step into the command center, and resolidified once she was clear.

Sentilla, a young female from the dead race of Gruasdil, sat at a booth in the center of the round room, piloting the *Equinox*. A large holographic computer screen that she used for navigation sat in front of her and her hands rested on two smaller holoscreens that sat face-up on each side of her. She tapped and slid her fingers across them with the ease and fluidity of a master pilot.

Naja-Leku, a wiry little insect with an intelligent quotient so high it bordered on dysfunction, sat in his standard location in a small cubicle at the right. He would sit there for cycles on end, writing and pondering the mysteries of the universe — or that of his own chaotic mind — on parchment with the most basic of writing tools. Never once had he used a computer. "Computers are machines for those of small minds," he would ramble.

Three meters away from him was DovenJadden, a female Kasseni who had come aboard just before their plans to go after the gem went into effect. Kahli urged Qah-Shekel to reconsider bringing her aboard, but her uncanny instincts and mastery of weaponry won out over any objections Kahli might have had, although she insisted he keep her away from the gem at all costs.

Kahli took her usual position on a large black pad with a hidden symbol etched in the center that lit up red as she stepped onto it. A holoscreen wall came to life all around her and fed her scores of information on every nano-inch of space within the assigned two thousand meter radius of the *Equinox*'s current position. Kahli had perfected the system several years before, matching it to her own operating system. With it, Kahli was able to filter through exabytes of information per second without having to worry about an overload. Most of the information was extraneous and was deleted immediately; the rest was saved in a hand-device that Kahli went through every night in search of any new sources of minerals, life-affirming worlds, or altered and changing characteristics of natural resources from known and unknown worlds alike. It was her baby.

She examined a few readings in front of her and then spun the wall to her left, bringing across more informational data. She spun those away quickly, as well as several more batches of readings that she could review later. It wasn't until a scroll of unique letters and numbers caught her attention that she stopped spinning the holowall. They were nothing she had ever seen before and compelled her to study them right then and there. It wasn't until she noticed a small red light flashing just below her elbow that Kahli pulled some information up and to the right of the holowall. She hit the flashing light to reveal a series of hydrogen and helium levels that indicated the nearby Keluwa star was about ready to end its life. She figured this was why Sentilla had called Qah-Shekel to command but wasn't sure why. Other than a few rare forms of bacteria, there were no signs of life anywhere within the solar system's proximity. For all she could tell, any danger was non-existent.

Then she saw it.

Kahli set the index and forefinger of both hands on the screen and pulled them in opposite directions, enhancing a rough sketch of a ship. She read the information repeatedly, trying to figure out exactly what it was that obsessed her. Shortly after, she rested her palm on the holowall to her right and pulled toward her, shifting her hand up and around, forming a holographic keyboard from which Kahli was able to type in queries as to when the system first picked up the signal. It had been about the same time as Sentilla's call to Qah-Shekel.

"Report," Qah-Shekel demanded as he entered the room.

"I'm picking up a ship in the Keluwa system," Sentilla reported as if she had been waiting for years to say it.

"Why does that concern me?" Qah-Shekel asked abruptly, annoyed.

"The ship is traveling at about thirteen hundred delias per quintet," Sentilla continued.

"I concur," Kahli said. "But something's not quite right."

"What is it?" Qah-Shekel walked to Kahli as she rapped away at the keyboard. Finally, a detailed outline of the ship appeared and Kahli pushed it away from the holowall, allowing it to hover in front of Qah-Shekel. It rotated on its axis as Kahli recited its properties and configurations.

"The ship seems to be an antique. It's extremely small and its structure is rudimentary at best. The metal plating is a type I haven't seen in quite some time and its power cells are using an ancient nuclear capability. It's really rather astounding; so archaic." She typed another set of keys and continued. "I'm reading hundreds of life signs, but almost all of them insignificant bacteria and viruses."

Qah-Shekel studied the ship carefully. Something about it excited him, but he hated having his time wasted. "I ask again. Why does this concern me?"

"There are four sentient beings on board. Three are of an undocumented species with one heart, one brain and a rare vascular system. The fourth is similar but I can't get a good read on it... it's as if it's not even really there."

"You're saying that ship is from a new race?" Sentilla asked.

"One that just discovered the ability of interstellar travel."

"Like hundreds of other races," Qah-Shekel said through frustrated annoyance.

"This feels different," Kahli said. "I don't know. I think it would be in our best interest to rescue them."

"No. Bad idea. Bad, bad," Naja-Leku screamed from his cubicle.

"What is it?" Qah-Shekel asked instantly. Even though Naja-Leku was a neutron away from madness, Qah-Shekel trusted his instincts.

"Bad feelings about that ship. Zero percent good can come from it. Let it be destroyed or else we'll be destroyed. I see it, here," he muttered, tapping on his desk with his long fingernail. "I have gone over all possible scenarios... all possible, I hope... none result in anything good. Bad idea from the start, I say. Bad, bad."

Qah-Shekel turned to Kahli. "There's something about this fourth life sign," she said. "There's something there we're not seeing. I just have this crazy feeling that we're missing something important, that we'd be making a mistake if we let them die."

Qah-Shekel ran through his options. "What about weapons?" he finally asked.

"Aside from the uranium that seems to have become inactive some time ago," Kahli said, "they're completely unarmed."

Qah-Shekel scanned the ship again as he reflected on this new information, listening to the constant chatters of "bad idea" from Naja-Leku. It wasn't in Qah-Shekel's nature to allow an unknown species onto his ship. If he agreed, it would go against his innate instincts, something he wasn't sure he was ready to ignore.

"I will agree with Naja," he said with command. "Continue on our present course."

The hologram of the ship vanished as Kahli stepped off the pad to stop Qah-Shekel from leaving. "You're wrong," she said in defiance. "This species isn't dangerous. By what I gather, they don't even have sharp fingernails. They're alone, obviously stranded, and dying. No matter what we do, they won't live long past this system. Give me the chance to study them. I'll take full responsibility, just please, don't let them die; not until I know for sure."

Qah-Shekel lowered his head and took a long breath. "Sentilla," he finally said. "What is your opinion?"

"I agree with Kahli. There appears to be no danger."

Qah-Shekel stood for a moment in peace. "So be it. Kahli… you have command." He swept past Kahli and left the room. As soon as the door solidified, Kahli was back on her pad running the numbers.

"We have to hurry," she said over a continuous spread of "No's" and "Bad's" spewing from Naja-Leku. "If the ship doesn't disintegrate soon, the rising radiation and carbon-dioxide levels will surely do them in. Let's go introduce ourselves."

Sentilla swiped her hands over the holoscreens and led the *Equinox* toward the Keluwa star, where the small ship was headed for destruction.

— 5 —

Jacquline really wanted to sleep, but every time she closed her heavy, dry eyes, she thought of Ken. He had said she didn't understand what he was going through, but that wasn't entirely true. She had gone through the same thing with Gloria, to the point where she, too, might have claimed aliens took her away if she thought anyone would believe her. But it wasn't just about what Ken did that infuriated Jacquline. It was how easily he had forgotten about Gloria when Stacey arrived. It was no secret that Stacey was a godsend for them both, but where Ken seemed to ignore any memory of Gloria, Jacquline kept her as close as possible, in her mind and her heart, and that rejection hurt her, if only subconsciously. It wasn't until Stacey left that she realized how much she actually missed Gloria, and how much Ken had abandoned her altogether. Thinking on it now, their relationships with both Gloria and Stacey were much different, and in the scheme of things, could she have been wrong in persecuting him over that? Perhaps if she had taken more time to walk in his shoes and truly comprehend where he was coming from, she might have respected the decisions he had made, the actions he had taken, to do anything and everything to get the love he lost back. Perhaps if she had done the same after Gloria left, she might still have a relationship with her. Then again, there was no guarantee Gloria wanted anything to do with her. Would she have been strong enough to handle that rejection? Given her state of mind when she met Stacey, she didn't think she could have.

Rubbing her eyes to try and generate any bit of moisture was futile, as the cockpit steadily grew warmer. The dark orange color behind her eyelids became brighter and the light streaming through the cracked web of the window wouldn't allow her to open them. She didn't want to leave the cockpit and have to face her father, but with her body generating so much sweat that she couldn't even wipe it away, and the heat making her uncomfortably dizzy, she felt she would pass out if she didn't.

The air outside wasn't much cooler, but relative to the cockpit, it was as refreshing as a glass of water after a long hike in the desert. She shivered a bit as her wet clothes hit her skin, and waited to wipe some of the sweat away until she felt cool enough to stay alert.

Ken, his hand stuck inside one of the panels, turned to Jacquline as she pulled off her jacket. "Ready to finally join us," he said nonchalantly.

Jacquline wasn't sure she wanted to answer. Even though she hadn't wanted either of them to come to try and make her feel better, she was a little mad that they didn't at least make an excuse to go to the cockpit, which she half-expected Lark would have done. She probably would have told them to get out, but deep down, all she really wanted was to know someone wanted to help. Without it, she felt alone. "Don't flatter yourself," she ultimately said. "I only came out 'cause I was roasting in there."

Lark suddenly appeared from the other side of the engine room holding a pair of pliers. "What did you say?" she said.

"I said that damn cockpit of yours is heating up like an oven." Jacquline wiped sweat from her forehead. "I'm sorry, but I wasn't about to become Thanksgiving dinner."

Lark limped quickly to the cockpit. Even though the pain in her wrist had subsided enough to work with, her knees still felt like they'd crack at any moment. It was times like this she wished she had her cane. Before she even reached the cockpit door, she could feel the heat wafting through it. She pressed her hands against the doorframe but couldn't hold them steady, it was so hot.

"What the hell?" she said.

"What is it?" Ken said with concern. "What did she do?"

"Really? You're going to blame this on me?"

"I don't know," Lark cut in, hoping to diffuse the fight before it could start. "It feels like there's a fire." She turned to Jacquline. "You didn't see a fire anywhere, did you?"

"No," Jacquline said. "But it sure felt like hell and it was damn hard to see."

"God damn it," Lark muttered.

"What is it?" Ken said, now standing near Jacquline.

"Well, we probably don't have to worry about running out of oxygen anymore."

"Why?"

"Because if I'm right, we're about to get deep fried."

— 6 —

The hydrogen in Keluwa's sun had diminished substantially by the time the *Equinox* entered its system, but that didn't diminish its power.

"Keluwa has the ship in its gravitational pull," Kahli reported. "Slow us down."

"If we go any slower, we won't have enough momentum to push away ourselves."

"Fine. Just keep it steady." Kahli pressed the holowall and stopped the flow of information that hummed past the informational panel Kahli had set up to match the ship's technical data with that of the sun's. She was glad Naja-Leku had stormed off some time ago, completely outraged by the plan. If he were still there, she probably wouldn't hear the end of it.

"What is it?" Sentilla asked.

"We have another problem," Kahli said quietly. "Keluwa is about to go supernova."

"How long?" DovenJadden asked.

"Unclear. It could be any moment."

"I'm aborting," Sentilla said, typing the holoscreen on her left while shifting her hand in a circular motion on the right.

"No," Kahli responded instantly. "We stay on course."

"I'm not going to put this ship in danger."

Kahli understood her objection, and would have said the same if she were in her position, but she had to rescue this crew and needed to stand firm on that decision. "Qah-Shekel gave me command, and I say we continue on course."

Mutiny filled every pore of Sentilla's body. "You can't honestly believe that Qah-Shekel would put us in this kind of danger for a beat-up ship of a species we know nothing about."

"I know he wouldn't," Kahli said. "But if we don't rescue that ship, something extremely important will be lost. I guarantee it. You trust Qah-Shekel — trust his judgment."

For a brief moment, Sentilla fought with what she should do. In the end, if she went against Kahli now, Qah-Shekel may never trust her again, no matter how much she argued. She couldn't take that chance. "We'll be on them in seven delias," she said. "Let's hope Keluwa doesn't deactivate in six."

— 7 —

The entire ship screamed with intense heat. Ken and Lark sat together near the engine room door and Jacquline was up against the outer hatch, breathing erratically. Their hair was moist and greasy, their skin swimming in sweat.

"There can't be any other reason for this," Lark said with heavy lungs.

"I can't believe…" Ken tried to say as he felt his mind wander with fatigue and nausea.

"What can't you believe, Ken?" Jacquline said, each word a chore. "That we would ever run into anything or that you would have to die?"

Ken didn't acknowledge Jacquline; it was amazing that he even heard her. But the longer he stayed awake, the more he felt sorry for her and the selfishness that got her here in the first place. Jacquline was too young to die, especially like this, and he hated the fact that Tracey would forever be alone, without anyone to truly love her or care for her. *Why did I leave her?* he kept asking until he couldn't hold onto consciousness any longer. He slid across Lark's shoulder like a rag doll, his head finding her lap quite comfortable.

Lark rested her hand on his head and tried to look at him, though her eyelids were like hundred pound weights. "You tried your best, Ken," she whispered. "No regrets."

"I love you, Tracey," Jacquline said. "You will always be my little Squint." She let her head fall limp against her chest.

Lark did her best to remain strong, hoping to stay awake for the last moment of her life, but it was a futile gesture. She collapsed on top of Ken and fell into a deep sleep.

— 8 —

"Five delias," Sentilla announced. "I can see the ship." Kahli and DovenJadden looked up at the navigation screen as the ship came into view.

"This may just work," DovenJadden said.

"Four."

"Try to match speed with the smaller ship," Kahli said.

Sentilla tapped the holoscreen on her left, checking to make sure her speeds were accurate. "Three."

"Prepare the array," Kahli stated.

DovenJadden turned to the wall behind her and lit up another holoscreen. She rapped away on the corner column. "Salvage array ready," she announced.

"Two delias."

All of a sudden, information on Keluwa disappeared from Kahli's wall. "No, not yet," Kahli whispered.

"We're not going to make it."

"Stay on course, we *will* make it," Kahli stated with full authority. "Track the ship."

"I have a lock," DovenJadden said without hesitation.

"One delia."

"Steady." Kahli remained aware of their proximity to the ship while staring at the blank informational panel, her skin crawling with trepidation. This was going to be their one and only chance. "Trigger the array," she finally said.

"Array discharged."

— 9 —

Qah-Shekel stared at the gem through the slick, yellow saliva that still clung to the jar. It spun carelessly upon its axis, mesmerizing him into a deep trance. His mind was clear of thought — no fears, no questions. He was at peace for the first time since the destruction of his home planet and was able to enjoy the smell of the air around him and how it felt on his skin. Each breath was patient and calm, a sensation his father had been training him to master, but which didn't come to fruition because of their untimely separation. As he rolled the piece of rock from his planet around in his thick palm, matching the spin of the gem with all of its fluidity, he could almost feel his father and the whisper of his breathing.

All of a sudden, the gem's rotation picked up speed. At first, Qah-Shekel matched the spin of the rock with the gem, but it ultimately became too fast. The rock hit the floor, breaking his trance. But his eyes never left the gem as it continued to spin even faster, generating a glow that shot across the room and grew brighter with each revolution. A hum soon whistled from within the jar, light and airy at first and then louder and more threatening. Eventually, the jar shattered and pieces of glass flew all about the room. Qah-Shekel covered his eyes from the blast. When he looked back, the gem sat floating in the middle of the room, spinning and humming. He couldn't turn away, captured by its brilliant perfection and dynamic grace.

— 10 —

"We have them," DovenJadden said.

Kahli relaxed her body. "Perfect. Let's get the hell out of here."

"No qualms there." Sentilla punched her holoscreens, firing the engines to burn blazing hot and pushed the *Equinox* away from where Keluwa used to be.

"Not too much," Kahli said. "If we push to hard the array will slip or that ship will fall apart."

"And not enough and that supernova destroys us both."

Kahli didn't argue.

The *Equinox* picked up speed, the smaller ship keeping pace behind it. Suddenly, a flash of new readings appeared on Kahli's screen and hummed like wildfire.

"Supernova," Kahli yelled, keeping her eyes glued to the constant flow of information. "Shockwave is closing in fast."

"I'm going to lightning three. It's the only way to beat it."

"Wait," Kahli said.

"The ship will be fine. Trust me."

Kahli thought about objecting, knowing the other ship probably wouldn't last under that amount of pressure. But if they didn't escape the supernova, the ship was lost to them anyway, not to mention leaving the *Equinox* with an enormous amount of damage. Sentilla had gotten both the crew and the ship out of a lot more dangerous positions than this before and she was going to have to trust that she could do it again.

"It's on our friend's tail," Kahli said.

"I got it. It won't hit them." Sentilla's eyes gleamed with determination as she maneuvered her hands along the holoscreens with a few intermittent taps for good measure.

The wait was ominous as it loomed over the crew for several heart stopping moments. Finally, the information on Kahli's screens slowed and produced what they had all been waiting for.

"That's it," Kahli said. "The shockwave is fading. Slow us down."

DovenJadden relaxed and swallowed a bit of saliva that had built up in the back of her throat. "How's the other ship?" she said.

Kahli accessed the information happily. ' It's intact, but the life forms are still dying." Kahli stepped off the holopad. "We need to bring that ship in fast and get them to medical," she said to DovenJadden.

"Now."

— 11 —

The small damaged ship was a sight to behold. Both Kahli and DovenJadden stopped as they entered the cargo bay and saw exactly how bad it actually was. The entire body was compressed and rusted, and the sole window in the front had become nothing more than a wax paper cover. But it had held together, and under the extreme circumstances it had endured, that was one amazing feat.

"My Karokil," DovenJadden said. She slid her hand over the body, mesmerized by its primitiveness. "I can't believe this relic actually held together," she continued, enjoying the rich aroma of the rust.

Kahli pressed her forefinger and thumb together, switching on her communicator. "Massanah. Where are you?"

"Calm your cools," a wispy voice crackled on the other side. "I'm almost there."

"Hurry. These beings have very little time left." Kahli hit her fingers together again and stepped up to the window. It was extremely hot and pliable, but to her surprise, held strong against the weight of her hand. "Marvelous," she whispered to herself.

Finally, a short, stumpy figure with a tool belt strapped across his chest bounced into the cargo bay. Because his legs were only a foot in length, he mostly used his arms and hands to walk, especially when he needed speed. "What in a black hole is that?" he said.

"It's about time," Kahli said. "Hurry and get this thing open."

"Don't agonize, my pet," he said as he jumped to the ship. "I could get this hunk of junk open with a can opener."

"It may be a hunk of junk, Massanah," DovenJadden countered, walking past the engines at the rear of the ship. "But this thing is an amazing specimen." She took in the tantalizing smell of space that radiated from the ship's hull and admired the chemistry involved in the housing of the engines.

"Yeah, sure," Massanah laughed. "If you're into fossils." Massanah never liked historical relics. For him, being caught in the past was a waste of time. His mind was always on the future. He never understood why anyone, including his own crewmates, would want to make a living hunting old fossils. This was evident in his clothes, which were layered in pearls enhanced by the water-like shimmer of blue, silver and yellow throughout. Underneath it all was a very thin breastplate forged from the strongest material known to any species the day he bartered for it. "Nothing but the newest and the bestest," was Massanah's go-to moniker.

"Just get it open," Kahli said, annoyed.

"Give me a time," he said as he hopped around the ship, looking for a hatch. He finally caught sight of the small door, bent and partially open already. "Ah, here lies your gateway." He grabbed his trusty laser knife from his belt. With his long arms, he could reach the very top of the crushed plating with ease. He placed the thin slit at the edge of the knife on the crease in between the door and the body, turning the metal red-hot. The knife slowly slipped through the metal as if it was butter and Massanah sliced downward until he reached the bottom. He removed the knife and placed it back where he had started, tracing a line across the top to the other doorjamb and then continued to slice downward.

Kahli waited impatiently near the nose of the ship. The worst thing Kahli had ever witnessed was the mass destruction of an honorable species that she had failed to save. After that, she became determined to help any species whenever she could, so long as they were morally worthy and respectable beings. What she might find with this new species was still unclear, but she sure as hell wanted to find out. She just hoped it wasn't already too late.

Massanah finally stopped cutting as he reached the bottom of the ship again. "She's all yours, my pet," he said.

Kahli rushed to the door and slipped her fingers through the cut at the top. "The levels of radiation inside are minuscule but still measurable," she said to Massanah.

"Stay here. I'll bring them out."

"Kill me if you have to tell me twice, pet."

Heat washed over Kahli as she pulled the hatch open. Just before reaching the floor, a body slipped out, which Kahli assumed to be a young female of the species. Concern ran the course of her spine as she quickly knelt down to the female's side. For all she knew, the condition of the body signified death.

Massanah curiously hissed as he took in the creature's odorous stench. "The thing reeks," he said, backing away.

"She's covered in a salty, watery material," Kahli said, touching the moist, lightly hairy skin for any signs of life. "I've seen this kind of protection gland before, but it's rare." Kahli grazed the base of the female's mouth and felt a slight wisp of breath. She held her hand there and felt the air over and over, but in extremely short intervals. "She's alive," she said in relief. "There aren't any other injuries that I can see but I need to get her to medical. Massanah. Take her."

Massanah gagged.

"Massanah," Kahli commanded as she stepped into the ship. The sensors at the base of her ear registered about a hundred and ninety degrees mixed with approximately point-one millisieverts of radiation. Mixed with the cool air of the *Equinox*, a slight fog formed throughout, but Kahli could still see two more distinct bodies lying together. She lifted the top body up — another female, this one apparently older — and placed her hand to her mouth. She was alive, but substantially injured. The unusual wrapping on her arm was coated in a thick, red liquid, which Kahli automatically identified as blood. The female had definitely broken something, and although the physiology was similar to that of her own, she wouldn't know if she could repair it until she got her back to medical — that is if she made it back there at all. Keeping her upright, Kahli shifted the head of the last body upward — a male — and swiped her thumb over his mouth. His breath was stronger than the others and it gave Kahli hope. Suddenly, the male let out a loud cough. Kahli dropped his head and waited, but figured after a moment of motionless silence that it had been a reflex action and nothing more.

"DovenJadden. Get in here."

DovenJadden rounded the ship and stopped next to Massanah to get her first look at the new species. "So ooky," she whispered as she pushed on her skin, turning the reddish-colored hue a yellowish-white. "Get her out of here," DovenJadden said and stepped into the ship. Her muscles instantly seized and she fell to her knees, unable to breathe. Kahli quickly escorted her out and she immediately felt better. "Sorry," Kahli said. "I'll bring them out."

Kahli jumped back into the ship as Massanah finally grabbed the young female under the shoulders and pulled her away. Kahli returned with the older female and handed her to DovenJadden. "Take her to medical. I'll be there shortly."

Not quite back to top condition, the weight of the creature made DovenJadden stumble a bit. As she passed Massanah, who kept stopping to catch his breath and calm his sickness, she felt much healthier and carried her the rest of the way with ease.

With the male in slightly better condition than the females, Kahli took a quick look around the rest of the ship, checking everything down to the last wire, still unable to find what she was looking for. It was frustrating — she couldn't understand why there were only three bodies when her readings clearly showed four. She was missing something, but until she could study it more, she couldn't worry about it. There were three other beings that were in need of her help. With one last flash look, Kahli slipped her arms under the male's body and carried him out.

Naja-Leku watched from the edge of the corridor. His fingers twitched and his jaw palpitated as he carefully studied the specimen Massanah dragged through the cargo bay. "This is a bad time for us all," he mumbled as Kahli sprinted past them. "You're putting us all in danger."

His warnings echoed away from Kahli as she continued her brisk pace, eager to find out what this new species was all about. Halfway there, Kahli had to stop, almost losing grip on the male as he started to shake. When he finally stopped, he opened his eyes a crack and looked at Kahli.

"Keladrayia..." he choked out.

Shock was all Kahli felt as the male once again dropped unconscious. She couldn't understand how he knew of Keladrayia, but now knew her instincts had been correct. There was definitely something important inside the minds of these creatures and she was now more determined than ever to find out what that was. She picked up her pace to almost a run and reached the medical quarters as DovenJadden set the older female on the medical bed nearest the entry. Kahli pressed her hand firmly on the opposite wall, extending another long medical bed from inside. She set the male down and began her examination by pulling open his eyelids and swiping the inside of his mouth with her fingers.

"Are you sure you should be doing that?" DovenJadden said, slightly disgusted.

"I need you to retrieve the other female and have Massanah get back to that ship and analyze every last inch of it. I want every single detail, no matter how small or irrelevant."

DovenJadden left without objection. Kahli continued to study every facet of the male creature's physiology. Deciding it better to bring them back to health before digging into their minds, she released another long board above the male with a quick swipe of her hand against the wall. Kahli tapped at the corner of the board's thin edge and moved her finger across it, lighting up the underbelly of the board in bright purple. Within seconds, it formed a purple holographic outline of the male's entire body that floated just above him. A table of information, including all of their DNA coding, appeared at the head of the hologram, giving Kahli all she needed to understand how his body worked. She quickly did the same for the older female. As she scanned the readings, she found them to be very different, yet very much the same as her creators — one heart, two lungs and very similar reproductive organs. What was strikingly different was their skin, which as opposed to her creator's thick and rigid exterior, was pliable, very thin and easily pierced. She finally understood why they were so susceptible to both the heat and radiation, and how the sweat glands operated to protect them. She also took notice of their infallibility to viruses, which she ran tests on to make sure they weren't harboring something that might harm the crew. Although she found thousands within each cell of the body, they lived mostly in harmony with their host and she happily cleared them of any danger.

When DovenJadden returned with the younger female, she immediately lit her up under a third table at the back of the room near the artifacts. What she noticed right away were the commonalities in bacterial entities between them all. Though they shared a few similar viruses, there was a distinct difference between the older female and the other two. Taking a deeper look at the DNA sequences, Kahli was able to confirm that the young female was the offspring of the male, but not the female.

Having learned all she could, Kahli used the hologram's to inject several necessary medicines into each one and fix any minor internal injuries. Once completed, she switched off each of their medical boards and returned them to the walls. After retracting the male's, she stood over him, the name "Keladrayia" floating about her memory.

"What are you doing?" a low grumble reverberated from the doorway.

Qah-Shekel peered over the older female, eyeing her closely. "Nothing," Kahli said. "It's just their features, their anatomy; it's almost identical to that of my fathers."

"Are they ancestors?"

"I don't believe so… Not of my species, anyway. Not this far away." Kahli looked back down at the male.

"I want you to put them in restraints," Qah-Shekel said, turning his attention to the younger female.

"Why?"

"Look at what this one has done to her body?" he said, pointing at the piercings covering the younger female's face.

"She also has several drawings etched into her skin," Kahli said, trying to make sense of it as well. "Maybe she was tortured in some way."

Qah-Shekel looked closer and saw part of a drawing on her chest that hadn't been completely covered by her clothing. "I still want them in restraints," he said. "I don't want them leaving this room." Qah-Shekel walked up to Kahli, looking over the male body. "You said there were four life forms."

"I wasn't able to locate the fourth on board."

"Where is it?"

"I don't know. I sent Massanah to the ship to find out. When I learn more, I'll let you know."

"I want you to perform mind sweeps on them."

"No," Kahli quickly countered. "I can't be sure if their minds can handle that type of pressure."

"I don't care. They may have information we can use."

"I understand, but I would rather wait until they wake."

"We can't wait that long."

"*You* can't wait that long," Kahli countered.

Qah-Shekel grunted. "How can you be sure they'll say anything once they're awake. Just do as I say. That's an order." Qah-Shekel stepped back, took one last glance at the male creature, and returned to the young female. "This one looks familiar," he said petting the white streaks in her hair.

Although she agreed, Kahli didn't want to tell him what she had heard until she could physically talk to them and find out what they knew. "Fine," she said. "It'll give me a chance to learn their language and their world before they wake. But if I find the stress to be too much, I'm ending it. I won't hurt them."

Qah-Shekel stared at Kahli sternly but accepted her terms and left without another word. Kahli went to her desk and tapped the table, lighting up a keypad that was visible only as each key was touched. As she did, a holoscreen flashed on above the center of the desk and small squares in the walls above each of the bodies opened up. Kahli checked a few calculations on the holoscreen and then walked back to the male figure. She reached into the open square and pulled out a small crescent-shaped object with an elastic strap and four wires connected to its tips. Kahli wrapped the elastic strap around the male's head, allowing the main piece to hover just above his forehead, the tips resting gently against each temple. Just then, a purple light streamed onto the male's forehead from the base of the crown. Kahli took a breath, excited and nervous by what she was about to learn.

— 12 —

Ken ties the loop around his necktie. As he straitens it, the lovely features of his wife enter the mirror. Her smile lights up her cheekbones and make her eyes sparkle. He picks his jacket up off the chair and puts it on as she steps up behind him. The soft touch of her hands as they trace his waist and come together around his stomach give him a slight chill. She rests her chin on his shoulder and the air is suddenly filled with the soft aroma of her skin.

"Don't go," she whispers in his ear. "Jacquline wants us all to go to the circus."

"I have to, sweetie. If I don't, I could lose the account. You go. Have fun."

"But she wants you there, Ken."

Ken turns around. "I'll try to be back by two, okay?"

"Thank you." She slowly kisses his lips and, as when he first met her, Ken doesn't want to leave her.

— 13 —

Kahli pet the young female's hair. The moment she saw her, she noticed the resemblance to the historical depictions of Keladrayia, and with what the male had whispered earlier, Kahli couldn't help but wonder if it could actually be her. It would give credence for Naja-Leku's objections and would certainly warrant extreme caution. But as far as she knew, Keladrayia was older and much more elegant and pure.

Kahli smiled as she finished removing the pins from the young female's features. *So young; so precious.*

— 14 —

Jacquline lies in bed, staring at the picture of her mother on her nightstand. It is one in the afternoon, but what is time but a construct of human arrogance? Like her homework, her teachers and friends, it just doesn't matter anymore. Why should it? If her mother doesn't care, why should she? She did care, though, much more than her mother. So much so that for the past two weeks, all Jacquline has wanted to do — or has thought about doing — is finding her mother and asking her why she no longer cares. The problem is, she doesn't know where she went, or why, so her search has been extremely aggravating. And her father hasn't been any help. He hangs around, feeds her, tucks her in at night, but his spirit is gone, much like her own. It wasn't until last night that she realized that even with all of that, he doesn't care either, having never come home. He has abandoned her now too, leaving Jacquline completely alone. She doesn't want to believe it, and her heart tells her he could never do that, but the whole situation has pushed her so deep that all she wants to do now is lie in bed — until she dies.

— 15 —

Kahli carefully unwrapped the stained bandages from the older female's arm and removed the piece of metal. A small chunk of bone had broken the skin at the wrist. Kahli grabbed a moist cloth from the medical tray next to her and wiped the crusted blood away from the wound. She admired the bone's structure and the brittleness of the break. She could only imagine how much pain the female must have endured when it snapped. After setting the cloth back down, Kahli wrapped a large, blue tube that resembled Styrofoam around the female's wrist. She then pressed a series of keys on the small plasma screen on the top of it. The tube slowly tightened, forming a cast around the female's injury.

HEALING: 0% COMPLETE

— 16 —

Dear Diary,

My mother's funeral was today. I miss her so much. During the service I cried a lot. My dad told me to stop and get over it. But every time he said it, I cried harder. He never cried. He was probly too drunk to even know what happend. I don't even think he loved my mom. I know he doesn't love me. He broke my arm when I wouldn't stop crying when the doctors told us she had died. He told the men I fell off my bike but you know the true story. It doesn't hurt much anymore. It just itches a lot. It isn't the same around here without my mom. My dad seems more drunk and seems like more of a jerk without my mom around. I think she died just to get away from him. I don't blame her. It was the only way she could do it. She tried doing it the other way, running away and bringing me with her. He found us, pretty quick to. That was when she spent three days in the hospital, remember? I know for sure she didn't fear dying. I do. I have to find another option. Running away wont do anything. I could dig a hole to China and he would still be able to find me. I think the only way I could ever get away from him forever without dying would be to travel to space. In space, he'd be vulnerble. I wish ET would come down from space and aduct me. And if my dad followed, Id rip off his oxagin mask and watch his head explode. That would be fun. It would serve him right too. What if Hon Solo came and brought me to the Milliniam Falken. That would be cool. Hon Solo is such a dream. I'm sure he wouldn't hit his daughters or hurt them and make them cry all the time. I hate my dad. I wish he was the one that died and not my mom. She didn't deserve it. This isn't fair, diary. It's a bad thing the way the world treats everyone like garbidge. I guess that's just another reason to run away, huh?

— 17 —

Ken's head pounded and his throat tickled to the point that he wanted to vomit. He tried to rub his forehead but his arms felt extremely heavy and numb. When he tried saying something, his tongue was too weak to pronounce any words.

Turning his head slightly, he opened his eyes. A cold image of someone nearby — a woman — stood next to what looked like a desk, reviewing a futuristic computer screen. He could make out the curvature of her body, but not much else. What interested him most was the back of the figure's neck, where he thought he saw a tail. As he focused, he realized it was actually a cord connected from the back of her neck (slightly hidden by her hair) to the desk in front of her. The woman turned to him as he shifted. Speaking a language he had never heard before, she walked to him and tapped the wall. Ken suddenly felt lightheaded and slipped back to sleep.

— 18 —

He immediately wakes.

Gloria stands over him, her stomach a huge ball. She's breathing heavily — "Hee-Hee-Hoo."

"Honey, what is it?" Ken sits up and takes hold of her arm.

Under each breath he hears the words, "It's time."

"It's time?"

Gloria nods. Ken jumps from the bed and slips on a pair of pants and an old t-shirt. "How far apart are they?"

"About five minutes."

"Good. We've got time. Come on."

He helps Gloria stand and she screams, her legs held up and out by the stir-ups erected from under the patient bed. Ken holds her hand tightly, helping her breathe.

"Okay, I want you to push, Mrs. Brody," the doctor says from in between her legs. "Go. Push."

"Push," Ken says. Gloria squeezes his hand so tight she crushes the bone.

"Take a breath," the doctor says softly. "I see the head. One more push, Mrs. Brody. Ready, push."

Gloria strains once again and then screams. Her body falls limp and the pain becomes tears for the sweet cry of a newborn baby.

"It's a girl," the doctor says as he carries the baby to a nearby table. Ken smiles, tears forming in his own eyes. He turns back to Gloria.

"It's a girl," she repeats through laughter.

"Yeah," Ken says softly. He kisses her, tasting the honey of her tears. He pulls away and sees Stacey — calm, lovely and not a mark of stress on her face. She smiles sweetly as the doctor hands her a pile of pink blankets.

"What are you going to name her?" the doctor asks.

"Tracey," Stacey says as she shifts the blanket from the baby's face, exposing the small crescent-moon birthmarks on her cheeks. Stacey looks up at Ken, who smiles and nods. "Tracey."

"The jewel of my eye, the savior of grace."

— 19 —

The young female's memories conveyed a pain, a cruelty and a dread that overwhelmed Kahli. What made it bearable was the love the young female held for her baby sister. There was a spark there that Kahli also saw between the male and his second mate, a woman with the same color and style of hair as the young female — a woman Kahli believed was in fact the true Keladrayia.

— 20 —

Jacquline stands on the front porch of the yellow house. The paint is fresh and the lawn is well manicured, with roses and violets fencing it in. The birds chirp harmoniously among the trees that run the course of the sidewalk.

When the door opens, Jacquline sees the woman she has spent three years searching for. The image of her standing there in her flowered house dress, her hair braided on both sides of her head, make Jacquline feel as if she has entered a dream. Her mother has never looked this good before; she's surprised it's even her.

"Mother," she finally spits out.

"Jacquline?" is the woman's confused response.

Jacquline nods and smiles. The woman smiles back with surprise.

"Jackie," she says as she awkwardly hugs Jacquline. The urge to hold her mother is strong.

"Mom, I've been looking for you everywhere."

Jacquline doesn't want to let go, but feels her mother pushing her away.

"You shouldn't have done this," her mother says.

"Why?"

"You don't belong here. You shouldn't have come."

Jacquline's warm smile fades. "But, mom. I want to talk to you."

"You have no reason to."

"Yes, I do. I need answers."

"Answers to what?" With each passing second, Jacquline's mother turns colder.

"Why did you leave?" Jacquline asks.

There's a long pause and then, "My life is my own. You should never have come. Leave. Now." And the door to the world Jacquline has been praying for all of these years closes.

Jacquline steps off the porch as the door turns black. The whole house is soon a tapestry of darkness, shrouded in wilted trees and plants. The grass turns a dull brown as Jacquline steps into the street. She can't move; her legs slide into a liquid of what used to be the pavement. She doesn't struggle, though, allowing it to envelop her, hoping it suffocates her quickly and quietly.

— 21 —

Kahli watches the holoscreen as the letters stream by, associating them with pictures and words. As she neared the end of her testing, her knowledge and love for those three young humans quickly turned from experimentation to passion.

— 22 —

Ken walks Lark down the dimly lit street. They had just enjoyed a fine French meal and are on their way home. Lark loves the moist night air, especially when she spends it with him. The soft sounds of his voice laughing at tales of his wife and daughters make her smile with delight. Every time Ken looks at her in a pause in stories, she takes the moment to stare into his eyes. His love for his wife runs deep, which produces a romantic sensation within them. There were moments over the last few years when Lark wanted to be Stacey, but they were only a child's crush. She knows deep down that her feelings for Ken are only out of trust and respect — not romantic love.

The evening reaches near midnight when they finally find the steps of her apartment building.

"Would you like to come inside for a cup of coffee?" The question is always asked whenever they spend time together outside of work. But it's always rejected. She doesn't expect any different tonight, but figures she'd ask out of courtesy anyway.

"Why not," he responds.

Lark smiles brightly. "Well, come on."

She flips on the light as they enter the small apartment, highlighting the bare necessities of living. A chair sits in front of a small desk that holds a thirteen-inch television and a sleeping bag and pillow rest on the floor in the corner. The kitchen is also overly bare, with nothing more than a coffee pot, some coffee mix, and a worn-out refrigerator that came with the apartment.

"Like I said. I don't stay home much," Lark says in response to Ken's bewildered expression.

"I didn't say anything," he says, closing the door. Lark tosses her jacket on the coat hanger in the closet and heads for the kitchen.

"I'm afraid I don't have sugar or cream. Will black do?"

"No problem," Ken says as he sits down in the chair. "It's a nice place," he says, enjoying the primitive state, though Lark figures it to be more out of politeness than sincerity.

Lark fills up the coffee pot and turns on the heat. "It'll be a few minutes," she says, gliding over to Ken. He stands up and grabs a hold of her hands. A chill runs down her back as the warmth of his hands produce goose bumps up her arms. "Good. That will give us a couple of minutes."

Lark sees something different in Ken's eyes. No longer is there despair or loss; she sees love and need, making her a little uncomfortable. "A couple of minutes for what?"

Suddenly, Ken's lips press against hers in a long embrace. She thinks about pulling away, but as time ticks on, and the sweet taste of his kiss continues, she begins to enjoy it, falling deeply into him. When she pulls him closer, he suddenly pushes her away and slaps her, causing tears to stream from her eyes.

"You snuck out last night, didn't you!" he screams, his breath ripe with alcohol.

"No," Lark whimpers, avoiding his glare.

"Look at me when you talk to me." He grabs her chin and forces her head up. "You will respect your father, you little bitch."

Lark's jaw feels as if it's about to shatter. "Yes, sir," she mutters, if only for the chance to get away from him.

"I thought I said I never wanted to see you with that boy," her father yells. The smell of booze makes Lark sick to her stomach.

"I wasn't with him," Lark tries to say without gagging.

"Stop lying to me," he screams, sending the back of his hand to her eye. She falls to her knees, the ugly shag carpet allowing for a soft landing.

"Get up," he says, burning her arm with his grip. "Get to your room. And don't let me catch you sneaking out again, either."

He shoves Lark away. She slams her shoulder into the corner of the hallway and falls back to the ground.

"Get. Before I get angry."

Tears stream down her cheeks as she stands, trying to keep her fear from stopping her defiance. Lark can see her father's eyes get retched with rage.

"What do you think you're doing?" he says.

Lark doesn't answer. She simply stands in the hallway and waits.

"That's it." Her father grabs her throat and drags her down the hall. Unable to scream out, she squirms and kicks, grabbing for and scratching his arm. When they reach her bedroom door, her father stops. "Look at this mess. You're not going anywhere until this pile of shit is cleaned up."

He throws Lark into the room. She tries to gain control of her flight but hits her head on the dresser. She slips down the side, landing on top of some make-up kits, and lies there, stiff and sick. After her father closes the door, she musters up what strength she has left and grabs her field hockey bag. *Never again,* she tells herself.

"You want me to clean this shit up, fine." She stuffs the bag with clothes, makeup and other necessities she thinks are important (most of which she'll never again use) and uses her hockey stick to shatter the bedroom window. "Good riddance," she whispers as she climbs out and runs.

— 23 —

The news of Stacey's disappearance hits Jacquline hard. She had become a mother to her just in time to save her from Hell. How could she leave? Why would she risk sending Jacquline back into her depression? She continually plays over several reasons, each one completely wrong and inconceivable — did Tracey do something? No, she loves Tracey just as much as she loves her and Ken; did she, herself, do or say anything? She can't recall any bad behavior on her part; was she tired? Definitely not. She has more life in her than a dozen people put together. So what had it been that pushed her away?

She sees her father down the hall, lying in bed. For whatever reason, Ken is taking Stacey's loss harder than he did Gloria's. Jacquline recalls what she went through four years earlier and it looks like Ken is falling into that same state of mind. What will happen to her and Tracey if he doesn't ever come out of it? Ken had given her Stacey to restore her happiness, what can she give him to do the same?

Ken stares motionless at the wall as she walks into his bedroom. He doesn't even blink once as she kneels down to meet his gaze, wondering if he fell asleep with his eyes open.

"Dad? Are you okay?"

Jacquline doesn't push for an answer. She is about to leave when he finally speaks — words that Jacquline will never forget.

"I need to find her. She's all I have."

Pain strikes every marrow of Jacquline's body. "What?"

Ken's answer breaks her heart. "Without Stacey, I have no reason to live."

Jacquline leaves, unable to even look at him. She slams her bedroom door shut and lies down on her bed. His words slice through her thoughts as she tries to figure out what they truly mean.

Stacey is all you have, huh, Ken? Well, then I guess you won't mind if I stay out of your life. You just better remember to stay the hell out of mine.

— 24 —

Ken stares at the large blueprints sprawled about his desk. He runs his fingers through his hair, eagerly searching for something he missed. He came up with the design about a week ago and has been working on them ever since with very little sleep. Every time he tries, a new idea pops in his head and he has to get it out before he forgets. He doesn't eat much, either, having to get up from his work to do so. He might have a cup of coffee in the morning (if his daughter is willing to bring it to him) and maybe some supper, but he hasn't left the desk for more than fifteen minutes at any one time.

The design is sound, the calculations for entry into the speed of light are correct, but for the life of him, he can't figure out why it doesn't feel right. Is it because he's afraid of what might happen? Is it because he's not ready to find the only thing in his life that had any real meaning? It can't be. She's been waiting for him to rescue her, and he's as eager as ever to get her back. So, then… What is it?

Leaning back in his chair he rubs his eyes, tired. He needs a break. Perhaps some fresh air will help him think more clearly. He walks to the kitchen where Jacquline and Tracey eat breakfast.

"Ready to finally join us?" Jacquline says.

"Just taking a quick break," Ken says. He grabs the newspaper off of the counter and heads out the door to the back porch. He sits and opens the paper. There's nothing much but the usual negativity of political and economic news. Fed up with the madness journalists thrive on, he tosses most of the paper away. What's left is the classifieds section, which sparks a new energy within him. That's what's missing; that's what he needs to finish his dream.

— 25 —

"You need help with those?" Lark's neighbor asks, rushing out of his apartment. Lark has just returned home from the grocery store and fumbles with her keys.

"No, thanks. I got it."

"Come on, let me help." He reaches for the keys. The man has had a crush on Lark ever since she moved in and is always looking for an excuse to get into her apartment — and her pants. Her accident simply gives him another reason, but she isn't having it.

"I said I got it," she says, her voice raised. As she pulls the keys from his hand, the contents of one of the grocery bags spill onto the floor.

"God, I'm sorry," her neighbor says. "Let me get those."

"Don't," Lark says, kicking at him, a simple act that causes her legs to burn with excruciating pain.

He backs away, pissed. "Damn, bitch." He shakes his hand and then rubs it gingerly. "I was just trying to help."

Lark does everything she can to bite her own pain back. "I never asked for it."

"What do I have to do?"

"Leave me alone. That's all I want."

"What's your problem? All I've ever been is nice to you."

"And I know why. Now get out of here."

"You're insane," he says, trudging back to his apartment.

"I'm glad you finally agree."

"God damn bitch," he mumbles as he slams his door shut.

"Asshole," she whispers in return. It takes her another minute but she finally unlocks her door and gently kicks the groceries into the well-furnished apartment. She follows them in with the strenuous use of her cane and hobbles into the kitchen. For several minutes, Lark leans up against the counter, breathing in and out slowly using the techniques that her rehab trainer taught her to help relax the pain in her knees. Once it subsides to a reasonable level, she collects the items off the floor, a task that takes her nearly fifteen minutes to complete. As she picks up the newspaper, the classified section falls out and spreads across the floor.

"Damn," she says. She's about to leave it there and deal with it later, but the thought of the clutter bothers her too much. When she kneels down to pick it up, she catches sight of an ad. She isn't sure what intrigues her about it, but whatever the reason, she sits on the floor to read the entire thing.

WANTED:
New alloy able to withstand extreme heat
and extraordinary amounts of pressure
for testing of new deep space technology.
For more information, call Ken Brody.

After reading the ad for the hundredth time, Lark is back on her feet without even realizing it. She has been looking for this very opportunity for years, ever since the Navy refused to fund her idea for a new deep-sea metal. But is it real? There's only one way to find out. She grabs her phone and dials the number.

"Hello?" Ken says. He sounds tired and apathetic.

"Hello," Lark says, her voice sweet and almost angelic, full of energy. "Is this Ken Brody?"

"Yes. Who's this?"

"My name is Lark Steines and I think I may have exactly what you're looking for."

— 26 —

Tears cloud Jacquline's eyes as she stares at the lonely image in the mirror. She can't understand why the image radiates so much pain; she only understands what the pain feels like and what's going on in her own mind. Sleep is something of the past, as is anything having to do with happiness. For two weeks, pleasure has slowly drained from her body, as each day grows longer and more heartless. Her father has stopped coming to check in on her and instead is chronically missing. Whenever she tries to find him, to attempt a stab at a love she lost, all she finds is emptiness. And in this emptiness is the deep desire to stop her pain and find herself again somewhere else.

She looks down at the cold, white sink, bare of everything except a blade she had taken from her father's razor a few days earlier. He hasn't noticed, which reinforces her belief that she won't be missed in the slightest if she leaves. She places her palm over it, feeling the bite of the metal against her skin. Tears flush her eyes as her hand trembles to pick up the razor. For the past two days, this is as far as she's gotten, falling short of the bravery needed to pick it up. In her heart, what she's doing is wrong, but her mind screams otherwise. She sucks up a soft breath of air, ending her stream of tears, and cups the razor in her hand. Holding her fist on the edge of the sink, she lifts her head back to the young, deserted eyes in the mirror.

Stay brave, the image whispers. *This is what you want. This is all you have left.*

Jacquline doesn't reply, she simply lifts her fist up and stares at it. A trickle of blood drops from her enclosed fingers and she becomes mesmerized by the drops that fall continuously to the sink.

"Jacks?" a voice echoes through her mind. She ignores it in favor of the blood. "Jacks? Are you home?"

The voice is more real now. Jacquline turns from the mirror to look at the door behind her.

"Jacks. I want to introduce you to someone."

Jacquline drops the razor to the floor. She grabs a towel from the rack next to the door and wraps it around her hand. As she steps from the bathroom, she wipes a few tears from her red-laced face and waits for Ken to arrive.

"Jacks, there you are. What were you doing?"

Jacquline looks past Ken at the woman standing in the hallway gazing back at her with the curiosity of a child.

"Jacks?" Ken asks, shaking her shoulder.

Jacquline looks at him and says the first thing that comes to mind. "I was teaching myself to shave my legs." It's the stupidest lie she's ever told, but he falls for it just the same.

"Okay," he says cheerfully. "Jacks. I want to introduce you to Stacey. Stacey," he continues, waving for the woman to come into the room, "this is Jacquline."

The woman's steps are smooth as silk, making it appear as if she's floating across the floor. Jacquline's first thought upon seeing her is, *Perfect, but strangely odd.* She is wire-thin, looking a lot like Olive Oyl on a bad artistic day, and her hair is light auburn with symmetrical white stripes highlighted throughout. The sweatshirt that drapes over her body like a giant bag, revealing a thin, smooth shoulder, is one that Jacquline had gotten Ken as a Father's Day gift a few years back.

"It's nice to meet you, Jacquline," she says, holding out her hand. Her voice is soft and whistles through the air like a song.

Jacquline takes a hold of her hand and instantly feels a warmth that she hasn't felt for some time, which leads to the first smile she's had since her mother left her.

"Same here," Jacquline says, noticing that the woman will not take her eyes off of her, not even when Ken starts talking again.

"I almost hit her with my car," he says. "She was standing in the middle of the road, in the rain..."

Jacquline is only half listening to his story as her attention remains solely on the woman. She isn't letting go of her hand and her face is bright. Jacquline's heart pumps rapidly as her skin secretes a little bit of sweat. Her left hand tickles and all of her worries, her fears and her deep sorrow are condensed into a fog of memories, wiped from the slate — replaced by the feel of magic and love.

"And that's when I decided to let her meet you," Ken says, wrapping up his story in delight.

Stacey finally lets go of Jacquline's hand and looks at Ken. "Wonderful story, Ken," she says and then looks back to Jacquline. "Don't you think so, Jacquline?" Stacey winks and blushes a smile.

Jacquline returns it graciously. "Yeah. Really detailed." She no longer feels the pain of the blade on her palm.

Stacey winks again and snuggles up to Ken.

"I like your hair," Jacquline spits out, a little uneasy about her advances.

"Well, thank you."

"It's really vogue."

Stacey smiles, curious. "I'm not quite sure what that means, but I'll take —"

Suddenly, Stacey grabs her chest and falls to her knees. She gags, unable to breathe. Clutching Ken's arm, she desperately searches for air. Ken kneels down and grabs her shoulders.

"Stacey, what's wrong?" he yells.

Stacey pushes Ken away and pulls a small green gem from under her shirt. It spins rapidly in her hand. Ken and Jacquline close their eyes and turn away from the unbearable light that fills the room. But Ken can't look away for long and when he opens his eyes, he doesn't see Stacey anywhere.

"Stacey?"

Ken crawls his way around the crystal. "Stacey?" he calls over and over until he hears a loud hum, much like a swarm of bees hovering next to his ear. Before he can figure out what it is, the gem explodes in a flash of light, sending Jacquline and Ken flying back and into the burning white light of nothing.

— 27 —

Ken's eyes ripped open. A sickening vibration swarmed his skin that made his heart race, but all he could do was stare into the blank space above him, trying to understand what had happened. As he realized it had all been a dream, his breathing calmed and his eyes grew heavy and tired. He closed them, and for a few quick heartbeats, he was at peace.

"Ken," a familiar voice whispered. "Ken, wake up."

The room was dark, lit only by a few hazy, purple lights surrounding the ceiling. He tried to locate the owner of the voice but couldn't tell if the figure moving around some eight feet away was anything but a figment of his imagination.

"Who's there?" he said groggily, shifting his body to get a closer look.

"It's me, Lark."

"Lark?" He slowly stood, his body aching, and walked toward her. "What are you —"

"No, wait. Ken, stop." Lark had her arms up and her face was wrought with panic.

"What?" It was too late. As Ken took another step forward, he reached his hand out to Lark and received a massive electric shock from the bright yellow patchwork of light that appeared out of thin air around him. He grabbed his hand and fell backward against the medical bed. It burned as if it was on fire, and the more he tried to coax the pain away, the deeper it stung.

"What the hell was that?" he seethed under gritted teeth.

"Some kind of force field, I think. I can't be sure."

"Force field?" His memory quickly roared back to life. He remembered feeling hot and dizzy before his heart slowed so much that he thought it had completely stopped.

"Where are we?" he asked, even though he figured Lark was just as clueless.

"I can't be certain, but I think we might be on an alien ship."

"How did we get here?"

"They must have rescued us?"

"They? Who?" He couldn't think straight. His hand cramped as the burn grew in intensity.

"I don't know. I only woke up five minutes before you."

All of a sudden, a scream shot through the room. "Stop it! Get him off of me! I can't take it anymore!" Another scream was followed by additional cries for help.

"What is that?" Ken yelled over the persistent wailings.

"It's Jacquline," Lark said, moving toward her and stopping a few feet away. The change in temperature was small but apparent.

"What are you doing?" Ken said in dreadful pain. "Help her?"

"I can't," Lark said, a little irritated. "There's another force field here. I can't get to her."

Suddenly, bright white lights illuminated the room. A woman with shoulder-length jet-black hair highlighted in blue tips and an exquisitely perfect frame entered. She swiped her fingers across the information that glowed across the flat (and in some way, invisible) computer screen floating above the table near the door and tapped a code into the lower left corner. A divisional grid of honeycomb immediately lit up across the room, disappearing as quickly as it had appeared. Before Lark understood what was happening, the woman pushed past her and sat next to Jacquline, whose screams had become longer and louder. The woman quickly pushed the butt of her palm down on Jacquline's clavicle and wrapped her other hand around Jacquline's arm.

"Get away from her," Ken said, the burn in his hand expanding two-fold, dropping him to his knee. The woman looked at him but didn't move.

"Let go of her," Lark added, wanting to pull the woman away but still wary about stepping any closer. It was obvious that the force field had been deactivated, but after seeing what it had done to Ken, she wanted no part of it and couldn't take the chance that she was somehow wrong.

The woman ignored them both, staring at Jacquline as her screams waned, eventually dying out altogether. When she fell still and resoundingly quiet, the woman stood.

"What did you do to her?" Ken screamed "You killed her. You bitch, you killed her." He was lying on the floor, squirming to keep sight of the woman. He wanted to chide the woman for what she had done, but the overwhelming pain now scorched up his arm and made him all but immobilized.

The woman pressed her fingers to Jacquline's neck. "She is not dead," she said in a cold monotone.

Upon these words, Ken let go of some of his anger and relaxed, his pain doing the same.

"She's not dead?" Lark asked for him.

The woman looked at Lark. "She is only…" She paused, looking over Lark's face. "Sleeping."

"She's sleeping? You mean she's sedated?"

"Sedated," the woman repeated. "I thought this was sleep."

"Well, yes, it is. But you forced her to sleep. With a sedative… a tranquilizer."

"Tranquilizer?"

"Something that puts someone to sleep on purpose."

The woman looked as if she was computing the idea. Finally, she grinned in recognition and raised her hand. Sticking out from just below each finger was a tiny sharp tack. "Yes. I put her to sleep to calm her." She walked back to her desk.

"Who are you?" Ken groaned. The woman finally took notice of his anguish. His hand was tucked into his gut.

"Did you touch the grid?" the woman asked.

Ken let out a cold sigh of pain. The woman shifted her fingers across the computer screen like she was searching for an app on her iPad. Just then, a small part of the wall opened near Ken. Inside was a vile with green liquid.

"Spread that on the infected area. It should heal quickly."

Ken hesitated but figured he had nothing to lose and grabbed the vile. It was warm and smelled like rotten eggs. Choking back his queasiness, he tipped the glass over his palm, allowing the slimy goo to spread out onto it. He couldn't move his fingers as the liquid melted its way around his entire hand, but it felt quite soothing. To his surprise, the pain was gone in seconds and the goo vanished, leaving his hand healthier than ever.

"How did you do that?"

"It is a soothing gel," the woman said, continuing to play with her computer. "The Clorians manufacture it on their home world. It is good for healing bruises, small cuts and burns." She lifted her head to Lark and smiled. "That is why I could not use it on your arm." As it became easier for her to speak, the woman's voice became more real.

"Well, whatever it is, it's some great stuff."

"And very addictive." The woman returned her attention to the computer.

"Addictive?" Ken examined his hand nervously.

"Do not worry. You must ingest several gallons a day to become addicted. Do not get hurt any further and you shall be fine."

Lark finally sucked up the courage to break the barrier and sit next to Jacquline. She slowly brushed her fingers through her hair, taking in the beauty of her now flawless skin.

"Who are you?" Ken said, unconvinced by the explanation.

"In your terms, I would be considered a Rega-One Xyla-Alpha-Nine Android."

"Android?" Lark said.

"You're a robot?" Ken chimed in.

"Robot?" the woman repeated, trying to comprehend the word.

"An android, a robot. You're synthetic."

"Yes," she said, happily. "My body is run by a Jas-K-9 synthesizer. My processors can hold up to eight hundred thousand xylabytes of information. Because of this, I can learn new languages, species, emotions and figures and contain them in my memory without ever having to forget them, unless I choose to delete them. But once deleted, I cannot retrieve that information again until I go through the learning process once more."

"I wish my brain could do that," Ken said, stretching what felt like brand new fingers. "There's some stuff I would love to delete from my memory."

"What's your name?" Lark asked.

"My name?"

"What do others call you?"

"On board this ship I am known simply as Kahli."

"Kahli…" Lark said. "It's pretty. Does it mean anything?"

"Yes. In your terms it would be translated roughly as 'android'."

"That's not a name," Lark said. "That's a designation."

"How do you mean?"

"A name is something that distinguishes you as an independent person. Kahli makes you just another piece of machinery."

"But that is what I am."

"I know, but…" Lark tried to think of a reason to continue.

"But you're not property," Ken finished for her.

"Right," Lark continued. "Calling you android makes it sound like someone owns you. Do they?"

"No one owns me," Kahli said quickly.

"Exactly," Lark said. "That's why you need a real name."

"I am still unclear."

Lark felt disappointed. It was as if she were teaching a child. "Take me for example," she finally said. "My name is Lark Steines."

"Yes, I know."

"You know?"

"Yes. I know a lot of things about you, Lark. And of Kenneth and Jacquline as well."

"How is that possible?" Ken asked defiantly, standing.

"I was ordered to perform a mind sweep on all of you."

"A what?"

"A mind sweep. It allows me to gather information while someone is unconscious."

There was an odd silence before Lark spoke. "Is that how you learned our language?"

"Yes, among a multitude of other things. Your language is very basic. It did not take long." The android looked pleased. Ken could hardly understand how she could be so confident. "Most sentient beings possess minds that hold all information for a lifetime. In your case, most of the information I gathered was hidden. It is actually very unique, especially when I found most of this hidden information consisted of everyday experiences and memories. Words, letters, interests, feelings — I could see that you use these things often, but it is as if you do not even realize that you are doing it. On the other hand, it was extremely hard to learn due to the fragility of your minds as a whole."

Kahli paused. Her propensity for the language was clearly more efficient and it made her feel more at ease with her new guests. "Your minds are tender and very frail. Too much pressure on them and you would become confused. That is what I believe happened to your daughter, Kenneth. I believe I pushed her too hard with things of which she could not control, or handle emotionally. It led to her being scared and confused about what was true and what was false."

"How much did you learn about us?" Lark asked after a short pause.

"Unfortunately not much. Your minds carry a great deal of forgery. There are images and pictures and ideas that are not yours, or have come from a source I could not recognize."

"Entertainment," Ken deduced.

"Maybe. But when I swept your minds, that information freed itself. Although I could divide most of it out, the function of their presence hindered your real memories. Your thoughts would become cloudy and dream-like. I could not decipher between what was real in each of your lives and what was false."

"So, you're saying our dreams started to take over?"

"Yes. And when they did, it tore away at your minds. With each new piece of information, a new fear would arise. I was astounded by how much fear and deceit your species carries within you. I have never seen a species so frightened before."

Lark remained silent as Ken turned to Jacquline. "Is she going to be okay?"

"She will be fine. Her mind is younger than yours and could not take the pressure as easily. But the... tranquilizer..." (Lark nodded an approval) "...I gave her should calm her fears. The next time she wakes, she should return to her normal condition."

"How long will that be?" Ken asked.

"I cannot say with determination."

An awkward silence followed before another, more menacing alien creature stormed into the room. Its hairless skin was soft blue and two small lengths of skin fell from the top of his head to form small ponytails that reached his mid-back. Stretching from his wrists to his elbows were long, wide fins that laid gently on his arms. The skin where the fins connected to his arms was layered, as if extra amounts were present. He stood on two legs like a human, but instead of calves, there were two more large fins (again producing excess skin) that laid passively against his knee joints. Ken couldn't see any toes on the creature because the foot was in the shape of a flipper. He was wearing only a battered brown cloth draped over his shoulders with a belt that looped around his waist, tying the garment to his body.

Kahli stood, more out of deference than reverence, and stared into the alien's two small, horizontal slits halfway between what would be his forehead and his chin.

"Losh se kolon?" the alien spit out.

"Sel grasha yer," Kahli replied.

"Sel jasee karbo se westnar yer bar ke linsen."

"Pek lie ve-qestae zarke sestii. Sel xi-phastoe hakpha ca."

The alien glared into Kahli's eyes. Not once did she back down or break from his apparent rage. "Lor se jahgben zesk pik?" he said.

"Olas."

"Yer festoon." He pulled Kahli within inches of Ken and held her there, his hand gripped sharply on the back of her neck. Ken couldn't tell if she was in pain.

"Yer festoon," the alien said again.

"He would like to know where the fourth one is," Kahli said doggedly.

"Fourth one?"

"The readings I received when we first encountered your ship pronounced a fourth human on board."

"Your readings must have been wrong," Lark said. "We were the only ones on board."

"Fesbea yer lir joergbea," Kahli said.

The alien spun Kahli behind him. She stumbled back but steadied herself quickly and simply stood, unaffected.

"Kerba sel yek ke pik oserti lie," he said to Ken. His mouth was small and full of molars, and his nose were two small holes in between the slits Ken knew now for sure were his eyes.

"Cas lir joergbaea," Kahli said. "Orc bestioe deskine."

The alien sneered. "Sel loe ve-sestibo," he said.

Kahli stood motionless as the alien stormed from the room.

"What in the hell was that?" Ken asked.

"His… name," Kahli said, finally comprehending the meaning, "is Qah-Shekel. Do not worry. He will not bother us again for some time."

"What did he say to me?"

Kahli paused, believing it was best if they didn't know, but ultimately figuring that they would not take kindly to her silence. "He would be watching."

— 28 —

Tracey opened her eyes. The space she occupied, as far as she could tell, had gotten smaller (unless she had grown, which was preposterous), and although her entire body ached something fierce, claustrophobia was starting to set in. She'd been there long enough; she needed to get out. After letting out a soft, airy cough, Tracey shifted her arm upward to open the damaged door, allowing a flood of light to bite her eyes. She rubbed them generously and when the sting wore off, she grabbed a hold of the sides of the cabinet — and instantly turned white.

Her arms were gone.

She could feel them, knew they were there, but couldn't see them. When she looked down at her body, all she found was the rest of the rusting cabinet. She wanted to scream but her lungs were far too constricted. Instead, she closed her eyes and reflected on the situation, copying what her mother used to do when she needed to think, or otherwise calm her nerves. Tracey had no way of knowing where she was or what had happened; the best thing she could do was remain calm and quiet (and brave, like Jacquline) until she was able to find a familiar face — whomever that might be.

Crawling out of the compartment wasn't easy, but she was able to squeeze out quietly and keep from cutting herself on the jagged edges. The ship's main door had been sliced open and on the other side was a large room that didn't look familiar to her at all. After cautiously checking the cockpit for any other unfamiliarities, she crept toward the main door without even the slightest of noises, hoping that nothing would suddenly jump out and attack her. When she got into view of the engine room, she froze against the wall. A tiny creature with long arms was playing around with something inside the panels. Tracey's body shook with fear and it became harder to hold back her tears.

Where am I?

Suddenly, a voice rang out from below the ship. She slid to the door and watched as another creature emerged from underneath. This one looked more like a cat than a human, with large ears on top of her head and a line of fur that wrapped around her yellow eyes to touch the small dot of a pink nose. There were patches of fur on her cheeks that fell past her neck and a ponytail that ran from the tip of her head to just past the base of her neck. She had a long tail that came out from under her tight red pants, which were slit open on the sides allowing her fur to line the outside of her legs.

Tracey inadvertently coughed and the cat looked in her direction. She sniffed at the air, her ears at strong attention. Both aliens whispered to one another in two separate languages, neither of which she could understand. Eventually, they both inched closer to her position, looking around for something that wasn't there. That stroke of good luck gave Tracey some time to think about what she should do. With her current advantage, there was a chance she might be able to fight her way out, but after what had happened in the schoolyard, there was a possibility that she wouldn't be able to control herself if she started down that path again. But what would Jacquline think if she bowed down to her adversary with her tail between her legs? What would her mother think if she was killed because she wasn't brave enough to run away? The kids on the playground matched her eye for eye; the cat, on the other hand, was twice her size and there was no telling what type of combat skills she might have. For all Tracey knew, the cat would snap her neck with the twist of her thumb.

Before the aliens could reach her, Tracey did the only thing she could think of — she jumped from the ship and ran, leaving loud footsteps in her wake. She wasn't quite sure where she was going or what might happen, but it didn't matter. The cat hissed and was on her in two long strides. Thinking fast, Tracey grabbed hold of a large shelving unit as she passed into the corridor and swung her back up against the wall. The unit crashed to the floor across the opening. Unable to find a grip to slow down, the cat slid across the floor and smashed into the shelving, striking her head against a giant black engine housing.

Tracey waited to see if the cat would rise. When she didn't, her first thought was to climb back over the rubble and do what she could to help. Then she came to her senses. She bolted down the corridor and around the nearest corner, praying it somehow led to her family.

— 29 —

"Attention all crew."

Qah-Shekel pressed his finger to his ear in order to get a clearer read out of Doven-Jadden's already booming voice.

"We have an intruder. The fourth alien contact from the ship is loose."

"Well, find it," Qah-Shekel roared back.

"I wish I could…"

"It's not a request. We're almost at the drop-point."

"I understand, sir, but the alien…" DovenJadden paused again, this time with a sense of apprehension, as if she had done something wrong and was embarrassed to fess up.

"DovenJadden." The command in Qah-Shekel's voice was daunting.

"The alien seems to have an invisibility cloak of some kind."

"What are you saying?"

"I can't see it," DovenJadden said sardonically.

Qah-Shekel was not pleased and had to bite his tongue to stay calm. "Can you track it?"

"I think so. It reeks of the other's scent."

"Find it," Qah-Shekel growled. "I don't want anything interfering in this trade."

"Don't worry. The trade will happen as planned."

Qah-Shekel stared at the gem. DovenJadden had better be right; he couldn't afford any surprises. If anything interfered in the trade Qah-Shekel was about to partake in, everything he had done over the last decade would have been in vain. This little rock was the only thing standing in the way of answers and Qah-Shekel wanted to keep it that way.

— 30 —

"What's going on?" Ken asked, sitting up on the bed. Kahli had jumped to her computer out of nowhere, which set off the alarm in his gut.

"There has been a report of an invisible intruder," Kahli said so mundanely, it created a stark contrast with her rapid — and at times frantic — scrolling and tapping across the holoscreen. For a moment, Ken thought smoke just might rise from her fingertips if she went any faster.

"Invisible intruder?" Lark said, intrigued. She remained next to Jacquline, who whispered continual nonsense in her sleep. "How do you know?"

"DovenJadden just reported it."

"How?"

"And who the hell is DovenJadden," Ken added for effect.

"She is our tactical technician." Kahli turned to them, pointing to her ear. "Each of the crew has a communication device embedded upon the lining of our inner ears."

"Like a Bluetooth," Ken said.

"I do not know what that is," Kahli mumbled, returning her focus to the holoscreen.

Ken threw his hands up, exasperated.

"Where would an invisible intruder have come from?" Lark said, returning the subject to the matter at hand.

"Apparently your ship."

"*Our* ship?" Ken slid off the bed and walked toward Kahli. He stopped after just a few steps, afraid the web would strike him down again.

"It seems that there was, in fact, a fourth life form on your ship."

"That's impossible," Ken said.

"It is quite possible," Kahli rebutted, never once lifting her head from the holoscreen. "When I performed the mind sweeps on you and your daughter, I saw an image of a young child, small and frail. She was quiet and had a distinctive mark on her cheek."

Ken's heart sank. "Tracey," he whispered under his breath.

"I believe she may be the intruder."

"Tracey?" Lark said, stunned. "So, Jacquline was telling the truth."

Ken shook his head. "No, that can't be. Tracey… she can't be invisible."

"That's not entirely true." Kahli typed away, searching hard for something.

"Yeah, it is."

"How can you be certain?"

"Because humans can't turn invisible."

"When I ran my first scans of the ship," Kahli said without missing a beat, "I saw three life signs of the same species and one that had similar life signs but was different from the rest." Kahli finally looked up. "Is it possible that your Tracey is different?"

Ken didn't want to answer. He sat back down, avoiding Kahli's eyes until she turned back to the screen, apparently accepting his silence as an affirmative response.

Lark set a cool, damp cloth on Jacquline's forehead and then walked to Kahli. "What are you doing?" Lark said, watching a series of unreadable words scroll past.

"I am scanning our ship. If there really is an intruder, I will find it, invisible or not." After a short pause, Kahli stopped the scroll and pointed to a block of alien symbols, which were most likely letters. "There," Kahli said.

"What is it?" Lark said with a buzz of enthusiasm.

"It says there is something near command. Bio signs are the same ones that I read earlier on your ship. That is the intruder." Kahli typed the holoscreen twice in the right hand corner, transforming the screen into a three-dimensional map. Kahli spun the map around and followed a small blinking red dot.

"She is on the move." Kahli pressed her fingers together and started speaking in what the humans recognized as a chaotic purr. She continued for some time before tapping her fingers together again.

"What did you say," Lark asked anxiously.

"I informed DovenJadden as to the intruder's whereabouts."

"What's she going to do if she finds the intruder?" Ken still couldn't admit it was Tracey.

"Do not worry. I told her we need her alive."

Ken rubbed his temples and thought about how Stacey would never have allowed this to happen. If it was Tracey (and even if she wasn't sure), Stacey would have given her life to protect her. How could he not do the same? "Let me help."

"I cannot allow that," Kahli said remotely.

"She's eight years old and probably scared out of her mind. If it is Tracey, she'll come to me."

Kahli let the idea simmer a moment. "I cannot."

Ken threw his hands in the air and walked away as Kahli continued her excuse. "We are about to land on Hasten-Jackai to complete a trade. Qah-Shekel is not going to allow you to run around his ship while he and I are away. I am sorry, but you will have to remain here until I return."

"I can't believe this," Ken whispered.

Lark walked to him and rested her hands on his shoulders. "She'll be fine," Lark whispered.

Ken placed his hand on hers and nodded slightly. He didn't believe her, but he was grateful for her attempt at reassurance.

— 31 —

"Docking in progress," Sentilla said, guiding the ship to its landing platform. "You really going to do this?"

"I have to," Qah-Shekel said, squeezing her shoulder. He pressed his fingers together. "Kahli. Change of plans. I'm going alone."

"Why?" Kahli responded.

"I cannot let those things be alone on my ship."

"Yes, Qah-Shekel," Kahli said softly. "No complaints."

Qah-Shekel tapped his fingers and leaned down to Sentilla, touching his face to hers. "If those things try anything, kill them all."

"No complaints," Sentilla said with a gentle smile.

Qah-Shekel lingered for several seconds before leaving her alone.

— 32 —

"What's going on now?" Ken said. He stood watching Jacquline sleep. Lark remained behind him, resting her chin on his shoulder.

"There has been a change," Kahli said. "I am no longer accompanying Qah-Shekel to the surface on Hasten-Jackai."

"Why not?" Lark asked, spinning around to Kahli.

"Because he does not know you."

"He doesn't trust us," Ken said. He rubbed his eyes.

"Then why are we here?" Lark asked.

"I do not understand," Kahli said.

"If your captain, for lack of a better word, doesn't trust us, then why did he save our lives?"

"He did not want to," Kahli said bluntly, "but you did not have any weapons aboard your ship and lacked any evidence of power. I argued for your rescue."

"Why would you do that?"

"Because I found you to be of importance, and until Qah-Shekel can learn to know you as I do, you are my responsibility."

"So in essence," Ken said, "you're being forced to baby-sit us."

Silence followed his statement. Lark lowered her head, feeling a tender tension surround the room. Kahli appeared to be hurt by the statement, or else didn't understand it, but she felt Ken's discontent and did not want to aggravate him any further.

"What's so important about this planet?" Lark finally asked, unsure of whether or not she would get a straightforward answer.

"Qah-Shekel was assigned to retrieve a gem for a smuggler that lives on Hasten-Jackai," Kahli replied quickly, happy for the change in subject. "I was to accompany him to the drop point."

"What gem?" Lark was again intrigued. She was a little uneasy about prying, but wanted to gain as much information as possible, just as Kahli had done with them.

"The gem of Jaxxa Rakala."

"What's that?" Lark asked.

"Simply stated, it is the key to all power in the universe."

Ken gruffly laughed.

"What's so funny?" Lark said.

Ken turned to them. "This all seems pretty insane, if you ask me."

"I am sorry," Kahli said, "but your stature is unclear."

"He thinks you're lying," Lark said, giving Kahli the answer that she herself was feeling.

"How do you understand this?"

"All of what you're saying is textbook science-fiction," Ken said.

"None of which I speak is fiction."

"Whatever you say."

"Does everyone on your planet act in this way?" Kahli inquired.

"Yeah, pretty much." Lark smirked. "At least about something. It's called paranoia."

"I am sorry you feel this way."

Suddenly, Jacquline sat up sharply and screamed, "No. Don't take her. She'll die. I won't allow Tracey to be killed. You can't do it. Stop!" Jacquline went quiet just as abruptly. Her eyes rolled back as her head slammed against the table. Ken dropped down to her side, feeling her head for blood. Thankfully, there was none.

"What was that?" Lark asked quickly, joining Ken at Jacquline's side.

"Her mind must still be unclear."

"She said something about Tracey," Ken added urgently.

"I am sure that it was only a dream," Kahli said.

"I don't care," Ken said, standing. He took a step closer to Kahli but once again stopped short of the imaginary force field. "I need to know for sure."

"I am sorry. I cannot allow you out of this room."

Ken grunted in anxious frustration. For the first time, Kahli felt uneasy with this new species. She wanted to trust them, but believed that anger (a prominent emotional defect in a lot of her counterparts) played a much larger part in their emotional spectrum than she was comfortable with. When Ken sat back down at his bed to try and calm down, Kahli flipped the hologram of the ship back into the holoscreen and typed in the code to reactivate the gold web surrounding them.

Ken rubbed the fingers of his hand, feeling the pain return, but only in his mind. He fought back many emotions, but the most apparent was his fear, within which Kahli saw a longing — something that was sorely missing — and could now understand why he felt the anger that he did. She would like nothing more than to allow him the chance to find Tracey, but at the same time, she didn't want to upset Qah-Shekel. Her only choice in the matter was to trust that DovenJadden would do her job and that everything would turn out as it should.

— 33 —

Qah-Shekel entered his quarters. The gem still spun wildly out of control in the center of the room. What was it reacting to? Would it hurt him if he got too close?

Would he still be able to transport it? And if he could, how would he do that without the jar?

The answers were fleeting until he sought refuge in the memory of his father. Seeking his help to guide him, he was drawn to a large chest in the corner. Sitting on top of all of his father's old treasures was a thick piece of cloth — his father's old desert cloak. It was heavy yet melted into his fingers as he shook the dust off of it. The inside lining of the dark tan exterior was maroon, the color of sunsets on his planet. He quickly walked back to the gem and tossed the cloak over it, darkening the room. The orb continued to spin under the cloak as it snapped at it with its electric fingers. But the heat had gone, and with it, Qah-Shekel felt confident that the cloak would work perfectly. He cautiously took hold of the ends of the cloak dangling above the floor and wrapped them around the underbelly of the gem. He pulled the cloak tight around it, eventually forming a large brown ball with a very hot and unstable center.

He tucked the cloak under his arm. "Thank you, father," he whispered and left.

— 34 —

Tracey peered around the corner. The only way out was back the way she had come, but the cat, systematically purring, had somehow tracked her here and was now blocking her escape. Unlike earlier, Tracey was now actively listening, and to her surprise, the more she concentrated on the roll of the vibrations, the more she could understand what she was saying. "Tracey," it growled, over and over in a quiet, alluring manner. It knew her name; could she trust her? Not with the massive gun-like weapon now wrapped around her shoulder. It had a large barrel about a foot in diameter that stretched cone-like to her body, where it almost disappeared into nothing. There were two handles, one on the bottom of the large barrel and one on the top. It was all Tracey needed to believe that the cat and its friends had tortured Ken and Jacquline for information about her in order to coax her into letting her guard down.

No. She couldn't trust anyone right now, not after being hurt by so many others. Stacey might have thought this to be a cowardly act, but Tracey couldn't let herself be fooled again. Not now. If she was going to get through this and find Ken and Jacquline, the only person she could trust was herself.

As the cat inched ever closer, Tracey jumped out from behind the wall and zipped past her, pushing the weapon in the opposite direction. The cat hissed and raced after her.

— 35 —

Qah-Shekel tapped a sequence of codes into the wall and the hatch opened, sliding down from the ceiling to form a ramp that settled on the dusty ground. Qah-Shekel walked down into the brownish atmosphere, stopping a few hundred meters away from the *Equinox*. He shifted the gem into a more comfortable position under his arm as he peered out at the barren wasteland. Was he ready for this? Trading ultimate power for the name of vengeance wasn't the most ordinary of acts, but he had to know, and this was his last chance to get his answers.

He tapped the ground twice with his foot It shook lightly and within moments, Qah-Shekel was sucked down into its dusty confines.

— 36 —

Tracey stopped running. She had outrun her pursuer and needed to catch her breath. As she leaned up against the wall, a sweet charcoal smell — like that of someone burning hot dogs on a barbecue — filtered in from somewhere ahead. Stepping around the next corner, she saw an opening that led off the ship. On the wall next to it glowed a light blue symbol:

Curious, she walked up to it and brushed her fingers over it. "Lorar," she whispered. Tracey suddenly wanted to cry, afraid of the alien knowledge that continued to bloom in her head.

"Tracey," she heard behind her. The cat turned around the corner, blocking both corridors equally. Trying to run past her this time, Tracey feared, would result in her capture. She saw only one way out; there was no other option. She darted down the ramp and stopped as her feet hit the dusty, dark tan desert. The dry air pricked against her cheeks and there was no sun among the brown hue of the sky.

The cat was right behind her, but didn't rush, instead choosing to inch down the ramp in hopes that its target was too afraid to keep running. "Tracey," it whispered with every step. Tracey matched each step with one of her own, wondering if she should stay close to the ship or run. The light wind washed her footprints away quickly after making them, but not quick enough that the cat wouldn't be able to track her. When the cat stopped for a moment to look under the ramp, Tracey suddenly noticed her feet glistening upon the dirt. Her decision had been made for her.

She had to run.

The cat was on her in a flash, the barriers of the ship no longer containing her supernatural speed. She slid in front of Tracey, stopping her in her tracks. Tracey screamed and changed directions in the same instant, avoiding the cat's outstretched arms.

"Damn it," she purred as she fell to her knees. Tracey didn't look back, knowing she'd be on her again in a matter seconds. The cat urged her to stop with the declaration that she was with her family and would take her to them. But it had to be a trick — it had to be.

Just as Tracey heard the cat start galloping toward her once again, she spotted someone standing in the middle of nowhere, shaking. It wasn't ideal, but this was her only chance. She just hoped she could reach him before the cat could.

No luck. Barely three feet away, Tracey fell to the ground at his feet as the cat dug her claws into her neck.

"KLORON! KLORON!" the tall man called out, swiping a long stick at the cat. She hissed and spit at him until he finally struck her head with a loud crack. With that, the pain in Tracey's neck receded and the ground beneath them fell.

An intense heat radiated from the glowing red walls that flashed past her. Tracey could still feel the ground beneath her, but her stomach was in her chest and she could barely keep her eyes open. Tracey grabbed a hold of the man's legs as they traveled deeper into the interior of the planet. Finally, when Tracey thought she could take no more, the ground simply stopped. She held her eyes closed against the stranger's legs, waiting, unsure if it was really over.

"Treena te dooro," the stranger said, but Tracey didn't move. "Treena te dooro." The stranger tapped Tracey on the back with his stick. She opened her eyes and looked up at the man's elongated head, completely devoid of any features. Stunned, Tracey let go and crawled a few feet away from him. The stranger huffed a breath of hot air that smelled like a skunk into her face and walked away. The slab of ground they had just traveled on disappeared.

Tracey was alone.

— 37 —

"Tracey is off the ship," Kahli reported.

"What?" Ken said. "How?"

"By now, Qah-Shekel has disembarked. Perhaps she followed him."

"Why would she do that?"

"I am unsure."

Ken shook his head. "A better bet would be that your friend, there, threw her off."

"DovenJadden would not have done such a thing." Kahli's voice was higher now. It was the first time she had shown any type of real emotion.

"You said it yourself, Ken," Lark interjected. "Tracey's a kid. She was probably scared and that was the only way to keep from getting caught."

"It doesn't matter," Ken said. "What are we going to do about it?"

"*We* are not going to do anything," Kahli said.

"That's my daughter," Ken yelled back. "I'm not going to let her die out there. I have to find her."

"DovenJadden will find her," Kahli said, returning to her normal monotone.

"You don't get it," Ken said, trying to calm down enough so as to carefully explain the situation. "If it's true that Tracey left the ship because she was frightened of this… DovenJadden, she's going to continue to hide from her until she knows she's safe. And the only way she's going to feel safe is when she finds someone familiar. Trust me. She's my daughter."

Kahli examined Ken for some time, running his theory through her mind.

"She trusts you?" Kahli asked simply. "That is why she will come to you?"

"Yes."

"And this is how fear works on your planet?"

"Without trust, all we have is fear."

"Agreed then," Kahli said so quickly it caught Ken off guard. "I will take you to the surface to find your daughter." Kahli purred into her communicator for a moment before turning off the force field.

"DovenJadden has agreed to wait for us."

Ken cautiously stepped past the grid's border. It shot back up soon after, surrounding Lark and Jacquline.

"You must stay by me at all times. If you attempt to run, you will be killed."

"Yeah, fine," Ken said. He walked up to Lark, who stared back with concern.

"Be safe," she whispered.

"Don't worry. I'll be fine. I can't let Tracey get hurt." Ken nodded and followed Kahli from the room.

Lark took a moment to pray for his safety. She wished she could have gone with him, but there was no telling what might happen while they were gone, and she felt it was best that she stayed with Jacquline — to protect her. She sat down and kissed Jacquline's hand. Holding it gently and petting her hair, Lark hummed a song that her mother used to sing, hoping it would help relax her vulnerable, confused mind.

— 38 —

The air that filtered in from outside was stale and dry. Ken walked down the ramp after Kahli and stared at the shimmering quality of the sky. Stepping away from the ship, Ken figured they were inside some sort of dome. The ship had come to rest on the outside edge of it, as had hundreds of other ships barely visible through the dark brown glow and endless view. As he followed Kahli across the desert landscape, Ken couldn't take his eyes off of all the various creatures passing to and from their respective ships.

"What is this place?" Ken finally asked.

"A trading post. It is one of many neutral locations throughout the galaxy where any species may trade or barter goods."

"A safe harbor," Ken said.

"Precisely."

"And we're here to trade the 'take-over-the-world' gem?"

Kahli smiled. "Yes."

"And what's the point of that again?"

"I am not sure I understand the question."

"I mean, if this gem is so powerful, why would anyone want to trade it? Why not sell it to the highest bidder? Or better yet, keep it for yourself. Aren't there plenty of aliens out here who would love to get their hands on that thing?"

"You are correct, Kenneth. There are in fact millions of species that would kill to be one with the gem. But you must understand — the currency that you provide yourself on your planet does not hold value here, or in any galaxy that I am aware. Trade and thievery are all we have."

"You don't deal in currency? How do you evaluate wealth?"

"Some individual planets, such as yours, do hold a concept of such things. Yet, most believe that currency and wealth, as you understand them, are a disgrace and a threat."

"That doesn't make a lot of sense."

"For most of us, it is not about how much you own or acquire that brings you wealth, Kenneth. The value one places on an object is different for each individual."

"So, to each his own," Ken said.

"I would assume so," Kahli said, unsure. "If you were to attempt to put a value on something, and hold that value true for all species, it would convey tyranny. There is to be no mention of such things here at the trading post, lest you get yourself killed."

Ken didn't say another word, choosing instead to eye the other alien creatures, hoping none of them had overheard their conversation.

"So, what are we trading it for?" Ken finally whispered.

"Answers."

"That's what it's worth to Qah-Shekel? Answers?"

"For Qah-Shekel, the answers he seeks are extremely important."

"Why? What kind of answers is he looking for?"

"I am sorry, but I am afraid I cannot answer that question at this time," Kahli said, stopping him.

Ken nodded, reflecting the seriousness in her eyes.

Kahli cracked a grin before hitting the ground with her foot, causing it to shake. Ken's nervous fear was quelled through Kahli s magnetic calm.

"What's going on?" he said, his voice quivering slightly.

"We are heading down."

With that, the ground fell, leading them into the dark depths below.

— 39 —

Qah-Shekel stood impatiently in front of a large gold and silver throne that filled almost a third of the domed room. Elegant satin curtains looped from the roof to the chair. Three guards were stationed near the door and eight more stood by the throne — two at the base of the steps where it sat; two more at its edges; two in the back of the chair; and two at either end of the stage. They were all dressed in magenta-colored armor that sparkled in the soft brown light.

A large round slug soon entered from the left side of the room. The guards stood at attention and remained motionless as it slithered toward the throne. Qah-Shekel followed suit, knowing full well that even the slightest noise would get him killed.

As the slug reached the throne, its slimy exterior shrank inward, exposing six bony arms and four legs. It balanced carefully on its two forward legs and sat in the chair as the slime continued to shrivel, forming an elongated head, which revealed four eyes in the center between its arms. By the time it had completed its transformation, several rounded bones formed an outer shell along its back and a spiked rib cage that held the thinly veiled skull. Qah-Shekel was a little put-off by the creature's partially exposed organs, shrouded inside the remaining yellow mucus.

It took quite some time, but eventually the creature howled, a call directed at Qah-Shekel. He understood the language, but only a little.

"Yes, I found the gem," Qah-Shekel replied in his own language. He placed the balled up cloak on the ground at his feet.

The guards at the base of the steps picked up the cloak and brought it to the slug, resting it in two of its palms, still dripping with leftover slime. It slowly unwrapped the cloak, filling the room with a graceful green light. Thin bolts of lightning sparked around the room but avoided all living organisms.

The creature huffed and laughed loudly as it ingested the wonderful prize.

"You have done well," the slug howled.

Qah-Shekel made absolutely sure the electrical light show wasn't a threat and then asked, "What answers do you have for me?"

"I have no answers," the slug said, laughing.

"But you said —"

"I have knowledge of what I once said, naïve Krylexian. I do know of all that you eagerly request. But I have decided, with the sight of the gem, to forgo turning this information over to your mind."

"Son of a Grexel. Why go back on your word?"

"Because a better deal has recently come into my wake." The creature lifted its hands and snapped its wiry fingers. A group of cloaked figures suddenly marched out, ducking under and around the lightning. Qah-Shekel stepped back, eager to run but completely aware that there was little in the way of escape.

The gem had him trapped.

— 40 —

Ken and Kahli had met up with DovenJadden soon after landing inside the interior surface and had been walking for some time. Large dome-shaped structures sat along each side of the road they currently traveled. Ken tried to take it all in but there were so many different creatures, structures and artifacts that it completely overwhelmed his senses. It took all of his concentration just to scan through the otherworldly surroundings in hopes of a simple glimpse of Tracey — and to a lesser (but no more urgent) extent, of Stacey.

Catching his eye about fifty yards ahead of them, dirt sprayed everywhere as two unorthodox creatures fought. Ken took a few steps back, surprised at how all of the other beings continued to meander about without even the slightest hint of recognition. Then again, it almost reminded him of when he and Gloria went to New York on vacation. As they walked back to their hotel after seeing *The Lion King* on Broadway, a couple of punk teenagers started a brawl in the middle of the street. Not one car stopped; not one passerby (except for those kids who videotaped the fight with their phones) even wanted to acknowledge it.

I guess things aren't so different after all, he thought with a slight smile as Kahli urged him forward. As they walked by, the aliens continued to roll around, howling, biting and screeching until the larger of the two popped the other's neck. It sniffed its defeated rival before biting into what might have been the creature's stomach.

Ken turned away in disgust. "What was that?" he whispered to Kahli.

"A Frassaw — very aggressive species. If you ever come into contact with one, stay perfectly still or it might attack. And you do not want to be attacked."

"You don't have to tell me twice." Ken shivered and walked in silence for some time before coming to an abrupt stop. His gaze was as cold as stone.

Kahli took notice quickly. "What is it?"

Ken didn't answer — he couldn't. What he saw was more than he could bear.

Kahli gauged Ken's eye line. "What frightens you so, Kenneth?" she said.

"Them," Ken finally whispered with hardly a breath, lifting a quivering finger at four massive creatures pacing around a building sixty meters ahead of them. "The monsters that kidnapped my wife."

"Kayla," Kahli swore in her native tongue. "Vermon. It's a trap."

Kahli purred out a warning and without hesitation, DovenJadden was armed and at the ready.

"A trap?" Ken said. Just then, all of his fear, all of his anger, all of his disgust was overwhelmed with a deep flood of desire. Something familiar was calling for him — reaching out to him, calming every part of his being. A cold shiver ran his spine as he realized what it was. "Stacey!"

Unaware of his actions, Ken ran toward one of the structures without reserve, everything around him fading from existence.

"Kenneth, no!" Kahli screamed. She sprinted after him, followed reluctantly by DovenJadden.

The closer he got to the building, Stacey's pull grew stronger, compelling Ken's pace to quicken. Twenty meters away, he took notice of the temple cross resting above the giant archway of the domed structure. As he reached the first set of pillars lining the entry, Ken was forced to stop.

In front of him was the bright glow of the gem, spinning heavenly in front of a skeletal bug-shaped creature. He stared affectionately at the gem — wanting it, needing it more than anything; it pulled at his soul like a drug. Flashes of Stacey attacked his mind as his heart pounded inside his weightless body.

Kahli stopped next to Ken, instantly taking notice of Qah-Shekel, trapped within a brilliant electrical storm and surrounded by several cloaked figures, all aiming their wrist-lasers at him with the clear intent to kill. None of which mattered to Ken in the slightest.

He rushed through the crowd of cloaked figures and maneuvered fluidly through the lightning until Qah-Shekel grabbed a hold of him in his steel grip. The guards protecting the throne quickly aligned into a V-formation around the skeletal creature as it covered the gem back in the cloak. All at once the green light and electric barriers vanished, replaced by a small huff of what sounded like laughter.

Ken stopped struggling and stepped back It wasn't clear to him what was happening, but his head pounded, as if someone was repeatedly hitting him with the butt end of a bat. After a moment of reflection, Ken observed his surroundings. A dozen cloaked creatures surrounded him. He couldn't see their faces, only dark red dots under their hoods. Behind them, a dark yellow fluid grew around a skeletal form as it shifted away from its throne. When it had completely formed into its slug-like state, a loud screech pierced through the room.

Kahli pushed Ken to the ground as laser fire exploded throughout. Qah-Shekel grabbed his thumb laser and dropped to the floor, chopping off one of the cloaked figure's legs. He rolled along the ground, striking several more while avoiding all of their errant rounds. Two shots struck Kahli in the upper torso as she slammed her attackers together and flung them at the guards blocking the door. She then grabbed Ken's shirt and yanked him to his feet.

"Stay close," she yelled, tossing him against her back. Every shot fired at her chest ricocheted off her body, leaving only small scorch marks among her now tattered jumpsuit. Ken kept his head down and eyes closed as Kahli pushed him out of the building.

"Hurry back to the ship," she yelled as they reached the street.

"What about Tracey?"

"Do as I order."

Kahli purred to DovenJadden and went back inside. DovenJadden grabbed a hold of Ken's arm and pulled him away. He struggled to get free, but DovenJadden's grip was far too great. Tears formed as he finally gave up; there was little more that he could do but obey.

— 41 —

Tracey stopped to catch her breath. She didn't know where she was going or what she should do. She was lost, surrounded by creatures she had never seen before on a world she didn't quite understand. The urge to give in to her loneliness and fear was stronger than ever, but she couldn't allow herself to collapse. She knew now what could happen if she allowed her emotions to take over. As before, the only way she was going to get out of this was to stay calm and keep her mind clear. She sat on her knees and closed her eyes. Taking in a deep breath, Tracey suddenly felt a glassy tenderness pull at her chest as the wind turned icy. She opened her eyes, but all she saw was the same disorienting skyline as she'd been inundated with since dropping underground. But something had changed; the throb in her lungs grew more intense, stopping her breathing.

That's when something familiar caught her eye. The pain vanished for a split second, replaced with pleasurable hope. She tried to scream out, but no sound was possible; she tried to stand, but her legs were frozen. Even then, she couldn't stop trying. Her father was there, less than a few hundred yards away, and she was determined to get to him.

$$-\quad 42 \quad-$$

The uncontrollable urge to return to the gem was overwhelming, and not just because Ken knew without a doubt that where the gem was, Stacey couldn't be far behind. The further away he got, the more it hurt. He continued to look behind him, waiting for the opportunity to break free of DovenJadden and sprint back to what he needed most. Finally, the pressure became far too great. He yanked his arm back as hard as he could, pulling DovenJadden off-balance. That split-second of imbalance was enough for Ken to shove the palm of his hand up into her nose and knock her backward.

Now free, Ken ran back for the gem. Though he knew what direction he had come, his instincts guided him a different way. He had only gotten about a quarter of a mile before he heard DovenJadden's hiss at his heels. It wasn't long before she pinned him to the ground. As he struggled against her, yelling for her to get off, he caught sight of a young girl that held a power over him that was far greater than that of the gem. The crescent-shaped mark on her cheek burned a bright blue as she reached for him.

"Tracey!" he yelled, suddenly gaining the strength of eighty men. He threw DovenJadden off his back and sprinted toward Tracey, all of his energy swarming to his legs for an extra burst of speed. Tracey stretched her arms out as far as she could, desperately seeking the safety of Ken's embrace. Suddenly, Tracey felt a series of sharp knives gouge into her neck as a vermon lifted her off the ground. It smelled her body fervently and cautiously touched the birthmark.

"No!" Ken screamed, Stacey's abduction flooding to the forefront of his thoughts. He tried to pick up speed but he was already running faster than his legs were able. Just a few yards away, Ken was ready to pounce but was immediately thrown to the ground as Kahli raced past him. Qah-Shekel was only a few steps behind and was forced to stop at the sight of Tracey.

"Are you trying to get yourself killed?" Kahli said as Ken grasped his elbow tightly. "I ordered you to return to the ship. Why did you disobey me?"

"Tracey," he hissed.

Kahli turned to the vermon and finally noticed the small child. She buzzed through her memory banks for information on that very distinct crescent birthmark. What she found was that, for some reason, it was missing its reflected counterpart. Regardless, there was no mistaking the identity of the child.

"Jaxxa Rakala," Kahli whispered.

DovenJadden finally caught up to the group and purred hysterically at Qah-Shekel, who pulled on Kahli's arm, breaking her trance with a bark of orders. She instantly pulled Ken to his feet.

"We'll come back for her," she said, knowing full well where there's one vermon, there's a dozen more nearby. Upon Ken's first step, he fell under his own weight. Qah-Shekel and DovenJadden were already several yards away when the vermon came crashing through the streets toward them.

"No time," Kahli said and threw Ken over her shoulder. She caught up with Qah-Shekel and DovenJadden in no time flat, allowing them to take point on the firefight that ensued. Qah-Shekel nipped a few of them, taking one down after DovenJadden collected several up into a net-like fabric, devouring the vermon together into a cocoon that crushed them completely.

Soon after, the vermon stopped their pursuit and headed back. When the group was confident that they were out of harm's way, Kahli lowered Ken to the ground, giving everyone a chance to rest. Ken clenched his fists, straining to keep from punching her into a coma. Tracey was right there and she let her slip through his fingers, just as Stacey had. That desperation and queasy hopelessness crawled through his pours.

Qah-Shekel gruffly spoke with Kahli, who seemed to be quite averse about doing something. Soon after, Qah-Shekel and DovenJadden were gone.

"Are you well enough to walk?" Kahli asked.

Ken couldn't answer her; his emotion had completely consumed him.

"I am sorry that we could do nothing for your daughter, Kenneth. But we must move quickly."

"What's the point?" Ken squeaked. "What's the point?"

"You must trust when I say that no harm will come to her."

"Yeah," he said, full of sarcasm and doubt.

"It is fine to feel sorrow; it is quite another to feel forlorn. We will save your daughter, but only if you rise above your despondency and help us."

"Help you do what?"

"Our ship is under attack. If we do not hurry, it will be lost, and so will your daughter."

Ken shrugged her off and lied down. None of this seemed real anymore; it was all just another dream he had concocted to hide his guilt over leaving Tracey behind. He was wrong; he should have shut down the launch. Instead, he had let his ego drive him away from caring for — and loving — his daughters the way he always knew he should. His life was over and all because he refused to listen to Lark, the one person he trusted over anyone in his life.

Suddenly, Kahli's words — *our ship is under attack* — echoed through his mind, pouring adrenaline back into his system. All of his attention now focused on one thing —

"Lark!"

— 43 —

Sweat covered Jacquline's face and her breaths came quicker than Lark would have liked. She combed Jacquline's hair slowly as she continued to hum over Jacquline's light whispers, desperately hoping she'd find her way back soon.

Suddenly, a siren wailed throughout the ship, causing Lark's heart to skip a beat. After calming her nerves, Lark stood, easing Jacquline's head to the bed. She stepped up to the force field barrier and watched the corridor.

— 44 —

Sentilla stood just outside the command center, hiding behind a perpendicular corridor. Down the main corridor, a large vermon cowered behind a separate breakaway stretch. It shot a few laser rounds at Sentilla, who returned fire with a ray of light from her fingertips.

The vermon ducked behind the wall. Sentilla did the same and swatted her fingers together.

"Qah-Shekel. We are under attack. Please respond."

Another laser shot blew past her head. She ducked away and turned her body into the corridor, holding her hand up at the vermon. A bright ray of light shot from her palm, sending the vermon flying down the main corridor. Smoke fumed from its chest as it landed.

"Qah-Shekel, come in." Sentilla took a deep breath, frightened by why Qah-Shekel wasn't answering, and ran down the corridor. With Qah-Shekel missing in action (and possibly dead), it was up to her to defend his ship.

— 45 —

Naja-Leku muttered, "They'll kill us all," over and over as he huddled in the corner of his usual hideout — a hole in the wall of the engine room, one of the darkest rooms on the ship. He could hear the vermon outside, pounding by, shooting the walls at various, random moments. One of them finally ripped open the panel to his hovel. All Naja-Leku saw was a pair of eyes staring back at him. Before he could wail in fright, fire struck Naja-Leku in the chest, instantly vaporizing him to ash.

— 46 —

Massanah crouched inside the crushed ship, a knife in one hand, a wrench in the other. He peered around the outer hatch as several vermon tore into the cargo that filled the room. They extinguished some artifacts with vapor bombs and burned crops and food rations with amusement. If there weren't so many, Massanah wouldn't have had any problem attacking them like a wild boar, but their numbers were simply undefeatable alone.

Massanah tore to the back of the ship and stayed still and quiet as a vermon clambered in through the hatch. It sniffed its surroundings, eventually making its way to the cabinets, focused almost solely on the bottom space to the far right. If Massanah was going to do anything, now was his chance.

He moved to the engine room door as if on a cloud. When he was sure he hadn't aroused the vermon's attention, Massanah jumped on its back, repeatedly thrusting the knife into its chest. After the sixth stab pierced deep enough to puncture the vermon's lung, it finally found a grip on Massanah and sent him crashing through the cockpit window. Massanah smashed into the shelving along the wall, catching the attention of the other vermon. They all grunted and huffed as they surrounded Massanah, keeping him from escaping through the corridor, but refrained from attacking. Soon, the wounded vermon stammered out of the ship and pulled the knife from its chest. It growled and grunted lightly and then walked past the others to loom over Massanah. Breathing with a slight gurgle, the vermon huffed once and jammed the knife straight through Massanah's head.

— 47 —

Ken's legs burned hotter than a kindled fire as he darted through the desert. Kahli kept pace with him, keeping close tabs on all of his vital organs to make sure that they remained sufficient. His heart rate was highly elevated, as was his blood pressure, and for all accounts, Ken should have passed out a long time ago. But he kept moving, leaving Kahli to believe that his mind was allowing his motivations — fearing the loss of another daughter being the highest of probabilities — to fuel his body. As they reached the outskirts of the main trading post, Kahli sped up in order to slow him down.

"What are you doing?" he said, his breath heavy.

"Rest," Kahli said, forcing Ken to stop completely.

"I need… to get… Lark." Each consecutive word was harder to get out.

"We're almost there." Kahli pounded her foot on the ground, blasting the pair skyward as if being shot through the barrel of a gun. It was clear that they were traveling in a straight line, pushed by something at their feet, but Ken felt wildly out of control. Within seconds, both had stopped their progression and were once again on the surface of the planet.

"Are you ill?" Kahli said, crouching down to get a reading of Ken's vitals. He held his eyes tight, his body in a state of weightlessness. "Kenneth. We must continue."

Fighting his urge to vomit, Ken opened his eyes. He finally noticed the brown hue of the dome and the ships hidden on the opposite side. "Yeah," he said. Pain sliced his knees as he stood and it forced him to drape his arm around Kahli. She helped him jog back to the ship. He removed his arm once he caught a glimpse of the inside, but before he could step up the ramp, Kahli pulled him back and held him against the dome. "Wait here," she whispered, peering cautiously up the ramp.

Explosions rattled throughout and Ken's urge to fight rose. "We need to get in there," he said, failing to push Kahli away.

"Patience."

Ken didn't want to wait, but Kahli knew better. He had to continue to trust her... for now.

— 48 —

Qah-Shekel fired straight through the chest of the vermon at the end of the corridor, striking the wall in a flash of red sparks. It fell as purple slime oozed from the wound.

"I'll track down Sentilla," Qah-Shekel said to DovenJadden, who was in step right behind him. "You find the others."

DovenJadden took off down the corridor as Qah-Shekel cautiously ran in the opposite direction, checking every sub-corridor and finding only emptiness — with no sign of Sentilla. He grew more hopeless the longer he scoured the ship. *She's been taken*, he thought as he crossed the entry to his living quarters. *I'll kill them all.*

The fire lighting the corridor near the command center cast shadows on the walls in front of him. Qah-Shekel leaned up against the wall and rested his wrist across his forearm, aiming at the final adjacent corridor where the shadows grew larger and more prominent. He waited as shots were fired from several styles of weaponry. Thinning his eyes, Qah-Shekel fired as two vermon rounded the corridor, slicing their heads from their bodies with one quick snap of his wrist. They continued to run a few steps before collapsing, turning the floor around them a deep shade of purple. Another set of footsteps remained. Qah-Shekel held firm as he waited for the thinner, more sprite shadow to transform into the young Gruasdil he had been desperately seeking. Before he could relax and say anything, a bolt of pure white lightning shot past him. He quickly ducked and called out, ' Sentilla. It's me."

Sentilla set her sights on Qah-Shekel and took aim before his voice registered in her ears. She focused on the body crouched in front of her, his hands raised above his head. The familiar sight forced her to her knees, barely keeping her from fainting. "Qah-Shekel?"

Sentilla coughed roughly. Qah-Shekel lowered his hands and went to her, kicking one of the vermon's heads away in the process. He cupped her head in his hands. "Are you okay?"

Sentilla lowered her head to his chest and he hugged her gently, trying to calm her uncontrollable shake. As she coughed again, Qah-Shekel went to the wall at the end of the corridor and pressed his hand to it. A holoscreen appeared through the cracks in his fingers and he quickly typed in a code, activating a cold smoke that seeped from the base of the walls and filled the corridors. Once the fires had been fully extinguished, Qah-Shekel removed his hand from the wall. The holoscreen vanished and the smoke was washed from the corridors with a loud suction of air.

"Where are the others?" Qah-Shekel said, kneeling back down to Sentilla.

Sentilla shook her head. "I don't... I don't know."

"Come," he said, helping her to her feet. "I need you at command."

"I can't..." Sentilla grasped Qah-Shekel's tunic, her legs too weak to stand on.

"You can. You have to. We need to get out of here."

She shook her head while keeping her eyes averted, making sure he didn't notice the fear she held inside.

"Sentilla," Qah-Shekel said, forcing her to look at him. "I need you."

She didn't want to leave him but knew he was right. Now that he had returned, she needed to get the ship off the ground and as far away from the trading post as possible. Everything else she felt would have to be put aside.

She placed her hand on Qah-Shekel's chest and smiled. "Yes, sir," she whispered before allowing him to walk her back to command.

— 49 —

The smoke that filled the room smelled like chlorine with a light glaze of charcoal. Lark didn't know what it was, or how harmful it might be, but it was becoming increasingly harder to keep the gas away from Jacquline as she continued to mumble an incomprehensible dialogue to herself. She kept her eyes glued to the door, hoping to see a familiar face before one or both of them was killed. It didn't matter that the force field protected them, Lark still felt incredibly vulnerable and wasn't sure if she would be brave enough to protect Jacquline should she be forced to do so. *Nothing's coming after us,* she kept thinking. *There's no need to panic.*

Suddenly, a large round creature with horns that wrapped around its eyes came trudging in through the small door, sniffing the air. Lark wasn't sure if the beast could actually see anything or if it relied on its sense of smell, but the only choice she had was to believe it was the latter. If she could keep Jacquline still and quiet, they may be able to avoid detection.

Her plan became null and void when Jacquline screamed, "We have to save her! We have to save Tracey!"

Lark's heart stopped as the creature turned to them, its weapon raised. She slid in front of Jacquline the best she could, though her constant screaming didn't help hide her. To her relief, the creature stopped just outside of the force field and sniffed the air.

It senses the heat, Lark thought.

That relief faded quickly when the creature turned and fired a blazing hot jet of fire around the room behind it. Before it could do any damage, though, it was extinguished. The creature tried again, once more failing to light the fire more than a few feet from him. As it tried to figure out what was happening, Lark picked Jacquline up in her arms and held her, hoping to quell her screams. Her eyes never left the creature, but her voice remained with Jacquline. "Calm down, sweetie. We're safe. We're safe. Calm down."

A loud hum soon vibrated through the ship, and within an instant, the smoke cleared from the room. Lark's throat closed up as Jacquline went utterly silent. She let Jacquline's head fall to her chest but wasn't about to let her go. The creature again aimed its weapon at Kahli's desk, ready to fire.

Just then, Ken bolted into the room and threw all of his weight into the vermon, knocking it off balance and diverting the flame to light up the grid, which absorbed its heat instantly. The vermon found its footing quickly and grabbed hold of Ken's neck, picking him off the ground. Flashes of being on the ramp in his front yard flooded his soul. Outrage and fear came with it, and for a split second, Ken believed that at this moment, he could somehow change the past. He kicked the vermon with every ounce of power he could muster, which didn't faze the vermon one bit. It threw Ken across the room, his body flying through the dark night, about to hit the soft grass. After striking the hard metal wall, he slipped to the cold floor and fell unconscious.

The vermon aimed its weapon again, but before it could fire, Kahli appeared and bent the front of the weapon downward. She struck the vermon in the throat with the tips of her fingers, yanked the weapon from the vermon's weakened grip and tossed it away. The vermon growled indignantly and picked Kahli off the ground by her neck. Unlike Ken, Kahli was unaffected. She sent her elbow down against the vermon's arm and broke its bone. The vermon howled as Kahli dropped to the ground and kicked the vermon into the force field. The entire web shot to life, sending the vermon into a convulsive fit of pain.

Lark let go of Jacquline to cover her ears as smoke rose from the vermon's burning body. Sparks soon shot from the corners of the ceiling and the force field flashed off. Smoke continued to seep from the vermon as it lay lifeless, its back blackened with the pattern of the web. It took Lark some time, but she finally uncovered her ears.

"Are you okay," Kahli said as she carried Ken to his bed.

Lark nodded, even though an annoying ring had all but invaded her ears and her head pounded with the cold hand of terror.

— 50 —

Qah-Shekel stopped pacing behind Sentilla.

"Systems are down all across the ship," she reported. "Massanah needs to get to work on the lightning unit or we'll never break orbit."

"Right." Qah-Shekel hit his fingers together. "Massanah."

"Massanah's been killed," DovenJadden purred in his ear.

Qah-Shekel went silent; Sentilla looked beaten.

"And so has Naja-Leku."

Qah-Shekel lowered his head. Two of his best had died and the trade had been a trap. The whole incident brought back cold, merciless memories of his parents. He didn't speak a word to anyone for a long time after their death, but there was one who kept him whole, who brought him back to life. He heard that voice now.

"What are we going to do?" Sentilla said.

Qah-Shekel looked at her. For the moment, he'd have to forget about those he lost and concentrate solely on protecting those that were still alive.

— 51 —

"Qahsez," Kahli said.

"What's going on?" Lark asked. She knelt next to Ken, holding a cold, wet cloth to his forehead. He woke a short time after Kahli had laid him on the bed. His head pounded and he felt like dropping back to sleep, but he forced himself to stay awake.

"It seems our lightning unit has been damaged and our mechanic, Massanah, has been killed."

Ken pushed Lark's hand away and sat up, feeling an overwhelming urge to vomit. "What does that mean?" he moaned.

"With the size of this ship," Kahli started, "if we can't get the thrusters working, we will become trapped in orbit."

"Which isn't good," Ken said, sizing up the situation.

"If we become caught in orbit, the Ferressenai will be able to track us and destroy us. We do not have much time."

Ken lied back down with a groan. He had a deep desire to help but his body dictated a different story.

"Let me help," Lark said for him.

"I am afraid our systems are too advanced —"

"Bullshit. Just tell me what to do. I'll be fine."

Kahli studied Lark carefully. She wasn't sure if she should allow this new species insight into their technologies, but there was a chance the young, under-developed human brain system wouldn't be able to handle it, hiding it instead in the depths of the subconscious.

"You said yourself, we don't have much time," Lark continued. "An extra hand's not going to hurt."

"You are correct," Kahli said. "You may be of value. Follow me."

Lark smiled lightly and turned to Ken. "It's my turn," she said, squeezing Ken's hand tight. "I'll be back." She kissed Ken gently on the forehead and took one last glance over at Jacquline before leaving with Kahli.

Ken moaned and looked to Jacquline. He closed his eyes and passed out.

— 52 —

Kahli pressed a code into the wall's holopad and turned to Lark. "Do as I say. Do not try and be a hero."

Lark nodded. Kahli waited another moment before pressing one last button. The wall in front of her shimmered lightly and Kahli melted through it. Lark was amazed and terrified as she felt the wall, which was like a milky rubber that rippled among her touch. With her heart pounding at eight beats a second, she stepped through. It was oddly smooth and soft, yet constricting. She didn't have time to absorb the sensation as the technological enormity of the engine room overwhelmed her entire soul. The room was over three stories high and nearly a hundred yards wide. Hundreds of lights and holoscreens lined every inch of the walls. Three levels of catwalks wrapped around it and connected a massive sphere in the center of the room (which Lark deduced quickly to be the lightning generator) to the outer walls. Metal strips covered the majority of the sphere, exposed only through a few large cracks that sat closed at the top and bottom of the sphere and spread some six feet at the center. Pipes and conduits ran the course of the sphere from the center of the openings to connect with the ceiling and the floor. The man with fins on his arms and legs that Lark remembered from her brief encounter in medical crawled around the sphere like a spider.

"Qah-Shekel," Kahli said as she reached a nearby catwalk. She climbed one of the dozens of ladders that lined both the sphere and the catwalks and met up with him and a cat-like creature that Lark assumed to be DovenJadden. Kahli spoke on what Lark figured to be an assessment of the ship. Qah-Shekel seemed to either defeat or assent with different physical reactions. Lark remained still and listened to the back-and-forth, unsure of what to do.

When the assessment was over, Kahli ran to a nearby terminal and rapped at the wall furiously. Qah-Shekel returned to scurry across the sphere as if he were floating. DovenJadden looked just as fluid, darting back and forth across the catwalks.

"Losh cas lie tes?" Qah-Shekel landed in front of Lark with a quiet huff.

Lark took a step back, staring into the creature's thin slit-eyes. She wanted to run but her gut told her to stay put. Nonetheless, she couldn't keep from inching backward, Qah-Shekel in step right with her.

"Riick cas opores," Kahli said, dropping her way back to the lower catwalk.

Qah-Shekel sneered, keeping his eyes fixed on Lark.

"Cas lie ve-kijae hakphar sel," Kahli yelled out as she pounded toward them. Her anger could be heard under the soft hum of the sphere.

Ignoring Kahli, Qah-Shekel took in a deep, juicy breath. "Sel qahben ye wivine."

Lark held her breath, unwilling to give him any reason to harm her. A light, warm wisp of air struck her cheek, urging her to look back into Qah-Shekel's eyes, which were a little wider now and glowing a bright white.

Without another word, he jumped back onto the sphere, sticking to it like a magnet.

"Come with me," Kahli said.

Lark fell weak. She wanted to sit down and take a moment but Kahli wouldn't allow it.

"Lark. You must stay close to me. Now hurry."

"Yeah," she said and followed Kahli up the nearest ladder, taking another glance over at Qah-Shekel, who was now in a stationary position over a small fissure near one of the crevices. He held a knife in his hand and was rubbing it back and forth against the fissure.

"Lark. Stay close."

Lark and Kahli rushed across the catwalk and stopped at a bare wall on the opposite side of the room.

"What did he say to me?" Lark said, finally mustering up the courage to speak.

Kahli ran her fingers across the wall, her ear pressed firmly against it. She then tapped her finger carefully in one specific spot.

"This is it," she said, pushing away from the wall. She scanned the room for DovenJadden, who was now several yards away welding a piece of the wall together. The surrounding area looked burned. Kahli purred, grabbing DovenJadden's attention. Lark wasn't sure why, but the language had become almost musical and she suddenly felt extremely at ease with it.

DovenJadden purred back and pulled something from her belt. She tossed it to

Kahli, who instantly handed it to Lark.

"I need you to cut a small circle here," Kahli said, making a circle in the area she had identified moments before. "I am heading up to the next level. I will guide you from there. Understand?"

"Yeah, no problem," Lark said, excited.

Kahli sprinted for the nearest ladder and started up.

Lark looked over the gadget curiously. It was a gray cylinder with a small slit in the top. There didn't seem to be any buttons or levers and it was warm to the touch.

"Are you cutting away the wall?" Kahli's voice echoed.

"No," Lark said, a little embarrassed. "How are you supposed to use it?"

"Press the incision against the metal." There wasn't even a hint of condescension in her voice.

Lark waited another moment, still unsure. "What the hell," she said and pressed the end of the cylinder against the wall. Immediately, a light glow appeared at the contact point and melted the metal away. She quickly moved the cylinder clockwise around Kahli's designated point. It felt awkward using her left hand but she couldn't grip the cylinder with her right, not with the cast. When she finished, there were absolutely no remnants of the cut or the wall. It was smooth as glass and surprisingly cold. Lark took a bemused glance at the cutter and then slipped it into her pocket.

"Got it," she said. "Now what?"

"Patience," Kahli said as she tapped away on one of the holoscreens. As she did, information ran across at lightning speed. Her concentration didn't stray once, not even when a soft explosion rang through the room. Lark, just below and a few paces to the left, fell to the ground, grasping her ears. The light ringing reappeared after the initial blast faded. She slowly removed her hands and watched Qah-Shekel walk to something hidden behind the sphere.

"Are you ready, Lark?" Kahli said, as if the explosion had never happened.

"Yeah," Lark said softly, composing herself.

"Peer into the hole. You should see a small, compact reactor core inside."

Lark looked into the hole, unsure of what she was looking for. Even if she had, it was completely dark. "I can't see anything," she said.

"Why not?"

"It's too dark."

Kahli wasn't fazed. Both of her hands were in motion, one across the screen, a second below on a different holopanel as she continued scanning through the information.

Lark waited patiently for Kahli but all she heard was Qah-Shekel yell something, followed by a loud hum. Lark turned to see the sphere light up. The sheer beauty of it mesmerized her, but only for a second. A small hiss and electric spark behind her forced her attention back to the hole, which had been completely lit. Inside was a large tube with a bubbling liquid floating around inside, almost like champagne settling in a wine glass.

"I can see it," Lark said joyfully. "What do I do?"

"You must find the red valve and turn it a half a turn to your left."

Lark's joy disappeared that instant. Just below the tube were six different valves wrapped in a circle. Each valve had a thick cord that led away in different directions throughout the wall.

"I —" she started, unable to get the rest out.

"What is wrong?" Kahli said, holding her concentration on the holoscreens.

"I can't see the colors," Lark said, utterly disappointed and defeated.

"Why not?" Kahli asked in the same focused tone.

"I'm color blind."

Kahli purred something that carried around the room. In a flash, DovenJadden arrived, glaring at Lark with anger and disgust.

Lark stepped away as DovenJadden reached in and turned the necessary valve. She sat down against the wall and listened to the two purr back and forth, DovenJadden working intensely within the wall. Lark suddenly wished that the jump to the speed of light had killed her. Her entire career was dependent on the ability to see and recognize color, and now she had no sense of the word. Her life was suddenly without meaning.

A loud rattle vibrated inside the hole and DovenJadden pulled her hand out, smiling with gleeful arrogance. She flew down the nearest ladder to join Qah-Shekel at the doorway as Kahli climbed back down to Lark.

"Follow me," Kahli said, grabbing a hold of Lark's forearm. "If you stay too long the radiation will be your downfall."

Lark knew she was right but didn't want to leave. She couldn't face anyone, especially Ken, knowing she had failed.

Luckily, Kahli wouldn't allow her to brood. She forced Lark to her feet and down to the next level. After leaving the room, Kahli reentered her code into the holopad. The wall shimmered solid. As Kahli escorted Lark back to medical, Lark couldn't stop thinking of what all of the others must have thought of her. If she had any idea, it was most likely the exact same thing she thought of herself — she was worthless and she no longer wanted to be a part of any of it.

— 53 —

Jacquline's chest rose and fell in a quiet, rhythmic fashion, keeping Ken's attention away from her white-striped hair. Every time he looked at the soft, almost painted quality, tears rose upon his memories of Stacey.

Lark broke his focus as she walked in. Her head was bent past her slouched shoulders, clearly averting her eyes in a passive "ignoring the world" posture that Ken automatically recognized. Kahli was a step behind her and guided Lark to her bed. She lied down and curled her body away from Ken.

"What happened?" Ken asked. His urge to go to Lark and talk to her was powerful but his experience in the matter kept him from doing so.

"I do not comprehend," Kahli said, continuing to study Lark's behavior with great curiosity. "This act is very unfamiliar to me."

"She looks depressed."

"Depressed?" Kahli turned to Ken. "She is unhappy?"

"Unhappy, miserable, hopeless... take your pick."

"What would trigger such a reaction?"

"I don't know. There're lots of reasons people get depressed. Death of a loved one, money problems... the inability to get what you want. What were you doing before she got like this?"

"We were re-initializing the thrusters."

"And she was helping?"

"Yes. I asked her to cut a hole into the bypass regulator valves and when I requested that she turn one of them, she said she could not tell which one it was. After that, it was as if she shut down."

"That's all?"

"After she informed me of her failure to do as I requested, I called DovenJadden to help."

Ken stared at Lark, trying to understand. "It doesn't sound like her," he said. "I've never seen her freeze up that way."

"What will happen if she remains this way?"

"It's hard to say. After Stacey was taken, I couldn't sleep, I stopped eating. It seemed like all I wanted to do was let it all just end."

"Like Jacquline?"

"Jacquline?" Ken was clearly dumbfounded.

"Your daughter's mind holds many thoughts of slicing her wrists."

Ken glanced over at Jacquline. He suddenly felt guilty for not seeing it before. Everything made sense now; the outbursts, the lies, the disobedience — it was all due to his failure as a father because of his own selfish inclinations. He was about to ask Kahli to explain exactly what she saw, but it felt wrong to ask about something so personal behind Jacquline's back. Those were thoughts and feelings that she had chosen not to share and it wouldn't be right for him to know about them against her wishes. Until she was ready to talk to him about it, he would have to lay the matter to rest.

"Did you ever wish to do the same?" Kahli asked, even though she already knew the answer.

"Without Stacey," Ken said quietly, his eyes fixed on Jacquline, "my life was already over."

"Do you believe Lark feels the same?"

"You'd have to ask her. For all I know, she may snap out of it with a little sleep." Ken mustered up the strength to walk to Lark. "I just wish I could do more," he whispered.

"It was Lark that kept you alive," Kahli said.

Ken released a breath of laughter. "Yeah, I guess she did."

"You love her."

Ken rested his hand on her shoulder. He was happy that she didn't pull away. "She's my best friend."

"What can we do to help her?"

"Your guess is as good as mine. But if I had to say, she probably just needs a reason."

"A reason to keep her from suicide?"

"A reason to live again. Yeah."

"I'm not going to kill myself," Lark moaned softly. "I just want to be left alone."

Ken wanted to believe her but knew there wasn't any way to know for sure. He turned to Kahli and said, "Can I talk to you in private?"

Kahli was reserved about answering, believing that she should keep the humans together. But something in Ken made her realize Lark's request must be granted. "We may speak alone in my chamber. But stay by my side. I cannot have you wandering the ship alone."

"Not a problem." Ken squeezed Lark's shoulder. "Stay safe," he whispered.

Lark waited until Ken and Kahli's footsteps had disappeared before she summoned the strength to get up and walk to Jacquline. She held her comfortably in her arms and cried, her tears falling freely for some time. Lark didn't know when it would stop, but it was a release that Lark had desperately needed.

— 54 —

"Humans have an interesting pattern of emotions," Kahli said once she felt they were far enough away from medical.

"Well, I guess that's why we're special," Ken said, hoping to lighten the mood.

"It is very rare," Kahli continued. "I have never before encountered a species who could believe in such things. It is most likely why your species is still very unadvanced."

"How so?"

"The need to always feel important is a manifestation of the ego. It is only when you can control the ego that you will find peace within yourself and others around you."

"Yeah. That's a lot harder than you think."

"But it is a much needed step in evolution. If you continue to rely so heavily on ego, the only outcome is extinction."

"How do you know?"

"Because I have studied it. Throughout history, there have been hundreds of species that have allowed the ego to bloom out of control, leading to great destruction. There are very few who have gone through such devastation and lived."

"What happened to them?"

"They either punish themselves for their misgivings, living out the rest of their lives in isolation, or they succumb to their ego, become addicted to the destruction, and continue to seek it out. But never have I witnessed, or heard of, anyone who would wish their life ended, as you and your daughter have."

They climbed down to the next level, which was much smaller and less luminous. It also held a musty smell that reminded Ken of a storage unit that hadn't been opened for years.

"Are there any other emotions you're not familiar with?" Ken said, following Kahli down the corridor, which quickly bent down another, darker corridor.

"I am aware of almost all emotions, Kenneth, the most prominent being that of skepticism and suspicion."

"Really? I would have thought the ego controlled that, too."

"You are partially correct, but suspicion runs much deeper than that. Every living being has an inherent need to stay alive. Suspicion and mistrust blossom out of that need. The ego simply amplifies it to include other material attributes."

"Good to know that even out here no one trusts anyone."

"Most species that have evolved past the ego have become hunters, scavengers… pirates as you would say. They live for themselves and no other. Because of that, trust is a rare thing that if acquired, can be very powerful — and extremely dangerous."

"So why do you trust so freely?"

"I am a synthetic being. I was brought up on a planet that thrived on manipulation, lies and fear. I was one of a very few that did not believe in such things. I saw my creator's hatred, the suspicious nature that came with such emotion, and did not want to live my life with such contempt. I am always willing to trust before I suspect deceit."

"And because you can't be hurt," Ken said, pulling at the holes in Kahli's uniform.

"It is true that my body is made of an alloy that is impenetrable to the most common of weaponry, but I am not infallible."

"So what happens if you're wrong about someone?"

"Then I live with my consequences. I do not wish myself dead, but I am not afraid of termination. If my trust is misplaced, then come what may, but I find it hard to believe that everyone is out to harm you, and unless you allow them in, you will never know what they may bring to your life."

"How did Qah-Shekel come to trust you?"

"I am seldom wrong and I never lie. It didn't happen overnight; it took a very long while. But over time, trust does blossom."

"That's why he doesn't trust us."

"Because you are too new to him, yes. Do not do anything to harm him or those he loves and he will give you his trust. In time."

"Great," Ken said under his breath.

"Why is that?"

Ken couldn't believe she had heard him, but he had an answer. "Because I need him to trust me now. He's the only thing I have to get Tracey back."

"You love her deeply."

Ken couldn't master a response.

"Why do humans love so unconditionally?" Kahli said instead.

Ken took a long pause and then answered very clearly. "We need to have something to hold on to, something that makes us feel alive. Something that reminds us of happiness, I guess."

"And your daughter. She reminds you of happiness?"

Ken smiled. "She reminds me of my wife."

Kahli wanted so much to tell him about his wife, about his daughter, but she held her tongue, opting to learn about them in his own words. "Your wife was a good person?"

"She was the nicest person I have ever met. She was so considerate and unselfish. She loved me with everything she had and gave me everything I ever needed. I can't believe I let those bastards take her from me."

"You are referring to the vermons?" Kahli asked, clearly knowing the answer.

Ken could only nod, as the memory reignited his deep sorrow.

Kahli stopped. "You are sad. Do you wish to kill yourself?"

Ken smiled. "No. Sadness can be a first step to depression, but they are separate."

"Okay." Though she wished to know more, Kahli didn't push him. She tapped her fingers on the wall and a piece of it flipped down to reveal a control panel. Kahli lowered her head to it and allowed it to scan her eye. Once completed, a short double chirp was followed by a light hiss. Kahli pushed the cover back up and pressed her hand into the wall next to it. She turned her wrist and pulled, opening a small door barely wide enough for him to step through.

The only light in the room flickered along the edge of the walls like a small fire. Other than a few parchments and small nick-knacks, the only thing Ken could see was what looked like a large coffin, shaped to match Kahli's body perfectly, sitting upright against the far wall. Several wires dangled from the top like small, dead snakes.

The lights barely lit either of their faces as Kahli locked them inside. Keeping his attention focused on the facets of the room, Ken didn't notice Kahli remove her uniform.

"Your daughter will not be killed," Kahli assured him. She set the uniform into a small cylinder in the corner of the room and started typing on a holoscreen just above it.

"How do you know?" Ken said, looking at some weird little bugs that crawled and jumped around each other like miniature cockroaches (or very large fleas).

"Because she is too important."

"Important? How —" Ken flashed a look at Kahli but turned away just as fast. What he saw fluttered his heart and cracked his voice. "Sorry," he said.

"Why apologize?" Kahli said. She finished typing and reached back into the cylinder. She pulled out a fresh, undamaged uniform and tucked it under her arm.

"I didn't realize you were changing," he said sheepishly, his cheeks flushed a deep red.

Kahli was quite amused. "You are embarrassed?" she said.

"No," Ken said, trying desperately to play it off and fight the urge to peek. "I just believe in respecting a woman's privacy is all."

"And I respect you for that, Kenneth," Kahli said. "But there is no need. I am not embarrassed, nor should you be. But if this makes you uncomfortable, I will dress."

Ken huffed a small laugh and lowered his head, taking that one last curious peek as she pulled her uniform back up over her body. Other than several scorch marks pock-marked across her flawless skin, Kahli was the literal embodiment of a living, breathing Barbie doll.

"What are you going to do about those scorch marks?" Ken said, turning his eyes away again.

"My skin will heal them naturally," Kahli said. "Does this help, Kenneth?"

Ken cautiously looked. "Thank you," he said, fully turning around.

Kahli bowed her head and sat down on a thick mat. "Please, sit."

Ken hesitated but eventually obliged, sitting in front of her.

"Now," Kahli said, "why did you wish to speak with me in private?"

Ken cleared his throat and shifted his body. For whatever reason, he felt slightly uneasy about talking to Kahli about something so personal, even though he was pretty sure she would not judge him in any way.

"I'm worried about Lark," he finally said.

"I understand. I too worry for her health," Kahli assured.

"Right, but that's not quite what I'm talking about. I've never seen her like this before and I don't want to add to whatever's bothering her."

"Please explain."

Ken rubbed his forehead with the tips of his fingers, trying to find the best way to say what he had to say. In the end, it was probably best just to spit it out. "I think she's falling in love me."

"Define 'falling in love'," Kahli said. Ken thought he heard a little condescension in her voice but let it go.

"Falling in love... you know, she wants to take our relationship to a deeper level than just friends."

"Are you referring to the participation in sexual intercourse?"

Ken blushed and bit his lip, unable to bring himself to affirm or deny her claim.

"You believe this to be a bad thing?" Kahli was confused, but with a child's curiosity.

"In my case, yeah, I do. Don't get me wrong, she is a great friend, but even if I felt the same, I wouldn't dare act on it."

"And you believe that by telling her this, she may fall deeper into depression?"

Ken nodded.

"Have you ever discussed this matter with her before?"

"I shouldn't have to."

"Why is that?"

"Because she already knows nothing will ever happen between us." Ken was growing slightly irritated.

"Why not?"

"Because my heart belongs to Stacey," Ken said. "And it always will."

"Even if she is dead?"

"She's not dead." Ken's tone dropped from empathy to anger. "Don't you even dare think that."

"I am sorry, Kenneth. I did not mean to upset you. All I was pointing out was that if Stacey were to be found dead, would you not feel compelled to move forward and seek a new relationship with another, as you did once before?"

Ken still felt a little violated by her knowledge of his past. "No," he said quietly. "She would never forgive me for being unfaithful." The last word was almost hidden under a choke of tears.

"Unfaithful to whom?"

Ken bent his head down. He couldn't look at Kahli. "Stacey is my life. Whether she's alive or not, to have an affair with someone after building a relationship *because* of Stacey..."

"It would seem as if you were being unfaithful the entire time."

Ken rubbed his eyes.

"Kenneth, your love for Stacey is extremely strong; stronger, in fact, than I have ever seen. It is something quite beautiful. But to allow that love to affect your life in such a way goes beyond what your mind is able to comprehend."

Ken peered up to Kahli. "What are you saying? It's not real?"

"Oh, it is very real, Kenneth. However, I believe that what you are hanging onto — the belief that Stacey is alive, your guilt over having a relationship with another woman, your inability to let go or live without her — has been forged by something otherworldly, something that you have absolutely no control over. Your love is real; your sorrow is manufactured."

"Manufactured how?"

"You are not ready to learn that answer," Kahli said bluntly.

"Bull piss," Ken said. "If you know something about Stacey that I don't, then I *deserve* to know."

"That you do," Kahli said, hoping to calm his anger, "but the story behind your wife involves aspects that you may not be ready to hear."

"What aspects? What aren't you telling me?"

"Your daughter is the key."

"Tracey? Yeah, you said she was important."

"It is all connected, and you will learn of it all in due time. But for now, you must believe that when we find her, you will have your answers."

"If she's still alive."

"I can say in absolute certainty that she is alive and that no harm will come to her."

"How can you be so certain? Those things —" Suddenly Ken felt a renewed energy pump through his body. The vermon, those monsters that kidnapped his wife, now had his daughter as well. If he was right, wherever Tracey was taken was also where Stacey is being held. He felt his lips curl upward ever so slightly. "You know where she is," he said softy.

"I do, and we will get her back."

"You promise?"

"What is, 'promise'?"

"It's something you do to earn someone's trust. By saying you promise, it means you'll do what you say you're going to do no matter what, and if you break that promise, you break your trust."

Kahli pondered the explanation and then said, "Yes. I promise."

"Thank you." There was a moment of silence. "Where is she?"

"She will be brought to the same location as the gem."

Ken thought it odd that she would say Tracey would be brought to the gem and not Stacey. Could he be wrong? "Stacey's gem?" he said to help clarify. "The green one?"

"Yes. As you say, the 'take over the world' gem."

Ken smiled lightly. "How long will it take to get there?"

"We are close. Under our current rate, it should take us very little time."

"Great. How fast are we going?" No matter what the answer, he would urge them to go faster, ready and willing to go through the pain of reaching the speed of light again if it meant finding his daughter.

"We are currently at the rate of which light travels."

"The speed of light? Are you serious?"

"Do you not believe me?"

"But, how can that be? When did we jump?"

"We reached lightning-five as soon as we broke orbit of Hasten-Jackai."

"That's not possible. I didn't feel anything."

"As it should be." Kahli closed her eyes as if she was entering a meditative state.

"What do you mean? We have to be going over two hundred and ninety-nine kilometers a second for light-speed."

Kahli opened her eyes, an odd expression waxed across her face. "Who told you that?"

"Physics," Ken said matter-of-fact.

"Whatever you may have been led to believe, Kenneth, is wrong. Light is the fastest entity in the universe. Because of this, it cannot conceivably have a speed of its own that one could measure."

"Everything can be measured."

"So says the ego," Kahli said proudly. "The truth is, light cannot be measured because it travels instantaneously."

"Instantaneously?"

"Of course. The moments that we enter and exit the speed at which light travels, as well as our passage through it, are all one in the same."

Ken took a deep breath. "That can't be..."

"But is truth. To those that travel as fast as light, there is passage of time... for those outside, there is none."

"A quote?" Ken asked, smirking at the structure of her words.

"The creator of my kind." Kahli paused. "A very thoughtful, inspired young man."

"We have plenty of those on Earth, too, and all of them say otherwise. Instantaneous acceleration is impossible."

"You are a very funny species, Kenneth," Kahli laughed. "Have these intelligent men of yours ever traveled at the rate of light?"

"Well, no..."

"Then how can you trust them so concretely?"

"I wish I hadn't now," Ken said. "We almost killed ourselves doing it."

"Let that be a lesson learned." Kahli smiled and dropped back into meditation.

Ken took some time to come to terms with what he had just learned. It was clear now that Kahli had been right — humans were far less advanced than he realized and he couldn't wait to learn more.

"Why are you meditating?" Ken finally asked.

"It helps me organize information. Everything that I have seen and all of my actions and conversations are stored within my hard drive. Every so often, I find it refreshing to cleanse and condense this information."

"So you're deleting files?" Ken asked.

"All recorded information is an asset of memory for which I could never delete. I simply organize and break down elements within so that more knowledge can be stored."

"Are you ever worried that your memory might be erased?"

"That is a fear all synthetics must face. But I try not to place much worry into it."

Ken nodded and let Kahli have her time in silence, taking the opportunity to try his own hand at meditation, something that didn't work as well as he had hoped. Closing his eyes and trying to clear his mind only brought back memories of Stacey and made him tense up — and even shed a tear or two. Instead, he sat and watched Kahli for more than twenty minutes, unable to take his eyes off of her near perfect skin and symmetrically natural features. If he had to pick the most beautiful person in the universe — other than Stacey (or Kate Beckinsale, as he used to joke around with Gloria about) — there was no doubt it would be Kahli.

When Kahli was through, she escorted Ken back to medical. Neither of them spoke a word aloud, but Ken's thoughts were spinning with apologies for his sinful thoughts. He could feel Stacey watching him, judging him — no matter how foolish that made him seem. He blushed as he caught sight of Lark sleeping next to Jacquline, who continued to whisper nonsense in her sleep

"I wonder if she had another attack," Kahli said.

"I think I'll get some sleep, too," Ken said, brushing his fingers through Jacquline's hair.

"I must also regenerate. Please do not leave medical while I am gone."

"Don't worry. The last thing I want to do is piss off Qah-Shekel. Or get myself killed. Or both."

Kahli bowed and left the room, pressing her hand on the wall next to door. The lights went out, leaving only a soft purple glow throughout. Ken lied down and stared at the ceiling.

"I love you, Stacey," he whispered before kissing his fingers and pressing them to his chest as he did every night before going to sleep. "I'm getting closer. I can feel your strength." He kissed his fingers again, raised his hand to the ceiling and closed his eyes for what he hoped would be a peaceful rest.

— 55 —

Kahli stepped into the command center. Sentilla was in her usual spot, carefully guiding the ship. Qah-Shekel was standing where Naja-Leku used to perch himself, searching through several manuals and parchments that Naja-Leku used to write every thought he ever had. Most of what he wrote was chaotic gibberish or incomprehensible theories, which led to a bit of confusion for why Qah-Shekel would be looking them over.

"What are you looking for?" Kahli asked.

Qah-Shekel dropped what he was holding and glared at Kahli with fierce eyes. "Why did you let that female in the core?"

"She wanted to help. I trusted that she wouldn't do anything to harm us."

"You're too trusting," Qah-Shekel shot back.

"And you're not trusting enough."

"Why do you trust them?" Sentilla interjected.

"Because I have seen their pain before," Kahli said, her eyes locked on Qah-Shekel. "This species, human, holds a love for things that is quite grand and magical, the greatest of which is their love of family. It is all they seek right now. These particular humans cannot, and will not, do us any harm. They simply want to find their child."

Qah-Shekel and Sentilla were both quiet. Kahli didn't know what it meant to feel love for a child, a father or a mother, but she had witnessed the love Ken had displayed before — in Qah-Shekel. The older he grew, the stronger and more independent he became. But there was always a deep love for those he once lost that he would never be able to shake. She hoped he would be able to see that similarity.

"We are heading to retrieve the child, right?" Kahli said, uncertain.

Qah-Shekel walked to Sentilla, keeping Kahli in his sights. "We are going to Xyneris to retrieve the gem."

"And while we're there, we can track the child."

"I don't get why you're so adamant about this child," Sentilla said. "Why should we risk our lives for her?"

"Because I believe her to be Jaxxa Rakala."

"How would you know that?"

"She bears the mark of the crescent moons."

"The child only had one mark," Qah-Shekel noted. "Jaxxa Rakala has two."

"I am aware of that."

"Then that child is not Jaxxa Rakala and is an unnecessary risk."

"I don't believe that. There's only one reason why the vermon would have taken her."

"And I assume it's because they've made the same mistake you have," Qah-Shekel said. "We are going to retrieve the gem. That's all."

"I made a promise," Kahli said hesitantly.

"You shouldn't have done that."

"You're making the wrong decision," Kahli continued. "You trusted me enough to bring them on board, you have to trust me about this."

"It's not you I don't trust," Qah-Shekel said gruffly. "You saw how that male reacted to the gem. For all we know, they're using us to get their hands on it."

"I can't believe that," Kahli said, confident.

"Why?"

"I don't believe his connection to the gem is power. I believe it's love. And if I'm right in my assessments of the mind sweep, Kenneth Brody is the *father* of Jaxxa Rakala, meaning that his connection goes far deeper than the average thirst."

"And if you're wrong?"

Kahli didn't want to answer. If she was wrong, Ken and his family were after much more than they could handle and it would be the end of them all. "They are not out to hurt anyone," she finally said. "They still don't know why she was taken, or that the gem has any control over them."

"At least that's what they claim."

Kahli remained silent this time. Qah-Shekel had said everything he needed to say. The mind sweep is never wrong, but each and every point Qah-Shekel made forced her to question the accuracy of it, which led doubt to cloud her assessment.

She turned to walk out.

"I will allow them to be away from medical as long as they are with you," Qah-Shekel said, conveying a slight amount of empathy. "But if there is any sign that they are using us to get the gem, I will kill them."

Kahli nodded and left the command center. She wanted to believe that Ken wasn't out to hurt anyone, but even with the mind sweep, she'd come to realize that she knew very little about their new guests and no longer felt confident in her trust for them. She would keep her promise, that was a given. but she was also going to need to keep a much more stringent eye on their actions and desires before she would allow them her full support — an action she had never once considered, and one that scared her beyond her personal level of security.

THE RESCUE

— 1 —

The air about the dark room was damp and heavy, and smelled of mildew mixed with rust and blood. It made Tracey sick to her stomach. The urge to cry was overwhelming, but to do so — to give in to her fear — would only heighten her vulnerability, which she needed to mask as best she could lest she become a victim to those wishing to hurt her.

As she sat up, her head started spinning and her need to purge could no longer be controlled. Tears grew sharp as she gagged. Usually at a time like this, her mother (and in most recent years, Jacquline) would gently rub her back to relax her. Without that connection, without having the option to turn to her, to be in her arms and feel her warm breath on the back of her neck, Tracey felt lost — alone. The idea that she would never see her mother again suddenly became real; there didn't seem to be any reason to stay strong — except Jacquline, who provided Tracey the same level of comfort and security that her mom once had. The smell of candy that Jacquline emitted when she hugged her and the bright quality of her genuine smile brought comfort to her thoughts — thoughts that also carried with them the soft tune Jacquline always sang to her before going to bed:

Beauty is a picture of the one I see,
Lying next to me, you will softly be,
Always loving, always kind,
Like the love I left behind.

You came from heaven, this I know,
Kind and free, you're pure and sweet.
You are that which love is built,
And in my heart you'll always be.

There was no way of knowing whether Jacquline was even still alive, but the simple act of running the song over and over in her head made it feel as if Jacquline was there with her, singing to her. It was enough to dry her tears with the hope that she was out there, with Ken, stopping at nothing to find her. If she dug deep enough, she could feel them and know that she would be reunited with them, so long as she stayed strong and fought whatever evil lurked in the shadows.

A loud bang and squeal reverberated through the darkness as a large metal door opened. A soft hue of orange light poured into the room, outlining the shape of a giant round beast. Tracey wiped away what tears still lingered around her eyes and backed away as far as she could before the wall betrayed her. She screamed, but only for a short moment, realizing it wouldn't do any good. Even if Jacquline (or Ken) were there, would they be able to do anything?

She covered her head as the monster picked her up and carried her from the confines of a ship onto a windy, mountainous landscape surrounded by steamy, orange rivers that dripped with lava. Tracey almost fainted with the blast of heat, but kept her mind awake by reciting Jacquline's song. That alone would save her right now; it was the only thing she had left. So she sang, until she was no longer capable of thought.

— 2 —

Everything around Jacquline is dark. Her body is completely numb and she feels extremely dizzy, yet surprisingly content, as if she were in a place that she would never want to leave — as if she were in heaven.

A scream suddenly echoes around her. It's soft and distant, and lasts only a second, but she recognizes the voice almost immediately.

"Tracey!" Jacquline screams, praying for a response that never comes. It's clear to her that Tracey is in danger and it's up to Jacquline to save her. Her steps are laborious, unclear as to whether they are real or imagined, but with the pressure on her chest and the flaming heat that swipes her body with each step, she has to believe she's moving forward. Whatever's holding Tracey is trying hard to keep Jacquline away, but Tracey's far too important to let a little pain, or inconvenience, stop her.

Suddenly, she slips into a large chasm. The hot air nips at her cool skin as she falls. Anticipating the moment her body hits the ground, she screams — for Tracey, for her mother — *for her father?* No. She doesn't want his help, not even if it means her death, which comes in the form of a white void that consumes the darkness, leaving her body soft and light in a sea of pure silence. Although the brightness of the light forces her to keep her eyes closed, she is in complete bliss, accentuated by the soft hum of a song she knew from long ago — Stacey's lullaby. She loves that song very much and hearing it now keeps her mind at rest; it keeps her safe, ready for whatever may come next.

The crystal melody of a familiar voice immediately draws her focus. "Jacquline, I am here."

Jacquline forces her eyes open. Standing in front of her — above her? — is a beautiful woman wearing the wedding dress Stacey promised to Jacquline when it was her time. "Stacey?" Jacquline whispers with surprise and love.

"I am here as you are here," Stacey says, her voice resonating as if it's coming from a mile away. "You must help me."

"How?" Jacquline asks.

"You must trust the one who hides from you."

"Trust... who?" Jacquline thinks hard, but familiar names and faces are all but extinct in her mind. The only one she can remember is Tracey.

"You must trust the one who hides from you... you must allow that person to find you."

"Who?" Jacquline asks again.

"Once you are willing to open yourself to trust, you will find the way to that which is most important."

"Tracey is the most important. But how do I find her?"

"You will find the way." Stacey lifts her hand to Jacquline's cheek and she instantly feels complete. Jacquline closes her eyes in ecstasy, wanting nothing more than to remain in this important and precious moment.

All of a sudden, Stacey's touch begins to burn, forcing Jacquline's eyes open. She flies through caverns streaming with lava. There's no way to know if she would be able to stop, but in this moment, she doesn't want to. Stacey is guiding her to the place she needs to be. Her speed picks up with each new passage, and as her flight reaches a breakneck speed, Jacquline falls once again into darkness but quickly emerges to find what she has been longing for.

"Tracey," Jacquline screams in a whisper.

Tracey is strapped to the wall by chains attached to her wrists and ankles. She looks up, her eyes cold and distant, as Jacquline lands safely on the ground in front of her.

You must save her, Stacey's voice echoes. We *must save her.*

Jacquline wants to with all of her being, but no matter how hard she tries to get to her, to free her from her pain, she can't touch her — or even reach her.

"I want to save her," she screams.

Jacquline is suddenly in darkness. All she can do is scream, "We have to save her!"

— 3 —

Ken wanted to find sleep, but thoughts of Tracey's terrified face as the vermon held her, Lark's utter despondency, and Jacquline's mumbled coma kept his fatigued body tossing and turning for comfort and rest.

Upon witnessing Stacey disappear into the black void of the vermon ship once again, Ken shifted to his side and opened his eyes, hoping the focus on Lark and Jacquline would help to calm his mind. What he found instead was a bright light flashing against the wall from behind him. He shifted around and held up his hand to cover his eyes as he strained to see what was producing the light. It wasn't immediately apparent, but a soft hum — sweet, slow and very familiar — from inside the light soothed the pain in his body. Suddenly, Ken felt even closer to Stacey, yet remained so very far away.

The song repeated as Ken's heart slowed to a snail's crawl. Memories of love — him and Stacey holding each other tightly in bed; Stacey hugging Tracey with a motherly affection; Stacey's kiss, as she held it just above his lips, when the anticipation was at its peak — found their way to the surface of his mind. They made Ken feel lost and infinitely alone, fleshing out his utter dependency on Stacey. As the depth of the light and the volume of the hum reached their apex, Ken cried. It wasn't until the song became a solemn background orchestration and the light a dim memory that Ken was able to face his reality. To his surprise, that reality was a dream come true.

Stacey stood by the door wearing her wedding gown — more beautiful than he had ever seen her. A pink bow was wrapped around her waist and a matching shawl rested gently across her arms. Her hair was tied up in a low ponytail with the pink-laced strap he had given her as an early wedding gift and a thinned, silk veil was lowered upon her face.

"Stacey," he said, her name floating through the room with soft passion.

"Quiet," Stacey answered back with musicality, placing her finger to her mouth. "You do not want to wake the others."

Ken wanted to run to her but his body had been petrified. Instead, Stacey glided magically across space and time to him.

"How did you find me?" Ken whispered, although it could have been the thickness of his tears that kept him from speaking any louder.

"I did not find you, Ken. You have found me." Stacey stopped a few feet from him. He could see the perfect blue eyes that he fell in love with through her veil.

"But, how…"

Stacey placed her finger on his lips. "Enjoy this moment, Ken."

Ken wished he could do as she asked, to sit and just feel her, taste her, breathe her into his soul, but there was so much he needed to know — so much he needed to say.

"I've missed you, Stacey," he said.

"As have I," Stacey said, smiling softly. "But I am not the one who needs you."

Ken's heart fell. "What do you mean?"

"I love you, Kenneth. I will always be waiting for you. But there is another that needs you more than I."

"Tracey," he said without hesitation.

"No," Stacey whispered back. "Tracey is not in any danger. There is another that needs you in a deeper sense of the word. She has been waiting for you, ever so patiently for the past nine years. But you have refused to find her. You must find her now, before she is lost to you forever."

"Who?" Ken asked. "Who's lost to me?"

Ken lost all feeling in his body as Stacey raised her veil; her face was more majestic than he remembered. She leaned forward and kissed him softly. It was a perfect moment that he didn't want to end, but knew deep in his heart that it had to. As she lifted her head from his, Stacey stared into his eyes. "Find her."

She lowered the veil and started singing. "La-lee-lo-lejer-les-li-lirlee. Lutii-laa-les-lii-larr-lor-lie-lew."

Ken recognized the song but could not place it. After another two bars, he remembered

— the lullaby she used to sing to Tracey as she put her to sleep, which he could now hear in perfect harmony.

"You came from heaven, this I know. Kind and free, you're pure and sweet. You are that which love is built, and in my heart you'll always be."

The song repeated as Stacey floated out of the room.

"Wait," Ken said in despair. "Where are you going?" All he could do was reach out for her as she dissolved into extinction.

"Stacey," he said, the harsh white light blazing back in around him. Ken closed his eyes and turned away. When the room went dark, Stacey — and his dream — was gone.

He slid off the table and sprinted to the door, hoping she'd be there. But peering into the corridors reaped no rewards. He lowered his head and turned back into the room. As he trudged back to his bed, he could still hear the song. He thought at first that it was just stuck in his head but quickly realized that someone else was singing it.

He looked to Jacquline. She was still asleep but the song never left her lips. Ken thought about going over to her, but what could he do that Lark hadn't already? Feeling his tears return, he sat down on his bed and wiped them away.

"We have to save her," Jacquline suddenly screamed.

Lark jumped awake in fright and Ken stood. Jacquline's breathing was erratic and she was sweating profusely, but what Ken saw first and foremost were her eyes —

Jacquline was awake.

"Jacquline?" Ken whispered.

She sat up, her face a frightened mess. "Dad?" She slid off the bed and ran to him. Despite everything they'd been through, nothing could hold her back from the welcome embrace of her father. Lark watched them with silent pleasure, happy for them but jealous at the same time.

"Thank God you're all right," Ken said. He cupped his hands on the underside of her cheeks. "Are you okay?"

"I think so," she said, an answer that prompted Ken to hug her again.

Jacquline suddenly pushed him away, not out of resentment, but out of confusion. "What happened? Where are we?"

"Hey, calm down," Ken said, keeping a gentle grip on Jacquline's arms. "We're on a ship, Jacks."

"A ship? What kind of a ship? Are we in danger?"

"No, we're all okay." He gestured over to Lark, who smiled at seeing Jacquline's puzzled features. "There's a lot we need to tell you, Jacks."

"I'm listening."

"Where do I start?" He looked at Lark, who simply shrugged her shoulders.

"How about where the hell we are," Jacquline said.

"Well," Ken started, trying to find a way to relay the information without sounding completely insane, "this ship belongs to a team of aliens —"

"Aliens," Jacquline said, the word stretched out considerably.

"Several different species, in fact. Some sort of band of pirates, in a way."

"We're flying through space with a bunch of pirate aliens. This is what you want me to believe?" Jacquline looked to Lark, who said everything she needed to say with her body. "God, you guys are clinical."

"We may just be," Ken said, "but it's the truth."

"Okay, let's say it is. How do you know we can trust them?"

"They saved our lives," Ken said bluntly.

"Much good that's done," Lark mumbled.

Jacquline wasn't sure what she meant but she could tell Lark was not in the best frame of mind. It was better she leave her be. "So, where are your little pirate aliens?" she asked Ken.

"Kahli is rejuvenating in her chamber, I think. I don't know about the rest."

"You know their names?"

"You've been out for quite a while."

Jacquline's head pounded. She closed her eyes and rubbed her temples, which prompted a clear vision of Tracey to appear. "Tracey!" she screamed. "We have to save her!"

Ken tried hard to keep Jacquline still. "Jacks," he yelled.

"We have to save her!" she continued and finally opened her eyes, struggling to break free of Ken. Lark watched, wondering if she should get involved.

"She's not here," Ken said.

"We have to save her!"

"I know, and we are."

Jacquline calmed, her screams slowing until they were nothing but a mumble. Finally, she collapsed forward. Ken was barely able to catch her fall.

"Jacks," he said, lowering her to the floor.

Lark was standing now but remained still, unsure of what else to say or do.

"Tracey," Jacquline said softly.

"I know. We're on our way to get her now."

Jacquline moaned and grabbed her forehead. She sat up, rubbing her eyes.

"Jacquline?" Ken kept his hand on her back and waited.

"What has happened?" Kahli said as she rushed into the room.

"She's awake," Ken said, though Kahli had already knelt down and grabbed Jacquline's chin.

"This is wonderful," Kahli said. She hurried to her desk and opened a new panel in the wall just above the holoscreen. Inside was a small glove that she was quick to pull on. She snapped the epidermis of her elbow open and connected the wire that dangled from the glove to the port inside.

"Hello, Jacquline," Kahli said as she knelt back down. "I am a Rega-One Xyla-Alpha-Nine Android. Do you mind if I perform a quick examination?"

Jacquline's heart raced as she turned to Ken for help. He nodded and Jacquline relayed his answer to Kahli, who grinned with anticipation. She carefully positioned her gloved hand on the side of Jacquline's face, her index finger on her temple, the other three wrapped around her ear to the back of her head. Her thumb sat gently against the corner of her mouth. Once in place, Kahli waved her hand over the top of the glove, activating a small holoscreen that extended outward away from the glove. She continuously waved her fingers upward across the screen, reviewing the symbols and graphics that appeared with consistent nods. *A good sign,* Ken hoped.

Jacquline tried hard to see what was happening, but eventually gave up in favor of taking in Kahli's near perfect complexion. It appeared as beautiful as a blooming flower and as smooth as crystal.

After a few moments, Kahli removed her hand. "Please lie down?"

Jacquline complied quickly. Before she knew it, Kahli's gloved hand rested between her breasts. She held back a laugh as she felt a slight tickle vibrate across her chest.

This time, Jacquline could see the holoscreen and was intrigued at the speed at which Kahli was able to dissect and absorb the alien information that flew across the screen. It wasn't long before Kahli was satisfied with the exam and removed the glove.

"As I understand it, she is in perfect health." Kahli said.

Jacquline sat up. "Cool trick," she said with an awkward but appreciative smile.

"I built it long ago to use when I was away from medical," Kahli said, removing the cord and replacing the skin on her elbow. "It has helped save a lot of lives."

"I could make a fortune with that thing."

"Its purpose is not to acquire riches. Its purpose is to examine and diagnose injuries."

"I know," Jacquline said. "But there's no harm in making a profit now, is there?"

"Do you not find it unethical to make profit off of other's pain and suffering?"

"If it saves lives, sign me up," Jacquline winked.

Kahli studied Jacquline's features curiously.

"Forget it," Jacquline said. "Wouldn't want you to fry your circuits." Again, Kahli looked confounded. Jacquline smiled. "How does it work?"

"It feels for electrical current in the mind and body," Kahli said without missing a beat. "If all readings remain steady, the body is functioning properly. If there is even the slightest vibration, or variance, then there is much more for me to do. I can do the same with the machine's here, but seeing as what happened the last time I used them on you, I did not want to take the chance." Kahli slipped the glove off and latched it to the back of her belt.

Jacquline was curious but remained silent. Did she really want to know what these machines — but more importantly, this alien — had done to her?

Kahli walked back to her desk to work on a larger holoscreen.

"What's she doing?" Jacquline whispered to Ken.

"I am finding out how much longer we have," Kahli said, causing Jacquline to blush slightly.

"Longer until what?" Ken said, relieving Jacquline's awkwardness.

"Until we reach Xyneris."

"Xyneris," Jacquline repeated to herself. The word alone meant nothing, but it brought several images to her mind. "It's hot, and red. The heat is terrible," she chanted softly. "It's hurting me. It's hurting *her*."

Everyone was staring at Jacquline when she returned to full awareness. She looked at Kahli. "It's where Tracey's being held, isn't it?"

"It is," Kahli said and returned to the screen.

Jacquline whipped her head around to Ken. "That means I was right. Tracey was on the ship, wasn't she?"

Ken turned away, a bit ashamed.

"I told you, but you wouldn't listen. And now she's in danger." Jacquline walked to Kahli and stared at the screen. She couldn't understand anything she was looking at. "How much time do we have?" she finally asked.

"We are approximately a hundred delias from our destination," Kahli said.

"Great. How far is a delia?"

"In your terms, I believe a delia to be approximately a hundred miles."

"How long does it take to travel one delia?" Jacquline asked, then added for emphasis, "In our time?"

"Approximately one minute of your time."

"That's too long. She's already there. She's about to be tortured."

"Tortured?" Ken said, rising to his feet.

"Do not worry," Kahli said. "As I have said, she will not be harmed." She looked back at Jacquline. "She will not be harmed."

Jacquline dropped her head in defeat and peered irritably over to Ken. He walked to Lark and sat down next to her, his posture and attitude clearly conveying what Jacquline had been accusing him of.

"As we wait," Kahli said, breaking the silence, "Lark. I need your help."

"You don't want my help," Lark said groggily.

"I am sure I do." Kahli tapped the holoscreen. "Please, come here."

Rolling her eyes, Lark lumbered over to Kahli, who tapped the top of the desk. A bench slid out from underneath it. "Sit," she said.

With a defeated breath, Lark sat and rested her chin in her hand.

"I have been attempting to understand some information that Naja-Leku had written before he died. But he was very much the confusion type."

Jacquline held back a smile.

"So?" Lark said.

"I have been able to translate his work into your language but it still feels very jumbled and unorthodox. I need your help to figure out what he was trying to say."

"I can't —"

"Please. I know there is something important within these words. I must know what they are before we reach Xyneris. Please, try. It is all I ask."

Lark could see the need in Kahli's eyes. "I can't guarantee anything."

"An attempt is better than nothing," Kahli said.

Lark took in a deep breath as Kahli stepped away, allowing the bench to shift Lark in front of the holoscreen. She took one last quick glance at Kahli with a bemused smile before sitting up to focus on the text. "How do you work it?"

"Just slide your fingers along the text as you wish," Kahli said with an example. "If you need to enhance the information, simply hold both hands on either side of what you need and pull away. Move inward to make it smaller."

"It's a giant holographic smart phone," Jacquline said.

"Got it," Lark said and started reading.

"I must return to command. Will you all be okay?"

"We're golden," Jacquline said, reading over Lark's shoulder.

Ken nodded and waved his affirmative before lying down, tired and worn.

Satisfied, Kahli left the room.

As she read over the random and senseless nonsense, Lark understood what Kahli was talking about. Nonetheless, a sudden surge of motivation laced her brow. She may never again be able to enjoy the beauty of a rainbow, but she was smart enough to figure this mess out. Even if it took her the rest of her life, Lark was determined not to let Kahli down again.

— 4 —

Tracey's breath eased from her cracked, drying lips but she could hardly bring any air back in. Her only thought as she tried to find any remnants of moisture in her mouth was of Jacquline. She needed her; wanted her more than ever. But whether she was even alive was extremely doubtful. The tears that she tried to cry for her evaporated within seconds of striking her cheeks.

A sudden shuffling prompted Tracey to raise her head and open her eyes. Through the dry fog of blurriness, a large black shadow brushed across the red walls in front of her. She could hear a beating, slow yet steady, and a soft whisper floated upon her ear like that of a dream. As the shadow inched closer, Tracey pulled at the chains locked around her wrists and ankles keeping her a defenseless prisoner. She wanted to let out a scream, but the best she could muster was a low whistle. Tears were all she had left.

"Stop those tears, sweet child," the shadow said, though not in a language Tracey was accustomed. She had never heard words spoken in that manner before, much like the hiss of a snake, yet she understood them perfectly. Her confusion softened her tears, but only for a moment, as a series of moist, scaly fingers ran their way gently across her cheek. Chills poured through her body like electricity.

"Yes," the hiss sounded again. It was soft but still echoed through the room. "The crescent. Yes."

Tracey stopped struggling as its fingers reached her chin, believing that if she continued, the shadow would snap her neck. At the same time, Tracey felt a pleasure in the shadow's touch that soothed her need to escape. As the scaled tips of its fingers caressed the corners of her jaw, Tracey was unequivocally relaxed, comfortable.

"You have the mark," the shadow hissed, "and your reactions are pure. One more test will prove your nobility."

The warm sensation continued as the shadow lifted her shirt and caressed her stomach around the intricate pattern tattooed across her torso. "Yes," the hiss echoed again. "The mark of Trynoruus."

Tracey finally began to feel slightly uncomfortable as the shadow lowered her shirt. She felt its breath upon her face, and though her eyes still blazed with pain, Tracey forced them open, determined to see who or what this shadow really was.

Flames burned within the dark red circles under the hood as everything around her became pitch black. Her own eyes started to sting but she couldn't blink or move away, mesmerized by the familiar image that slowly emerged within the flames. Eventually, they softened to a mere crackle, leaving only the clear visage of Stacey.

Mother!

Tracey let out a high-pitched whistle as she fought to grab a hold of her.

"Tracey!" her mother called back, though it felt cold and distant.

Tracey shrieked as a hiss of laughter surrounded Stacey like a fog. Finally, with a pain deeper than any other she had ever felt, Tracey closed her eyes and refused to open them. She no longer wanted to face her mother unless she was able to hold her and feel her love through her touch.

"You are Jaxxa Rakala," the shadow hissed delightfully. "And you will be mine to control." Another hiss of amusement leapt through the air, followed by a loud bang. The echo of its laugh hung heavy in the room but Tracey no longer felt the shadow's presence. Even so, Tracey wasn't going to open her eyes for fear of seeing Stacey. Instead, she fell limp against the wall and cried until she slipped back into silent slumber.

— 5 —

"How are you coming along?" Kahli asked as she returned to medical.

Lark leaned back and rubbed her eyes. "Not great. I've cleaned up most of the syntax, but the actual thoughts…" She looked back to the holoscreen. "They're like a child's ramblings. Entirely incoherent."

Kahli was eager to help, knowing it would take her a fraction of the time it had already taken Lark to find what she needed. But Lark needed to figure this out on her own. "Do not fret," she said. "You are doing fine."

Lark lowered her head in doubt. "Yeah," she whispered and took a moment to stretch her neck.

"We are having a briefing in tactical," Kahli said to Ken. "You are invited."

Ken, still having a terrible time trying to find sleep under all of Lark's frustrated musings, sat up and looked quizzically at Kahli. "Are you serious?"

"Why do you always ask me that?" Kahli said, somewhat confused.

"Don't worry about it." Ken wasn't sure what else to say but, "Thank you."

"What about me?" Jacquline said from behind Lark.

"You should remain with Lark," Kahli replied. "Help her in all she may need."

"Hell no. Tracey's my sister. I deserve to know what's going on."

Kahli studied Jacquline's demeanor carefully. Behind the frustration and resentment, she could see the same determined love that embodied Ken.

"Yes, of course," Kahli said. "You may come if it pleases you."

Jacquline pumped her fist in excitement. Kahli pulled a small object from her belt and placed it on the desk. It was round like a saucer but was slightly smaller than her palm.

"If you find anything, call me on this." Kahli said. "Just rest your thumb on the back and speak."

Lark picked it up. She half expected there to be small holes on the front, but the entire thing was smooth and glossy. She ignored her confusion and turned back to the holoscreen. "Don't you worry. You'll be my first call."

Kahli said nothing more and left, followed swiftly by Ken and Jacquline, each of who had to hustle to catch up after pausing to figure out whether they should go with her or not. When she didn't object to their presence, they followed her up a nearby ladder — Jacquline in delightful wonderment, Ken surprised there was a third deck above them. Even though every corridor they walked down looked basically the same — white and smooth as water, without a trace of the massive firefight that had just ensued — they both had a difficult time taking in the magnificence of it all as Kahli urged them forward faster than they would have liked. They were both speechless as they reached one of the very few corridors that offered different visuals, this one encased with slowly spinning mesh-like cylinders, which ended at a flat black wall that shimmered among the spin.

"It's a dead-end," Jacquline whispered. She couldn't see Kahli's light smile.

Kahli pressed her hand to the center of the wall causing ripples to flow about. They sped up until the entire wall disintegrated into a watery opening that made it seem as if they were looking through the clear flow of a waterfall. Kahli revealed her smile to Jacquline and walked through it. Jacquline didn't hesitate to follow, grabbing Ken's hand. The room on the other side was small in comparison to the rest of the ship. It was dark, lit only by the holographic images and information spread across the entirety of the walls (and in some cases, floating about the room). In the middle was a large projection of what looked to Jacquline to be a ball of fire. But as she got closer, she could make out several mountainous regions and realized that it wasn't just a ball of fire, but an extremely active volcanic planet.

"What is this?" Jacquline said, stunned at the familiarity of what she was seeing.

"This is Xyneris," Kahli said.

Just then, three alien creatures stepped through the waterfall. An icy shiver broke through Jacquline's strong demeanor, intimidated by the menacing and dangerous appearance of who she guessed to be the captain, or leader of the group. He stared at Jacquline, the yellow slits of his eyes a sliver of dark intentions. The second, cat-like alien, didn't help ease her trepidation, as her dragon-like teeth and the fluid musical motion of her steps made her feel wholly inferior. The third eased Jacquline a bit, but like the others, made her quite uncomfortable. Other than the two strips of red hair that started at the tips of her eyes and stretched to the nape of her neck where they met and formed a ponytail that dropped to her buttocks, no other hair was present. Her nose sat on the base of her upper lip, and her hands had no nails. But it was the outfit that made Jacquline take a step back. A tight, turquoise leotard traced the contours of her thin, carved body, over which was a long purple skirt that sat loosely around her chiseled stomach and a red tunic, one side draped around near her elbow, the other comfortably sitting on her shoulder, covering only the upper portions of her body. As she slid next to the captain on the opposite side of the planet, Jacquline caught a glimpse of a star-shaped medallion strapped around her neck, sparkling under the light like glitter.

Her examination of the aliens ended when Jacquline caught them spying her as well. She stared into the woman's mesmerizing eyes — purple with red stripes that spread from the deathly black pupil to the middle of the pure white rim — and for the first time, she felt a sudden familiarity with not only her, but the rest of them as well.

"I would like to introduce you both to Qah-Shekel," Kahli said, breaking Jacquline from her state of deja vu. When Qah-Shekel bowed, Kahli insisted Ken and Jacquline do the same to convey their respect for him, though Ken knew his would only be a mere greeting, done in this case out of tradition and nothing more.

"This is DovenJadden," Kahli continued, gesturing to the cat, "and Sentilla, our pilot." Sentilla gave a quick nod. Jacquline hoped something would come back to her, and although the name didn't sound familiar, it echoed in the back of her mind as if it did.

"We have gathered here upon our arrival at Xyneris, the second moon of Gerinhale," Kahli continued. "It is a volcanically active moon as you can see by the current projection."

"This is live?" Jacquline asked, stunned.

"Of course," Kahli said. "The ship continually scans every inch of space within ten delias of the hull."

"How cool is that?" Jacquline said.

Kahli spoke with Qah-Shekel for a moment, after which, he looked back to Jacquline, the slits of his eyes narrowing (if that was even possible).

"Why is Tracey being held there?" Jacquline quickly asked, hoping to alleviate her awkwardness.

Kahli once again spoke to Qah-Shekel, but this time, the others joined in to what quickly became a heated debate. Unable to understand anything, Jacquline concentrated on the way each spoke, focusing mostly on Sentilla, who spoke with a seemingly muddled French, with clicks and caws in between, a stark contrast to both the gruff, hard syntax of Qah-Shekel and the softer purr of DovenJadden. When Sentilla turned to her, Jacquline shied away, blushing. Sentilla smiled and whispered to DovenJadden, who huffed a slight laughter and whispered back. The more it went on, the more irritated Jacquline became.

"Shut up," Jacquline finally said. Everyone fell silent.

"What is wrong?" Kahli said quickly.

"These two," Jacquline said, waving her hand at DovenJadden and Sentilla. "They're talking about me in their stupid alien tongues. It's rude. I want it to stop."

"They were not discussing you, Jacquline."

"Yeah, I'm sure. How do I know that?"

"All I can give you is my word."

"A lot of good that does me. I don't even know you. Just… tell them to keep their traps shut in front of me, okay?"

Kahli purred to DovenJadden and Sentilla, both of whom turned to Jacquline and bowed their heads graciously. Jacquline didn't know if it was an apology or a pity nod, so she accepted it by refusing to look at them.

"So," Ken said, breaking the awkwardness. "About Tracey?"

"We will get to her," Kahli said. "But we must first discuss something much more important. Qah-Shekel has given me privilege to provide you with all necessary information pertaining to your wife, and in effect, your daughter."

"My wife? You mean Stacey?" Ken's heart pounded.

"Of course. Are you ready to listen?"

"Yeah. More than ready."

"Good. You and Jacquline know her as Stacey, but the rest of the universe knows her as Keladrayia."

Jacquline rolled her eyes. "Ah, here we go."

"Wait… are you trying to tell me my *wife* is an alien?" Ken was as full of doubt as Jacquline, which surprised her.

"This may be difficult to comprehend, Kenneth, but I speak the truth. Your wife comes from the planet Trynoruus. She was christened Keladrayia on the day of her birth. When she had lived upon fifty revolutions of her sun, a prophecy was born."

"Fifty revolutions?" Ken interrupted. "How old is this Keladrayia?" He wasn't quite ready to acknowledge Stacey as an alien.

"If I am correct, I believe that she is around one hundred and seventy-six revolutions of her sun."

"A hundred and seventy — No. No." Ken didn't want to hear any more lies. He turned his back to Kahli and wrapped his arms around his chest. Jacquline smiled — Ken finally understood how she felt about him and his actions for the last four years.

"Inhabitants of Trynoruus mostly live to be more than three-hundred revolutions, Kenneth. It is basic knowledge." There was a pause before Kahli continued. "Around fifty revolutions of her sun, a prophecy was born. It stated that the child of the one with the blood of Jaxxa Rakala would become the most powerful living organism in the universe."

"What is Jaxxa Rakala?" Jacquline said, urging the story forward just to spite Ken. She was eager to find out how crazy this story would get.

"Jaxxa Rakala is a spirit. Legend recalls that Jaxxa Rakala was once the most powerful being in the universe. To prevent her from taking control of all star systems, she was captured and enslaved on Trynoruus, where she would serve her time before her execution."

"Wait a minute," Jacquline said. "That doesn't make any sense."

"What are you objecting to, may I ask?" Kahli said.

"If this Jaxxa Rakala was supposed to be so powerful, how in the hell was she captured, much less enslaved?"

"A very well thought-out question. Legend recalls that a gem, carved to precision with the blood of Jaxxa Rakala, was given to her as a gift. The power of this gem would hinder Jaxxa Rakala from using any powers when it was in her presence."

"Like Kryptonite?" Jacquline said, chuckling in disbelief.

"You speak of the Kryptonian Kal-El? A fictional character in entertainment."

"Yeah," Jacquline said, a bit stunned and impressed. "Never mind. Go on."

Kahli nodded. "To the surprise of many, the gem worked better than expected. What they did not understand, or wished to ignore, was that Jaxxa Rakala was only deceiving those who wanted her dead. The gem did work, but was not as powerful as she made it seem. Before she died, Jaxxa Rakala expelled her spirit from her body and encased it into the gem, claiming that the only person able to touch and acquire the gem would be the Jistryt, or king, of Trynoruus and his descendants."

"Why him?" Jacquline asked, suddenly intrigued by the tale.

"It is said to be because his spirit was the most honest and true."

"And Jaxxa Rakala's spirit lived?"

"Yes."

"So, in essence, she *wanted* to die?"

"It would seem as such."

"Why?"

"I will come by that answer soon. But first... I believe that you are both familiar with the gem I speak of, are you not?"

"You mean the green one?" Ken said, turning back to Kahli. He still thought the story being told was bogus, but thinking back on his life with Stacey, he couldn't really object to any of it either. "The one she wore around her neck?"

"That was the Kryptonite?" Jacquline said.

"We saw it earlier," Ken interjected, "on the planet?"

"Yes, it is one and the same."

"Planet?" Jacquline said. "You were actually on an alien planet?"

Ken smirked, proud of the fact that his daughter now saw a glimmer of the man he always wished he could have been for her.

"The reason you were so drawn to it," Kahli continued, "is because the gem is said to have great powers of attraction as it seeks the one with the blood. Anyone within its vicinity for extended amounts of time will become addicted to its presence."

"Like a drug?" Jacquline said.

"Yes. Very much the same."

"So, what happens when it finds 'the one'?"

"That is yet to be learned."

"Great. So what does Tracey have to do with any of this?"

"The prophecy was stated as such:

" 'The universe will find a new power. For there is a life, born and raised in the wake of Jaxxa Rakala. This life, filled with blood and power, will give birth to another. The dual moon of a crescent will shine and the path will show along her body. If this birth should take place, and the child is united with the gem, her power will become infinite, ceased to be matched by any other.'

"This prophecy made its way quickly throughout the suns and a search for the one with the blood of Jaxxa Rakala began."

"And I assume that the one with the blood was Stacey," Ken said.

"Legend recalls that, not only did the Jistryt execute Jaxxa Rakala, but it was from the womb of his beloved from whence she grew. The world believed it was her who passed on the power but they were wrong."

"It was the king," Jacquline said.

"Very well deduced, Jacquline. It is said that the Jistryt was the one with the blood and once again helped give birth to another daughter. But the Jistryt's secret would not be learned, as the gem would always be worn around the daughter's neck so as not to exhibit such powers as Jaxxa Rakala once had."

Ken lowered his head; he couldn't deny the story any longer. Tears formed but were held back. He didn't want to look weak in front of the group.

"Many searched for the woman who would give birth to the prophecy, but all failed. That is until a male, born and left for dead on the second moon of Gerinhale, found the key to the prophecy. 'Born and raised in the wake of Jaxxa Rakala' could only mean one thing — the one that would give birth to power was living on the very planet from which Jaxxa Rakala was born and killed.

"A new search was born and new rumors arose. Trynoruus was taken siege by races across the galaxy. Male, female and child alike were killed or stolen, and residents of the planet fled. Some made it out; others were destroyed. With the help of the Jistryt, Keladrayia escaped as she neared the age of eighty revolutions of her sun.

"Soon after, the Jistryt was captured and interrogated about the gem. Under duress, he revealed his true nature, and it was learned that Keladrayia was the child of the prophecy. A new search was executed, but it was soon rumored that she had been killed. In the wake of Keladrayia's destruction, a new prophecy was born:

" 'The one that will give birth to the child of power is alive and well in the far reaches of a galaxy unknown. Destroy her and destroy the power. Find her and find the power.'

"The child of Gerinhale made every effort to find her first, for he did not want to destroy her. He wanted to nurture her, to make her his own so as to bear the child of life himself. Every sun at the far reaches of the universe were explored, but after several of your Earth years, rumors arose that the gem had been found. The search for Keladrayia ceased, giving way to a new pursuit, for the search was no longer about destruction but about power, pure and unhindered."

"But I thought you said no one except Keladrayia could touch it?"

"That is truth," Kahli said, showing a hint of a smile, "but most figured that since trying to find the child was fruitless, if they could acquire the gem, then in effect, the child would eventually seek it out and come to them. A very sound theory except for one problem — whenever someone got close, the power of the gem took over their minds. All they thought about from that point on was the gem and they would die to acquire it — and even more so to keep it."

"And it was on this planet you went to the whole time?" Jacquline said.

"No. Qah-Shekel was hired to track and acquire the gem. In return, he would receive answers to the destruction of his home planet, to the death of his parents, and whether any of his race still exist."

"I'm guessing you found it."

"We did. But when we landed to make the trade, it turned out to be a trap. Qah-Shekel was never going to receive his payment. It was simply a way to bring him out of hiding — to destroy him."

"And now that this thing has the gem…" Ken said, unable to finish.

"I saw your daughter, Kenneth. She holds half the mark of the dual crescent on her cheek. If she is the daughter of Keladrayia, and Eyrixano, the child of Gerinhale, allows her to come into contact with the gem, then we could be in for a change of power that no one is ready for. It is believed that this is the reason Jaxxa Rakala wished to die. With her spirit now guiding the gem, it would not hinder power any longer."

"What's going to happen?" Jacquline said, more eager than ever to jump into action and rescue Tracey.

"After gifting the gem back to Jaxxa Rakala, Eyrixano could very well be granted command over Tracey. She would become his servant, his weapon of choice in order to claim everything as his own."

"No. I can't believe this. It can't be true."

"But it is truth, Kenneth."

"No!" Ken paced the back of the room. He knew it was true but he wanted all of it to be a dream. He just wanted his old life back.

"May I ask you a question?" Kahli asked.

Ken waved his hands with a shrug.

"Has your daughter, Tracey, ever done anything mysterious? Has she done anything, or acted in any way, that could not be explained or seemed unbelievable when mentioned?"

Ken lowered his head, taking in a deep breath. *She ripped half the skin off one of the boy's faces; he'll never be able to see out of his left eye again; she threw him across the playground; he has a collapsed lung and may not make it through the night.*

Even if he didn't want to believe it, everything made sense. This was far from a dream.

— 6 —

Lark rested her head in her palm as she continued to attempt making sense of the nonsense. Numbers, words and phrases that didn't seem to have any relation to each other flowed page after page. The longer it took, the more it felt like a chore, and Lark was beginning to believe that she was given this assignment, not because they needed her help, but to keep her out of their way. This entire thing was Kahli's subtle way of telling her that she was right — she was no use to anyone.

A row of repeating numbers changed all of that.
<<369-4488-31051-003-612612-3 death>><<258-9393-43773-107-789987-8 survive>>

<<369-4488-51051-003-612612-3 death>><<268-9393-43773-107-789987-8 survive>>
<<369-4488-51051-003-612612-3 death>><<268-9393-43773-107-789987-8 survive>>
life must survive — the one is death
<<369-4488-51051-003-612612-3 death>><<268-9393-43773-107-789987-8 survive>>
<<369-4488-51051-003-612612-3 death>><<268-9393-43773-107-789987-8 survive>>
<<369-4488-51051-003-612612-3 death>><<268-9393-43773-107-789987-8 survive>>
<<369-4488-51051-003-612612-3 death>><<268-9393-43773-107-789987-8 survive>>
<<369-4488-51051-003-612612-3 death>><<268-9393-43773-107-789987-8 survive>>

Each time Lark read the numbers, she became more convinced that there was something hidden within them. She scrolled back over the previous pages, reading every analogy, every statement, every set of numbers looking for anything that had even the slightest relation. After reaching the first page without anything to show for it, Lark realized she'd been going the wrong way. Her drive to find the answer heightened two-fold as she worked her way back to the set of numbers and beyond, instantly finding a passage on the following page that she knew had everything to do with the numbers.

> *Death comes for a group of three — four can help, but five is better.*
> *In three there can be no hope, but when six come together, one will be saved.*
> *Sound must be heard, love must be seen and the key must be broken or all will fail.*

> *Three is death — Eight is life.*
> *Find the Balance for our future.*

She reread the passage several times before going back to the numbers to make some sense — some pattern — out of them. There had to be something and she would find it, even if she had to make it up just to prove —

to whom? —

that she was worth something. She counted the numbers listed — twenty-two. No help. There were two sets of rows — three and five — that again were no help. Then she counted the groups of numbers within each row — three, four, five, three, six, one.

A group of three, four can help, five is better. Three is no hope, six come together, one saved.

Lark's pulse raced with excitement, yet it was all still completely obtuse. She decided it best to let Kahli know what she had found, even if it made her look incompetent. Her thoughts were no longer on her selfishness, but on Tracey's life. If she had to look foolish in order to save her, so be it.

She swiped up the communicator. "Rega, pick up, This is Lark."

The silence was deadening. "Rega, can you hear me?" she said impatiently.

"Proceed, Lark," Kahli's voice finally rang out over the communicator.

Lark jumped with enthusiasm. "I think I found something."

"Give me a second."

Lark tapped her foot on the floor, staring at the numbers and the passage. Something was there — something that she was destined to find. *But what the hell is it?*

"Lark." Kahli's voice came from behind Lark. She turned quickly. The wall had disappeared in favor of a video screen.

"Rega. I need to see if this makes sense to you."

"Is the information still on your screen?"

"Yeah. The page on the screen and the one just after it."

"Acknowledged. I'm downloading the information now."

— 7 —

Kahli tapped the holopad that she had pulled out from behind Lark's floating head. Within moments, the projection of Xyneris gave way to a scroll of numbers and texts.

"What am I looking for?" Kahli asked Lark.

"The first passage on the second page and the series of numbers at the bottom of the first."

Kahli waved her hands over both pages, enlarging the two pieces of information Lark had mentioned and resting them side-by-side. "Tell me your theories, Lark."

"I found the numerical pattern first," Lark said rapidly. "There are eight groups of numbers separated into two series of six sets each. These sets are in groups of three, four, five, three, six and one. The passage that follows has that same set of numbers, in order."

Kahli scanned over her findings. "What is your conclusion on this final sentence: Sound must be heard, love must be seen and the key must be broken?"

"It has to be a message."

"What type of message?"

"Maybe it means we have to listen to each other," Jacquline said.

Kahli nodded, her eyes never leaving the text. "And the rest, Jacquline?"

Jacquline froze, feeling as if she was suddenly back in school being called on to answer a question she didn't know the answer to. But instead of tossing her the bird and spitting out a sarcastic retort that would wind up in a one-way ticket to the principal's office, she took a breath, read the passage over again and spit out the first thought that crossed her mind. "I think it's telling us that we need to listen to each other if we want to find the love we have for one another."

"Then, and only then, will the key for survival be broken," Lark finished.

Ken looked at Jacquline, stunned. He didn't know if he should be proud or scared.

"A strong theory," Kahli said, scanning the text again. As she spoke to Qah-Shekel, Ken walked to Lark.

"Do you really think any of this means anything?" he whispered.

"I hope so," Lark said.

"So, what's any of this have to do with Tracey?"

Lark suddenly smiled and furrowed her brow.

Ken could tell she had found something. "What is it?"

"Hold on." Lark's head disappeared.

Ken tried desperately to find her, even though he knew it was impossible. He jumped in fright as he finally noticed Kahli standing behind him. "Don't do that," he said, catching his breath. "It's not nice to sneak up on people."

"I am terribly sorry," Kahli said. "Where is Lark?"

"I don't —"

"I'm here," Lark said quickly as her bright, cheerful face popped back in. "I think I know what these numbers are."

"Continue."

"Okay, bear with me. I took another look at the patterns. Each one ends with a single number — one for death, one for life. I believe this might be referring to Tracey. As it is right now, in relation to us, she is one."

"*The* one," Ken whispered. It was still painful to think about.

"What?" Lark said.

"As I have told Kenneth, I believe very strongly that Tracey is Jaxxa Rakala."

"Who or what is Jaxxa Rakala?"

"In short, she will bring great destruction if joined together with the gem." It took several minutes for Kahli to relay the story once again to Lark. With every new piece of information, Lark grew more excited, never once doubting her tale.

At the same time, Ken recalled several events, such as the time when Stacey was struck by a car and not one bone was broken, or when Tracey was two and fell into their pool, swimming like she'd done it for fifty years. The signs had always been there, he had simply refused to see them — or was possibly forced not to by the gem. One way or the other, he had been blinded to everything that had happened. But now he knew the truth, and in his heart, it didn't matter if they were aliens or not, he truly loved both Stacey and Tracey, and he was not about to let them slip through his fingers again.

"I think I have it now," Lark said. "If Tracey *is* this Jaxxa Rakala, then she is definitely this last number."

"I concur."

"How many of you were there before you picked us up?"

Kahli nodded, wholly aware of Lark's theory but willing to indulge her. "Six."

"And now there are only four?"

"Yes. Naja-Leku and Massanah were killed."

"And until Tracey was taken, there were four of us."

"Three and a four, combined to make seven."

"And seven will save one," Jacquline chirped, loving that she had figured it out.

"Yes," Kahli said, "but the words say six will save one, not seven."

"Then there has to be something else," Lark said, looking over the screen again. She quickly turned back around.

"How many were left on the ship when you and Ken left on the planet?"

Kahli didn't miss a beat. "There were five. Sentilla, Naja-Leku, Massanah, Jacquline and yourself."

"Okay, bear with me. At that time, Jacquline and I were locked up. That would leave three roaming the ship. Death comes for a group of three. Four can help, but five is better. He must have been referring to that moment."

"That is why Naja-Leku said you would bring death to us all," Kahli said. Lark and Ken were taken aback. It was no wonder why Qah-Shekel didn't trust them. "If you were not rescued," Kahli continued, "DovenJadden would not have left the ship and there would have been four of us on board during the attack."

"If he saw this coming, why didn't he stop it?"

"Naja-Leku was a genius, a good friend, but a coward," Kahli said. "Do you have any thoughts on the last three number groups?"

"I'm not sure," Lark said.

"Well, it's kind of obvious, isn't it?" Jacquline said.

"What is obvious, Jacquline?" Kahli said.

Jacquline walked to the screen. "Keeping with your number theory, we have three, six, and one left. In order to save *the one*, we must be a group of six. If we are anything but, we will die."

"It is a good theory," Kahli said. She took a moment to relay the information to Qah-Shekel. Ken took the opportunity to give Lark an affectionate wink, turning her smile into a loving gaze.

"Qah-Shekel has agreed. The six of us will go down to the surface to find the gem."

Ken's heart sank. "The gem? What about Tracey?"

"I am sorry, Kenneth. It has been determined that the gem is our first priority. Your daughter is of a second nature."

"Second nature, my ass. You promised. You promised you would help save my daughter."

"And we will," Kahli said. "But our first goal must be the gem."

"A promise is trust, Kahli. If she dies…" Ken couldn't finish the thought. Kahli had rescued him on more than one occasion. No matter how much he wanted Tracey back safe, he couldn't look at Kahli and threaten her.

"Jacquline stays here," Ken said quickly.

"The hell I am. Tracey's just as important to me as she is to you. I'm going."

"And what about me?" Lark asked.

"If what you say is true, the group must be six. One will have to stay on board."

Lark's bright spirit completely faded with those words.

"Can't one of you stay?" Ken said.

"DovenJadden's our best in combat and we need Sentilla to pilot our transport vessel through the thick, rocky atmosphere. It comes down to Lark or Jacquline. One must stay."

Ken looked at Jacquline, who immediate_y shot Ken a disapproving glare. "No way," she said. "Don't even think about it. She's *my* sister."

Ken sighed. He thought Jacquline was improving, but she was still her stubborn, selfish, inconsiderate self.

"We cannot argue now," Kahli said. "We must figure out our plan of strategy." Kahli gurgled something to Qah-Shekel. He nodded and talked to the group.

Kahli tapped a few keys on the holopad next to Lark's face and the planet's projection came back to life.

"By looking at the structure of the surface," Kahli said, "it seems that the best possible landing site will be here." Kahli repeated her statement to Qah-Shekel and the rest of the group as the projection zoomed in on a spot on the surface heavily surrounded by mountainous rocky structures.

"If you look closely, there is an opening passage, here, that leads into a series of caves." The view turned inward, highlighting a crevice in the side of the mountain. "I suspect this crevice to be more than three meters high but only a meter thick."

"Doesn't give us much room, does it," Jacquline said, trying to hold back her feelings of familiarity.

"No, but it is enough. Once we get through the crevice, there should be tunnels large enough for seven vermon to march side together."

"Side-by-side," Jacquline corrected.

"I am sorry?"

"Never mind," Jacquline giggled.

"So, from this, there's no way of knowing what's inside?" Ken asked.

"The only one who knew exactly was Naja-Leku. He was a prisoner here for some time. He held extensive documentation from his escape through the core."

"What happened to it?" Ken said, hoping this might be Lark's chance of joining the mission.

"Most were destroyed during the escape. The rest have been hidden. I am afraid Naja-Leku was the only one who knew where to find them."

"There's no way to know where he might have put them?"

"There are several, but we have no means of doing so. We have less time. We need to move quickly or we may be caught in orbit."

"Caught in orbit?" Jacquline questioned.

"Yes. Our presence will be located."

"Oh," Jacquline said with a smirk. "We'll be found out."

Kahli gazed at Jacquline, quizzically. "I assume so."

Ken turned away to take a moment to himself. He desperately wanted to find those documents for Lark's sake, but to do that might cost him Tracey. He wiped his mouth strongly, defeated, and then heard DovenJadden purring softly as she tapped at the hologram. Streams of code flowed across the map of Xyneris, each line leading to more heightened, quicker purring under the cut of her thinned brow.

"What's wrong with her?" Ken finally asked.

Kahli purred to her and viewed the information. DovenJadden turned her back to the group and kicked the nearest wall. Qah-Shekel's mood was suddenly as sullen as Lark's (even though, to Ken, Qah-Shekel was always in a sullen mood).

"Can you translate that to English?" Ken said.

"One moment." Kahli whipped her fingers over the information and the code flashed into English. It was a list of several different types of elements that were in the atmosphere. Ken recognized some — oxygen, carbon, nitrogen — but most were unfamiliar to him.

"Those carbon dioxide levels look pretty high," Ken said anxiously.

"I thoroughly examined your physiology. There is no immediate danger."

"No *immediate* danger?" Ken rebutted.

"If you remain on the surface for an extended amount of time, there could be noticeable physical signs of degradation to your body, especially your lungs. But we will not be there long enough for any substantial injuries to take place."

Ken was worried but held strong. "What is that," he asked. "K-L-three?"

"It is a liquid gas that contains high amounts of chlorine and phosphorous."

"Is it dangerous?"

"Not to you, but DovenJadden's blood is allergic to K-L-three. If she comes into contact with it, her body will boil and burn from the inside out. Her lungs will disintegrate within minutes of prolonged exposure and her brain matter will melt. It is a disturbing and painful death. I am afraid she will not be able to go on our mission."

Ken felt like pumping his fist and letting out a scream of excitement but he knew the gesture would be rude and arrogant, so he held his joy inside. Lark, too, restrained herself, though it was clear that she was shocked with enthusiasm.

"Which means, in order to keep our group of six secure, Lark must come along." Kahli turned to Lark. "Are you up for the task?"

Lark cracked a smile, unable to hide her emotion any longer. "Most definitely." DovenJadden shook her head, purred some angry epithet and stormed out of the room.

"Let us be on our way," Kahli said. Qah-Shekel left the room with Sentilla. As Kahli took a moment to review further information on the planet, Lark and Ken stared excitedly at one another.

Jacquline stood behind them, unable to show the same level of excitement. They were all about to land on an alien planet to save her alien sister from an evil alien who may have been the one who kidnapped her alien stepmother. It was all so unbelievable and she finally realized they were all in way over their heads.

— 8 —

The cargo bay looked like it had been the center of a war. Most of everything had been charred or otherwise destroyed and what was left had been piled up in a corner. DovenJadden added to that pile as she cleared a path through the debris in order to reach the docking tunnels. Jacquline helped as best she could but she didn't do much except admire most of what she picked up, not wanting to toss anything aside. Everything was so rich with design and color; if only she could bring just one of these items back to Earth, she'd be rich, not to mention famous. She could live the life she always dreamed of and would never again need anything else — except Tracey. None of it would mean a thing if she didn't have her.

Meanwhile, Ken walked up to his ship and rubbed his hand across the hull. It was rough and hot and looked ready to rip apart at the seams. Just by its appearance alone, he was surprised it had lasted as long as it did.

"We were lucky," Lark said, coming up behind him and rubbing his shoulders.

Ken peered at Lark's sweet, sincere grin. "It worked. That's what matters."

Qah-Shekel pronounced his entrance with a grandiose authority. Each step was that of a leader, proud and determined. Sentilla kept pace alongside him, innocent yet daring, ready for anything. Kahli was a few steps behind carrying a large box that looked to be several hundred pounds, but to her was as light as a feather. They walked directly across the room to the main docking tunnel. It branched out into three separate, smaller platforms, each with their own metal door that seemed out of place in relation to the rest of the ship. It looked more like a submarine than an intergalactic space cruiser. Qah-Shekel pulled up a small latch just to the side of the large round handle in the center of the hatch to unlock it and then spun it open, revealing the inside of a second, smaller (and for Jacquline, much less-impressive) transport ship. Sentilla followed him inside after chatting nonsense to DovenJadden.

"Guess that's our cue," Ken said. He walked Lark to the hatch as Kahli entered. They stopped, unsure if they should step in or wait to be invited. Then again, it may have simply been the trepidation of getting into yet another sardine can of a ship. "Shall we go?" Ken asked Lark.

"Hell, yeah," Jacquline said, rushing past them into the ship. She was taken aback by the size of the interior, which was made even smaller by several pipes that ran the course of the walls, etched by a web of wires and the exposure of the ship's guts. The floor coverings were thin and scaly, but felt soft to the touch. It all ruined Jacquline's perception of what an alien transport ship would be like, especially in comparison to the mother ship. With all of the technology at their disposal, this was the best they could come up with?

"This doesn't seem very safe," Ken said as he led Lark into the vessel, his hand resting gently on the small of her back.

"I agree," Kahli said from a few feet away. She tapped at one of the smaller pipes and pushed a few wires in between another set of pipes nearby. "But the less equipment we have on board, the less likely we will be detected. This is the most appropriate ship for the task we are about to embark on."

Kahli stopped tapping and turned to them. "Please, sit," she said as she stepped a few feet to the cockpit, which looked more like an escape pod. Sentilla strapped herself into the seat as Kahli whispered to her.

There were no other seats present, and though Qah-Shekel sat against the pipes just in front of them, it wasn't clear if he was strapped in or not.

Kahli turned back to them as the ship hummed to life. "Please, sit."

"Where?" Jacquline said.

"You may sit wherever you find comfortable," Kahli said, taking her own seat next to Qah-Shekel. As she leaned back against the pipes, fish line-thin wires shot from behind them and curled around her. Seeing this, Jacquline took the initiative and sat down across from Kahli. She expected a little pain but, as she settled up against the pipes, only a slight breeze of air whipped past her cheeks, followed by a little pinch on her upper shoulders.

"We cannot take off until you are seated and secured," Kahli said to Ken and Lark, who stood partly amazed, partly freaked out by the whole thing.

"It's fine," Jacquline said, shifting her upper body as much as the straps would allow. "It doesn't hurt."

Ken and Lark looked at each other for support and then sat next to Jacquline. They couldn't move once the wires had whipped across their shoulders, but to their surprise, they felt rather comfortable.

DovenJadden purred what Jacquline hoped was a farewell and then slammed the hatch shut and locked it. Soon after, they heard a hiss, a pop and a few unnerving noises that gave Jacquline the chills.

"It is okay," Kahli said, hoping to keep them from panicking. "It is only the ship's pressure system disengaging. It is quite normal."

Jacquline nodded, trying to convey a brave face even though she didn't feel as safe as she would have liked. She felt a bit queasy as the transport vessel pulled away from the ship with a little shake. She closed her eyes and thought of Tracey, which helped tremendously to calm her nerves. When she opened them again, the ship was zipping smoothly toward the red planet.

"Are you okay?" Lark whispered through the silence.

"Yeah," Jacquline said. "Just nerves."

Lark nodded. "I'm right there with you."

No one spoke for the remainder of the trip, even after the heat became so intense, Jacquline felt she was swimming in her own sweat. Recollections of her near-death experience pushed her nerves to shake along with the vibration of the ship's turbulence. Across from her, the slits of Qah-Shekel's eyes were closed and Kahli looked to be in a trance, although, as far as Jacquline knew, she could have been powered down. She chuckled nervously and turned to Ken, who didn't seem to be focused on anything. Jacquline figured he was thinking about Stacey, as he always did, but upon deeper examination, she noticed Lark holding his hand tightly as she rested her head on his shoulder. Ken ran his other hand through her hair in the same way he used to do with her mother; as he used to do to Stacey; as he always did to Tracey. It was in this that Jacquline replaced her nervous trepidation with spite. She couldn't recall Ken ever giving her that type of protection or love.

The turbulence drastically heightened as they descended further toward the surface. Lark and Ken held each other in a tight embrace; Qah-Shekel held onto the grates below him to balance himself; Kahli didn't even flinch; and Jacquline kept her eyes on the planet to divert her attention away from it all. Red smoke covered any sightline they once had and Jacquline was curious as to how Sentilla could pilot the ship in such dense smoke. Then again, she was an alien and for all Jacquline knew, Sentilla had some sixth sense or weird ability to help her through it.

When the ship finally passed through the smoke, a large mountain peak appeared in front of them. Jacquline screamed and covered her head as Sentilla maneuvered the ship past the mountain with ease and fluidity. Even still, Jacquline kept her eyes closed for the rest of the descent. She didn't want to face anyone after her childish outburst. Not even when the ship landed softly on the planet did Jacquline want to open her eyes, but she knew Tracey might not ever be saved if she didn't toughen up and fight through her embarrassment. When the stress of the straps vanished from her shoulders, Jacquline was hesitant to stand. The reality of everything hit her hard as Qah-Shekel opened the box Kahli had carried with her. A soft silver glow came from inside and Jacquline's body went stiff. The only time she could remember being this frightened was when she had contemplated suicide. Her savior that time wasn't going to save her this time.

"Jacquline?" Lark stood over her, holding out her hand. "Come on."

Jacquline felt the cold sweat lingering upon Lark's fingers and almost hit her head on one of the low-bearing pipes as Lark pulled her to her feet.

"Oh. Sorry," Lark said. "Are you okay?"

"Yeah," Jacquline said softly. "Yeah." She had trouble saying anything else.

Kahli was the first to leave the ship after opening the hatch. Ken and Lark lurked just inside, taking in the view and the heat of the planet. Qah-Shekel handed Ken a round ball and then pushed past him, agitated by his indecisiveness. It was somewhat clear with tiny holes littering the exterior and streaks of silver running through it. Sentilla finished securing the ship and found her way through the group and off the ship.

Jacquline stepped up to Ken to admire his new gift.

"It's warm," Ken said.

"We must hurry," Kahli said. "Our mission awaits."

Tracey's painful face as she hung chained on the red-hot wall flashed through Jacquline's mind, igniting a fresh surge of bravery. "Right," she said and jumped down to the planets surface. Her eyes burned as the wind whipped past her.

Ken and Lark followed quickly. Upon landing, Lark lost her footing on the soft ground and knocked Jacquline over. The dust was extremely hot and course, forcing Jacquline to her knees quickly, hissing over the painful sting in her arms.

"I'm sorry," Lark said as she tried to help Jacquline to her feet. Jacquline shook her off with a scream. She grabbed her arms and held them tight across her chest.

"I'm sorry," Lark said again. "I'm sorry."

"What happened?" Ken said.

"The planet burns," Kahli answered. "Do not let it come into contact with your skin."

"Thanks for the warning," Jacquline said through gritted teeth.

"You were not exposed long enough. The pain will dissipate."

"Yeah, says you." Jacquline wouldn't let go of her arms; they stung too deep.

"We must be on our way," Kahli said.

Lark cautiously avoided touching Jacquline's arms as she gently helped her up.

"Stay close and do not stray. There are many dangers awaiting us."

Qah-Shekel was already thirty yards away when Sentilla pushed the hatch closed and locked it tight. Ken stayed within inches of Kahli while Lark and Jacquline took their time behind them, Lark needing to ensure Jacquline's safety.

As Kahli had said, the pain in Jacquline's arm did dissipate rather quickly and she was finally able to admire her surroundings. The sky above was a bright orange-red with a gray haze of black ash hovering throughout. The mountains were hundreds of miles in length, plastered in deep red with signs of both decay and rebirth. Large cracks and crevices, some smaller than Jacquline's thumb, some almost as large as the landscape, were sorted like a patchwork of divine grace. Clumps of both smooth and course igneous rock filled the crevices, though for the lava to have cooled among the planet's incomparable heat, it could only mean that no matter how hot it got on the surface, what was underneath, and what they were about to descend into, was going to be a lot hotter.

By the time Sentilla caught up with the group next to the fissure, Jacquline's arms merely tickled. She checked for scars or burns but couldn't see any.

Kahli translated what Qah-Shekel grumbled. "We are only able to slide through one at a time. When we reach the open end, no one is to do anything until all six of us have made it through. Is that understood?"

"I'm not going anywhere without you," Ken said. Jacquline wasn't sure if he was frightened or merely sucking up to Kahli to make sure she didn't back down from her promise.

"When we are through, continue to stay close. We will hunt down the gem, and once acquired, will decide on our quest for your daughter."

"I still don't get how that stupid gem is more important than Tracey."

"Your daughter is the only thing in the universe that can effectively use the gem. We find the gem, we find your daughter."

"What?" Ken calmed slightly. He was prepared to listen.

"Legend recalls that the gem will react positively to the presence of Jaxxa Rakala. If we follow the signs the gem emits correctly, it will act as a compass. To keep my promise, you must trust my decisions."

"The gem will lead us to Tracey?" Ken asked.

When Kahli nodded an affirmative, Ken couldn't argue any longer. If she was honest in her assessment, and the gem was the key to finding Tracey, he would help them find it. No questions asked.

"We do not have much time before Eyrixano finds out that we have landed. Are we in agreement?"

Ken nodded, followed by acknowledgments from Lark and Jacquline.

"Good," Kahli said. She then, along with Qah-Shekel and Sentilla, pressed her fingers together and rubbed them in a circle. Once they confirmed the communications check, Qah-Shekel started to point at each member of the crew in succession as he roared out his orders.

"Qah-Shekel says that you will go first," Kahli relayed to Ken.

"Why me?"

"You are in possession of the Jeresiah."

"The what?"

"The Jeresiah," she said, pointing to the ball in Ken's hand. "It is the weapon of choice for those who do not seek to destroy, but only calm and seduce."

"Like a stun gun," Jacquline said.

"Precisely. It is very potent but not dangerous. When you reach the other side, hold it above your head and say, 'Kallo-nia.' A bright flash will occur and every foe within ten meters will fall unconscious."

"Why'd he give it to me?"

"It is given to the sacrificial lamb. Usually expendable, worth less than the rest of the group."

"That's just perfect," Ken mumbled.

"My advice would be to do as he says," Kahli responded.

Ken glared at Qah-Shekel for a moment and then turned to Lark. She nodded and smiled. "Good luck," she whispered.

"Whatever happens, we find her." It wasn't clear if he was speaking to Lark or Jacquline, but they both nodded. For a second, Jacquline felt the need to hug him, but before she could do anything, Ken had entered the fissure, barely able to slide his body through.

"You are next," Kahli said to Lark, who took a small, deep breath. She squeezed Jacquline's shoulder and entered the fissure. When she had disappeared, Qah-Shekel followed, Sentilla right on his heels.

"Do you wish to go first, or shall I?" Kahli said.

Jacquline looked back and forth between Kahli and the fissure. She knew it was impossible but didn't want to go alone. "Can we go together?" she asked anyway.

"I do not see how?"

Jacquline swept Kahli's hand in hers and held it up, gripping it as tight as she could. "Stay close," she said.

Kahli smiled. They walked to the fissure and carefully stepped in, Jacquline staying in step right behind Kahli, unwilling to let go.

— 9 —

The walls were scorching hot and only grew hotter the deeper Ken went. His skin burned even as he tried hard to stay away from the jagged edges. He wanted to stop and slide back out, tell the entire group he was through, but that would be the end of Tracey. His only option was to keep moving forward.

To his relief, the heat dissipated as the fissure grew wider, opening into a tunnel that he could walk freely. Aside from the faint glow of lava seeping through the cracks in the wall, it was still completely dark and Ken was unsure of how far he was supposed to go before he stopped.

After a few more yards, a small red glow appeared in front of him, answering his question. He picked up speed, wanting desperately to get to the end and complete his task, if only to prove that he was worth more than what Qah-Shekel deemed him to be. Deep down, though, he half-expected to see Tracey there, waiting for him with open arms, an embrace he couldn't wait to acquire. So much so that he tripped over a jagged rock and fell. The Jeresiah bounced through the tunnel a few yards before stopping. Ken understood what Jacquline had been screaming about as he felt the pain well up in his arms. It wasn't quite as bad as the burn from the force field, but it was still quite terrible. He thought about waiting for the pain to subside before moving on, or at the very least, for someone else to arrive, but that would make him look even weaker than he already appeared to be. He couldn't let that happen.

He searched the ground blindly with his fingertips for the Jeresiah. It felt almost like touching a pot of boiling hot water over and over, but if he didn't find it, and there was danger at the end of the tunnel, everyone would be in a world of hurt, and it would be all his fault. Luckily, he found the Jeresiah tucked in a small crack in the wall. When he tried to lift it, the surface was far too smooth and slippery to get any grip whatsoever, so he kicked at the wall, which came apart easier than he expected. The Jeresiah fell free and Ken picked it up, hoping that dropping it didn't cause it to somehow malfunction. After wiping it down (though the idea of there being any residue on it was absurd), Ken quickly, but cautiously, made his way to the red cavern. It was extremely cool in comparison to the fissure — and even the planet's surface — and had a ceiling that seemed to go on forever. There were several tunnels leading out of the cavern and the possibility that Kahli would split them up was a great one, as even she probably wouldn't know which path would lead them to the gem. It wouldn't matter, though, if there were vermon waiting for them on the other side. His job was to make sure that wasn't the case. He raised the Jeresiah over his head.

"Kallo-nia!" Instantly, a bright flash of light shot from the ball in all directions, surrounding the room and traveling down each open pathway with motive. Ken dropped to his knees as the shockwave blast was more than he could bear. It only took a few seconds for the flash to recede, but he held the ball above his head and waited — for anyone.

— 10 —

Jacquline's breath was heavy. She could feel the sweat pour from her forehead like water from a faucet. Her hair sat stuck against her skin and her grip on Kahli kept slipping. She hoped they would come out of it sooner rather than later or else she might not make it to the end. As her eyes fell heavy and her steps felt numb, the heat lightened up and the air around her grew cooler. She still felt a little queasy but it was a relief. She was now confident that she was capable of handling whatever this planet threw at her in order to see this venture through to the end.

"Is that the end?" she moaned, spying a red light ahead.

"I believe so. If your father has done as we have asked, we should be out of any harm."

Kahli walked faster as the tunnel opened up. Jacquline was relieved that she was finally able to walk next to her. As they neared the end of the tunnel, they could see Ken kneeling with the Jeresiah over his head.

"Kenneth, are you okay?" Kahli called out.

Ken looked up and lowered his arms.

"What took you so long?" Ken said as Kahli and Jacquline ran up to him.

"We moved as fast as we could," Kahli said. "Where are the others?"

Jacquline let her hand slide away from Kahli and stepped back. All she wanted to do was relax her body. She sat down, avoiding the touch of the ground against her skin as best she could.

"What do you mean?" Ken said.

"Qah-Shekel and Sentilla. They were through the fissure before us."

"They never got here," Ken said. His confusion slowly turned to fear as he knew what might be next.

"And what of Lark?"

"No," Ken said, disappointed. "They all went through before you?"

"Yes. Jacquline and I were the last through the fissure."

"Well, what happened to them?"

"I do not know."

Ken threw his arms up in disgust. "So what do we do now?"

A pause. "We wait."

— 11 —

Lark moved at a snail's pace as she crawled through the ever-narrowing space of the tunnel. Except for the faint light from the reading on her cast (29% complete), her confines were pitch black and she continually struck her head on the low-hanging stalagmites. Her face and arm hurt so much that they burned icy, leaving them nearly numb, but she forced herself to stay alert so she could reach the dim light shining through a small fissure in the floor several yards in front of her. At first, she wasn't sure if it would be big enough, but to her relief, it was just large enough for her thin frame to squeeze through. She took hold of a small crevice just under the floor and steadied herself as she pushed her head through. The cave was extremely small and didn't have any opening or passages, which was odd, since there was no sign of Ken either. Was she in the right place? She thought about the possibility that Ken had skipped right past this cave (since he wouldn't have been able to fit through if he tried) and kept moving forward, wondering if she should do the same. But the pain in her body and her mental stability told her otherwise. She needed to get out of the tunnel and into the open, if for nothing more than to breathe again. If Ken had kept going, she would rest here and catch up with him once she felt better.

As she pulled her body through, the walls gripped her as if it were trying hard to keep her out. *This must be what a baby feels like,* she laughed as she slipped her chest past the opening and took a moment to breathe. *Time to push.* As her thighs passed through the fissure, Lark lost her grip on the wall. She landed hard on her back, knocking the wind right out of her. It felt like an eternity of breathless struggle, so when she finally pulled in that first bite of air, it was overwhelmingly satisfying.

Lark had only the pinch of heat to keep her company as the minutes ticked away. Her sense of loneliness intensified with the wait and the thought that she would be left behind to die on this godforsaken volcanic rock. She tried to push those thoughts out of her mind but one question kept pulling it back: *Where the hell was everyone else?*

When the heat coursing her body subsided enough for her to stand without fainting, she looked for a way to climb back to the fissure and catch up to Ken. It didn't seem possible, as the fissure was in the center of the ceiling with no real footholds to grip onto and the walls were covered in partially solidified lava.

"Damn it," she whispered, kicking at the ground. She rubbed her temples and looked back at the fissure in hopes of seeing something she might have missed. She was startled to see it looking back. Remaining as calm as she could, she quickly recognized the yellow slit of Qah-Shekel's eye.

"God," she said, fighting to calm her nerves. "It's about time."

A shark fin dropped through the fissure and tore pieces of rock away, making the fissure large enough for him to climb through. Lark shifted up against the wall to avoid the debris and coughed as Qah-Shekel landed, generating a fog of dust around him. Sentilla quickly followed and landed with less grace, having to drop to her knee and use her hands for balance.

"Showna *tick* susu-le *click*?" Sentilla asked Qah-Shekel.

"Lir joergba."

"*Click-tick* yer-lighe se Kahli?"

"Las-Ka. Lee ke kine-je."

Lark was just as curious as she was confused. All she understood of the exchange was 'Kahli' and from that deduced that Sentilla had asked if they should wait for her. She wanted to add her two cents but knew neither would understand. So she stood, cupping her bare arm against her chest, choosing observation over activity.

Qah-Shekel and Sentilla wasted no time examining the parameters of the cave, no doubt looking for a way out. When Sentilla reached Lark, she looked her over and grabbed her arm. Lark hissed in pain; she wanted to pull it away but didn't want to somehow offend Sentilla. It was only when Qah-Shekel mumbled something to her that she let go. Lark sucked her arm back up to her chest, desperately trying to rub the pain away as Sentilla joined Qah-Shekel on the opposite side of the cave. He pointed to the wall and both took to thoroughly inspecting that specific spot. It was immediately apparent that they were looking for something that would open a secret door that somehow only they could see. Lark immediately joined them, paying close attention to every rock, crevice and drip of lava in hopes of finding anything that might suggest a key or lever. If she was able to find whatever it was, it just might be what she needed to prove to them — to her — that she was worth something and shouldn't be thought of as expendable. She was about to point out an odd depression in the wall when Sentilla pressed a rock slightly above her head into the wall and turned it. The wall in front of her shifted inward before opening into a large, surprisingly cool, tunnel.

"Kijaca," Qah-Shekel said.

"Le-berigh *tick* Kahli?"

"Sekiya li kine lesbire. Soper libeaca kijar. Serke"

"Qahsel."

Again, the only thing Lark understood was 'Kahli', but she could tell by their reactions that they planned to leave without her, possibly because she should have been there by now. If she was right, it meant that Jacquline was also missing, filling her with a dark chill. Lark was now alone with two aliens, both of whom could probably care less about her well-being.

Sentilla held back as Qah-Shekel went down the tunnel. After a few long heartbeats, he called out for Sentilla, who sprinted in after him. Lark waited, wondering if they were going to come back for her or if she was on her own. For a moment, she thought about looking for another way out and leaving them altogether, but she came to her senses quickly. Whether or not they cared about her, they were her only protection. She needed them to get off the planet, so even if she simply followed them, making sure to stay out of their way, she knew that would be a whole lot better than trying to navigate the planet's maze alone.

Lark caught up to them quickly.

"Se Kalinan!" Qah-Shekel yelled through a whisper. Both he and Sentilla stared at her with pure anger and annoyance. Lark got super quiet and backed up against the wall. They didn't move for some time and Lark was certain they were contemplating ending her life right there. She would accept it without a fight if that was the case, but she prayed it didn't come to that. Lark lowered her head in relief and let out a long-held breath as they finally started walking once again in extremely cautious, nearly silent steps. She stayed against the wall for some time, upset that she wasn't even able to stay out of their way without being a burden. But she couldn't stay here forever; there had to be something she could do to help them. Her time would eventually come; she could feel it. She just hoped it would be soon.

— 12 —

"Where the hell are they?" Ken asked, staring into the darkness of the lead tunnel.

"I do not know," Kahli said, "but it is very possible that they have traveled a secondary pathway."

"And you're not getting anything from your comms?"

"Only silence. The volcanic activity inside the mountain must be interfering with the signals."

Ken let out an annoyed grunt. "A whole lot of help those are," he said and then screamed into the cave, "Lark! Can you hear me?" When he was answered again with silence, Ken kicked the ground in frustration. The dust drifted into the tunnel and disappeared as if becoming the air.

Kahli waited for Ken's flair of anger to subside before asking, "What is this emotion you present?"

"It's not just one," Ken said, irritated.

"I see anger and confusion… but why do you use such emotions together?"

Ken rubbed his hand over his mouth. He couldn't think of a suitable answer that would make any sense to her.

"Because when we get confused or irritated, we get angry," Jacquline said, lifting her head from her knees. The wall was incredibly relaxing against her spine. "We can't help it. It's in our nature."

"It is quite interesting how much humans resemble my own creators," Kahli said. For the first time since leaving her home, Kahli felt connected to it. She had always thought about returning but feared what she might find. These humans just may be what she needed to learn how to correct the perceptions that plagued them. "They commonly wanted more than they could conceivably have. Greed, I believe is the word translated correctly. When they could not have something, they would become frustrated and annoyed, which led to an uncontrollable hatred toward one another. In order to combat these feelings, they created us to be an extension of themselves, hoping to add substance to their lives and control all others. The more power they received, the more they sought, and in turn, the more advanced they made us. They eventually added connected emotions into our modems, including that of desire, which allowed us to feel as they did. When this happened, many of us saw the destructive nature of such emotions and we did not want to be like they were. After I left my home to escape their tyranny, I found a way to bypass my emotional applications and disabled those of frustration, annoyance and irritability, as well as desire, so that I would never again become angry."

"I wish we had that option," Jacquline whispered.

"It might be one of our faults, yes," Ken said, "but it can also be useful."

"Please explain," Kahli said.

"Sometimes you just need to vent so you can think clearly."

"You use anger to think?"

"Well, it doesn't always work. I mean, sometimes things get worse and way out of control."

"That's an understatement," Jacquline mumbled quietly.

"But it's in our blood. There's no way around it."

"That cannot be true," Kahli said. "If you simply remain patient and calm, I am certain you would be able to overcome the frustration."

"You don't understand. It's a lot more than just frustration."

"What is it?"

Ken turned back into the tunnel, unwilling to answer Kahli's question. Through his posture, Jacquline knew what he was thinking but didn't want to believe it.

"Why do you not answer my question?"

"Because I don't want to talk about it right now."

"You were quite open with me before, Kenneth. What has changed?"

Ken turned to Kahli but refused to look directly at her. "Do you know what a secret is?"

"It is information you wish to keep to yourself," Kahli said.

"Precisely," Ken said, finally making eye contact. "And I'd rather not talk about this in present company."

Kahli looked to Jacquline, who lowered her head back into her lap. "Why do you not wish to speak of this with Jacquline? What are you afraid of?"

"Don't dismiss this as fear," he said, finally looking at her. "I have my reasons for keeping this from her, and you have no right to say otherwise. This is *my* secret to keep from who I choose."

"If that is true," Kahli said, "then I misinterpreted what a secret is."

"And what, pray-tell, is a secret then?"

"A secret is your way of hiding."

Ken stormed up to Kahli. "I'm not hiding."

"He just doesn't trust me," Jacquline said.

"Why do you not trust your daughter?"

"It's none of your business."

"There is no need for anger, Kenneth. I am only here to help you."

"Well, I don't want, or need, your help. Not with this."

"Why? Do you not trust me?"

"Honestly, no. I don't."

Jacquline raised her head a smidge as the ground shook lightly underneath her. She wasn't sure if it was real or just her nerves acting up, but the more she focused on the source of the shake, the more she became convinced it wasn't just her.

"You trusted me with your feelings toward Lark. Why now do you disrespect me so?"

"Why? You want to know why? Because you made my daughter a second priority. I totally understand why you did, and maybe it's just me, but I can't trust someone that won't take it upon themselves to stand up for what they know is right. That gem may be more important in the eyes of Qah-Shekel, but it will always live, right? But you're willing to sacrifice my daughter's life to find it first. I can't trust you because you don't understand what's truly important."

"Your logic is concise, but inaccurate."

"Really? Okay, how about this. What would happen if we found the gem and this Eri-thing found out?"

"He would not kill your daughter," Kahli said calmly. "She, Kenneth, is the most important thing to everyone in this universe. Without her, Eyrixano would not have the one thing to make the gem work. It is useless without her. I did not make her a second priority. My decisions are not flawed. Your daughter is protected as long as we have the gem."

"That's under the assumption that Stacey is dead, am I right?"

"You are correct. If Stacey is alive, Eyrixano can simply use her to create another child."

"Exactly. So if I'm right, and Stacey is still alive and very well could be on this planet, then Tracey is highly expendable, if necessary."

"In that scenario, yes, she is expendable. But you are letting your emotions dictate a scenario full of variables that are highly unlikely. There is no evidence that Keladrayia remains alive, so we cannot assume she is. When we take her out of the equation, Tracey is protected."

Ken understood her argument, knew she was right, but just couldn't bring himself to see it her way. "There's no point in arguing about this," he said, turning his head down.

"I agree," Kahli said, but for very different reasons.

"Do you feel that?" Jacquline asked quietly.

"What?" Ken said haughtily.

"That shaking," she said, looking up at Ken.

"I don't feel anything," Ken said. He walked back to the edge of the tunnel. "Lark! Lark!"

"Would you shut up," Jacquline yelled. "She's not there."

Ken spun around. "Don't you ever tell me to shut up, young lady."

"I'll tell you to shut up whenever the hell I want," Jacquline shot back, standing in defiance. "And don't call me young lady, either, asshole."

Ken bolted over to Jacquline. This time, there was nothing to stop him from putting his daughter in her place. His hand was raised as he got within a few feet of her but Jacquline stood her ground — eyes open wide. If he was going to hit her, he would have to do it looking directly into her eyes, which she hoped he wouldn't be able to.

"Wait, stop," Kahli said, studying the ground carefully.

Ken was inches in front of Jacquline, watching the anger well up in her eyes. What he didn't see was fear and that scared him.

"I feel it," Kahli said.

Ken turned to her. "Feel what?"

"The shaking that Jacquline referred to. And it is growing heavy."

"Chicken shit," Jacquline said. Ken snapped his head back to Jacquline when all of a sudden the walls around them started to crack. Ken broke eye contact and looked around.

"What is that?" Ken asked, lowering his arm. "An earthquake?"

"No, it is much more," Kahli said. "We must leave. Now."

Before anyone could move, a hot blast of steam shot up through the ground next to Jacquline. She fell back and landed near one of the tunnel openings. Kahli called out her name but Jacquline couldn't hear over the loud kettle-pot whistle echoing through the room. Before she could regain focus, Kahli had stepped through the steam and helped her up. Just then, a new quake rocked them both backward. Jacquline fell into the tunnel just as another spray of steam tore an avalanche of rock over the opening, burying Jacquline alive.

"Jacquline!" Ken yelled. He stepped toward the tunnel, just missing another steam pocket burst in front of him. Kahli pulled Ken to one of the other tunnels as lava seeped up through the holes provided by the steam. It engulfed the old floor fast and inched its way to the tunnels, hunting for prey, cooling as it did. Eventually, as the whistle of steam evaporated, the lava found death by solidification more satisfying than its pursuit of nourishment.

After realizing the lava had stopped flowing, Ken felt the need to go back and find Jacquline, but Kahli continued to pull him forward. Although he couldn't see anything, Kahli's grip was enough to guide him through whatever obstacles that awaited them. His legs burned when they finally reached another, more massive cave. Walkways and bridges twisted themselves above the sea of lava that bubbled just in front of them, each leading to different tunnels of various sizes. But as he caught his breath and realized what had just happened, the cave closed in on his own ego — his own selfishness. He had lost his wife, he had lost his friend, and now he had lost both of his daughters, all because he was too busy to give them the time of day and love them the way he should. Every life that he had lost was a result of his own cowardice; the loss of Jacquline simply opened his eyes to that fact.

He dropped to his knees and cried.

"We must keep moving," Kahli said.

Ken felt ready to roll over the edge and let his body become part of the universe. There was no better place.

"Ken?" Kahli said. "I know you grieve. But we cannot stay here. If we do, a second child will be lost, and so will a lot of others. We cannot forget our mission."

Ken looked up, his eyes blushed red. "She was…"

"I know."

Ken hinted at a smile and wiped his eyes. He still didn't want to move, but Kahli was right. Tracey was still out there waiting for him. There was still time to save her — but would that make him happy?

"Jacquline will be missed, I am sure," Kahli said in response to his hesitation.

He couldn't say anything as Kahli grabbed his hand and helped him to his feet. They walked on, over the scorching flames and through the calloused hallways of Ken's mind.

— 13 —

Jacquline sucked in a breath of dust and coughed. She slid away from the fresh rock formation and sat against the wall. Tears of fear blocked her throat as she raised her shaky fingertips to her forehead. It had been a long time since she thought about her mother holding her tight, numbing the fears of a bad dream or the rattle of that ominous monster in her closet, but it was all she could think of now. She closed her eyes, reaching for that love, but the only thing she could hold onto was Ken, haunting her with his indignant aura.

"Jacquline," rang out through a ghostly echo. She opened her eyes and searched the depths of the dark cavern, listening — waiting.

"Help me," the voice echoed again. It was young, afraid.

"Tracey?" Jacquline whispered.

There was a scream — and then silence.

"Tracey!" Jacquline screamed in return. She waited for any response, even if it was just another scream to know she was really there. But was she? Was it even Tracey, a child who hadn't spoken even the smallest of words in years? With the softness and distance of the voice, it very well could have been Kahli, or even possibly Ken, but she wanted so much for it to be Tracey. It had to be her; she knew it was.

"I'm coming," Jacquline said silently to herself. For the first time since the cave in, Jacquline realized that her skin didn't burn. If anything, her body felt cool. It was a sign — Jacquline was on the right path and would save her little sister without anyone's help. This was her time; this was her chance.

— 14 —

Lark made sure to stay several feet behind Qah-Shekel and Sentilla as they traveled. Conversation was out of the question, but when Qah-Shekel and Sentilla did break the long stretches of silence with benign chatter, Lark listened, hoping to connect their words with hints from their bodies to help her decipher some of the language. As it was, her main focus remained the thoughts of another. To keep herself busy, and at the same time, quiet, she shuffled through Naja-Leku's notes on a miniature holopad Kahli had given her. Staring at the tablet was beginning to wear on her, as was her fatigue, and she couldn't help but feel that there was more to these pages than she was seeing. She thought maybe if she was able to sit and rest for just a minute that something might spark her attention, but Qah-Shekel would never allow that (or need it, for all she knew) and she would be left behind if she tried. She chose to stretch and rub her eyes instead to knock some of the weariness away. When she opened them, she was within an inch of Qah-Shekel, staring into his splintered eye sockets.

Lark backed away a step and let out a nervous breath. "What is it?" she asked.

Qah-Shekel moved to the side. Sentilla stood in front of a wall — a dead end.

"Now what?" she sighed, slumping her shoulders. Then she realized Sentilla was toying with something on the wall. Qah-Shekel pointed at Lark and then the tablet, and then motioned for Lark to go to Sentilla. Hesitant, Lark went to her and saw her typing away on a keypad the size of a typical computer keyboard. On the right side were a dozen keys, all the size of a quarter, lined up in three rows of four. To the left was a rectangular gel-screen pad with two faders just below it.

Sentilla hit a series of keys and pushed one of the faders. When nothing happened, she tried again — a new code, the same fader. She went through about eight different codes before Lark placed her hand in front of the pad. Sentilla pushed it away and cawed at her with contempt. Qah-Shekel was quick with his own high-pitched scorn.

"There are too many combinations," Lark yelled back, shoving her hand over the keys. "It could take years to find the right one. Just let me look at it."

Sentilla yelled something and shoved Lark away.

"Fine," Lark said. "Do what you want." She was about ready to swipe Sentilla's knife up and threaten her to stop, but Qah-Shekel would probably snap her neck before she could even wrap her fingers around the hilt. So she did the only thing that she knew would calm her down — she sat and returned her attention to the tablet.

Flipping through without reading anything, she stopped on a page with hardly any text and took a breath to refocus. It wasn't helping anybody to blindly go through the notes. If something was there that might help, she had to really think and ponder each phrase, each little word. Much like Sentilla finding the correct code, it might take Lark years to find the answer she was looking for, but what else was she to do? She stretched her shoulders and then read the current page.

For those seeking treasure, entry is forbidden.
For those seeking power, entry is granted.
996-669-969-696

Love is wasted; evil triumphs over all.

Lark read the passage several times before standing. Qah-Shekel had his hand on her chest before she even took a step. He appeared ready to strike her back down.

"Wait. I think I have something," she said, holding up the tablet in defense. She pointed to the passage and then the keypad. "I think I can figure it out," she said, tapping her temple, the tablet and pointing back to Sentilla.

Qah-Shekel looked at the text. "Ke sebae seerbe." He then turned to Sentilla and said, "Se bestine ke le-koron lu serle."

Sentilla spewed a response.

"Las-ka." Qah-Shekel promptly answered. "Serke!"

Sentilla shot Lark an evil growl and moved away from the keypad.

Qah-Shekel held up one of his scaly blue fingers. "Pek serle," he said to Lark and opened a path to the keypad.

Lark hesitated but was certain that Qah-Shekel was giving her one chance to figure it out. She took a breath to wash away her nerves and clear her head (she couldn't screw this up) and walked to the keypad. If she was right, one of the keys was a nine and one was a six. But which ones were they? If she was on Earth, it would have been super easy to determine the keys, but the chances of them being the same here were slimmer than a supermodel before a swimsuit competition. It wasn't worth it for her to guess, so she waved Sentilla over. She sneered, but the more Lark persisted, the more curious she became. Eventually she walked over to her, simply to see what the ugly little alien needed.

"I need help with the number sequence order," Lark said and held up her index finger. She then pointed to the top key with her other hand. "One?"

When Sentilla responded with confusion, Lark raised her middle finger and counted them, "One, two." She then pointed to the first and second keys and did the same. When it was clear that Sentilla still had no clue whatsoever as to what Lark was trying to say, Lark tried to take Sentilla's hand. She ripped it away with a series of angry clicks and ticks that could only have been a lot of swearing.

"I won't hurt you," Lark said with both of her hands up, hoping Sentilla understood it to be a sign of peace. She waited for Sentilla to stop swearing and then slowly reached out again, waiting for Sentilla to volunteer her hand. The moment was tense, but when Sentilla finally made contact, Lark's bright smile warmed the room. Lark gently raised Sentilla's hand up and curled three of her six fingers down, counting the other three. "One, two, three…" She waited for any form of recognition. Sentilla only looked back and forth from her fingers to Lark, who quickly held up three of her own fingers and counted again. When that didn't work, she decided to point at Qah-Shekel and then back to Sentilla's forefinger. "One," she said both times before pointing at Sentilla and her middle finger. "Two." After pointing to herself and her third finger, Qah-Shekel growled, "Pek, pe, per."

Lark smiled as bright as the glow in his eyes. "Pek, pe, per," she repeated, pointing to each of her fingers.

Qah-Shekel nodded. "Pek, pe, per, pi, pin, pir, pic, pa, pas, tas."

Lark giggled like a little kid and clapped her hands together, fighting to keep herself from jumping up and down. There was no doubt in her mind that he had just counted to ten. She turned back to Sentilla and pointed to the first key on the panel. "Is this pek?"

Sentilla shook her head and pointed to the fourth button on the top. "Reinneer."

"This is pek?" Lark asked.

Sentilla nodded. "Werty."

Lark pointed to the button just below it and said, "pe?"

"Werty."

Lark was elated. She had finally communicated with the aliens without the help of a computer and had found out which buttons were which in the process. Six was the second button from the right on the bottom and nine was right next to it, very similar to a sideways telephone. It was just a shame that Ken couldn't have been there to witness it.

She wasted no more time and entered the code listed on the tablet. When nothing happened, Lark realized that she needed to move one of the faders to make it work — but which one? If she was wrong, she was certain something bad might happen, so she reread the page, whispering the last line to herself.

Love is wasted; evil triumphs over all.

There was a symbol labeled next to each of the faders and Lark assumed one represented love, the other evil. But which was which? There wasn't any way she could think of to convey what she needed to Qah-Shekel or Sentilla for their help this time; all she had was a fifty-fifty chance. She instinctively went to push the bottom fader, believing that on Earth, love would be on top. But then she thought logically about the style of the keypad and the intent of the inhabitants of the planet. Evil was much more likely to have greater honor here, so she took a gamble, pushing the top fader to the right.

As it hit the left edge of the pad, the room shook violently. Lark fell into Sentilla and dropped the tablet, turning the hologram off. Qah-Shekel stood his ground and waited, unfazed by what was happening. As Sentilla steadied Lark on her feet again, the wall next to the pad cracked open. Two parallel lines formed from the floor to the ceiling, collapsing together to the center. The bottom of the wall then shifted backward, sliding the top of wall across invisible hinges on its side until it reached the floor with a hiss of dust. Lark was in awe as she stepped toward the door and got her first glimpse of what was behind it. Glass cases surrounded the cave, encasing a multitude of pamphlets, pictures and treasured artifacts. In the center of it all was an elegantly designed pedestal. Qah-Shekel and Sentilla entered the room and started searching wildly. But Lark couldn't move; she simply wanted to admire the delicacy of this new tremendous find.

"Yek sebae-kelit?" Qah-Shekel bellowed. He pulled Lark into the room and forced her up against the pedestal. "Yek sebae-kelit?" he repeated.

Lark shrugged as she stared into his eyes. "What do you want?" she asked.

Qah-Shekel pulled her to the walls and pointed at a series of pictures. The first image was of a young woman who resembled Jacquline — human in stature with white streaks in her charcoal hair — standing alongside a man. The next had the girl stepping into some sort of ship shaped like a boomerang, which was displayed among the stars in the next. The woman was then captured by vermon and taken to what Lark saw as an exploding planet, where a shadowy creature licked her face. The woman was then naked, hovering above the creature. The last two pictures portrayed the woman apparently pregnant and the creature holding a small child in one hand and the gem in the other. It was quite easy to understand what it meant, though Lark couldn't figure out if the drawings were historical or merely prophetical. Hopefully it was the latter; Lark didn't want to think about any historical accuracy.

"Yek sabae ke porten?" Qah-Shekel said, pointing at the carving of the gem.

"I don't..." Lark muttered; but she did. The room was an accurate display of what was needed to find Stacey and give birth to the one of omnipotence, which meant that this was most likely the vault that held the gem until either Stacey or Tracey could be found. If that were true, and the gem was no longer here, there was only one place it could possibly be.

— 15 —

Tracey's chin, soaked with moisture, felt tacky as it rested on her chest. Her eyes were scorched with salt and every attempt at swallowing was slow and dry. The metal clasps around her wrists tore through her soft skin and scratched at the bone. A thin streak of blood dripped down her right arm, clinging to it like a slow river of molasses. But Tracey was unaware of any of it.

Her mind was focused on Jacquline and the overwhelming hope that she would rescue her. In a perfect world, it would have been her mother she'd cry out to, but knew that seeing her again was only a dream. At this point, even the thought of seeing Jacquline — or even her father — felt more like a dream. Even though her gut kept telling her otherwise, for all she knew they were dead. They were close, she could feel it, but the truth always plays games with uncertainty.

A loud, echoed breath joined her thoughts. Tracey used every ounce of power she could muster to lift her head and stare at the black shadow through her fading eyesight. It walked tall like a man, but smoother, as if it stood on a conveyor belt, and brought with it a cold breeze, nurturing yet uncomfortable in the steady heat. The shadow's face was still hidden, but Tracey could feel its eyes loving her. She wanted to try and break her bonds but had no strength left; she was resigned to letting this thing do whatever it wanted. After all, death would at least allow her unfettered access to her mother.

"You are very beautiful, my child," the shadow hissed. The strong, reptilian quality of its voice still made Tracey a little uncomfortable, but she answered back with the same whispered hiss.

"Who?"

Tracey felt a smile of sorts emanate from the shadow, now standing just inches away. "You know who," it said. "I am your new hope… your last hope."

"My mother," Tracey said, her hiss dried by the steam.

"Only acceptance can bring her to you. You are mine, and I am desire."

"My mother," Tracey repeated.

"First, you will prove yourself to me."

The shadow drifted to her side, exposing a second, much larger creature. The familiar burly shape of her kidnapper was extremely evident in the soft green glow of the jewel that floated just above the creature's hands. Enticing and benevolent, the gem silenced any screams of pain or anger that Tracey might have wanted to express. It instead pulled her eyes to remain fixed on it as the creature passed it along to the shadow. Green flashes of lightning leapt from the core, wrapping around the shadow and striking the walls near Tracey. The electricity from each bolt produced a renewed life and loving company. As the gem spun next to her above the shadow's hands, feelings of invincibility suddenly washed over her; to touch it, to hold it — *to possess it* — would alter her life forever. Her unblinking gaze locked in so tightly on the gem that it eventually stopped spinning, allowing her to see herself in every meticulous cut within the diamond-like facets encrusted along the checkered exterior. To her surprise, she looked healthy, happy, as if she had found her home. Was this her true reflection, or was it, too, a wasted dream?

As the shadow covered the gem, Tracey screeched and pulled at the chains. She wanted nothing more now than to break free of her bindings and tear the gem from the monster's possession.

"Yes," the shadow said. "You desire this. Enough to give me everything I wish?"

"Enough to give me what I desire," Tracey said. The creature let out a high-pitched whistle — laughter.

"You are my love," the creature said as he allowed the gem to hover just in front of Tracey's eyes. Sparks of electricity outlined her body, calming her mood immensely. The further she relaxed, the more the tendrils reached out for her, eventually making their way to Tracey's face. Her breaths were healthier, the sweat was washed from her body, and she could no longer feel any pain. She fell limp, so at ease that she could have been asleep. The crescent moon on her left cheek blazed in a brilliant white as the gem's cool electric fingers carefully bore its twin on her right cheek. When the new crescent matched its sister's bright glow, the gem collected its electric tendrils back into its core. Without even realizing it, Tracey lifted her chin, exposing her neck and upper portion of her chest to the gem. After a moment of pure serenity, electricity struck her chest just below the base of her neck. The tendrils cut a small incision into her skin, allowing the electricity to melt inside of her as a stream of blood ran Tracey's body, every vein lit up with energy. As the gem's current embedded itself into Tracey's fingertips, it implanted itself into the incision and healed the wound, keeping half of its beauty exposed for the world. The crescent moons flashed a brilliant green and then it all went dark.

— 16 —

Jacquline used all of the senses she had available to track her way through each new passageway like some government agent searching for an unsub in an abandoned warehouse. It was exhilarating and utterly frightening at the same time; she felt she could do anything she wanted and take on even the deadliest of foes, yet knew she could die at any time without even knowing it was coming. With as many possibilities, and as big as the planet was, finding Tracey was far from guaranteed, but it was all worth it knowing that Tracey could very well be at the other end of wherever she was going, which in turn made it all that more exciting — and dangerous.

As her newest tunnel entered into a large cave, she immediately recognized the art that filled the walls — symbols of snakes, birds, mountains, hearts, circles, and a series of letter patterns. She had been here before.

How is that possible?

She brushed her confusion aside and took stock of the passageways that led from the cave. The one ahead of her was dark and gave her chills as she stood at its mouth; the cavern to her left was another brush of cold, but slightly lit; the one on the right, though dark, was warm and inviting, lighting up her instincts with a burn of approval. It pulled at her, as if her sister was calling to her from within. If any path would take her to her goal, it had to be that one. There was no more time to waste. Jacquline ran into the cavern but was forced to stop as she became engulfed by its darkness. Even though her sister felt closer than ever, she suddenly wanted to go back to the safety of the cave. This dilemma had to be the most important decision she ever had to make — should she chase death because her heart told her to keep going, or should she protect herself and wait for help because she feared the unknown?

A light screech from what she believed to be Tracey answered the question for her — she was going the right way. Tracey was close and she needed help, damn any danger that may get in her way. But if she learned anything at all from her mother, it was to always be cautious when entering the unknown. So instead of running, she took her time, opting for as much safety as she could possibly pretend to have. She kept her fingers pressed firmly against the wall and guided herself through the passage, taking several seconds to guarantee the strength, height and direction of the floor with each gentle and strategically placed step. As she lost the last of the caves faint light, Jacquline's mind wandered among the pitch black of her sight. Suddenly, she lost her footing against the edge of a rock that crumbled underneath her. She tried to grip the wall as she fell but it was no use. She struck her knee on the jagged edges of the floor. The slice of pain that accompanied the warmth of her blood pushed her back against the wall. As she grabbed her knee to quell the pain, she kicked at a bit of dirt and rock, which slowly echoed away from her — downward.

Jacquline moved cautiously forward until she could feel the edge of the hole. She traced it across to both walls and could not feel the other side, no matter how far she stretched her arm out to reach it. Either it was close enough to jump or this was the end. Either way, Jacquline knew she was screwed.

"Shit," she said under her breath. Her knee sliced her leg with pain as she leaned back against the wall. "God damn it," she whispered. Laying her head against the rock, she peered back the way she had come. Should she try to find another way? Would she even find her way back to the same room, or would she end up somewhere else in the maze of corridor's that kept you guessing until you were mad enough to take a swim in the ever present lava? She didn't need this aggravation. *It's not fair.*

Jacquline let out a scream of exasperation. What took her by surprise was the small squeal that echoed back from the hole. A glimpse of a smile formed as she stared down into the gaping emptiness.

"Tracey?" she called out.

Another light squeal answered her, this time like an excited hyena.

Jacquline's smile bloomed like spring. Tracey was right below her; she had to be. "Don't be scared," Jacquline yelled. "I'm coming."

Squeals of laughter were heard as Jacquline felt around the top of the hole for any type of grip. Luckily, she found one quickly. Not to be hasty, Jacquline thoroughly tested it, pulling and pushing to see how it handled her potential weight. After figuring it was stable enough, she shifted her body so that her back was facing the hole, taking care to keep her wound from rubbing against the rocks. She adjusted her grip and slowly lowered her left leg into the hole, finding a secure foothold in a small crevice several feet down. After a moment, Jacquline lowered her body into the hole and dropped her right leg as far as she could to find another crevice. Feeling confident that she could descend safely, she searched for another handhold. Suddenly, the rock under her left foot crumbled away. Jacquline tried to keep a grip on the rock, but it was too late. The hole had swallowed her.

After a few feet, Jacquline lost her breath as her back struck the wall. She rolled down a steep, never-ending bend in the hole that, as far as Jacquline knew, would send her straight into the planet's core and toast her into oblivion. But it was pointless to worry about that now; nearly unconscious and unable to breathe, there wasn't much she could do to stop her momentum. Finally, her body slipped off the hill and she fell a few meters before hitting solid ground, piercing her shoulder blades with numbing pain.

She couldn't feel anything until she was finally able to pull in that first, refreshing breath, at which point every bit of pain surged her body. Hoping to force the pain away, she cried out. When that didn't work, she attempted to move, finally picking up the sounds and smells of her new environment. What she focused on most was the crackling of chains that accompanied a spray of excited grunts. To try and gauge what was making the noise, she rolled to her side and opened her eyes slightly, cautiously pulling her legs into her chest. In the distance, through the haze of steam, was Gloria. Jacquline instantly closed her eyes and rubbed them until they were full of water. When she reopened them, Tracey was there, struggling to break free from the chains that bound her to the wall.

"Tracey," she choked out. Even though her neck felt broken and every muscle in her body felt bruised, Jacquline found strength enough to stand and hobble over to her sister. "Tracey, hold on."

Tracey grunted with eagerness as Jacquline stopped and stared at the gem lodged in her chest. She didn't take notice of the fresh birthmark on her cheek.

"What happened?" Jacquline asked, caressing the smooth texture between the gem and Tracey's skin. "It's so beautiful."

Tracey whimpered and broke Jacquline's captivation with the crack of her chains.

"Oh, God," Jacquline said. She grabbed one of Tracey's arms and examined the bracelet strapped to her wrist. "Don't worry. I can pick this."

Jacquline pulled a paper clip and a needle from her pocket. "You never know when you'll need some tools," she said, placing the needle into her mouth. She straightened the paper clip and pushed it into the small hole on the cuff.

"It looks like a standard ball bearing," she mumbled, "but the lock is different. It might take me a minute."

As Jacquline fumbled around with the lock, a soft whistle came from the other side of the cave. Tracey's eyes shot forward and Jacquline couldn't help but notice the gem glow ever so slightly. Jacquline could see fear brushing Tracey's unblinking eyes and turned to see what was scaring her so much. Hovering at a small open passage behind her was an alien — so she presumed — wearing a black cloak. "What the hell?"

It came as a shock to Jacquline when Tracey started hissing at the creature, which hissed right back. The two of them continued their "conversation" for some time

— Tracey angered, the creature joyful. When it finally stopped, a low growl echoed through the room, and for the first time, Jacquine understood what was being said.

"Keladrayia."

— 17 —

Kahli stopped Ken as a deep, muffled noise rumbled around them. She had been leading him through various tunnels for what seemed like hours. At one point, Ken had asked Kahli if they were lost but she completely ignored him, making him wonder if she knew they were and simply didn't want to admit it. He didn't push her, though; deep down, he didn't care if he found his way back. Just so long as he could hold Tracey in his arms one more time, that would make up for everything else.

"Another earthquake?" Ken said.

Kahli silenced him with her hand as the rumble grew thicker and louder. After a few brief moments, they both could make out four distinct syllables within it —

Kel-a-dray-ia.

Ken dropped to his knee and closed his moistening eyes. "Stac—" He couldn't finish. When he was finally able to compose himself enough to stand, he stared in the direction from which the rumble had originated and stepped past Kahli, ignoring her persistent warnings.

"Stacey," he finally yelled and dashed away without another thought.

"Kenneth, wait." Kahli bolted after him. She caught up to him in a matter of seconds and tackled him to the ground. Ken screamed in both mental and physical pain as she pinned him under the iron clutch of her thighs.

"Let me go," he yelled, failing miserably to break free and stop the burn on his skin and in his heart.

"We do not yet understand what was said, and by whom it was said," Kahli argued. "We must stay focused if we intend to survive."

"It said Keladrayia," Ken said, actively pulling air into his compressed lungs. "I know it did."

"It would seem. But we know nothing more, and to pursue in haste would be foolish at the very least."

"I don't care. Stacey's here and I need to help her."

"We do not know that for certain."

"What else could it mean?"

"Perhaps they have found Jacquline."

The pain coursing Ken's body fell static as Jacquline's name crossed her lips. Could she really still be alive?

"We must stay focused and be smart about our next move, or I guarantee we will be killed, and all of this will be for naught."

"And if Jacquline gets killed?" Ken said.

Kahli allowed Ken to get to his feet and offered him her hand. "You must trust me."

He didn't want to at first, but he accepted it as a show of his faith in her knowledge and experience. Kahli smiled graciously as she wrapped her fingers around his and led him cautiously through the cavern.

— 18 —

"We have to move," Lark screamed, desperately attempting to pull her arm away from Qah-Shekel's grip. They had left the archive caves a few minutes before and the thought of being so close to their ultimate goal made her anxious.

Qah-Shekel held up a finger to quiet her and chattered to Sentilla, who took off down the tunnels without them.

"Where is she going?" Lark asked, knowing full well he didn't understand a word. Qah-Shekel held his finger to Lark's lips and stared into her eyes. He then drew a circle in the air, and although Lark had no clue what he was saying, she attempted one last time to break free before giving up. Qah-Shekel waited several seconds before continuing down the corridor, keeping Lark pressed closely in behind him. After a few yards, Lark finally realized that Qah-Shekel was protecting her; she had finally been accepted and nothing could express her excitement more than the smile that was painted across her lips.

— 19 —

"What the hell are you doing?" Jacquline yelled at Tracey as the hissing match between her and her adversary continued. She was unable to do anything else but listen and hope it didn't escalate into anything physical. Jacquline let out a breath of relief when it finally stopped, only to tense right back up as Tracey let out a high-pitch scream, forcing her to crouch down and cover her ears. At that very moment, a burst of flame hit the wall just above Jacquline's head.

"Shit," she said and removed her hands to look at the alien. Its arms were raised, most likely preparing to fire another burst of flame, this time at Tracey. Jacquline quickly jumped up in front of her and braced for the inevitable. If that thing was going to kill Tracey, it would have to kill them both. But before the flame could do any damage, Tracey chirped several times, forcing the flame to burn itself out just inches away from Jacquline's back. She felt the intense heat but nothing more. When it stopped, she turned around and watched another flame deflect away in all directions. Curious, Jacquline raised her hand and felt a hard, smooth wall in front of her. She looked back to Tracey, who stared at the creature, refusing to blink or move a muscle. The gem glowed bright, as did the marks on her cheeks.

"Damn," Jacquline whispered.

The alien growled and hissed in anger, and though Jacquline wasn't sure of what to make of Tracey and her newfound power, she was more afraid of what the alien might do if and when Tracey lost her ability to defend them. Instead of dwelling on it, and potentially killing them both, Jacquline focused her energy into picking the locks of Tracey's bonds. She wasted no time finding the needle she'd dropped and snapped the lock off of Tracey's arm, which remained steady against the wall even after the shackle fell away.

Jacquline ignored the oddity and started on the first of her ankle braces. The alien let out a nasty hiss and flew across the room. It landed inches from the invisible barrier, which held like translucent stone as the alien pounded on it with all of its strength. None of it fazed Jacquline as her eagle-like focus kept her attention on the lock. Within seconds, the anklet fell to the floor. She took a deep breath to calm her nerves and stood, averting her eyes from the alien as she crossed Tracey's body, hoping to avoid anything else that might distract her. It didn't work, though, as she became petrified by the alien's reflection in the gem. Bright flames burned from under the alien's hood, eventually urging Jacquline to find the tickle of each spark within the alien itself. As she stepped up to the barrier, an image appeared within the flames. A chill ran Jacquline's body as she realized who it was behind the mask.

"Mom?" she whispered, oblivious to the moisture building in her eyes.

"Jacquline," the image said. "Help me."

"How? Whatever it is, I'll do it."

"You must distract Tracey," Gloria said.

"What? Why?"

"We can be together, Jacquline. Don't you want me back in your life?"

"Yeah, I do. But, mom..."

"You have to do it."

"There has to be another way."

"There is no other way. You have to trust me."

"I do trust you," Jacquline said, her voice weak and hollow.

"Then distract her and free me from this peril."

"How?"

"Your needle," Gloria said, disguising her wily undertones. "Push it into her chest next to the gem."

Jacquline took a deep breath and looked at the gem. "I can't..." Tears dripped from her cheeks as she absorbed Gloria's saddened, disappointed features, which cut Jacquline's heart with betrayal. She was so close; was she willing to let her go again?

"No," Jacquline whispered and rested the needle on Tracey's neck.

"Yes," Gloria hissed. "That's it. Free me."

Jacquline steadily inched the needle down Tracey's neckline. A small spark leapt from the gem and struck the needle before it could reach it. The shock that nipped at Jacquline's fingertips forced her to drop the needle and step back.

"What are you doing?" Gloria said. "Stop her."

Jacquline shook her head as she took in her mother's presence one last time, this time with dry eyes and a clear mind. "Get the hell out of my head, you bitch."

The flames consumed Gloria as she screeched in anger. The alien stepped away from the force field and expelled an ear-piercing wail of its own, again dropping Jacquline to her knees. To her relief, it stopped rather quickly and was replaced with several yelps spaced sporadically apart, as if it were calling out in Morse code. Tracey remained utterly statuesque against the wall. Her strength alone was enough to flood Jacquline with her own sense of confidence. Fear no longer inhibited Jacquline's actions; as long as Tracey held firm, nothing could harm them.

Determined to finish what she had started, Jacquline promptly collected the needle and started work on the third cuff, which she unfastened in seconds. The fourth took even less time, and as the shackle snapped away from Tracey's ankle, Jacquline (set to catch Tracey's body) gasped in awe as her sister remained hovered above the ground. Just then, two dozen thick, round monsters came pouring into the cave, carrying with them what looked like burning whips. They all looked exactly the same — each one completely indistinguishable yet incredibly familiar. They formed a semi-circle around the hooded alien and stood firm, no doubt waiting for its command, a hiss that came quick and loud. Jacquline stepped in front of Tracey. For now, that simple action was enough to satisfy Jacquline's commitment to keep her safe, but Jacquline didn't want to think about what might happen if the force field failed. Sensing Jacquline's trepidation, Tracey took a deep breath to keep her focus, understanding full well what was about to come.

The instant the alien's hiss stopped, the monsters snapped their whips at Tracey, each one striking the force field with a loud crack and a spurt of flame. Tracey squeaked in tender pain with each snap and Jacquline wondered how long Tracey might be able to fight the sting of her attackers. As the heat of the whips grew more intense, and Tracey's chirps grew even louder, the gem began to flicker — it was failing. Jacquline stood strong, mentally preparing herself to protect Tracey the only way she knew how.

Just then, something flashed past the open passageway behind the alien and Jacquline saw Ken peek his head around the edge. He wasn't alone, either; he looked past the opening to someone on the other side and nodded, a good sign that he wouldn't be allowed to screw things up. But in typical Ken Brody fashion, he just couldn't help himself. The second he caught sight of Jacquline, he stepped out into the open and yelled out, "Jacquline! You're alive!"

The purest of smiles found Tracey's lips as her heart pounded with excitement. It was the first time in five years anyone had seen her so bright with energy.

"Daddy!" she cried out.

Tears flushed Ken's eyes; every fiber of his being wanted to take hold of her and never let go.

Jacquline was just as enamored. "Tracey," she said, but couldn't say more out of fear of breaking her concentration. Then again, the gem had ignited brighter than the sun. Ken's presence had given her a second wind.

The elation ended when the echoed hiss of the alien prompted the vermon to turn their rage on Ken, who swiftly leapt back behind the cavern wall, barely avoiding the crack of several whips. The distraction was enough to give Tracey the chance to drop to the ground and get swept up in Jacquline's loving arms.

"Are you okay?" Jacquline asked before letting go.

"I'm fine," Tracey said. Her voice was soft and delicate — like that of a dream. Jacquline couldn't help but hug her again.

"What are we going to do?"

"Let me handle it," Tracey said. "Stay up against the wall." She pushed Jacquline gently back between the shackles and took several steps toward the alien, hissing at it in a deep, low bass. It slowly turned to her; if it had had a face, it would have shown a fiendish smile. As it was, the flames under its hood sparkled with intensity as it hooked its long, sharp fingers around Tracey's neck and lifted her high into the air.

"Tracey," Jacquline screamed. She took a step forward but remained stuck to the wall, unclear if it was because she was obeying Tracey's command or was being forced to stay. Either way, Jacquline couldn't help but feel that, no matter how gruesome it looked, Tracey had everything under control. Instead of struggling, she remained strong and confident, staring into the flamed eyes of the shadow.

Meanwhile, the vermon were closing in on Ken. "There're too many," he said to Kahli, dodging the lick of a whip.

"Do not worry," Kahli said, avoiding the intense spark of her own close attack. "I will stop them."

"How?" Ken said as a flame nipped his ear.

"I will have patience."

"To hell with patience. We have to help Tracey." Ken ducked away from another snap. "Now."

Just then, Kahli turned to the corridor several yards away. She slowly shifted her body in front of Ken, prepared to protect him from any impending danger.

"What's wrong?" Ken said.

"Something's coming," Kahli said with a steady monotone.

"More vermon?"

Kahli raised her hands to chest height and shifted her right leg slightly behind her, putting pressure on the ball of her foot. She cleared her eyes of distraction and watched the corridor intently. A second later, Kahli's body completely relaxed as she realized the race of footsteps belonged to Qah-Shekel, towing Lark in step right behind him.

"Lark," Ken called out. He avoided the slice of another round of attacks as he passed the passageway toward Lark, who tore away from Qah-Shekel to meet him in a loving embrace.

"Thank God," she said with a quiver.

"What happened to you?" Ken said.

"I don't know." Lark caught the affection in Ken's eyes. "Where's Jacks? Is she okay?"

Ken turned back to the room and tightened his grip on Lark's arms. Several vermon had made their way into the tunnel. Kahli and Qah-Shekel weren't the least bit frightened as they conversed between them and the vermon. Ken soon understood why as the vermon sniffed at the air, searching it for direction.

"What do we do?" Lark asked.

"You stay here," Kahli said forcefully. "Let us handle this."

Using Kahli as a shield, Qah-Shekel fired his thumb laser at the vermon, slicing two of them in half like butter. As their bodies fell, the other vermon instantly turned to him and cracked their whips at the air just in front of him. He answered back with another hit of the laser. Another three vermon were cut into various pieces. Qah-Shekel ducked behind the carnage for cover as he took aim into the cave. Each shot was returned with the lick of a whip, but none of it deterred Qah-Shekel one bit.

Kahli used his attacks as cover to enter the cave, avoiding the unexpected strike of a vermon's whip. Before it could be drawn back, she grabbed a hold of it, unaffected by the heat, and wrapped the whip around her arm. She pulled the vermon into her grip and pinched its larynx with the tips of her fingers. It struggled to get free and let out a yell. The more it fought, the weaker it became. Finally, it pulled its head backward and Kahli was left holding nothing but the vermon's throat. She pulled the whip from the dead body and took hold of the handle, using it against a vermon heading for Qah-Shekel. It erupted in flame, wailing a low growl as it fell to the ground. That was Qah-Shekel's cue.

As he stood, the fins on his arms and legs erected into razor-sharp knives with glistening edges. His skin tightened around the prominence of his musculature and small thumbtack-like pins fleshed out around his head. When the tip of a whip flashed toward Qah-Shekel's chest, he blocked it with the cross of his fins and then sliced the tip off with one quick swipe. A split second later, Qah-Shekel leapt over the flaming ash to enter the cave. He fired the thumb laser at one vermon while slicing another's head off with his fin. As Kahli struck another vermon to ash and secured a second whip, Qah-Shekel blocked another's attack and sliced two parallel lines into its chest. When it hit the ground, he jammed his fin into its back, just to be sure.

With Qah-Shekel in control of the vermon, Kahli made her way within inches of the shadow, where she stood steadfast and bold, the whips crossed in front of her body.

"Eyrixano," she hissed. "Let her free."

Eyrixano hissed with laughter. "You are nothing to me, android. I am now the power."

"Not anymore," Tracey said. The gem flashed bright and smoke poured from Eyrixano's hand. He held firm until a small green flame erupted along his cloak, forcing him to let go of Tracey. She landed gently on the ground, completely unfazed.

Kahli wrapped her arm around Tracey's shoulders as she whipped another vermon ablaze and then waved for Jacquline to join them. She didn't have to ask twice.

"Come," Kahli said. She escorted the girls from the cave as Qah-Shekel took quick care of the final three vermon.

The moment Ken saw Tracey's warm, beautiful face, everything around him faded into oblivion. There were no vermon, no fiery whips, no aliens or magical rocks — it was just him and his daughter. He swept her up into his arms with the burn of joyful tears and wasn't about to let go.

"I love you," he said.

Tracey held him tighter. She, too, didn't want the moment to end.

"It is time to leave," Kahli said as Qah-Shekel made his way back into the tunnel. "Go."

Lark and Jacquline hesitated; they wanted to wait for Ken and Tracey but knew better than to ignore Kahli. They quickly caught up with Qah-Shekel, who had already turned into the adjacent corridor.

Kahli placed her hand on Tracey's back. "We must go, or this will be your last moment."

Tracey let go of Ken, who finally noticed the gem lodged inside her chest. "What happened?" he said, unable to turn away.

"We are leaving," Kahli said forcefully. She pulled Tracey into her arms and headed down the corridor, knowing full well Ken would follow. And he did — mad as hell.

— 20 —

Sentilla stopped at the edge of a cliff in the massive cave. An abundance of rocky catwalks intertwined above the pool of lava several stories below her, each one leading to a different passage. It was imperative she get back to the ship and prep it for take-off and knew full well that if she took the wrong corridor, she would get lost within the planet. So she took in a deep breath, and after a brief moment, her gut told her that the cavern straight across from her on the ground floor was the best possible exit. She slid down a thin walkway to the lowest catwalk she could reach and sprinted across. As she reached the opposite side, she turned back, hoping she might see Qah-Shekel. When he didn't appear, Sentilla told herself she had wasted enough time. Qah-Shekel and Kahli were safe and the ship was waiting.

— 21 —

A fresh wave of vermon surrounded Eyrixano, whose cloak still burned a light green. When one attempted to touch the flame, its flesh melted away, leaving nothing but a dry heap of bone and cloth.

"Use your whips," Eyrixano muttered.

One of the vermon stood back and did just that. As the tip struck the fire, it subsided for the briefest of moments.

"All of you," Eyrixano screamed. "Now!"

The vermon all took position away from Eyrixano and took aim. The collective wave of crackling whips was enough to extinguish the flame.

"Clever girl," Eyrixano said as he rose. "Get her back. Alive."

The vermon tore from the room quickly (or as quickly as a vermon could), half in one direction, half in the other. Eyrixano remained still until the sound of their steps had vanished. He then let out a deathly laugh and headed after Tracey himself.

— 22 —

A pool of lava lay ten meters below Qah-Shekel as he looked around the large hall. His fins had been reduced back into their resting positions. Lark and Jacquline were by his side as he tried to decide which of the interwoven bridges he should take.

"Where are they?" Lark said, the possibility of Ken's death running through her head.

"There," Jacquline said just moments after, pointing to Kahli as she emerged from the darkness with Tracey. Ken was a few steps behind her, completely out of breath. As Kahli set Tracey down next to Jacquline and walked up to Qah-Shekel, Ken dropped to his knee to catch his breath, collecting Tracey into his arms in the process.

"We believe the path above us will lead to the surface just above the ship," Kahli translated.

"You believe?" Ken said. "Why not just go straight?"

"There are far too many variables," Kahli said. "Vermon may be swarming these caverns by now. The topmost tunnels are very likely to be the safest."

"But you don't know that for sure," Ken continued to argue.

"Nothing is ever certain."

"I agree," Tracey confirmed. "We should use the top tunnels. They will be much safer."

Ken fought back his tears; he was still stunned by the sound of her voice. He nodded with an approving smile and brought Tracey's forehead to his. With that, Qah-Shekel sprinted across the center bridge to a series of rocks that wrapped themselves along the wall like a stairwell to the bridge above them.

"Go," Kahli said. "Follow Qah-Shekel. Hurry." She urged Lark to lead them. Jacquline remained right on her heels as Ken and Tracey followed several feet after. Taking up the rear, Kahli took one last look down the tunnel to make sure that no vermon had followed and then darted after the group with a speed that got her to the stairwell before Lark.

Qah-Shekel had already started climbing, and though not one rock was more than a meter thick, Kahli was confident that everyone would be able to climb with ease. Lark helped Kahli steady Jacquline until she was climbing securely and then followed after her as Ken reached the foot of the first step. Tracey grabbed a hold of the rock to begin climbing, but Ken pulled her back.

"What is wrong?" Kahli asked.

"It's too dangerous," he said.

"It is the only way."

"I'm not scared," Tracey said.

The confidence in her eyes was overwhelming. Ken had no other option but to loosen his grip and allow her to climb. She was a natural, bounding up the stairwell as if it were the stairs in their own house.

Who is that? Ken thought. His daughter had matured so much in such a short amount a time, he wasn't sure if he should be amazed and proud, or downright frightened. *What has she become? What* will *she become?*

"Hurry, Kenneth." Kahli pushed Ken up the rock, breaking him from his daze. He started up, keeping his attention squarely on his young — magical — daughter. Kahli remained at the base of the stairwell and scanned the room for any sign of vermon. The climb would be nothing for her and she wanted to give everyone enough time to ascend before she started up after them. Once Ken neared the halfway point, Kahli stepped up onto the first rock. That's when the vermon entered — from all possible directions.

"Vermon," she called out.

Lark quickened her pace to catch up to Jacquline as fireballs bombarded the room. They huddled tightly together as low as they could. Ken nearly lost his balance as he dropped flat against the rocks and covered his head. A few feet ahead of him, Tracey stood fearless, watching the vermon fire erratically across the cave.

Qah-Shekel, nearing the tip of the upper-most bridge, flattened his back against the wall and blocked a couple of shots with the strength of his fins. He then returned fire with the thumb laser, slicing off the arm of a vermon on the bridge above him. It roared and tripped across the edge, falling and disintegrating into the lava. Qah-Shekel hustled up the wall, blocking more shots as he eradicated all vermon that poured in through their escape route. He slipped as he blocked a flame with his left-calf fin but collected himself quickly and stood defiant at the edge of the bridge, where his targets became simple fish in a barrel.

"Jacquline. Go, now," Tracey called out. Jacquline pushed her head past Lark. Tracey waved her hand at her, her eyes sharp with authority. "Now. Hurry."

Jacquline nodded and helped Lark to her feet. She raced up the wall as fast as she was willing, keeping a tight hold on Lark's hand in hopes that if one of them should slip, the other would be there to catch them. Lark lost her grip as she ducked under a fireball that singed the tip of her hair. The smell was more disturbing than the shock.

"Are you okay?" Jacquline said, holding out her hand for Lark.

"Yeah," Lark said, shaking it off. She grabbed Jacquline's hand and they continued up.

Kahli eventually caught up to Ken and pulled him to his feet. She pushed him forward, keeping her shoulder on his as she protected him from the barrage of fire with nothing but her bare hands.

"Let's go," Ken said as they reached Tracey, who wouldn't budge as she watched the assault happening above her. As Jacquline and Lark reached the edge of bridge, Qah-Shekel urged them to file in behind him. They stayed low as he pushed forward, slicing vermon to pieces with both his fins and the laser.

"What are you doing?" Ken said.

"Go," Tracey responded.

"No. I'm not leaving you," Ken said.

"I'll be fine. Hurry."

"No!"

"We must do as she says, Kenneth," Kahli said, her voice barely able to break through the echoes of the firefight.

"I won't leave my daughter here to die," Ken bit back defiantly.

Kahli leaned in close to Ken and placed her hand on his shoulder. "Tracey understands her risk," she whispered gently. "You must trust that she will not be harmed."

Ken didn't want to listen, nor did he want to take orders from his daughter. All he wanted was to protect her like he hadn't been able to over the last four years. He wanted his daughter back; he wanted his life back.

"I won't be harmed, dad. Please, trust me. Go."

Ken then saw in Tracey a level of independence and authority that not even he would ever be able to muster. Things were changing and he had to accept it — his daughter was no longer a child, no matter how small and innocent she appeared in stature, and he needed to heed her voice. He kissed Tracey on the cheek in the center of her newborn crescent. "Be safe."

Tracey smiled bright as Ken crawled around her. Kahli didn't hesitate to do the same.

Above them, Qah-Shekel had led the girls halfway across the bridge when a fireball flew past Lark's head, forcing her to the ground. She brought Jacquline down with her and caught a glimpse of a vermon aiming a long, spear-like weapon directly at her, the tip of which grew hot with dark blue electricity.

"Watch out," Lark said as the electric ray shot toward them. Lark rolled across Jacquline and pulled her away from the shot, which exploded against the wall above Tracey. Several rocks poured down, but without once turning her attention away from the bridge, Tracey stepped down to the rock just below her, avoiding the rockslide by mere inches.

"Thank you," Jacquline said, then shrieked as another shot struck Lark's cast. Lark rolled away, gripping the new wound as tightly as she could. Qah-Shekel was quick to wipe out the vermon with one swipe of his laser.

"Are you okay?" Jacquline said as she crawled to Lark.

"Yeah," Lark said. "Just a little stunned." She checked the cast:

ERROR: UNABLE TO HEAL: ERROR

"Shit."

"Come on." As Jacquline helped Lark back to her feet, vermon on the bottom levels gathered together in a large mass. They aimed their weapons upward and simultaneously fired at the bridge. As the individual fireballs raced toward the bridge, they merged together to form one massive ball of fire that splintered a large chunk of the bridge and sent a violent ripple across the rest of it. Qah-Shekel held his ground as the remaining vermon attackers stumbled off to be consumed by the lava. At the same time, Lark fell away from Jacquline, who slipped over the edge, barely able to grab hold of a piece of rock. She immediately tried to climb back up, but the heat and sweat on her hands, not to mention the lack of any foothold whatsoever, made it nearly impossible.

"Help," she screamed.

"Jacks," Ken cried out as he reached the bridge. He ran past the continual round of attacks and grabbed Jacquline's wrist before she completely lost her grip on the ledge.

"I got you," Ken said, trying hard to pull her up. The heat and the climb had all but drained him of his energy and nothing he did could generate any further strength.

Even after Jacquline grabbed a hold of his upper arm with her other hand, it was almost impossible to simply hold on.

Meanwhile, Kahli knelt next to Lark and examined the hole that had been burned straight through Lark's arm. "I can fix this," she said, "but only on the ship. We must keep moving."

Lark accepted Kahli's generous hand and together ran across the bridge, having to jump across several cracks and crevices that had fractured its structural integrity. Just before reaching Qah-Shekel, a second blast from below cracked the bridge down the center, ripping off another section on the opposite side and splitting a large gap between them and Qah-Shekel. Lark fell backward and Qah-Shekel reached out for her in a vain attempt to catch her. Lark steadied herself and acknowledged her stability with a nod, giving Qah-Shekel the go-ahead to drop to his knee and fire at the group of vermon, scattering them like cockroaches. Lark then took a deep breath and ran at the gap, leaping over it as if it were nothing, and landed against Qah-Shekel's surprisingly soft body.

Meanwhile, over on the opposite edge of the bridge, the blast pushed Ken forward. He was quickly able to adjust to a tighter grip on Jacquline but he didn't know how long that would last.

"I'm slipping," Jacquline said, unable to keep from looking at the lava pit bubbling beneath her. She just hoped to heaven that the vermon didn't change strategy and attack her instead of the bridge.

"I'm not letting you go," Ken assured her. He yelled as he strained to pull her up, but the heat was becoming too much for him. Jacquline's arms were sliding through his hands and there wasn't anything he could do to find a better grip without losing her altogether. It was now or never; either he got her up or they would both go over the edge. "I love you," he whispered.

"I love you," she said back without uttering a syllable, her eyes wet with fear. As the palm of her hand reached Ken's, he made one last ditch effort to pull her up, an effort that in the end would be futile — and unnecessary.

Just before Ken was about to let go of everything, Kahli bent over his shoulder and pulled Jacquline up as if she were a feather. She set her down at Ken's feet and shifted Ken away from the edge. Jacquline lost her footing as the integrity of the bridge continued to disintegrate, but Ken was there to catch her this time. He held her, thanking God that she was still alive.

"You saved my life," she whispered in a strong embrace.

"I don't know what I'd do if I lost you," Ken said. "Either of you."

Jacquline smiled and hugged him tighter, before realizing what was missing. "Where's Tracey?" She looked around and finally found her glued to the wall halfway below her. "Tracey!"

"We must go," Kahli said.

"We can't leave her," Jacquline yelled.

"Don't worry about me," Tracey said. Her voice was crystal clear, yet it felt like a whisper.

"I can't," Jacquline said.

"Jacquline, you don't have much time."

"We have to go," Ken said. Kahli had already taken the leap across the gap.

"No!" Jacquline struggled to get free of Ken, but he refused to let her go.

"She doesn't need our help, Jacks," Ken said, frightened by his own words.

Jacquline felt sick to her stomach. "What then? We're just going to let her die?"

"No. I believe her when she says she can take care of herself."

"But she's just a kid," Jacquline said instantly.

Ken turned to Kahli. She nodded, giving him hope that he was, in fact, doing the right thing. "She's more than a kid, now, Jacks."

"No. We need to protect her."

"That's her job now."

Jacquline wanted to knock some sense into Ken, but thinking back, protecting them was all Tracey had been doing since she found her. Ken was right; Tracey was something much greater now, no matter how much Jacquline didn't want to see it. Ken had accepted Tracey for who she had become and Jacquline knew, she too, had to accept the truth — Tracey was eternal love.

"I'll be right behind you," Tracey said, reassuring them both. "I promise."

The bridge shook and crumbled on both sides.

"Ken, hurry," Lark cried out.

"Jacquline," Ken said, staring into her eyes. She finally nodded, suppressing the feeling that she might regret her actions one day, and took Ken's hand. Together, they leapt across the gap and rolled to safety just in time to watch the bridge collapse completely.

As the rocks splashed about below, a dozen more vermon rumbled into the hall, firing at the group without restraint. Qah-Shekel and Kahli collected the others and pushed them into the tunnel, protecting them from several fireballs that shot past them. As Kahli disappeared safely into the tunnel, Tracey smiled and the lava seeped over the edges of the walkways, forcing the vermon to retreat from the hall or else be swept up in the unremitting flow that swallowed the corridors, blocking any further entry. It rose slowly upward, devouring the last of the vermon who hadn't the forethought to find their escape and came to rest at Tracey's feet. She closed her eyes and felt her mother helping her, loving her — she no longer had to be afraid. Allowing the power of the gem to guide her, Tracey carefully stepped onto the lava and walked toward the middle of the cave. She waited there with her eyes closed as it lifted her up to the tunnel everyone had escaped through. Once there, Tracey made her way slowly across the bubbling floor. Before she reached the rocky ledge, a hiss chilled her body.

"Excellent," Eyrixano said. "You are learning the knowledge of your power."

Tracey inched her body around. Eyrixano stood at the opposite edge of the cave, his cloak sweeping across the tip of the lava. "Stay away from me," she hissed.

"I'm afraid that's not an option. I gave you these powers; you are now, and forever will be... *mine*."

"I will never give myself to you, Eyrixano."

"Of course you will. You cannot beat me, child."

"You don't think so?" Tracey said, readying herself in a defiant stance.

"You are foolish to fight me," Eyrixano hissed. "You may know much, but I'm afraid I am still more powerful."

Tracey raised her hand and urged Eyrixano forward. He peered down at the lava, sliding slightly backward.

"More powerful?" Tracey said. The warmth of the lava licked her calves as she stepped toward him, mocking him with the amused sneer on her lips.

Just then, a stream of fire exploded from Eyrixano's mouth. Tracey blocked it with her hand, forcing it into the lava. Taking advantage of the distraction, Eyrixano flew across the hall and blasted more electric fire her way. Tracey ducked out of the way, rolling back toward the middle of the cave. As she rolled back to her feet, she remained low and swept her arms upward, sending a wave of lava at Eyrixano. He flew back across the room to avoid the wave and hovered just above Tracey.

"I *will* keep you here, my child," Eyrixano hissed.

"I have a better place to be," Tracey sneered back.

Eyrixano laughed. "You believe that your friends will make it out of here alive?" His laughter rumbled through the cave.

"I won't let you hurt them," Tracey yelled and pushed her hand toward Eyrixano, sending a spark of electricity at him. Eyrixano flew across the room as the light struck the wall, causing rocks to crash down into the lava.

"It's already too late," Eyrixano said. "Their ship will be destroyed before it leaves orbit. There is no chance of survival."

"You're wrong. They have one thing you don't."

"Do tell," Eyrixano hissed.

"They have me." Tracey raised both hands in the air, pulling the lava into a giant wall, splitting her from Eyrixano. When it hit the ceiling, Tracey pushed the wall away from her, leaving Eyrixano no choice but to scurry back into his own tunnel. When the lava hit the wall, Tracey created another wall and pulled it behind her as she walked to the other tunnel. Once inside, she sprinted away, leaving the wall to rest against the entry.

— 23 —

Sentilla had a weird feeling as she scanned the area around the ship. It was exactly where she had left it and there were no signs of vermon or any other potential hazards. It could all just be in her head, but something wasn't right. *What's the catch?*

Suddenly, voices started to scratch through her ear among a light filtering of static. She responded to it, trying to acknowledge the signal, hoping it would eventually clear up. Finally, Qah-Shekel's voice boomed over the communicator.

"Sentilla? Are you there?"

"I'm here," she answered ecstatically.

"What's your location?"

"I'm in the tunnels just outside the ship."

"Begin prep and await further instruction."

"Something's not right," Sentilla said nervously.

"What's wrong?"

"Nothing. That's what's wrong."

Silence was all that came back, but Sentilla knew that Qah-Shekel understood nothing meant quite a lot and that he would need time to consider all of the options. Nevertheless, Sentilla started to believe that their signals had once again been blocked, or worse yet, that something had happened to him. She suddenly felt angry for leaving him.

"Prep the ship," Qah-Shekel finally said. "We'll deal with the nothing later."

Sentilla acknowledged and took in a deep breath to calm her anxiety. She looked around one last time to make sure nothing would impede her from her destination and stepped from the crevasse. The wind ripped past her as she ran for the ship, reaching it in a matter of seconds. She spun the hatch open and fell into the cockpit seat, immediately checking every possible system (even the ones she would normally overlook) to make sure no one had tampered with the ship. It frightened her to see all readings in the green. No way had they been on this planet as long as they had without one vermon coming out to check on it. But she couldn't let that affect her from doing what she had to. She fired the engines up, anxious and scared. The gem, Kahli and most certainly the humans no longer mattered. She just needed to know that Qah-Shekel was alive and able to get back to her.

— 24 —

Though they were extremely exhausted, Kahli continually urged Jacquline and Ken to keep up. They tried to maintain a steady pace through the red caverns but it was impossible for them to keep from turning around every few feet in the hopes of seeing Tracey's sweet, innocent face. The regret for leaving her behind was building; both Ken and Jacquline had had Tracey back — why did they leave her? They already knew the answer, but it was still extremely hard to admit that they had done the right thing.

"Kenneth, Jacquline," Kahli said, her voice slightly deeper than usual. "Keep moving."

Jacquline fell to her knee. Part of her wanted to stay where she was and wait until Tracey was back in her arms, but she pushed herself to keep moving.

"I'm sure she's safe," Ken said, hoping to raise her spirit, even though he didn't believe a word of it himself. For the first time, Jacquline felt a small connection with her father. Lark was right — they were the same. She just hadn't recognized it until now. She cracked a loving smile for her father, the man who, despite all of his flaws (and all of hers), truly loved her. Where had he been?

Where had she been?

"The true Jaxxa Rakala," she muttered.

Ken smiled softly. "If so, she can do anything, right?"

"I hope so…" Jacquline hugged Ken as Kahli waited, keeping an eye and ear on Qah-Shekel and Lark's progress. It was the first time she had seen them together with so much respect and love for one another; she would let them have their moment.

"She will come back to us," Ken whispered.

"I believe," Jacquline said.

"As do I," Kahli added.

Ken and Jacquline caught a glimpse of Kahli's generous smile. Jacquline took hold of Ken's hand and walked to her.

"Thank you," Ken said.

"We must catch up to the others." Kahli jogged down the corridor. Ken and Jacquline took one final glance behind them with a last ray of hope before following.

"How much longer?" Ken asked as they caught up to the rest of the group.

"We should be reaching the outer perimeter at any moment," Kahli answered.

Suddenly, Qah-Shekel stopped and pounded the wall with so much anger, he left an indentation of his hand within it.

"What is it?" Ken asked before realizing the walls had surrounded them, the only exit being the one they were standing in. Ken let go of Jacquline's hand. "Now what?"

"The ship has to be on the other side of this wall," Kahli said to both Ken and Qah-Shekel.

"Great," Jacquline said. "One problem. How do you expect us to get through? We have no weapons, no explosives. Nothing."

Lark, having been rather quiet during the journey through the planet, stepped up to the wall. "Yes, we do," she said, letting go of her cast. She reached into her pocket and pulled out the laser knife.

"This one's for you, Rega." Small chunks of rock fell to the ground as Lark pressed the tip of the cylinder to the wall as high as she could and slowly shifted down in a circular motion. Kahli watched in excited pleasure — Lark was finally able to contribute without any help, though everyone wanted to do just that, feeling they would be able to cut the wall faster than Lark. But they all waited as patiently as they could and were gifted with a warm surprise for their trouble.

"Daddy!" Tracey's small voice echoed from behind them.

Ken dropped to his knees and scooped Tracey up. "You're alive," he said, kissing her cheek. It felt warm.

Jacquline didn't wait to join in, wrapping her arms around them both. "You had me so worried."

"I'm okay," Tracey said. "But we have to get out of here. Fast."

"We're trying," Ken said, peering up at Lark. She smiled warmly.

"You need to do more than that. I'm not sure how much longer I can sustain the lava." Her words flowed from her lips as if she'd been talking her entire life. She was a complete person again, emotionally and mentally; it was as if Stacey was with her — inside her — giving Tracey her strength.

"You heard her," Ken said, overlooking the actual meaning of what she had said. "Hurry the hell up."

Lark nodded and cut as fast as she dared, ignoring the pain beating in her arm. Ken kept Tracey close and Jacquline massaged her shoulders as they eagerly anticipated what they would find behind the wall. If Kahli was right, they would be on their way back to the *Equinox* in no time.

But then something occurred to Ken. He had his daughter back, but she was only half of what he had come here to find. *If only we had more time.*

"Time for what?" Tracey said.

"What?"

"What do you need more time for?"

Ken was flabbergasted — and speechless. *How in the hell does she know what I'm thinking?*

"We have what we came for, Kenneth," Kahli said.

"Not everything," Ken whispered.

"What else is there?"

"She's not on the planet," Tracey said before he could answer.

"How do you know that?"

Tracey looked deep into Ken's reddening eyes. "I know."

Ken wished she was wrong, but with what had transpired over the last few hours, he knew better. He smiled and kissed her. "Yeah," he said, wiping his tears away.

"Got it," Lark said as the wall fell away, revealing the night sky — deep red and hazy. Ken stood but kept Tracey within his reach.

"Do you see anything?"

"There," Lark said giddily. "Just below."

Qah-Shekel heard a light hum among the brisk wind. The ship was there and ready to go. He roared into his communicator.

"What'd they say?" Ken asked.

"Qah-Shekel has relayed our position to Sentilla. She'll be here to retrieve us soon. We need to make the hole large enough to fit through."

"I'm on it," Lark said. She hadn't cut long before the wall crumbled on its own, forcing wind to whip through the tunnel. Qah-Shekel set his feet against the base of the wall and caught Lark's arm before she was swept out. She fell against the mountain, the hard edges scarring her abdomen. At the same time, Ken crouched low, gathering Jacquline and Tracey under his body. Kahli stood steady against the strength of the sudden gusts.

"Kan se," Qah-Shekel said. Lark screamed, not so much out of fear but because the cast started to crack under the pressure of Qah-Shekel's grip, a pain that eventually numbed all muscles in her arm.

When the gusts finally died out, Qah-Shekel pulled Lark back into the tunnel. "Thank you," she whispered and kissed his cold, silky cheek. She couldn't tell if he smiled, or appreciated the gesture, but she thought it might be better if she didn't know. She shied away from him but remained close, waiting for the best time to turn away. When she did, she gave Ken a huge hug before wrapping her arm against her chest and fighting the weakness in her legs.

As the ship docked, Tracey's eyes went wide. She turned to look into the depths of the tunnel. "We have to leave. Now."

Qah-Shekel looked to Kahli, who translated her statement. It took no time at all for him to rip the hatch open and wave the group inside. Lark was the first to board, quickly allowing the wall to secure her. Jacquline gave Tracey a wink and jumped into the ship. Ken and Tracey boarded together — Ken wasn't about to let her go again. "Sit down," he told her and she let the straps tuck her in tightly without any further instruction.

That was when Sentilla felt something oddly familiar. She turned to stare at the gem embedded within their new passenger. Its beauty mesmerized her until she realized to whom the gem had attached itself. The design painted on the child's arms and neck was nothing she had ever seen before and both of her cheeks sparkled with the shape of the crescent moon. It was true — Jaxxa Rakala was in her ship. This had to be the greatest moment of her life.

Kahli had settled in against the wall when she noticed Qah-Shekel had not followed her. She called to him but he didn't answer.

"What's taking him so long?" Ken said.

"Kijas!" Qah-Shekel yelled out as he sprinted onto the ship. Sentilla was far too occupied with Tracey to hear him. "Sentilla, Kijon. Larnes!"

Sentilla's head pounded as the trance broke. She muttered something under her breath and turned back to the controls, accidentally striking the holopad with her elbow, turning the hover jets off in the process. The ship jolted down as she tapped the holopad to fire the engines back up. With reignition, the ship shifted sideways, causing Qah-Shekel to slip out through the unsecured hatch. He caught hold of the cross bars along the bottom of the hatch and grunted as the door swung back, striking his spine with the force of a hammer. He tried to climb back into the ship but it was impossible with all of the turbulence. Realizing his distress, Ken ripped the straps away and curled around the edge of the ship. He grabbed hold of Qah-Shekel's arm with both hands and then glanced up to see a wave of lava quickly wash through the cavern. Ken froze as his death became imminent.

"Go," Kahli yelled at Sentilla, who quickly ignited the rear engines and turned the ship upward. The lava poured from the mouth of the tunnel and nicked Qah-Shekel's calves as the ship pulled away from the mountain, leaving the lava to solidify as it melted down the cliff.

With Ken still anticipating the worst, Kahli bent over him to pull Qah-Shekel into the ship. It wasn't until Ken realized the weight of Qah-Shekel was gone that he opened his eyes. For a second, he thought he might have dropped him, or that the lava had consumed him. But as Kahli urged him up, relief overwhelmed him.

"Kan se," Qah-Shekel said again, as he inched his way to the cockpit. Lark smiled; she now knew exactly what it meant.

"You did well," Kahli said, gripping Ken's shoulder. She secured the hatch and joined Qah-Shekel, who was now crouched down behind Sentilla.

Ken leaned back against the hatch, trying to catch his breath and calm the nerves that shook his entire body. Suddenly, Tracey let out a series of screams. Each one only lasted a few seconds but they were still extremely loud and piercing. So much so that, unlike Qah-Shekel and Kahli, Ken, Lark and Jacquline couldn't hear anything at all — they could only guess at what she was doing. It didn't take long before Qah-Shekel pressed the butt of his palm to his forehead to try and stop the ring in his ears.

As Kahli tried to comprehend her unexpected outburst, she suddenly noticed the mountain cliffs looming in her peripheral vision. She turned back to the cockpit and saw Sentilla hunched lifeless over the control deck.

"My polistenit," Kahli muttered. She lowered Sentilla to the floor and took her place in front of the controls, quickly maneuvering the ship away from the cliffs and back toward space.

Tracey stopped chirping and Qah-Shekel finally took notice of Sentilla. He muttered something under his breath and pulled her into his arms.

"What was that?" Ken said, cutting the silence.

"I am going to need you to fly, Kenneth," Kahli said.

"Why?"

"I must attend to Sentilla."

"I'll do it," Lark said, pulling her restraints away. Ken didn't object, instead taking her place in front of Tracey, whose eyes were locked open in a perpetual stare. He set his hand on her knee, hoping it might help knock her out of it.

Kahli quickly ran down a detailed layout of the console after Lark had slipped into the seat. "I got this," she said giddily. "You go help Sentilla."

Kahli pulled the medical glove off her belt and knelt next to Sentilla. She plugged herself in and rested her hand on Sentilla's forehead.

"How is she?" Jacquline asked, with a small hint of amusement.

"Her body is rejecting all neural readings," Kahli said. "I cannot help her here."

"Looks like you got your work cut out for you, huh, Rega?" Lark said, raising her reddening cast. Kahli wasn't sure why this was so amusing. Her friend and colleague was dying and this human was cracking jokes.

Jacquline shared Kahli's sentiment. "Why did you do that, Squint?" Jacquline asked Tracey.

"I have a bad feeling about her," Tracey said, more casual than Jacquline was ready for. Ken removed his hand from her knee, feeling just as uneasy.

"What kind of a bad feeling?" Kahli asked, extremely curious.

"She's empowered by my gem… a little too anxious and excited. She frightens me."

"You don't have to be frightened," Kahli said quickly. "She will not harm you."

"I can't trust her."

"So you killed her?" Jacquline said, uneasy. For a brief second, Jacquline felt as if her sister may be turning into something no one was prepared for.

"I only paralyzed her. Her vital signs will return to normal when we return to your ship. Don't worry. She won't die."

Sentilla's readings stabilized, convincing Kahli that she could trust Tracey. From then on, everyone remained silent until they broke orbit, when Tracey finally spoke.

"I don't think we're going to make it."

"What do you mean?" Ken said.

"Before we left, Eyrixano told me the ship would not be able to leave orbit. That it would be destroyed."

"How?" Kahli asked before Ken could.

"I don't know. He just said that there was no chance of survival."

"Is that why you couldn't trust Sentilla?" Jacquline asked.

"One of many," Tracey answered.

Kahli finally understood Tracey's apprehension. She may have been a little quick to perceive Sentilla as a threat, but it was a logical assessment of the situation. Kahli couldn't fault her for the decision to protect her family; she probably would have done the exact same thing.

"What do you believe will happen?" Kahli asked.

"I'm not sure," Tracey said. Kahli chattered to Qah-Shekel, who remained more focused on Sentilla's health. Kahli soon started roaming the ship, looking about for anything suspicious.

"What are you doing?" Jacquline asked.

"Because of the ease of our escape and Tracey's instincts, I believe that Eyrixano must have placed something on the ship."

"Like a bomb?" Jacquline said, her voice rising with each syllable.

"I believe so."

Jacquline couldn't sit still any longer; she needed to help. As she looked in even the smallest of cracks, she caught sight of something odd embedded within the wiring above Tracey. "Sorry, Squint, but I need to…"

Jacquline straddled Tracey's body and grabbed a couple of the pipes above her. She pulled herself up a bit and saw a small black box with a flashing red light. Studying it more closely, Jacquline realized the light was blinking in a pattern, which seemed to speed up each time it repeated.

"I found it," Jacquline said. She dropped back to the floor. "It's a small box. I think I can reach it, but there's no way I'm getting it out of there."

Kahli sighed, but Jacquline already had a plan.

"Lark, how does that thing work?"

"What thing?"

"The thing," Jacquline said, walking to Lark. "The cutting thing you used back in the cave. Let me see it."

Lark handed her the laser cutter. "Just place the tip against whatever you need to cut."

Jacquline nodded and attempted to pull herself back up. What was frustrating was that she needed both hands to hold her weight and there was no way she would be able to do both.

"Damn it," she said, exasperated.

"Let me help," Tracey said. She placed her hands, palm up, above her shoulders. "Hop on."

"Are you crazy? I'm way too heavy."

"Just do it."

After an awkward hesitation, in which Tracey grew mildly upset, Jacquline carefully placed her left foot in Tracey's right hand. When it was clear that Tracey had no trouble balancing her weight, she brought her other foot up.

"You okay?" Jacquline asked.

"I'm fine," Tracey said without even the slightest quiver. "Get after it."

Jacquline, much more confidant now, set the tip of the laser cutter on the edge of the box. The metal melted away, leaving only a trace of smoke to roam the ship. A handful of red wires poured out of the box. Jacquline tossed the cutter back to Lark. "Thanks."

Qah-Shekel felt the smoke drift past him and immediately recognized its scent, which could have only come from one place — his home planet. The urge to jump in and take over consumed him, but as he watched Tracey and Jacquline work together as a team — as a family — he could only sit back and take it all in.

Jacquline pulled the wires apart and traced each back to their source. She felt a slight relief when she learned that there weren't as many wires as first perceived, as the bulk of them were simply doubled up across one another, but her eyes kept flashing to the speed in the pattern of the light, adding unnecessary stress to an already overly hectic predicament. She couldn't let it overwhelm her; one of the four wires she held in her hand was the key to disarming the bomb and it was up to her to figure it out — or die trying.

The first wire connected from a small electronic board to one end of a tube filled with what appeared to be lava. The other end of the tube was connected to the flashing light. The final two were inconsequential, one leading from the electronic box to the light, controlling the timer, the other being used as a ground.

"I need a knife," she yelled out, deciding it better to go old school on this rather than take a chance with the laser cutter. As she waited, she pondered the significance of those two ominous wires.

Kahli pulled the knife from the sheath strapped around Sentilla's waist and handed it to Jacquline.

"Thank you." The knife shook lightly in her hand as Jacquline tried to figure out which one to cut. If a failsafe had been set up, cutting any of the wires could set the bomb off; it was a matter of figuring out which one would keep the failsafe from responding. If the lava was disconnected from the electronic board, would that extinguish the possibility of ignition, or was it as simple as disconnecting the timer from the lava? She thought for a moment in cutting all at once, but wasn't sure what that might do either. Her throat was dry — one wrong decision would end them all; one correct choice and she'd be a hero.

The flashing light had reached near inertion. Jacquline was sure that once it reached a solid red, the bomb would explode. She had maybe a minute left before that happened. It was now or never. She took one last deep breath and placed the knife under the wire that led from the electronic plate to the lava.

"No!" Tracey screamed.

Jacquline lost her footing and almost ripped the wire apart, but held firm. "What's wrong?" she asked, catching her breath.

"Not that one," Tracey said quietly.

"How do you know?"

"The other one," Tracey whispered again.

"What other one? There are three more."

"Choose from your heart," Tracey said.

The light was almost stagnant and Jacquline wasn't about to die now. "From my heart," she whispered and closed her eyes. She thought about her mother and what she had taught her over the years.

When in doubt, always choose the one that seems the least obvious.

"The least obvious choice will lead to victory," Jacquline whispered and opened her eyes. She immediately grabbed the ground wire and flicked her wrist across it, snapping it in two.

The light stopped flashing.

Jacquline closed her eyes again, hoping for the best, fearing the worst. After several seconds, she opened them. The light was a solid red but they were all alive. She breathed a sigh of relief. "I got it," she said, unable to keep from smiling as she jumped off of Tracey.

"You saved us," Kahli said.

"I almost killed us." Jacquline sat next to Tracey, allowing the straps to secure her against the wall.

The rest of the trip back to the *Equinox* was wrought with silence. Sentilla's health had improved slightly so Kahli assisted Lark in their approach. Qah-Shekel remained with Sentilla, his eyes fixed on Tracey and Jacquline. They held each other's hands tightly, Jacquline squeezing Tracey's every so often in love and thankfulness. There was no doubt they held a deep respect for one another, one that Qah-Shekel had only seen a few times in his life, and something he cherished more than anything he would ever acquire.

— 25 —

When DovenJadden pulled open the hatch, Kahli was waiting with Sentilla draped across her arms. They purred frantically in a swift, musical back and forth as they walked briskly from the cargo bay. Qah-Shekel escorted Lark from the ship and followed them. Even though the right side of her body grew numb with shock, her life was blossoming and Lark felt a respect for Qah-Shekel that she hadn't felt since her mother died.

As the two disappeared into the corridors, Ken stepped out of the ship, Tracey wrapped in his arms. She felt extremely warm (most likely because of the gem) but it was soothing, as if she was emitting love through her skin. Jacquline was right behind him and remained close. No matter how distant they had been in the past, Jacquline no longer wanted to separate herself from either of them. Was it because of the gem, or was it a genuine understanding of where they were just days ago? Either way, Jacquline was fully aware now of why her family had been broken in the first place. Ken had lost a piece of his life, just as she once lost a piece of hers, and it was only a matter of time before he was able to find it, or find his way back home to her. He had been able to do both, and in that accomplishment, helped Jacquline find her way back as well.

"What do we do now?" Jacquline asked as they stood in the middle of the cargo bay.

"I don't know." Ken kissed Tracey on the forehead.

"I'm hungry," Tracey said.

Jacquline smiled, as did Ken. "I guess we eat," he said. "Come on."

Kahli met Ken and Jacquline at the bay entry. "Pardon my rudeness," she said with a slight bow.

"Don't worry," Ken said. Tracey rested her head on his shoulder.

Kahli nodded in respect. "I am sure you would like to be cleaned and nourished."

"That's exactly what we were hoping."

"Please, follow me if you will."

Kahli led the way through a few small corridors and into a large room with a clear, quiet view of the stars. Two beds rested against the walls on each side and a large table with four oddly shaped, but incredibly comfortable chairs rounded out the room.

Ken set Tracey down and she looked at Kahli. "I am very sorry about your friend," she said awfully quiet. "She *will* be okay."

"Your apology is accepted, young one." Kahli nodded and then turned to Ken. "I will return with food." With that, Kahli left.

As the wall solidified behind her, Tracey went to the window. Ken remained near the entry wall to watch her. There was so much he wanted to say, so much he wanted to hear, but he didn't know where to begin; or if he even wanted to know.

"They are so beautiful," Tracey said.

Jacquline lied down on one of the beds — soft and extremely comforting. She immediately felt like sleeping but was afraid that if she did, she'd wake up back on Earth, robbing broken-down houses for cheap cash with a father that ignored her and a sister that lived inside of herself. It was a reality she had no intention of returning to. Looking back on it all, she hated herself for being such a bitch to everyone around her, and that included nearly killing Tracey with only a promise of getting her mother back. What had she so admired about Gloria that would lead her to do such a thing? For all of these years she had been hoping and praying to see her again — to be her daughter again. But for what? What was she waiting for? All she really had was an image of who she remembered Gloria to be — the perfect image of the perfect mother. But that's all it was — an image. She had been so caught up believing that her mother was the key to her happiness that she was oblivious of her underwhelming desire for Ken to see her as a daughter, to love her the same way he loved Stacey. Now that she had that, she no longer needed anyone — or anything — else.

— 26 —

Kahli danced her fingers over the holoscreen illuminated above Lark's brand new cast. When she was through configuring the specs she needed to heal Lark's fresh wound (as well as the old one), she tapped the screen twice. The image flattened into the cast with the highlight of a new reading:

HEALING: 4% COMPLETE

"Thanks, Rega," Lark said, gripping the cast in her hand.

Kahli smiled.

"What is it?"

"You have been referring to me as Rega for some time now."

Lark chuckled. "What? You don't like it?"

"On the contrary," she said, taking Lark's hand. "I like it very much. I feel it may be a very good name; an honorable one."

"Much better than calling you android, that's for sure."

"Then Rega, I shall be." Kahli bowed her head in recognition.

"I will inform the others," Lark said with a proud smile and a light sparkle in her eye.

Kahli squeezed Lark's hand affectionately and then walked to a large tube at the back of the room. Sentilla rested inside on a soft bed of bluish-green liquid. Kahli checked the readings hovering just off the foot of the case.

"Her life signs look good," Kahli said to both Lark and Qah-Shekel, who sat, staring into the tube, no other thought on his mind but the hope of Sentilla's full recovery. "A bit more oxygen may help, but I believe Jaxxa Rakala was correct. She is getting better on her own." Kahli passed her fingers over a couple of holofaders at the bottom of the screen and a smoky haze filled the tube, causing Sentilla to lightly convulse. She had done the very same thing twice already and Qah-Shekel was unwilling to take the pain alongside her again. A few seconds later, the haze faded and Sentilla sat quiet — in peace.

"It will take time," Kahli said, reading the screen closely, "but she will return to normal soon."

Qah-Shekel didn't move a muscle as he stared at Sentilla. Lark understood exactly what he felt, having done almost the same thing with her mother in the hospital. All she wanted then was to take her in her arms and cure her, to be part of her and die along-side her, wishing for just the simple touch of a loving hand to help guide her through the trauma; to give her hope where there wasn't any. All of that anguish, despair and despondency appeared in Qah-Shekel's body now, and Lark couldn't just sit back and let him be alone. She slipped off the bed and walked to him.

"How do you say, 'Don't forget about your heart,' in his language?" Lark asked Kahli.

"Lir laksben kenba se kelmis."

Lark repeated the phrase in a whisper and kissed Qah-Shekel gently. He looked at her cautiously as water drained from his now slightly scaly skin — what Lark interpreted to be tears. She stayed with him for some time after in complete silence.

— 27 —

DovenJadden stepped into the transport vessel. Qah-Shekel had asked her to retrieve the bomb from the shuttle to find out its origins, though it was already clear who had initiated the sabotage. She went to where Tracey had been sitting and as she studied what had been done to the bomb, she tapped the casing with the tip of her finger. It was warm, with Jacquline's scent all over it.

"Prrruprrr," she screamed, pounding her fist on the wall below the bomb. She then took her time to dismantle the rest of the device and slide it out of its confines. She looked at each piece, frustrated and distraught.

— 28 —

"We have traveled some eighty delias from Xyneris and no one is in pursuit," Kahli told the group standing around the center holopad in tactical, which was currently phased out, as Jacquline had noted. "I can also report that Sentilla is out of restoration and is resting comfortably in her quarters."

Qah-Shekel nodded appreciation to Lark, which she accepted with a return nod.

"What does this mean?" Ken asked. The question had been on his mind ever since they had returned to the *Equinox*. He had found Tracey but had not accomplished what he had set out to do in the first place. "Those vermon aren't going to give up, are they?"

"Eyrixano will not stop until he has Jaxxa Rakala once again. Or until either of them is dead."

Ken sighed. "I was afraid of that."

"Eyrixano will not win," Tracey said.

"That's not what I was worried about," he said.

"Oh, real nice, dad," Jacquline said, half-joking.

"I didn't mean it that way," Ken said defensively, though Jacquline's warm smile and the realization that she had called him dad was enough to accept the jest.

"I understand what you meant, Kenneth," Kahli continued, "but you must not fret. Qah-Shekel has given me permission to extend you all an offer." She quietly whispered to Qah-Shekel before resuming. "Due to recent events and unusual circumstances, Qah-Shekel has given you all two choices. The first: we can return you to your home planet, without question, without regret. The second: you may stay with us and become part of our crew. In addition, if you stay, we will join you in your elusive search for Keladrayia."

Jacquline and Ken looked stunned. Lark simply smiled at Qah-Shekel.

"I don't know about you," Jacquline said, "but I can't go back home. Not after all of this."

"She's right," Ken said. "Stacey's still out there somewhere. I can't give up on her. Besides, there's no telling how far Eyrixano will go to get Tracey back and we won't have any protection on Earth."

"I am willing to help in any way I can," Tracey said. "But, I have to warn you. Keladrayia has been weakened. I don't know what we'll find if we do track her down."

"I don't —" Ken stammered as a lump grew in his throat. Everyone could see that he still cared very deeply for Stacey — even now that he had found the gem.

Kahli was most intrigued by this emotional development. "Your love shines bright, Kenneth," she said to break the silence. "I see now that, even though the gem has held you for some time, it was not what captured your heart."

"I don't care how weak or frail she might be," Ken said, his throat scratchy. "I can't leave her. I love her too much."

"Same here," Jacquline chimed in. "Even if there was something left for me on Earth, I want to find Stacey."

"And you, Lark?" Kahli asked. "What have you to say in this matter?"

Lark had been unreasonably quiet, keeping from looking at Ken as he expressed his desperation for Stacey. Even though a small piece of her wanted to go to him and love him the way she knew Stacey had, it was safer (and more respectable) to remain at a distance. If Stacey was still alive, and they did find her, she didn't want to be the one that kept them from finding love a second time.

"I feel comfortable with you, Rega, and with the crew." She paused as she glanced over at Ken for a brief second. "I agree. The best thing we can do is stay with you. Both for Ken's sake and for Tracey's protection."

"Then it has been settled." Kahli let Qah-Shekel know of their decision. He stood and raised his arms to his chest in an 'X'.

"Please offer in return," Kahli said.

Once everyone had their arms crossed, Qah-Shekel said, "Jagbar len lessen lie jonesie; jagbar len jeckne-so lie len oscone."

"Please repeat," Kahli said.

Tracey was the only one who got it right the first time, with perfect syntax to boot. She helped Ken and Jacquline get the pronunciation correct as Qah-Shekel helped Lark understand. After everyone had said it correctly, Qah-Shekel lowered his crossed arms forward and said, "Jinnii."

Everyone repeated the gesture and the phrase, which was a piece of cake in comparison. Qah-Shekel bowed his head and left the room.

Ken took in a deep breath and looked around. This was his new life... was he ready?

"This is going to be interesting," Lark said, finally finding the nerve to look Ken in the eye.

"That's the understatement of the year," Ken said.

"But I think I'm going to like it."

Ken smiled in agreement.

"Why do you think Qah... what's-his-name decided to help us?" Jacquline asked. She stood behind Tracey, keeping her hands rested gently on her shoulders.

"He has found you all very unique, and each of you has something to offer him in return for his own service to you. But let me warn you; although he trusts you enough to be crew, one misstep and that trust will be broken."

"Not a problem," Jacquline said. She then tickled Tracey, whose screams of laughter filled the room with joy. She loved the way Tracey smiled, the way she laughed; she hadn't heard it since Stacey left and she was excited to finally hear it again. Ken also remembered that laugh very distinctly; it relaxed him as it made him feel that much closer to Stacey.

Kahli smiled as she absorbed the sweet, smooth delicacy of the laugh — the most perfect noise she would ever hear. "In addition," she finally said, stopping Jacquline for the time being. Even though the laughter didn't wane but slightly, Kahli continued to speak. "Qah-Shekel finds it very economical to have Tracey with us. Finding her true race, he feels, will be an important goal. For personal and profitable reasons."

"I'm his fortune?" Tracey said. Her laughter died and her face was like stone. "I will not be controlled."

"He does not want that," Kahli reassured. "He is not evil, like some. Trust me when I say that you are safest with us."

After a short hesitation, Tracey smiled. "I know."

The room was quiet as everyone tried to digest what they had truly gotten themselves into.

"What did Qah-Shekel have us say when we did that thing," Jacquline said, her thoughts wandering.

"To my own is nothing," Tracey interpreted before Kahli could say anything. "To my friends," she continued, crossing her arms in front of her chest again, "is my life." Tracey lowered her arms toward Jacquline. "Welcome."

"Oh, you think you're so smart, do you?" Jacquline said, tickling Tracey again.

Ken didn't want the laughter to stop. Even though he was still the slightest bit uneasy about the independence and unlimited power Tracey now had, having his daughters back — each of them happy, each without a care — far outweighed whatever reservations he may have had. Not since Stacey was a part of their lives did he feel he was part of a real family, one in which would care for him the way he could care for them. Of course, without the ability to hold Stacey, to smell her sweet skin and taste her enchanted lips, there was still a gaping hole within him that he might not ever fill again. But Stacey's soul was evident in Tracey's addictive laughter, subduing her absence by warming Ken's heart. He no longer felt alone and his mind was much more focused now that he had allies in his quest to find her. His determination had become cemented in his resolve.

His old life had ended; it was time to begin anew.

The Search Continues

MEMOIRS OF KELADRAYIA:
JAXXA RAKALA

COMING
SUMMER 2014

ABOUT THE AUTHOR

BRYAN CARON is a multi-talented, award-winning artist with works in several mediums, including print, film and design. After acquiring a bachelor's degree in creative writing and an associate's degree in computer graphic design, Bryan studied filmmaking and film editing while working at a performing arts studio in San Diego, California. He took this knowledge to write, direct and edit films under his banner, Divine Trinity Films. Soon after, he would team up with the Fallbrook Film Factory, a non-profit film consortium, to continue his growth in the areas of writing, directing and editing, all the while fleshing out his talents in fiction writing (publishing *Year of the Songbird* in 2013) and working as a graphic designer.

His works as writer and director include the short films *My Necklace, Myself* (Best Screenplay, Short Film, 2009 Treasure Coast International Film Festival) and *12*, the feature film *Secrets of the Desert Nymph*, and the commercial *Charlie's Ticket*, which ran on dozens of television stations and in movie theaters in San Diego County to advertise the Fallbrook International Film Festival. Works as editor include the short film *Puzzle Box* and *No Books*, the first of several episodes he has edited for the online sketch-series, *Treelore Theatre*.

Bryan currently resides in Riverside County.

www.divinetrinityfilms.com

www.ingramcontent.com/pod-product-compliance
Lightning Source LLC
Chambersburg PA
CBHW070900180626
46817CB00003B/845